STOCKER'S
KITCHEN

D1212134

STOCKER'S KITCHEN

a novel by **Juliet Wittman**

Beck & Branch Publishers

Stocker's Kitchen

Copyright @ 2018 Juliet Wittman

This book is a work of fiction. Names, characters, places and incidents are the product of the author's imagination or are used fictitiously. Any resemblance to actual events, locales or persons, living or dead, is coincidental.

All rights reserved. Except as permitted by the U.S. Copyright Act of 1976, no part of this publication may be reproduced, distributed or transmitted in any form or by any means, or stored in a database or retrieval system, without the prior written permission of the publisher.

Cover design by Farmtopixel.com

Beck & Branch Publishers

ISBN 978-0-9972644-9-4

For Clark, Aubrey and Sabina

CHAPTER ONE

The kitchen was a cacophony of crashing pots and pans; no one could cook without slamming the pan onto the greasy old burner; whenever one of the commis opened the refrigerator door it banged against the back wall. Periodic howls of pain arose as someone or other cut or burned himself—no manly silent fortitude here. People were always thudding into each other—hard enough for the thudder to throw the thuddee off balance. On his cell phone, Harold berated his mother. No, no, no, mom. I never did. I'm coming round next week. I know I said that. I said I know I said that. Two or three people yelled Shurrup in unison; no change in Harold's tone. So why did you ask if you knew? I'm not coming. That's right, ma, I'm not coming. You know everything. And all the while, Bluetooth at his ear, he chopped onions, carrots, peppers, lemongrass, into chunks, brunoise, batons, near-transparent circles, hands quick and neat. Fuck it, ma. I'm not talking to you if... I didn't. Okay, you heard fuck you. That's not what I fucking said. Everyone's shoes scraped along the hard grime-slick on the floor, a floor that no one had tackled seriously for decades, vegetables—once appetizing and bright—dissolving into froth and slime and then subsiding to glue themselves to the generations of dying vegetables that had preceded them. What had that floor been once? Linoleum? Wood? Concrete? Nastiest thought of all: was it carpet, one of those hard-napped industrial carpets, before fallen refuse penetrated every crevice, worked its way between strands, and tamped the entirety down?

The place was the closest thing imaginable to hell, an ill-lit basement cavern that seemed fathoms deep, caught in the sizzling sulphur-spitting bowels of Mother Earth. It smelled of sulphur too, or at least of things burning—hair and feathers, flesh, ancient fragments of baked goods that had bonded to the inside of the ovens with the tenacity of a murderous lover stalking a rejecting woman and that somehow continued to emit a bitter stench though they had long ago carbonized.

They were careful with their knives, the kitchen staff. Those knives seldom crashed into anything except on purpose, when an aggravated sous-chef slid a tip into a line cook's flesh, the thick muscle at the top of an arm or thigh, between the shoulder blades. It wasn't hard to imagine how the blade cleaved flesh and ground on bone with so many creatures having been chopped up in this place—calves' heads de-fleshed, fishes opened up with v-shaped slits, beneath which viscera glistened, Stocker disassembling a chicken, swift, precise, and savage, his blade ploughing through skin and meat, the thrick-click when he found the sweet spot where joint connected to socket. A dropped knife sometimes penetrated the top of a running shoe, and then there'd be cursing and hopping, a sweaty hand closed over leather, blood seeping between fingers.

Curses, jabber, an Italian love song begun and aborted, rock pounding from the radio, and Stocker yelling nonstop, a stream of admonition and advice, salted with the insights he'd acquired recently. "No one gives head like a Chink. Male or female, don't matter. It's those pointy tongues." A gurgling snicker, followed by lurid, point-by-point description. Or, "Chefs are tops these days. Tell any bitch you work in my kitchen and you won't be able to peel her off your chest," and he might actually dance a few loosey-goosey, butt-swinging steps here. Sometimes a new commis would respond, starting a brag of his own or asking a question, perhaps congratulating Stocker on his prowess, but it did no good. Stocker didn't care who you were or what you had to say. Nothing could interrupt his flood of self-commendation and obscenity. When he joked, you'd better laugh. When he reproved, you looked servile and squint-eyed and pushed out a lot of "Yes, sirs"—loud and clear, dammit, or his relentless ear banging would never stop. Other than that, your participation wasn't required. You just focused on the food in your sauté pan or on your chopping board and listened, laughed, or smiled conspiratorially when required. His name? Stocker? Oh, yes, he knew it was ironic for a chef, here in this kitchen where huge pots bubbled perennially with savory, mysterious broths, but no one mentioned that or punned, and if a new recruit said something, anything about stock—Should I add chicken stock to this? Does the stockpot need replenishing? Or even, I don't put much stock in the guy's betting tips—there'd be a roar, as Stocker slammed down whatever he'd been handling: "What? Wassat?"

The old hands told the new ones that if you survived Stocker's kitchen, you could survive anything. It was worth holding your tongue and ducking your head for what he had to teach, and then you could go on to just about any kitchen you wanted, maybe start your own place.

Why didn't they close him down? Who knows. Perhaps the health department was afraid of him. Perhaps the inspectors were in on the conspiracy. They came. They looked around. They never saw rat droppings or cockroaches, the wet leaves suppurating in the sink, the blood on the counters. And when they wanted prime seats with their wives or girlfriends, they got them, and sat, and ate the best the kitchen had to offer and left without paying.

Stocker. No one knew his first name. Stocky as the name suggested. Always wearing the same stained gray workout pants under a voluminous apron, black baseball cap on his greasy-haired head. But the sheer deliciousness of his cooking. Oh, yes. Deep-flavored, subtle stews and delicate soufflés, meat that bloodied your teeth and shredded between them, or white and delicate as baby's flesh—there was nothing he couldn't do in that kitchen.

CHAPTER TWO

When he first saw Angela, Stocker was standing in the alley behind his restaurant, taking a cigarette break, savoring the gritty early spring air, the scents of exhaust and garbage. It was mother's milk to him, New York, it was meat and potatoes. He remembered coming to the city alone at the age of sixteen, on the run from a sterile lonely brutal life, walking out of Penn Station and standing geeky and alone in his too-large jacket with the too-small pants rubbing at his crotch—not that any of the people hurrying by would have noticed. Pulling on his cigarette, he tried to call up that skinny, shivering figure, that truncated, shorthand version of himself. He remembered how he'd finally found a place in a cheap flophouse, and how he'd walked the streets, day after day, amazed at all the black, white, Asian, and Latino people, the clatter of foreign languages against his ears. He'd never seen so many black people before, never been among black people; where he came from they kept to their side of the town, stood in a group at the lone bus stop, barely even looked at the white kids at their high school— not that he himself was there very often. He'd spent his first months in New York eating. Salamis from Italy and Hungary, baked goods from Europe, goat and halal chicken, empanadas and cupcakes, hot chocolate thick enough to stand a spoon in, dishes from Egypt, Iran, Afghanistan, Korea, Ethiopia, Palestine. Street food. Soul food. He ate his way up and down Broadway, through the East Side and the West, in hidden places around town. He watched people cook over red coals in braziers on the sidewalk, while others made music. Everywhere he went, cooks were willing to talk to him about their food, ingredients and preparation, things that puzzled them about the way Americans ate. Some even took him into their kitchens to show him how they did it.

He felt the wall against the knobs of his spine, sent an exhalation of smoke over his lower lip, hearing traffic, voices, the quietly sliding river behind the restaurant. A thin black cat was moving in the shadows. He watched until she melted back into them. The exhilaration of New York had never left him. This was the smart place, the place where the smart people lived, clever, neurotic, wealthy people who thought of the city as theirs and spent their time trying to impress each other. They didn't believe in themselves or trust that they were who they were, and they could be unseated by a word from someone else, someone more impressive, famous or simply confident. Stocker knew this; it meant they could be outdone. These people didn't really see the world around them, but he did: bums, junkies, and immigrants from other countries, walking through the streets, all of them bringing their otherness, that breath of something alien and distinct with them. He loved the jagged mix of accents he heard daily, the people yelling on street corners, the conmen selling cheap cosmetics and watches, Puerto Ricans, Koreans, Haitians. Everyone jostling up against everyone else in a swirling soup and fighting also to remain separate. You needed a lot of hide to live in a battering place like New York. Everything surprised him at first, but he soon took it all in stride. He wasn't afraid of crazy people. He figured he could take whatever the world threw at him. He knew the city was an archeological experiment, a place for reinvention where the powerful strolled and human refuse washed up. He knew that anything could happen here, whether an attack by a meth-crazed teenager or a beautiful girl riding slowly by on a white horse. The place was connected by webs more varied and subtle than anything he'd ever been able to imagine before. It had taken only a couple of months in New York for Stocker to drop his fantasies of a loving mother and accept the fact that there was no one here who cared enough even to hit or curse him, and while that knowledge was scary enough to jolt the breath out of his lungs, there was something about his aloneness, the absoluteness of it, the utter indifference of the great city, that filled him with pleasure. Stocker smiled as he stubbed out his cigarette. He was a king here now. He thrived on uncertainty and contradiction, and he knew who he was, having been hardened and blackened in flame a long time ago.

He was about to go inside—the cold was getting to him—when he noticed the woman progressing along the street at the end of the alley; her high heeled boots distorted her stride, so that she high-stepped and pitched her leg a little forward like a show pony. He hesitated a moment, then called out, Hey.

She turned, looked around without breaking her stride, kept walking.

Hey, girl, you.

Now she stopped and looked full at him. Her face was as narrow and angular as the cat's—foreign looking, he thought. Exotic. Maybe Japanese. She widened her eyes in query.

You hungry?

She hesitated, began shaking her head.

I'm the chef here. You hungry? You want to eat?

She stood for a moment, then decided, and began picking her way over the rough surface of the alley toward him, turning her ankle once on a pock in the asphalt, recovering her balance, continuing her high-legged pony strut. He gestured to the lit door, and she went in ahead of him, along the dark corridor until she stood at the entrance to the blaring kitchen. Everyone turned to look, but Stocker ignored them, ushering her through to the little room at the side with a line of lockers along one wall and the big rough table for staff dinners, marked with burns and coffee cup rings. Once she was inside, he was awkward. He went behind her to help get her coat off—it was deep purple, oddly cut, angular, fashionable, he supposed—and she turned, startled, and an awkward dance ensued as he attempted to rescue her arms from the sleeves.

He felt more himself as she took a seat at the table. She pushed off her boots with a brief sigh, and he caught a glimpse of the chipped red polish on her toenails. He knew what to do now. He raced into the kitchen filled with a sense of mission and excitement, grabbed one of the flaky cheese and tomato tarts he was serving that night, sprinkled herbs over the top—green on red, nice and vivid—and brought it out.

She thanked him and plunged her fork into the tart, splintering the crust. He ran back into the kitchen, shoving aside the sous chef, pulling the lids off pots and inhaling the savory steam. Would she like this? Perhaps this? Braised duck in a deep, whispering sauce, full of things that might speak to her: garlic, dark cherries soaked in wine, stock, roots. He thought at that moment of the creek near the farm where he grew up, the stretch where it widened into a small level lake, the bank he liked to sit on, the yellow narcissi that marched from the bank into the water, and the croaking of frogs in spring, so regular and unceasing that it was hard to believe it came from the throats of living things, so unceasing that eventually you stopped hearing and the sound became part of the tapestry and mystery of the place, the stick insects and shiny beetles skimming along the top of the water, the leaves dangling and dragging through it, and further below, beneath the swirling dark eddies, who knew what copulations, birthings, and dyings? A little of the duck for her then, the rosy breast slices fanned out on the plate, and beside them the dark leg meat in its winey, fruited sauce. Yes. And what might she like after that? What else might she like?

She ate. She didn't say much, just a brief thank you as each new dish came to the table, an array of plates garnished with sauces of various textures, a swirl of oil or a sprinkle of salt—pink salt from the Himalayas, black from Hawaii. Stocker's philosophy as a chef was that people should know what they were eating, ingredients should proclaim themselves clearly and one ingredient shouldn't morph suddenly into another, savory and sweet intermingling promiscuously, resulting in tastes you couldn't identify, and yet he couldn't stop himself from playing around, impetuously combining this with that, and somehow the tastes emerged cleanly from the murk anyway, like Venus rising shining from the surges of the sea.

What am I eating? she asked.

Normally he brushed the question off, but he told her. He explained the ingredients, their provenance, what they meant. She tried everything: digging duck slivers from the dark liquid, removing marrow from a calf's leg-bone, her forehead slightly furrowed, occasionally commenting—That surprised me. This was on the edge of overwhelming—but not quite. The little sharp crystal of salt—I liked that on my tongue.

He watched and periodically he got up to bring her something else: this will complement that, the saltiness here will counter the sweet juiciness there, do you see? Did you catch the hint of bitter?

She nodded. She did see. There was oil on her lips when she'd finished and instead of using the napkin, she darted out her tongue and ran it round her lips to capture the last of the flavor. It moved something in him, her attention to his food, a slow coiling in his intestines, nothing as obvious as desire, though it had to do with desire. Connection, and a deep happiness. At any rate, once she was done, and had finally used her napkin, leaving only a tiny smear of lipstick on it because the glistening coating she'd worn earlier had long since worn off, he asked, What's your name?

Angela.

Do you want to do something now? Take a walk maybe? They can get on without me in the kitchen for a while.

She said she had to go home, and stood up.

Will you come back? You should come back. I'll give you dinner any time you like. Any time, any night of the week.

She smiled. She didn't say anything.

I mean it. We've a good reputation here at my place. It's hard to get a reservation, sometimes people try for months. But you—you can eat here any time you want.

He stopped. We've a good reputation. It's hard to get a reservation. He was talking like an idiot.

She was struggling into her coat, and he didn't try to help this time. When it was on, she turned to him. I'll come back. The dinner was great. Thank you. You know, you never told me your name.

CHAPTER THREE

Stocker was standing over his ancient black pot at midnight, steam collecting wetly on the tip of his nose as he peered into the depths. The staff had all gone home, and he was alone with the hastily wiped-down counters, the sink, the hanging implements and pots and pans, the smell of onion and potato, the rustling of hidden mice and his thoughts about Angela. He replayed the meal he'd served her and the way she'd eaten it, saw the chipped red polish on her toes. Her hands. Her mouth. And for a second he thought—for no particular reason—about the cat, that skinny angular little creature skulking in the alley; it was as if there were a connection between the cat and this girl, this woman made of angles and shadows who had uttered soft little grunts of pleasure as she ate. With her febrile, vibrating energy, Angela hadn't seemed like an eater, but it turned out she was.

This stew he was making was for himself, it would never be served in his restaurant. Putting ingredients together, stirring, inhaling, this was his form of meditation and the kitchen his natural habitat, the environment he swam through waking and sleeping, the place where he spent crazed hot days in a maze of sensation, smelling, watching food change color and texture, listening to bubbling liquids and the searing of meats, tasting, tasting, tasting—though some of his fellow chefs said it was a miracle he could taste anything at all given the constant smoking, and it was true his mouth was always full of the flat bitter sensation of old smoke, between the crevices of his teeth and floating above his tongue. But there it was: somehow his food was stellar, at least according to the critics, stellar in a quite straightforward and specific way, with every taste distinct upon the palate, a phenomenon you could attribute to the vagaries of the food gods whom he worshipped without fail morning and evening through the feel of the tools in his hands and dough between his fingers. Oh, yes, Stocker did have gods, black looming figures thick with the effluence of centuries of cooking and feeding, the history of eating humanity from the Neanderthals around their fires, placing food in the midst of the circle and showing their teeth in a gesture that meant I'm no threat, I will share—this being the characteristic that made us uniquely human, Stocker believed. Not speech, not some misty ephemeral soul, not fidelity or love, but the willingness to share food. From which rose communities and civilizations, myths and stories, and great cities like this one, this city at the center of the universe and his adopted home.

Bumping against the sides of the stewpot, spinning toward the eddies in the middle and away again, vegetable parings, seeds and roots and leaves and pieces of bone slowly dissolved—there was no good stock or stew without bone, he thought. Filling his nostrils, filming his face with damp, the steam kept rising. He had learned everywhere he worked in New York. He learned first and most importantly from the brothers Salvatore, their lasagna, stacked high, layer on layer, globbed with sauce that delivered one hell of a punch and that you wanted to chew, thick with the tomatoes the brothers bought from the farmers' market and stewed for hours, a lasagna like a locker, huge and artless, filled with fat and flavor. He came in to Salvatore's at night sometimes and played with the food. Angelo and Santo didn't mind. They were mellow. They laughed and argued, their hair glistened, they flirted with the pretty girls—well, Angelo did; Santo was more taciturn. After that, he worked for a while at a steakhouse where they aged the beef for eight weeks until it dried on the outside and acquired that complex cheesy smell. He helped butcher the cows. As a boy, he'd helped cut up the family cow, Cherry after her ugly, messy death at his father's hands. He'd heard the spitting of her flesh as it hit his mother's hot frying pan and smelled the sickening rancid smell.

His wasn't a cuisine based on finesse; he didn't make sparkling clear consommés. His was a fierce dark mixing of elements. He didn't think it through, just combined this thing and that. He used whatever was at hand. Offal. Lungs and lights. Vegetable stems and parings. Things farm people knew not to waste. And now those thrifty things were fashionable and thin fashionable New Yorkers came into Stocker's Kitchen and nibbled at them. Gotcha. He wanted to laugh. He really did. He loved fat too, and would pilfer the cut-off edges of chops and steaks from plates that came back to the kitchen, exulting in the lusciousness, the sense of plenty, the way fat dissolved and coated his mouth.

He wasn't interested in the critics or the fashionable people. That was one of the reasons for his fame, the way he brushed off the world. Once he had shoved a model—he didn't know she was a model, though he could tell she was beautiful, well, sort of, not his kind of beautiful—nothing like Angela—but the kind of beautiful regular people recognized, people who seemed to live lives so lacking in energy and savor that it made him crazy to contemplate, people who strolled into his place and asked his waiters in polite but not to be argued with voices, to modify and change his dishes. The model had actually descended to his kitchen and berated him for having nothing low fat or gluten-free on the menu, and it turned out she was famous, a tall, lithe, pantherine creature who had taken New York by storm, and a customer filmed the shove and by the next day it had gone viral: Celebrity chef pushes Carna out of the kitchen.

Angela. If this were a musical, Stocker reflected, he'd be turning her name into a song about now, and capering around his kitchen singing. Could she like him? Could she possibly like him—noisy and vulgar as he was, a farter and a roarer?

He was vulgar, he knew, but that didn't make him stupid. He read incessantly; he was steeped in the mysteries of his art, and when he put a dish together, no matter how much smoke and ash lingered in his mouth, when he mixed almonds and rose water—those humble wild roses with their singlets of petals and scent of soap and country lanes mingling with the lingering bitter of the almonds—when he did this, he communed with the ghosts of medieval cooks in Europe and the Arabian cooks who preceded them. His sauces told stories of the Silk Road, the erotic and religious mysteries of spice, the sailors who hurled themselves onto the high seas, sails snapping, winds roaring, flying over waves as big as houses, bigger even than the dragons they imagined populating foreign shores, in search of nutmeg, peppercorns, and chocolate.

Did Angela understand anything of this, had she sensed it? And if she had, would it bring her back?

He grabbed a cutting board and dumped pieces of potato from it into his mixture, slightly browned now, but each one exactly the same size and shape: Harold's work. Stocker had never been to cooking school himself—the stupid futility of cooking school was one of his pet topics—but though he'd never say it aloud, he admired Harold's fast, precise hands and cooking school acquired technique.

The stew was dark brown and glossy. He ladled a portion into a bowl, took it to the staff room, and sat down. Warm bowl between his hands, he thought of Skeeters, the old shack by the highway where he and his parents had eaten Sunday supper every week, the crudely painted sign that showed a thick white soup plate with something reddish inside and a plume of rising steam that looked as solid as the plate itself. When he asked his parents about the name of the place, his mother said no one knew why it was called that; maybe someone named Skeeter had originally opened it, and in his mind he saw an ancient railroader, a cartoon figure with a thin beard and a knobby stick between his hands. For a long time, he half believed that Skeeter still haunted the bushes behind the diner, and if he squinched his eyes together hard enough and gazed out of the window, he'd see him.

They'd pull up at the same time each week in the ancient, rattling truck whose back doors were held in place with wire so that his mom had to come round to untwist the strands and let him out. He'd jump out onto the rutted ground, jolting his knees, and barely have time to inhale the freezing air before they were through the door and into the sweat-and-beef-smelling warmth of Skeeters. Jack Cody was behind the counter—everyone always used both names addressing him, never Jack, never Mr. Cody—owner and cook. He'd have laughed if you called him chef, laughter that shook the hard belly under his stained apron and displayed a mouthful of bad teeth.

When they were seated at their booth, Violet would come over—a cruel name, he reflected now, for such a big woman. Hey, she'd say, pulling the notepad from her apron pocket, holding her pencil ready above it, What can I do you for? and she'd laugh and sometimes put a damp hand on his hair, while he held very still, willing her to keep it there.

Violet. Fat ugly Violet, with her thinning hair and wandering eye, who had worked at Skeeter's since time began, or at least since any memory he had of time beginning. He stared down at a piece of cabbage leaf in his bowl, edges dissolving into dark liquid. Some of the kids said Violet was a witch and cringed away from the plates of food she set in front of them, but it was a perspective he'd never understood. You'll be wanting a cheeseburger, she'd say to him, and he'd nod, noting his parents' carefully neutral faces, aware that they disapproved of his gluttony but were resigned to suffering it this one night a week. He'd pay for it later; for days he'd get pared-down rations, bits and scraps of things, fighting the constant squirm of hunger in his belly while they reminded him: Violet. The cheeseburger. The fries. You stuffed yourself, remember?

He's got an appetite, Violet would say, smiling. Just look at him scarf down the food. More fries, hon? Yes, he'd say, but his parents would smile politely, his mother holding up a hand to cut off discussion: I think he's had enough. They were angry, mean-spirited people, his mother and father—or rather these imposters who posed as his parents. His dad believed the rod was the best teacher, or more specifically the thick belt with its cold metal buckle.

Without anyone asking, Violet would bring dessert, a huge slab of lemon meringue pie and set it in front of him, and he'd bend his face close and plunge his fork through the hardened foam of the meringue with its myriad tiny bubbles and into the sliding custard below, getting white and yellow all over his lips and cheeks, eating fast fast fast before his father could say, We didn't order the pie, and Violet respond quickly, It's on the house today. I think he's had enough—that was his mother, repeating infuriatingly. There was never enough. Meanwhile he was thrusting sticky pieces into his mouth and chasing smears of sweetness around the plate with his finger and wishing fat, ugly Violet would place her hand on his head again, and hold it there for a long time, and maybe take him home with her at the evening's end.

He stood up, set the bowl in the kitchen sink, pulled a jar of Folger's instant from its semi-secret corner—everyone on staff knew he drank the stuff; no one dared mention it. Stocker ate a lot of things he'd never serve to others. Cloves of raw garlic on black bread with salt for breakfast, fistfuls of Cheetos when he was stressed. For him, Folger's was the smell of childhood, of those rare peaceful moments when his mother fixed a cup of coffee and settled herself in front of the television or at the kitchen table with one of the dozens of catalogues that stuffed the mailbox daily. She ordered decorative plates with horses on them or a faux Wedgwood Romeo and Juliet mooning across a balcony railing. She bought china angels. The peaceful moments never lasted long. If he closed his eyes, he'd see his father yelling drunkenly, sweeping an arm across the shelf of angels, the pudgy figures tumbling, wings cracking as they hit the floor, bodies disintegrating into white chunks and a scatter of powder. He poured boiling water over his Folgers and went back to the table, took a swallow, lit a cigarette. Then he leaned back, closed his eyes, and summoned up again the image of Angela eating.

CHAPTER FOUR

Crystal took the heavy plates from the kitchen; she was used to the weight of the crockery now, though it had struck her as odd at first, coming from the Greek-run coffee shop where Stocker had encountered her—the plates were heavy there too, but on a different scale entirely—these felt weighted—and they didn't cost much, so dropping one wasn't a tragedy. Stocker's plates were specially made to feel earthen and rustic, glazed in dullish shades of bronze, orange and brown with flecks of vibrancy breaking through, and they cost a lot. She'd had trouble at first remembering to keep her thumbs off the carefully-wiped edges as she carried them from the kitchen to the dumb waiter. She remembered when she'd first met Stocker, his coming into her place for coffee and watching her wait tables for a while, then asking her to work at the new restaurant he was about to open—she'd vaguely heard about it through the trade grapevine, though not with any particular curiosity—and she remembered her disbelief at Stocker's offer: Don't know about that. Doesn't sound like my kind of place. She meant her weight, among other things. Crystal was tidy and economical in her movements, but substantial in frame, with wide hips and a big bottom. She made just enough in salary and tips where she was to get by, and she enjoyed joking with the owners, a pair of Greek brothers who were almost always on the premises, and flirting with her regulars. But the salary Stocker offered was large.

She mounted the steep, splintered steps, swung open the dining room door with her hip, and surveyed the place. She had laughed when Stocker first showed it to her—with pleasure and also because of the sense of contradiction and surprise it conveyed—the amber lighting and soothing woods that ranged in color from dark gold to ebony, the shadowed dining nooks, the elegantly inelegant tables and subtly-colored nubbly linens.

There was a funkiness to the room, but it was a carefully considered, warm and comfortable funkiness. It still threw her every time she made the transition to this calm space from the roaring, flaming, under-lit kitchen with its smells and the constant simmering, crackling, spluttering, shushing and slushy food sounds, the arguments and singing and the babble of every kind of accent from Scottish to Puerto Rican. Everyone broke together for smokes in the alley out back, joshing and fooling around as though they'd known each other forever, no matter where they came from. Perhaps it was just the relief of being out of the kitchen and in the cool evening air. But Stocker never took his break when the staff did; he smoked alone. Crystal didn't think he was being stand-offish. It was the way he was, essentially alone, encircled by aloneness despite all the noisiness around him, and all his own yelling, touching, rebuking, and farting, as well as the cackle that started crazed and high-pitched and descended quavering ferociously through a couple of octaves into a phlegmy chest rattle. She thought of his noisiness as a hard plastic shield like the nose guard around a salad bar. A nose guard! Hygiene! Still catching her breath at the top of the steps, Crystal snickered at her own comparison. Stocker's cooks were constantly licking spoons, sticking them back into simmering liquids, licking again; they barely wiped the boards after cutting up meat, and they sent their smoky, boozy, decay- and bad-stomach-scented breath sailing toward everything they touched.

Crystal put the plates on a trolley, and wheeled it to her table, set down her customers' plates, and stood discreetly aside to watch. Her customers—two professional-looking couples—were new here. They looked like people who could order up anything they wanted to eat at any time— mangoes from India, Alba truffles, a Food Network star to cater an at-home dinner party. They chattered a few minutes, then one of the women picked up her fork and conveyed a piece of meat to her mouth. Her expression changed.

Crystal knew why. She remembered the effect when she'd first tasted one of Stocker's creations. It began with a tease, a faint pixilation of the taste buds, and then descended into something more ordinary. A second mouthful, and the ordinary began to transmute. It was still ordinary, but now deeply and almost troublingly so. The taste reminded you of something you'd loved as a child, loved before words and logic and the ability to classify and define took over, something you couldn't quite put your finger on but that was as familiar as the smell of your own skin as you sank into welcoming darkness at night, something you'd once had whenever you wanted and without having to ask, and yet had somehow managed to lose. And after that, you'd gone through life searching and searching—though you hadn't realized it, not until this moment—and sometimes you came across a scent or taste that reminded you of it, that was almost it, but never quite. And now that you'd resigned yourself to your loss, here it was again, that sensation, following those prickly little preliminary surprises and sparks of flavor you couldn't quite name, here it was in your mouth, filling your senses and whispering to you about the old dog whose curly coat moved so miraculously under your childhood fingers, the taste of a thick grass stem after rain, the feel of your mother's hand pushing the hair from the side of your face.

She was only the messenger, the conduit, but it pleased her to do what she did. To pass from one reality to the other again and again: kitchen-stairs-dining room; dining room-stairs-kitchen. It had been hard at first to negotiate those stairs where you couldn't pass anyone coming in the other direction, but had to either back all the way down to the kitchen again or re-climb where you'd just descended, but she was used to it, used to pausing on the small square landing in front of the door to the restaurant to catch her breath and let the flush on her cheeks subside, used to retrieving the plates from the dumb waiter, keeping her broad fingers off the rims. She knew the dining room by heart. Her body knew exactly the number of steps it took to get from one table to another, how to avoid bruising table edges and carelessly pushed back chairs. She had the tone and rhythm of her performance down pat. Stocker could have hired young waitstaff, pretty young men and women, with glossy hair and narrow hips in sharp black trousers, but what he wanted was herself, Crystal, and also Karen, Katie, and Dot, all of them snatched from the kind of inconsequential eating place where you stopped for a quick nosh, a squishy bagel, fructose-sweetened baked goods, a cup of bitter coffee. She'd been here since the beginning. She'd helped recruit the others. She'd been skeptical at first about Stocker's plan to have fat motherly women moving among the tables; she knew enough about the restaurant business to know where someone like herself belonged, but he was adamant—he'd have put them in mustard colored uniforms with cheap nylon aprons if he could—and it turned out to be a good place to work. Not a whole lot of pretension to Stocker's restaurant, despite the steep prices and rave reviews. The sommelier was French and knew everything there was to know about wine, but he was also cheerful and round, and after a few drinks, he came up with absurd flights of French-English puns, and flirted a bit, and stroked her arm and told her she was beautiful. Stocker got the entire front of the house crew together monthly to sit at a table and listen while the sommelier poured wine, explained where it came from, told them what elements to look for and how to name them, and roared with laughter when she, Dot and Katie refused to spit out their mouthfuls. Ridiculous waste, said Dot. By now, Crystal could talk a bit about wine herself, and tell people what should taste nice with what. There were always some cheap decent wines around; Stocker made sure of it. He wanted people he felt comfortable with in the place. She didn't know much about his background, but she knew it was hard and rural, like her own. She'd once thought none of his ideas would attract the rich folk he needed to keep his restaurant going, but they came in droves, drawn at first by a *Times* article about his unusual background—Stocker hadn't given the reporter much, just enough. He'd talked about being abandoned as a baby and then adopted, the small, dusty farm where he grew up with its vegetable garden and one cow, going hungry—and then by spreading word of mouth. By now the set-up, the home-spun food with its oddly sophisticated underpinnings, the smells from the river that wafted through the French doors toward the back tables when the winds were right, and the waitresses who called everyone sweetie and hon had become perversely trendy.

####

Megan was grateful to be led to a table off at the side, right beside the glass doors fronting the dock and the river. They were slightly open; beyond the shadowy sidewalk and the bank, the river glinted, molten lights over darkness. She sat down. This part of the Hudson had been cleaned up, she'd read, so there probably weren't rotten fish in the water any more or used condoms or bloated, seaweed entangled bodies—images put in her mind by her anxious mother trying to dissuade her two months earlier from moving from Delaware to New York—but the light reflections flowed over the moving depths and you could imagine serpents undulating through the water toward the sea. Even in her sheltered spot, she felt conspicuous. But she was lonely, she passed the place every day, and she had finally yielded to the promise of warmth and comfort it offered. She pulled out the paperback she had in her purse, *Shadowed Heart*, and set it on the table in front of her. It was the kind of book she was ashamed of reading, but her loneliness was acute. Every time she read a novel, she measured herself against the heroine, always finding herself deficient. She wasn't wild at heart, sensually in tune with nature, a dark-haired, wraithlike Victorian figure of romance. Her hair was somewhere between dark blond and brown—the color, she always thought, of wet sand—and her face forgettable. There was nothing mysterious in her, just sloshing confusion, a sense of being unformed and unable to claim herself. So the book was trashy, but who cared? Who in this anonymous city knew her? The cover was coffee-colored, with a paler oval at the center that showed a woman with brown hair seated alone at a table, cradling a cup of coffee, an artistic curlicue of steam circling her face and creating the tendrilled outline of the oval. The woman's eyes were cast down. It was the picture that had drawn Megan to the book, the sense of isolation it communicated, and the blurb on the back that said this was a story about a young woman who had come to New York looking for excitement and fulfillment and been forced to work at a boring job in an office. It felt like her own story. She glanced again at the gleaming water, opened the book at her bookmark, caught a scrap of dialogue from a neighboring table—something about the right age for kindergarten—sighed, and began reading.

"Here you go." Someone set a menu in front of her, a homey middle-aged woman, breathing audibly. She was surprised. This place was supposed to be fashionable.

Would it be okay if I just got some kind of appetizer? Before the waitress could answer she added, I won't stay long with an appeasing smile.

Stay all you want, hon, and order whatever. That's what we're here for.

The electric yellow menu was dissected with a jagged black slash that looked almost cheeky, like a comment on the muted tones of the rest of the room. There were six or seven items in each category—appetizers, entrees, desserts. Goat meat, Megan read. Duck legs. Pigs' feet in jelly.

The waitress watched her study the menu. Why don't you try something different, she suggested. You never know what you'll like.

Pigs' feet?

Surprise yourself.

Megan ordered cauliflower soup, which sounded comforting and safe, then drew a breath and said, Okay. I'll try the pig's feet as well.

He has me eating all kinds of things since I've been working here, the waitress said. Stocker. The chef. You wouldn't believe the things I've eaten.

Megan was feeling more at ease now, and she smiled to herself about that, and about the fat, unexpectedly confiding waitress you'd expect to find at an old style coffee shop and not an expensive Manhattan eatery. The place was slowly filling up and the people at the neighboring table had moved on to someone's recent vacation in Turkey. Why don't you have a glass of wine with that? the waitress suggested, appearing at her side, and she did, and took a couple of sips followed by a spoonful of the soup, and then there was this sense that perhaps her life in New York would work out after all, perhaps she could bring her other world, her old one, here with her. The reassurance was there in the earthiness of the soup. Her pigs' feet arrived, small trotters dissolving in aspic, splashed with droplets of vinegar. As she ate, she turned back to her book, and the travails of the brown-haired heroine seemed at once more unreal and ridiculous than before, and at the same time, more moving.

The check, accompanied by a crisscross of pretzel-like twiglets flavored with something she couldn't identify and speckled with crystals of salt and sugar on a saucer, was quite a bit smaller than she'd expected. She glanced quickly at the waitress, who smiled and said, "Come by again, hon."

Outside, a cool rain had begun falling, just a few slow, heavy, splattering drops exploding on the sidewalk and in small thumps on the top of her head, as if someone were reproving her for something. And that was so ridiculous, the idea of someone reproving her for … what? For being who she was and in the place where she was, which was the wrong place, which required of her constant and unceasing adjustment, as if she were always racing forward toward an ever-receding circle of light, so close that half a skip would bring her into it yet never reachable. As the thumping raindrops multiplied into a sheet of water, washing over her face and soaking her clothes, she began to laugh, and then somehow to skip in that springy, body-swaying way she hadn't skipped since she was six, when she had never wondered for a moment who she was or whether she was good enough, smart enough, hip enough for the place where she lived. There were pigs' feet in her belly—poor little pigs, little baby pigs, she hated the idea of them dying to feed her—but there it was, they had died, and their feet were in her belly and rain was plashing on her head and on the shining sidewalk, the air freshening, car lights laying down their colored streaks on the road, and she was skipping along the street, her street, her street in Manhattan, toward the subway that would take her home to her apartment.

Clearing the table, Crystal felt a heaviness in her chest, as of something bruised and ragged-edged. The girl was lonely, that was obvious, and if she came back, Crystal would do her best to help. But her record as a nurturer was mixed. She saw herself all those years ago, standing over her twelve-year-old daughter, placing a large wet palm on the back of the little girl's blond head, pushing fiercely downward, saying, Eat, Jennifer. Eat your goddamn burger. I work hard enough to keep us fed. Some events move forward with you through time, stick like burrs no matter how hard you try to dislodge them, as vivid as the moment when they happened. Her unrelenting rage, the choking sounds her daughter made as she chewed, the pathetic half-masticated piece of burger she'd sicked up before Crystal relented—that was one of those events.

Crystal pulled the cloth off Megan's table in a single swift gesture.

They were over now, her years with Jennifer. No matter how deeply the memories grieved her, she could never go back and re-shape them.

Megan had a dream that night. She was back home in Delaware, sleeping in her childhood bed, and something woke her. The heavy scent of smoke. A crackling sound. Rousing herself, she realized her home was on fire. She called for her parents, but no one responded. Flames were surging into the hallway from the kitchen. Running outside, she saw that every house on the block was aflame. Then she was on the main street, people rushing by but not a single face she recognized, and a roaring, red-black tunnel of fire racing toward them all, flying black ash, hot wind searing her face. She ran with every speck of energy she could muster, though her legs felt heavy, almost rooted, and then it seemed there was someone or something on her back. Twisted, half-human, the thing had leapt onto her and was clinging to her neck, pressing on her windpipe. Everyone else had vanished, the street was empty, and the fire was almost on her. Step by useless step, she weakened, slowly filling with the sickening realization that the creature meant her to die, that she was dying. She became aware of a low, distant droning, and turned her head. A black motorcycle with a black-leather-clad rider was taking shape in the middle of wavering smoke and flame, rushing forward, and then, just as it seemed about to slam into her, whooshing past with such force that she staggered and almost fell. And in that moment, the moment of the motorbike's passing, she was free. The sheer force had blown the imp from her back. The rider didn't stop or hesitate, and his bike got smaller and smaller, dwindling to nothingness as it sped away.

Waking up took several long minutes; it took even longer for her to understand that she was safe. She turned on the bedside light and pulled the covers tight about her. And then she started wondering about the huge blind force that had saved her—not deliberately or out of compassion, but simply because it existed and had crossed her path at the exact moment when she needed it.

CHAPTER FIVE

A few nights later, Crystal stood at the sink, stacking the pots she'd used to prepare dinner and filling them with water to soak. The chops were finishing in the oven, and Jennifer would be here momentarily, her daughter Jennifer, from whom she had been estranged for a few years, the silence broken only by an occasional telephone call, and who had finally agreed that Crystal could visit her grandchildren in New Jersey the next weekend, but had insisted on coming by beforehand—to set the ground rules, Crystal assumed. Through the window above the sink, she faced the familiar faded brick wall across the way, punctuated by small square windows like her own, the bricks glowing as the sun set. There was a window directly opposite hers, offering glimpses of another life. The place belonged to an elderly couple whom she had decided—without quite knowing why—were Italian, a skinny man who sat wide-legged in his undershorts, a comfortable, cushiony woman. When the curtains were open, she could see them, eyes fixed on a television just below her line of sight, a curly little dog beside them on the sofa. Sometimes, when the man turned away momentarily, the woman slipped the dog a kernel of popcorn or a lick of her ice cream cone, a lick the dog took with great delicacy, never attempting to snatch the entire treat. For Crystal, there was a long-ago, wistful quality to these comfortable tableaux. But today the curtain was drawn.

She moved through the living room, cleared the empty coffee cup and cigarette pack from the TV tray—she allowed herself one cigarette a day—and began folding the quilt she draped over her legs at night, even in summer, because the air conditioning blasted cold air at her then, but going without it turned the apartment into a furnace. The quilt had been made by her grandmother Sarah, the one who had eventually left Alabama for New York to manage a Mexican restaurant—a journey that had struck Crystal as a marvel of independence and exoticism at the time and had lured her to the city herself years later—after her divorce—with 11-year-old Jennifer in tow. There had been problems between her and Jennifer all along, but they intensified with that move. Packing up their hot, poky little Auburn house, she hadn't understood the fierceness of Jennifer's attachment to her home, or the depth of the girl's belief that someday her father would return to live with them again.

Crystal held the quilt against her chest. Grandma Sarah had told her that its pattern, solid triangles of red, brown and beige all facing in the same direction, with one delicately flowered recurring patch for contrast, was called Flying Geese. She half-smiled at the sad irony of that, and began circling her already-tidy apartment, straightening the arrangement of china ornaments on the top of a bookshelf, the photographs scattered on end tables: baby Jennifer being tossed in the air by her father; Jennifer as a pudgy toddler in tap shoes. She picked up the toddler photo, remembering how, at three years old Jennifer would jump up and down when Crystal returned from work, arms up, wriggling with joy and excitement. Crystal remembered the feel of the little girl's body between her hands, squirming, firm and smooth, perfect and sweet as a plum. Now that child was a tight-lipped, impermeable young woman who wouldn't let her mother in no matter how gently Crystal knocked, or how hard she tried to keep her voice neutral and undemandingly loving, wouldn't give an inch even when Crystal tried—as she had time and time again—to say she was sorry.

There were two places set at the table, and Crystal had put a jar of flowers in the center, daisies. Stocker had volunteered to send home a couple of meals from the restaurant, but she'd said she wanted to do the cooking herself, though she accepted his offer of thick-cut lamb chops while sedulously ignoring his insistent advice on how to cook them. Opening the oven to check on the chops in her ancient cast iron skillet, she found herself filled with unreasoning happiness. Despite everything, Jennifer was coming. Jennifer Juniper. That was the song Crystal had sung pushing Jennifer on the swing, or holding her at night when she was scared or fretful and couldn't sleep: Jennifer Juniper lives upon the hill. Jennifer Juniper, sitting very still. She'd waltzed the baby around the living room singing when she and Jennifer's father still thought they were in love, when she found his drinking worldly and romantic rather than disgusting and he called her babe so proudly and possessively, walking beside her with a heavy arm draped across her shoulders.

It took a while for everything to turn sour. She remembered heated arguments with her mother who kept insisting, He should be supporting you, Crystal, you and Jennifer. At least he should be trying. And times when she crept over to his parents' house, shame-faced, to beg his mother to lend her a little money out of the red-and-white chicken-shaped change jar on the kitchen counter, and to please please please not tell Gary she'd asked. But she kept loving him for a long time nonetheless. She told herself she didn't mind his going out in the evening with friends or flirting with other women because, after all, it was she he came home to. At night, she'd sit in the rocking chair waiting for the sound of the car, the baby's cheek sticking to her sweaty breast as she nursed and sung, Is she sleeping? I don't think so. Is she breathing? Yes, very low, while Jennifer kept one round gray eye fixed on her mother's face.

And then he stopped coming home most nights, and eventually she had to go to work waitressing at the one Main Street restaurant while her mom babysat Jennifer, who soon began to prefer being in her grandparents' cozy house and ran off shrieking when Crystal came to get her. She's only four, her mother would say, observing Crystal's hurt and anger. Four year olds don't know squat, honey. She loves you deeper than you can know.

But it was all getting to be too much. There was Gary, at this point openly running around with their eighteen-year-old neighbor; she'd seen them walking down the street, his arm around her shoulders, strutting the way he once had with her, the teenager's hard young breasts pushing against her white T-shirt. There was no point in being angry. He wouldn't care. He wasn't trying to hide it. He paid Crystal no attention at all. She grew fat, weepy, and morose. Looking back now, she could see how all this must have affected Jennifer, but at the time she was drowning in misery, sodden with it, and all she could see was the next task, and the one following it, and all the things she needed to do to keep the two of them going.

Even in her darkest moments, Crystal didn't accuse herself of having been abusive toward Jennifer. Not that. Short-tempered, quick to yell, and occasionally administering a harder-than-intended slap, but never cruel, never someone who terrorized her child. Except she kept remembering how the little girl would sit very still as her mother moved about the house, watching wide-eyed, and she could still hear herself yelling I'm not angry with you Jenny, for Chrissake, it's not you—though she understood, even at the time, at least now and then, that a big angry person banging around a room is a threat whether she's directing her anger directly at you or not.

She touched one of the chops, decided it needed another few minutes. Slamming the oven door shut, she fought a wave of guilt and self-hatred. A memory was pressing insistently against her forehead, hard as she tried to push it back. It was roughly a year after they'd arrived in New York and they were fighting almost daily—about Jennifer's refusal to study, the ridiculous upcurling bangs she wore in an effort to look like the city kids, the vampire-dark nail polish. Crystal had hurried home from the diner, trying as always to get home before her daughter, carrying two hamburgers for their dinner. The subway had been even more hot and crowded than usual, and there'd been a long delay in a stifling tunnel. When she got home, Jennifer was flipping through a teen magazine. Crystal told her to come to the table and plunked a burger down in front of her. Jennifer poked at it.

"There's pickles, mom. You know I hate pickles."

"That's okay, Jen. Just take them out."

"It'll still taste of pickle."

Crystal felt her irritation rising and tried to fight it down. She said, I work all day to keep us in food. Jennifer grimaced theatrically, and Crystal's voice tightened. Now you're too good for what I bring home?

Jennifer took a tiny bite, and chewed, still turning pages.

"Come on, Jennifer. Stop playing around."

How long did the scene continue? It never stopped. Somewhere in her mind, it was still going on. Now and then, placing a plate in front of a customer at Stocker's, she'd see Jennifer's slumped shoulders again, the effortful way her jaw moved, as Crystal insisted, bite after miserable bite, that she finish that damn hamburger.

Half gone, and that wasn't enough, and then there was a long period—was it an hour, was it two, was it the entire evening?—when Jennifer sat at the table, the mutilated burger in front of her, crying quietly while Crystal tidied the rest of the dishes, rinsed them, and eventually sat down and read the newspaper, conspicuously ignoring the snuffling except to say every half hour or so, You're not leaving the table till that burger's gone.

Finally it was. Jennifer sat perfectly still for a minute or two, swallowing hard, and then the food started to come back up. Looking over, Crystal saw her throat move up and down convulsively, once, twice; a gurgling sound and there it was on the plate: a nasty, vomit-smelling little mound of chewed beef and dissolving white bread. She came up behind her daughter, a large woman filled with anger, and placed her hand on the back of Jennifer's head and pushed until the girl's face was almost in her plate, and said, lower jaw tensed, "You'll eat it. You'll eat it if it's the last thing you eat." At that moment she meant it—Jennifer would eat that burger if it was the last thing she did—and everything, Gary's betrayal and Jennifer's hostility, the hot subway, the man who'd yelled, "Hey girl," at the diner and held out his spit-slobbered glass for a refill, and the older one who'd pinched her butt then turned back to his friends with an expression of mocking pretend innocence as she whipped around to confront him, the loneliness of New York, the way her feet ached by evening and protested in the morning when she tried to squeeze them into the cheap plastic waitressing shoes, the overwhelming responsibility of keeping the two of them sheltered and fed in this strange city on her own—all of that was in the weight of the hand pushing at her daughter's head. She felt the silky hair on her palm, the hair she loved brushing, the little girl she loved, but love itself was corroding in her throat. "Dammit, Jennifer, eat." A moment passed. She spoke more softly; something was moving in her, some part of her was disengaging and telling her to stop, Just eat it, Jen. It'll be quicker and easier if you do it fast. Come on, Jennifer, you can't waste food. The girl forked up a bit of the part-masticated mass on her plate and choked it down. Swallowed again, subdued her retching, paused. But then Crystal thought, wasn't it her job to make Jennifer eat all of it? There were voices in her head, experts, grown-ups, the pastor at her church at home, saying children should obey, food shouldn't be thrown away, and once you've told your child to do something, you should never back down. If she were a good mother, she'd follow through, but she wasn't a very good mother obviously. And how could she be expected to be fair and firm and consistent when it took everything she had just to keep going? Come on, she said, eat what you've left, and then, as Jennifer miserably took another bite, Oh, okay, that's enough. She may have been violating a cardinal rule of childraising, but it was enough, and suddenly she was so tired she had to sit down. Jennifer threw an ascertaining look at her mother, grabbed her magazine, bolted from the chair and vanished into the bedroom, closing the door. Crystal sat for a moment to catch her breath and then rose heavily to her feet. She picked up the plate with its pathetic chewed remnants and carried it to the sink.

The doorbell rang, she opened the door, and there stood Jennifer. It was all Crystal could do not to wrap her arms around her, breathe her in. She was here. Her child was here, somewhere inside this composed young woman with her careful makeup and smooth blond hair. Many years ago, Jennifer had shaken off the messiness, flux and ambiguity of their life together. She had left New York as soon as she could for marriage to an accountant, a house in suburban New Jersey, and three children whom she home-schooled. Crystal hesitated, opened her arms, and saw Jennifer's mouth pinch slightly before she moved forward for a ritual embrace. I have iced tea, Crystal said, relieved that her touch had been accepted. Sweet the way you liked it back home.

Jennifer nodded. I can't stay long, mom.

Crystal hustled to get the food on the table. They exchanged a few comments, she asked about the children, and Jennifer told her about the older son's learning to ride a bike and the little one's fascination with trains. "About your visit," she said finally. "Dan didn't want you to come, but I told him you are their grandmother."

Crystal didn't say anything. She sawed at her chop, trying to sever the hard rim of fat from the meat, her knife thick and blunt and clumsy in her hand. If she'd been alone, she'd have picked the thing up, but she worried that her daughter would think she was turning into one of those pathetic solitary creatures, unselfconsciously ugly in her habits, gnawing at bones and leaving scraps to harden on the plate overnight.

"I persuaded him," Jennifer continued.

Was she supposed to be grateful? She tried. "Thank you, honey."

"So you'll stay over Saturday night, and he'll drive you back Sunday morning before the game."

"That'll be wonderful, Jen. Hey, perhaps you two would like to go out on a date and have me babysit?"

"No."

"Okay." They ate in silence for several minutes.

"We can just all watch TV together or something."

Crystal took in a breath. "You want a bit more potato, Jen?"

"No thanks, mom. I'm full."

"Coffee then?"

Crystal began clearing the dishes, and Jennifer got up to help. Crystal was always aware of the way people moved in kitchens, and in this cramped space—this was what surprised her—in her tiny kitchen they moved together neatly and companionably, never getting in each other's way, Jennifer stacking the dishwasher, Crystal measuring coffee into the filter, moved as they had through years of cookie making, heating leftovers, drying dishes, undeniably flesh of each other's flesh, undeniably mother and daughter, no matter how congealed and chilly the air between them, and despite the quivering, self-righteous rage she sensed at her daughter's core. She had spent so long trying to communicate through careful words and wordless tending, through offerings of food and drink, that she was different now, washed in the blood of the lamb, to use Jennifer's language, no longer the old Crystal with the angry mouth and hurtful hands. She found herself blinking back tears, breathing deeply and consciously as she poured water into the coffee maker. Yet still they worked in unison, sensing each other's movements and accommodating as they could never do in any other sphere.

When they were back at the table with their cups of coffee she said, "I'm not the way I was, Jennifer"—so much care and calculation in those few words. Jennifer shook her head, slightly. "Let's not." Minutes later, she picked up her shiny, unscuffed brown leather purse. "Well, it's quite a drive." She checked for her keys, turned and said, "Thanks for the chops, mom.

They were good," as if leaving a formal dinner party, moving slightly away to signal she wouldn't be receiving a second hug. "We'll be here to pick you up around ten."

When the door had closed behind her daughter, Crystal took the cups into the kitchen, and began rinsing them in the sink. The Italians had opened their curtain and cracked the window to savor the cool air. Hands in soapy water, she watched them, two old people on a faded couch facing an invisible television, a bowl of popcorn on the woman's lap, the dog seated beside her. The man said something, the woman got up and walked into the kitchen, and the dog levered itself painfully and arthritically up from the sofa and trotted gamely behind her, tail high, followed her still as she returned with two cans of soda. Crystal watched as the old man took his can, smiling slightly in thanks. Then she started the dishwasher and walked into the living room, settled into the armchair under the quilt with the Flying Geese and lit a Kent. She clicked on the television. Wifeswap. A woman was yelling at a man that he needed to have more fun in his life, and he was fuming that life was about much more than fun, and the song that had started up earlier was still running through her head. Do you like her? Yes, I do, Sir. Would you love her? Yes, I would, Sir. Watcha doing Jennifer, my love?

CHAPTER SIX

Angela did come back. The next Thursday she peered in through the kitchen door, and Stocker yelled at Harold to take over his sauté pan and raced to escort her to the staff room. And again the following Thursday, and the next. She had become comfortable with the arrangement by then, and she was tired. Thursday was her late night at work. She took off her shoes and plopped her feet on the table not far from her plate. She read the newspaper as she ate; she had stopped commenting on the food every time, asking what was in it, paying him compliments, but he liked watching her eat and took her unabashed greed as tribute. He sat and watched and listened to the faint sound of her mastication and thought about the muscle of her calf, spread a little on the table, and the faint smell of her feet. He wanted to kiss those feet, tongue the hot skin between her toes. He didn't care about crud. It was her crud, Angela's toe jam. He'd harvest the stuff and put it into one of his dishes if he could—that's what his cooking was about anyway, transmutation, the eternal dialogue between pleasure and disgust, nourishment and decay. He wanted to dive deep, take everything Angela was into himself, everything, not just smooth skin, wise eyes, thin little lips, breasts, waist, and small, tight buttocks, not just the sexy stuff, but also liver, lungs and heart, the half-digested contents of her stomach, her waste, everything—that was love in his eyes, never being repulsed by anything about the beloved. Who was the medieval idiot who said that woman was nothing but a sack of filth, that if a man considered for just a moment what she was made of he would never want to touch her, hold her in his arms or put his lips to hers. Fool, thought Stocker. Mimsy, prancing, weak-kneed fool. That was the point, embracing the entirety. His job was to mine Angela, take her into his body in both her familiarity and her otherness, understand her—not the understanding that comes with words and self-revelation and confessions about the past, but an understanding of the living creature beneath those witty, eccentric clothes and that cool mien that would throb along his veins. And once he'd done that, he'd fashion his tribute, the single dish that could contain and communicate her essence.

He looked back at her feet and said, You have bunions.

She lowered the paper. They stared at each other. Perhaps she was trying not to laugh; he wasn't sure. He placed his fingers on the bony lump at the side of her foot very gently. She winced, but she didn't move her foot away, and he began stroking in widening little circles, watching her face the whole time. After a few moments, she wiggled her toes, sighed deeply, and went back to her food—calf sweetbread in a truffled sauce with veal jus, carrots, celeriac. We humans are who we are, Stocker thought, watching the muscle move along the side of her jaw, because of the way we eat. Because we eat meat and because we cook our food—primitive man, cooking over those long-ago fires that he had first come upon by accident, wood burning after a lightning strike or an errant spark, and later learned to create for himself—perhaps the biggest and most important discovery of our entire human history. Cooking and eating meat, combined, caused our jaw muscles to shorten, and our snouts, and the twisting channels of the intestine, and we lost the gorilla gut pushing out in front. That one small thing, changing the way we took nourishment, caused an endless cascade of changes in the ways our bodies confronted the world and the ways in which the world responded.

Angela set down her knife and fork, gestured toward his stroking hand. "It's the shoes. They're not made for human beings."

"Why do you wear them? For the job?" She worked in a clothing shop a few blocks away, that much he knew.

"Well, sort of now. But I've always worn my shoes as high as I could stand. Since I was thirteen."

"Didn't your parents mind?"

"They didn't know. I kept my going out stuff hidden in the bottom of the closet and changed my clothes and put on makeup and snuck out at night."

He thought a follow-up question was in order, but he wasn't sure what it was. Angela sighed and slid her feet from the table. "Any coffee, Stocker?" He nodded and began to stand up. "Perhaps you could walk me home after that?"

A short time later, he was bustling along beside her, his usual rage for action subdued. He didn't have to talk. He felt proud; if he could see himself, he thought, he'd see his chest puffed out like a pouter pigeon's. He was only two or three inches taller than she; it was a ridiculous image; it made him laugh inwardly. But what he was feeling wasn't only pride. He thought about the pigeon huddled over her nest, head deep beneath her puffed out feathers, cooing gently, that liquid crooning sound deep in her breast as she protected her egg—and that egg was the fragility and splendor of his walking down the street with Angela. She was grumping about her shoes meanwhile, wondering why they couldn't be better engineered at the price, and then she stopped and leaned against him for balance, her shoulder against his, her left hand clutching his arm while with her right she fumbled at an ankle strap. He said something about the dangers of going barefoot on the dirty sidewalk, the possibility of glass or stones, dog shit, and she responded that she walked barefoot all the time along the gritty streets of New York and in California, where she grew up, on the hot sands of the beach. "The soles of my feet are so thick nothing penetrates," she said, turning up a foot for his inspection, awkward, hopping on the other, still clinging to his arm. "I stepped on a tack once—it went all the way in to the head—and it took me a couple more steps to even realize it."

She got the shoes off, caught her balance, then padded along beside him in silence for a while. A motorcycle roared by, the sound rising and dying away. They turned from Broadway onto a quieter side street. But always in the city, Stocker reflected, that sense of life being lived all around you, the invisible people behind the walls of the high, narrow buildings. He heard television sounds from an open window, one of those annoying female announcers; he couldn't make out her words, but the smug hortatory tones were familiar. Sometimes, alone in his apartment at night, he'd watch cooking contests, the kind with the slightly exotic, impossibly beautiful and far too thin hostess, raging at the way she and the judges humiliated the competing chefs, and thinking, Give me half an hour with you in my kitchen, you skinny bitch, and I'd show you cooking. It infuriated him, the chefs' servility. Why would you do it, he wondered. Why would you hand over yourself, your sacred calling, for a row of tight-assed pretentious idiots to pass judgment on? He glanced at Angela walking beside him, just as skinny and impermeable as the hostesses, but made of something else entirely, true to herself, true all the way down to the core. Angela's dignity didn't come from privilege, wealth, beauty, hours spent on workout machines. It came from the way she'd grown up, her urchin beginnings. In reality, Stocker had no idea how Angela had grown up, but he understood her toughness as a mirror image of his own, knew she'd been forced to shrink protectively inward as a child and hold herself tight, not be soft for a moment, and he knew also about the small, dark thing inside her, that imp of darkness and self-preservation that was often spiteful but was also her salvation because of the glimmers of humor, of joy and sensuality at its heart. All this he knew without her speaking a word, as she walked beside him barefoot, her hand in the curve of his elbow.

Angela's apartment was a small, spare box, with a mattress in one corner, a few pieces of furniture, a cubby at the front that served as a kitchen—a narrow stove, a cheap microwave. My boss owns this, she said. I was lucky to get it. He opened the buzzing brown box of a refrigerator and found eggs, a small carton of milk, a paper bag with a smear of grease on the side, and fruit in a bowl, kiwis and lychees. He approved. He liked the coolness of these fruits and the way they satisfied thirst without gushing juice or showing off a peach's vivid sensuality.

Leave it alone, Stocker. Close the fridge door.

He did. You're not a cook?

Coffee in the morning, that's about it. Maybe a scrambled egg Sunday.

He stored up the sparse details. They were like pieces of a puzzle, each to be scanned for meaning before he figured out where it fit.

She offered him a beer and he nodded. It was something to do. Then, beer in hand, he looked for a place to sit, seeing only a single wooden chair at the table and a sofa in front of the television.

You don't have people in much.

Uh-uh. She shook her head. Here. She gestured to the sofa, he sat, she lowered herself to the floor a few feet in front of him. He held up his beer can: You're not having any? She shook her head again.

He sipped, played with the tab, fidgeted on his chair. Seated cross-legged on the floor, Angela seemed perfectly composed. Stocker had only one way of dealing with discomfort or self-consciousness, but roaring round the place or telling obscenity-filled jokes didn't seem quite right. He felt physically smaller. She looked at him and laughed. You came here to fuck me, didn't you Stocker?

He set down his beer and stared.

Well, how about it? The bed's right over there.

She walked over to the mattress and sat down, watching him close-ly, patting the place beside her, and now he knew who he was again, and he bellowed and leapt at her, tumbled her back onto the mattress, snuffled in her neck, going fast, fast, fast and crazy knowing if he stopped and thought or hesitated for as much as a second he'd run out the door, and he only knew how to go at this thing head on like a wounded bull because he'd never really been with a woman before, in terms of having a relationship—sure, he'd had sex with women at drunken parties, with some female once who wanted to be a chef and thought this was the way to ingratiate herself—it didn't work; he didn't believe women should be in the kitchen, well, not in his kitchen—and a prostitute here or there when the longing became too strong. He hadn't been looking for more. He didn't think he could do it. Relate to a woman, be a man with a woman in a relationship. Not so fast, said Angela as he wriggled on top of her, her clothes half off, and his, not so fast, and she grabbed his rump, hard thin fingers digging into the meat of him, digging and wiggling like sharp-shelled little clams settling into sand—was it a poke or a tickle, pleasurable or painful? He couldn't tell. And then she was stroking, smooth strong strokes from the place where his flesh barely began to curve out and downward over the bulbous part, alternately poking and stroking, brushing past the shadowed groove between his buttocks, but never pausing and never moving between his legs, though by now he'd have given his life, his breath, his kitchen to have her touch his balls and penis. But she just kept stroking as his butt quivered and moved away from her fingers and toward her fingers, and he sighed and moaned, fleshy, garlicky moans, oh yes, of the flesh, fleshy, that was the point, that was the fucking point, that was the point of fucking. But then he'd had all he could take, and he cried out and grabbed her hair and pulled her backward by it onto the bed and got on top and pushed aside the thin strip of underwear covering—oh, finally—that secret part of hers, that small and secret and inward curling part with its entryway of hair, and parted her with his fingers, and greedily put his mouth to her and sucked at the sweet tender fishiness of that place, that place to which he was finally—and he hoped forever—staking claim.

####

Stocker began cooking for Angela, and his food changed. His new dishes were filled with a coruscating energy, almost roaring with life. It was all there, the rejoicing, the nourishment, the songs of the small green frogs courting their mates in the velvet darkness of a spring night. If his pastas could have leapt from their plates and capered, they would have; the small parcels of fried dough he liked to fill with savory surprises were so buoyed by the heated deliciousness within that they almost needed to be weighted down. The green energy of herbs pricked through his entrees. It was as if he were taking the foods apart, freeing the molecules and allowing the air between to vibrate. No one could say how he did it, but to eat these things was to feel a rush of joy, a sense that life had never been so full, the heart rising, breath quickening, memories unanchoring themselves from nooks and crannies of the brain and standing forth with startling clarity: old loves and deep quiet pleasures, moments of understanding—as when the jumble of black marks printed on a page cohered for the first time, and the child cried, I can read. I can read. The touch of a loving hand on your hair at bedtime, or falling asleep in the back of a car leaning against your mother, the hypnotic forward movement into the dark, the blurring as your eyes drifted shut, the comfort of her warm body. And Crystal, setting down the heavy plates before her customers and standing back, deferential and proud, because she knew what she was offering was ambrosia.

They were prepping for service one Thursday when Stocker, turning with a whisk in his hand, noticed someone sidling down the stairs, a pale nerdy boy with black hair flopping over his pimpled forehead, jean cuffs crusted with mud, clutching a paper shopping bag. Stocker wrinkled his nose inquisitorially; the boy descended a few more steps: I have morels.

You have morels? Stocker's arms opened as though he wanted to fold the youngster to his grubby, white-coated front. You have morels?

How many? A couple pounds?

I'm not sure. More, I think.

Okay, said Stocker, let's see. He gestured toward a clear space on the counter and the boy upended his bag, a patter of dirt, a silent fall of black, honeycombed mushrooms. Two of them rolled over the edge of the counter and onto the floor, and Harold reverently retrieved them. Stocker stood over the stash, inhaling, eyes closed. Oh, yes, he said. He picked up a mushroom, turned it in his fingers, put it to his nose, inhaled again.

Beautiful, he proclaimed. Where'd you get these?

The kid said nothing.

Not telling? Don't want to give away secrets? Okay, I don't blame you. How much d'you want? Here—he turned to Harold. Clean them off. Gently. No water.

Twenty a pound? said the boy.

Stocker sputtered and harrumphed—Stealing me blind, he said—but his heart wasn't in the complaint. He could feel the water collect in his mouth as he thought about what he'd do for Angela with those morels—scallops, perhaps. He imagined the way the morels would sponge up the dark humusy sauce, and how he'd balance the dish with something acid, just a little acid, and perhaps thin curls of orange zest scattered across the plate. He reached for his checkbook.

It was all there, everything working together, and he, Stocker, was the executor, he brought forth these wonders, and in his kitchen, for once, peace reigned, the Puerto Rican dishwasher humming under his breath, Harold's tone softer: Yeah, ma, I'll be there. No, honest. Everything moving. The dance of sauté pans over flame and the foods they contained curving upwards and downwards in a smooth, rhythmic arc, the bubbling surfaces of soups and stews, himself, prancing around the kitchen reciting dirty limericks, clopping his cooks so hard and gladly on the shoulder that they dropped their knives and wooden spoons, the pulsing of food between his palms, light and dry, wet and heavy, the living elasticity of dough and the wrist-bending weight of melon, the calmly repetitive movements and the adrenalin-spiked moments of tension, everything throbbing, transmuting, nothing at a standstill, stolid or satisfied, everything reaching in its own way for sublimity. And on Thursday evenings—this Thursday evening—Angela descending the stairs, high heels tapping, face alight with her own brand of grinning imp-like joy, waving to the cooks at their tasks in the kitchen before settling herself at the staff-room table to be fed.

CHAPTER SEVEN

Megan sometimes had dreams about dead people beneath the stage where she was performing. Their thoughts and emanations entered her body through the soles of her feet and rose up through her and out of her throat so that she became the conduit for their long-silenced voices. That was how it felt during those fleeting moments in class when she was acting and everything came together—like being possessed, like being part of something ancient and eternal. She loved acting, or at least she thought she did, but she wasn't at all sure she liked being watched. Except for those times when she truly became someone else and—miraculously—found herself flying, acting so well that all nervousness fled, and she could ignore the miserable little goblin in the back of her head that chattered incessantly about how untalented she was, how her dishonesty and blundering ineptness as an artist shamed the world. During those flying times, power coursed through her—the power of the words she spoke and the character she portrayed, and also of the charged silence pulsating between herself and the audience. That power, created by the dead and the living together, was infinite but it didn't belong to her. It used her, visited rarely and couldn't be willed into being. All she had to do was allow in a single question—was she speaking too loudly or sobbing too long? Was she being entirely authentic?—and the power evaporated.

For the last several months, she had sat in Mort's acting class, an echoing room on the fourth floor of a decrepit building with a raised platform on one end—heaven knows what the place had originally been used for—listening and watching. She had seen her fellow students rage, weep, bicker and kiss on that platform, and watched them sitting on the edge of it afterwards for the critique Mort called the blue period. Beautiful Bea had wept about a role she was sure she'd won, but hadn't, pudgy Doug fretted that his performance was wooden—which it had been. She had learned so much here about what it meant to be an actor. Some of her classmates worked from the outside in, taking on a limp, an accent, a smoker's cough to create their characters; others searched within for motivation and wouldn't make a move or utter a sound until they'd found the exact feeling they wanted and allowed it to swell until, uncontainable, it forced its way into their faces and out of their mouths. Mort preferred this approach, but he admitted external means could work too: if the anger you're supposed to feel doesn't come, he'd said, slam your fist on the table anyway and you're likely to find yourself filled with real rage. The best actors were so grounded and centered, he told them, so immersed in what they were doing that they could mesmerize an audience while simply sitting at a table drinking coffee. That was the magic of theatre, the way it transmuted the quotidian into art.

It was all new to Megan and miraculous, and this space was where the miracles happened, this funky room with dusty windows and the constant crooning of pigeons in the loft above. Piled against the back wall in stacks and untidy heaps were all kinds of things the students might need for their scenes: bits of furniture, a rack of clothing that included long skirts, bonnets, torn T-shirts, props like teapots, paintbrushes and walking sticks, an ancient sofa with the stuffing oozing out.

And her fellow students. Everyone knew who the real talents were—and who they weren't. Karen, stick-thin, talking endlessly about food but subsisting, as far as Megan could tell, on celery sticks with peanut butter; a short stocky Italian guy who figured he could find work in gangster shows but really wanted to do Shakespeare; handsome Devon, a model and unimaginably rich, whom everyone envied despite his obvious lack of talent. Did talent really matter? the gossip went. Devon was so gorgeous he was sure to end up a star eventually anyway—that fraught word star, always spoken with rage, envy, contempt and longing. And so would Lauren, the dark-haired girl who looked like a prom queen and had found an agent within two weeks of arriving in New York. These two were class royalty. And then there was Tracy, the new student who rarely smiled and whom everyone disliked. She could have been pretty, the students agreed during the beery after-class convocations at the Liffy, the corner bar where they discussed who was hiring and what directors looked for and which fellow student was promising and which would really be better off in some other profession. If only Tracy dressed in some color other than gray or brown, they lamented, and did something with her limp, straight hair. It was almost as if she didn't want to be attractive, didn't think any of them—or anyone else in her world—was worth the trouble of sprucing up for.

This evening, Tracy had a scene scheduled, the first she'd taken on. Megan watched as she walked slowly across to the exact center of the platform and turned to face them. She stood painfully upright, her hands dangling at her sides, her green nail polish making her fingers look fish-belly white. Megan saw Lauren and Devon exchange a look. This is from *The Bald Soprano* by Ionesco, said Tracy, her voice formal, gravelly, flat. She paused. Then:

The polypoids were burning in the wood.

A stone caught fire.

The castle caught fire.

The forest caught fire ...

The men caught fire

The women caught fire

In this place where emotion was the primary currency, Tracy was blank-faced and inexpressive. Yet somehow Megan found herself leaning forward, breath bated, listening. Every word Tracy spoke felt like a physical object, standing separate in the air, vibrating with indescribable significance. She closed her eyes momentarily and instantly the pursuing flames of her nightmare—the garishly lit Main Street, the racing black motorcycle with its faceless rider—flickered behind the lids.

The birds caught fire

The fish caught fire

The water caught fire

The sky caught fire

The ashes caught fire

The smoke caught fire

The fire caught fire

Everything caught fire

Caught fire, caught fire.

Tracy stopped. In the silence that followed, she moved to the front of the stage and sat down on the edge, awaiting the critique. Students usually appeared nervous during this blue period, but Tracy still showed no emotion—well, Megan thought, perhaps just a flicker of ... was it defiance? Where did this girl's boldness come from? That speech wasn't anything you could get your teeth into, not even a real monologue, just a weird scrap of something. Or nothing. And who did Ionesco these days anyway?

Mort cleared his throat. Why did you choose this piece? he asked.

Good, thought Megan. He had the same criticisms.

I don't know. I felt like it.

You felt like it?

I thought it was important.

Explain that to me.

I know the whole play's supposed to be about language, disintegration, meaninglessness, stuff like that. But that's not how it felt to me. When

I first read it I kept thinking about how there are times ... I don't know. This speech made me think about wars and displaced people and famine, terrible things happening in the world that most of us never even think about. How life is scary and precarious and you can't make any sense of it and Ionesco doesn't even try.

Yes, there are times when everything implodes, Mort said carefully. In history and in our private lives. Devastation. Chaos and catastrophe. Do you think that's what this speech is about?

Tracy shrugged. It's the maid speaking. Maybe she's pissed and overworked and just wants to blow everybody up.

Her tone was challenging, but Mort laughed. That works too. Very interesting, Tracy.

He was impressed, Megan thought. It didn't seem fair.

When class was over, the usual group of students congregated to discuss whether they wanted to go out for coffee or beer. This time their backs were conspicuously turned toward Megan. There was some code by which these people had identified and chosen each other and it wasn't one Megan could hope to crack. Sometimes they asked her and one or two others outside their circle to come with them, sometimes not. That night, she left rapidly, along with the other rejects. Tracy's voice was in her head as she left, went with her as she walked along the street toward Stocker's Kitchen. The men caught fire ... The women caught fire ... The birds caught fire. It was comforting to turn the corner to the restaurant, slide into its accustomed warmth and take up her table in the far corner, comforting to see Crystal approach with the black-stripe-slashed yellow menu in her hand. And even more comforting when Crystal returned a few minutes later with a wine glass and a half bottle and started pouring. Don't worry, hon, she said, as she did every time, it's on the house tonight.

Megan was leaving the restaurant after dinner when she saw a small cat slide around the side of the building. She crouched down and held out her hand, expecting that the cat would move away from her into the shadows but it came forward, and she felt the damp cool of its nose against the ends of her fingers. Her leftovers were in a sturdy cardboard box with the bold SK of the restaurant logo on it, and she pushed through the flap and felt around inside until she touched bone, pulled off a piece of chicken and held it out. After the briefest hesitation, the cat snatched at the morsel— she wanted to be polite, it seemed to Megan, but her need was too fierce— and a tooth snagged the end of Megan's finger, raising a dot of blood. Megan offered another scrap. Now the cat was close, purring, winding around her ankles. I'm lonely, she told the cat, plumping down on the restaurant doorstep, suddenly wanting to cry. Once the words were out, they became overwhelmingly true. The cat curved its skull to receive her cupping hand, and she felt the self-pitying tears surge as she told it wordlessly that she was a failure at acting, that she couldn't seem to do the work she wanted to in class because every scene she attempted came out wrong—the very same scenes she'd explored with so much joy and freedom in her own apartment. New York was too big for her, too scary. When she was around people, she could never find the right words to say; her classmates thought she was nothing; men paid her no attention; and when she opened her apartment door at night it was to a sick scatter of cockroaches—she could never get them under control—her bowl from the morning still in the sink, floating soggy circles of cereal. She didn't have her mother's easy knack for making a place comfortable, and she missed home. The cat was seated on her lap now, though still tensed and wary, and Megan had just started to think maybe she could pick the creature up and carry it back to the apartment, have a vet look it over, and then feed and care for it until the sunken sides plumped up and the black fur shone, when it sprang from her knees and, ignoring her call of kitty, kitty, kitty moved swiftly around the side of the building and vanished.

CHAPTER EIGHT

Kim bent over her sewing machine, the steady droning and the movement of the treadle, her hands guiding the cloth through—the machine was ancient, but it worked, and she didn't want a new one. It was one of the first things she'd acquired in the United States; she'd found it for a few dollars in a second-hand shop, a poor worn old thing, but it did her bidding. She was tired, the material blurred under her eyes, sometimes she almost nodded off, but she knew how to work past tiredness. In the living room Ron watched sports on TV; she heard the shouts and the crowd buzzing, the commercials with their sudden jump in volume, the high, inane voices. Sometimes she was glad of her own willful angry failure to understand the language. She didn't want to comprehend this crazy place, the alien white people with their idiotic and incessant grinning. He told her now and then that she didn't need to sew, he made enough to support them, but his salary wasn't that much, and anyway she didn't trust him. After all she'd been through, the sea voyage, the months in the camp, she needed to be independent and have something of her own. And there was a kind of peacefulness to the sewing, as if the task were doing her rather than her doing it. It kept her seated, foot moving, hunched into herself and hunched also against the small but persistent pain in her breastbone she hadn't told anyone about. She had had a lump in her breast for a long time. The morning she first found it—two years ago, maybe three—she'd fingered it over and over again, kept returning to it, then decided to pretend it wasn't there, and held her fingers rigidly away. But now she often touched the place when she was alone, almost tenderly, finding a comforting familiarity in it. Her lump. Her secret lump. And now this pain. The blouse she was working on was silk, the mauve-purple color of lilacs. Why would Angela never wear anything graceful, or kindly to the ends of your fingers when she lived at home? She, Kim, could make pretty things. She could make clothes that sold for good money—though mostly her work was hemming skirts and taking up pants for people too lazy and rich to do it for themselves. But sometimes she had something like this, material that was a pleasure to touch, and then she took pains to make every seam perfect, enjoying her own swift skill, even if it was a skill no one else prized. But Angela. Angela had never been able to accept what Kim sewed. She could have made her ugly daughter pretty, softened the harshness of her skinny body with this flowing stuff, helped redeem and make her happy. Ungrateful Angela, who could claim an easy, rightful place in a world where Kim was forever a stranger.

She remembered Angela in her early teens, walking through the door, her hair moussed extravagantly and pushed to the top of her head where it fell to one side with a few jaggedy uneven pieces sticking straight up, like something out of a comic strip, the entire thing held into place with a large red clip. Angela in a voluminous jacket intended for a grown man that she had no doubt picked out of a trashcan or found at a garage sale. Early on, when Angela was about seven—and before Ron found out—Kim had taken her daughter on food scavenging expeditions in dumpsters and behind supermarkets because it pained her to see perfectly good produce and boxes of cereal tossed out. It had made her crazy, life in Los Angeles, the luxury and the poverty all mixed together, all the expensive objects thrown out when she was living with five women in one room, working in a sweatshop, and with the images of life in the camp, the hungry children playing in the mud still so vivid in her mind. So there was nothing she could really say about Angela's teenage scrounging, and anyway, Angela just laughed and said, You taught me. Off-balance, Kim would start yelling, Why you have to dress like that? You look like monkey, and Angela would respond with insulting coolness, I like to look like this. This is me. And then she'd saunter into the kitchen, open and close the refrigerator door, sing out, Nothing to eat in here, and take off for the mall.

It would have been different with her other child, the son she'd conceived at seventeen when she was doing laundry for the military base in Saigon. One of the soldiers had started paying attention to her, a sweat-smelling man as solid as a tree and bigger than anyone she'd ever seen up close before. His name was Chuck. A silly name, like an exclamation or a plate falling and cracking. Chuck whispered to her in corners, met her outside as she left to walk home, brought food and gifts—bubble gum, syrupy sweet fruit cup—and eventually began putting his hands on her body. She was awed by the power of his uniform and the incomprehensible behemoth called America she glimpsed behind his shoulder. It went on for a while, the kissing and touching, and then he pushed her gently back against a wall one evening, fumbled at her clothes, and put himself inside her. She didn't mind. She liked the warmth, his smoothness and thickness pushing insistently against her. There was a short sharp pain, soon gone, and a smear of blood after he'd withdrawn.

Her mother knew what had happened the minute she walked into the house, but she didn't say anything, just took the rice and cigarettes Chuck had given them. Even when he left without a goodbye a few months later, just as she was beginning to wonder if she was pregnant, Kim couldn't be angry with him, or resentful. Nothing in her life had led her to believe the world owed her anything, or that she had any power to shape events. She understood her fumblings with Chuck would be considered shameful in this country, this place of ostentatious cleanliness and shine where dirt was kept hidden—though if you looked, you could see it clear enough: in the hungry scrabbling of an army of invisible poor people, trash blowing along the gutters, dirty gray dishcloths swiping at gleaming restaurant counters. No one could understand, least of all her husband and so-called daughter, the otherness of the place where she'd grown up. Hungry sometimes, tired, too cold or too hot, bedeviled by insects, cringing constantly at the sound of bullets and the sight of soldiers. But not unhappy. Not as she understood it.

Her mother was good to her after that first time with Chuck, washing gently between her legs as she trembled, giving her a little extra rice in the evening. As her pregnancy advanced, Kim stopped working at the base. She stayed home and helped in the house and outside among the vegetables. She was walking beside a field one afternoon when the pains began. She didn't go home, though her mother had prepared a place for the birth. Instead, she stepped off the path, pushed through some undergrowth, and lay down in a ditch. This child was hers, hers alone, and she would keep it to herself as long as she could.

She remembered the birth as easy, tranced and quiet: birdsong, tall grasses rustling by her head, and her son slipping into the world like a blessing. She hadn't thought clearly beforehand about what would happen next though sometimes she'd thought if she could smother the thing with her hands, none of it would have happened: Chuck inside her, the wall against her back, those long hot swelling months. But now the baby was in her arms, wet and slippery with blood—hers, his, she didn't know which—heartbreakingly small. He turned his head blindly toward her breast and she understood then that she was everything to him, sun and moon, food and sleep, life itself, and when he fixed his lips to her nipple a tenderness welled up in her dark and deep as heart's blood. They lay curled together, skin to skin, her cheek sticking to the top of his bloody head, that place where his soul resided. She had a name for him, Tuan, a name that began like a bird trill and ended in a sigh, but she didn't so much as whisper it for fear of alerting the ancestors, who might come at night to steal him. He would appeal to them, this white ghost baby, already half theirs.

Her mother came and led her to the house. She didn't look at the little boy, said nothing to Kim, her face expressionless. He would be a difficulty and a curse for the family. And she too feared the possessiveness of the ancestors. She made Kim lie down, built a fire under the bed to keep her warm, took care of her and fed her until she was able to rise and work around the house again. They didn't speak the boy's name for a month, or bite off his fingernails or cut his hair. They called him second son to confuse the spirits, and were careful not to appear too attached. Finally, they named him, and he could be openly adored, and now Kim carried him against her front, swaddled tightly, wherever she went, and he laughed when she blew kisses onto his stomach or played with his fingers, and she loved him all the more fiercely because he was a child of dust, and his life would be hard.

And despite all their care, she thought, moving the lilac silk through the thread guide of her sewing machine, the spirits took him in the end.

CHAPTER NINE

The pigeon was lying on the sidewalk where two huge gray wings of a bank building formed a sheltering corner. Sean imagined it flutter-dragging itself along to this place on faltering gray-pink legs, wings flapping for balance, and finally sagging down amid its own feathers. It crouched, almost unmoving, the head turning slightly now and then, the eyes black and opaque. He came closer; unblinking, the eyes focused on him. No sign in them of struggle or suffering; no complaint; no movement but a slight quiver running periodically through the body. The bird had given up; it was awaiting death. He was half aware that the stream of people moving along the sidewalk was parting and reforming around him, and he stood, as immobile as the bird, twinned with it, the seventeen-year-old boy lost and trembling, the trembling bird huddled in its feathers. And finally he bent—he had dealt with injured birds many times, several kinds of birds, taken them home and kept them in a shoebox in his bedroom, fed them with an eye dropper; he was a country boy and he understood wild things.

Few people thought of pigeons as wild. He knew that. But he also knew that the borderline between wild and civilized was artificial, man-made. It meant nothing to Sean who had seen a fox come to drink at their waterspout day after day, two summers in a row, and then sit down beside the spout, ears pricked, paws neatly tucked, placid as a domestic dog. He had noticed the pigeons during his first days here. They had made their accommodation with the grimy city, pecking at its refuse, walking among all the hurrying feet, cocky and fearless, their heads snapping back and forth like the heads of mechanical toys, their chests puffed out, undaunted by the trucks and smells of gasoline and exhaust and the people yelling into their cell phones. He fingered the ten-dollar bill in his pocket, the last of the one week's extra salary he'd gotten from Sal at the corner grocery. So sorry, Sal had said. You're a good kid and I like you. But it's not working out.

A cup of coffee and a donut, and the ten would be gone. He'd already been forced to move out of the shabby room in Brooklyn with the bathroom down the hall; he'd been sleeping on a bench in the park, huddled under newspapers and all the clothes he owned. But the pigeons managed. They knew the place, exploited its cracks and crevices, seduced its human inhabitants into sharing crusts of bread, reared their young on ledges, even knew enough to duck under a car for shelter when a hawk was soaring overhead. He'd watched and he'd seen.

This one, though, was in retreat. Almost oblivious to the world around it, it had returned to its own country waiting for whatever was to come, human cruelty, a hawk's tearing beak or just the final blanking out of consciousness. Sean stooped and picked the bird up, the bedraggled feathers, the scratch of feet in his palms, held it a few moments until it stilled and sank into his hands, half conscious, and slowly, carefully, pulled one wing out into a crescent, then the other, paused a moment to let the pigeon recover, then tested each leg the same slow, careful way. He saw no sign of injury or break. Whatever was ravaging and destroying this bird was inside it.

He looked up and started. He was surrounded. People had stopped and edged in to see what he was doing. Faces impinged, a circle of humanity enclosed him and the sick pigeon. He took all this in in a fast blur and looked quickly down again. It's gettin' better. This was a little boy, perhaps six, out on his own, jiggling up and down. Look, it's gettin' better. It likes you, and then an adult voice, a woman's, I'm gonna call the humane people. Sean's shoulders rose, he half turned his back. The bird was moving. Some fierce energy possessed it. He felt the strong pulse against his hands, and then it was surging upward, rising, wings flapping hard, and he heard an exhalation from the people around him, someone's hands clapping, and someone else saying, Yeah, there he goes. Go on, bird. Go on. Sean looked up. He saw the flapping outline against the pale blue oblong of sky framed by the canyon of buildings, rising and rising, and had time only to half realize that the flapping had become out of sync and grotesque before the pigeon fell heavily down to the sidewalk. He didn't need to touch it to know it was dead.

There was a murmuring, and the people who had surrounded him began moving away. The boy ran off between the buildings, people started talking on cell phones as they walked, the pigeon nothing now but a dirty heap of feathers riffling a little as the breeze passed over, lying half sideways, legs curled and clawed. Sean turned away and stood irresolute, wiped his hands along the sides of his pants. Hey, you, someone said. He looked up to see a stocky man in a black baseball cap. You. Fuzzy bunny looking guy. You need a job? Can you peel a potato?

####

A few days later, Sean hovered by the back wall of the kitchen. Figures loomed in the flame-lit semi-darkness, seeming to elongate elastically or shorten and fatten like cartoon characters. He saw a pile of what looked like animal entrails on a board, smelled garlic, vegetables, sweat, and aromas he couldn't identify. The activity was constant, and the noise an assault: whistling, someone cursing in Spanish, thumps, exclamations, metallic bangs, hoots of laughter. He watched for a while, but there was no order to anything as far as he could see and he couldn't imagine a way to insinuate himself further into the place. He moved back against the sheltering wall. He'd learned early that being seen was an almost inevitable prelude to insult.

Sean was slow. It wasn't that he didn't understand the froth of ideas always tossing around him, the sounds emanating from moving mouths, the startling inexplicable jerks of people's torsos and elbows. He did understand these things, and he understood speech, or at least its surface and most immediate significance. But he kept thinking that wasn't enough, that couldn't be all there was to it, the speaker wouldn't be going to all the trouble of verbalizing anything so meaningless, and so he'd turn the words over and over in his mind, his consciousness moving around them like lazy swirls of honey, searching for the actual and elusive truth they contained. He had always driven his family crazy. As a kid, he couldn't play a simple board game because for him each square quivered with just-out-of-reach meaning. His brother would set out the Chutes and Ladders board and Sean would get lost in the curve of the chutes, which he could sense subtly and persistently moving. He could become equally lost in the sugar-sweet smile of his sister's Barbie doll until she yelled, He's doing it again, mom. He won't stop staring at my doll. Make him stop.

His school years were filled with impatient teachers, tapping their fingers as they waited for answers and schoolmates who schemed constantly to intrude on his blurred, swimmy world by sliding objects down his back, bumping him hard in the corridor, hiding his books, snatching food from his plate, and once egging on the school's prettiest, most popular girl to tell him she'd been dreaming about him while they hovered within earshot. They loved to watch the violent way he started, to guffaw at his sudden intake of breath and the blotchy color rising on his face. Only one person, a teacher, spoke to him directly and kindly. Miss Lang kept him with her sometimes during lunch break and asked if he read books and what he thought about. She had black hair and olive skin, and he liked looking at her. She didn't mind that it took him endless seconds to formulate an answer to the simplest question, and she always seemed delighted when he finally found words. Mostly just comics, he told her. Or: I like the way things look in puddles. Tree branches and things. Buildings.

When he was sixteen, someone introduced him to pot, and then the world became less hard-edged and gabbling. The people he smoked with—finally—seemed to be moving in something close to his rhythm, and being among them was calming, like sinking into bed at night, pulling the blankets closely around himself and waiting for sleep.

Stocker bustled up to him. Hey, he said, It's you. Pigeon guy. You showed up. Okay, you'll be the commis. Know what that is? Sean shook his head and Stocker explained, It's the lowest of the low. You do the shit no one else wants to do, the grimy repetitive shit, the stuff that's smelly and hurts your hands and makes your eyes smart and your muscles sore. You up for that? Sean nodded.

Over the next few days, he tried, but it was hard. Dealing with living creatures, his hands were gentle and deft, but when he tried to shell peas the size of seed pearls, shuck oysters or devein shrimp, they became senseless clubs. Harold looked over one afternoon as Sean toiled at the sink over hard-boiled eggs, and noted the clumps of white sticking to the shells, the shaking of Sean's hands. He hesitated, then came to stand at the boy's elbow. It's not your fault, he said. They're way fresh. Eggs that fresh are hard to peel. Look, make a nice web of cracks. Keep the water running over them. And ... see?

After that, Harold began calling Sean over whenever things slowed down and stationing him in front of the cutting board. He'd demonstrate how to dice an onion, or tell if an avocado was ripe, then split it and pull out the stone. Still on the phone to his mother, he'd lean over and put his hand over Sean's to show him how to hold the knife, when to rock it, when to chop. Little by little, the others noticed. Kenneth, a gray-haired, middle-aged Scotsman seasoned by decades of kitchen work, had brought his own son George into the place a year earlier. Now father and son began quietly rescuing mangled bits of food from Sean's hands and fixing them. Within a few weeks, by some unspoken agreement, the entire staff had formed a protective cocoon around the boy. Stocker pretended not to notice. He understood the paradoxical power of Sean's vulnerability, knew there were only two possible responses to vulnerability that acute: protectiveness or attack. And, like Sean, Stocker had worked his way through kitchens, starting at seventeen, washing dishes, scraping goo from plates, filleting fish and tearing lettuce.

Sean was sitting on a stool in the corner one afternoon peeling potato after potato, the side of his hand cramping painfully. Stocker pulled up a chair, and sat beside him. Sean hunched down further.

You're mutilating it, Stocker said.

Sean's Sorry was so faint Stocker wasn't sure he'd heard anything.

You're wasting half the potato, gouging like that. What's the matter with you? You some kind of retard? Peel. Peeeeel, don't saw.

Sean made himself even smaller.

They cost money, potatoes, Stocker continued. You don't want to be wasting them. Look—he reached over, took the potato from Sean's hand—you peel away from yourself, okay? You keep peeling toward yourself the way you're doing and you're going fast, fast, fast for the service and next thing you know you've taken a chunk out of the side of your thumb. I know. I've been there.

Sean managed an Okay.

And sit the fuck up. Why are you all bent over like that? Have some respect for yourself. That's better. Go smooth. Peel smooth and away from yourself. Slow till you get the feeling for it; you can speed up later.

Sean tossed a peeled potato into the pot of water and Stocker grabbed it back out. For shit's sake, you think that's finished? It's got eyes all over. Get 'em. With the tip. No, the fucking tip. Every one of 'em—and peel off the greenish part too. He watched as Sean tried to comply. Christ, this thing's nothing but green. This potato's a crime. Wait till I see the supplier. You—why'd you stop? Keep peeling.

I'm trying.

Yup, you are. Very trying. Stocker snorted with laughter at his own joke. Okay, keep going, Fuzzy. Fuzzy Bunny. That's what I keep calling you because that's what you are, a little blinking, pink-eyed bunny. Okay, that's better. That's a bit better. Couple bushels more, and you'll have it, eh, Fuzzy?

Stocker fell silent, watched as the shaking of Sean's hands began to subside and the denuded tubers tumbled into their pail of water, one by one. He nodded. Wonderful things, potatoes, he said. Living things. You could plant that right now, that bit you've just cut out, and you'd get more potatoes. They came from Peru and traveled back to the old world courtesy of Mr. Columbus. No one there had ever seen a potato before. Can you imagine? You know why potatoes took on over there? An invading enemy could burn up your whole crop, but your potatoes would still be safe underground. Lifesavers, potatoes. Damn near killed the Irish though.

Can you imagine life without 'em now? Potato can mellow out a pushy taste, bring a dish together, thicken things up, soup, sauce ... and the taste, Fuzzy, the taste of a new little potato, raw, right out of the earth ... You ever eat one like that? Yuh? Good. You're a country kid, right? Well, you just keep peeling.

CHAPTER TEN

Stocker was standing in his usual spot in the alley, leaning against the wall, thinking about the duck farm he'd visited upstate that morning. Spring was turning into summer, but everything was still wet and cool. The farmers were an idealistic young couple named Greg and Jen. He'd trudged with them through sucking mud to the pond, caught the scent of last year's leaves decaying beneath the blades of new grass. The birds were everything he'd hoped for, big, lively, handsome creatures with a deep blue-green sheen on their necks, harlequins, cayuga, rouen. They came up, quacking, looking for food. At his elbow, Greg spoke softly and unceasingly, explaining his rearing practices as he reached repeatedly into his pocket for breadcrumbs: the natural pond the ducks enjoyed and the way they kept the edges clean of bugs and weeds while in turn, underwater, the fish disposed of the duck excrement. Maybe he'd try raising tilapia in that pond, Greg said—not for Stocker perhaps, but for someplace more down-market. I got no problem with tilapia, Stocker grunted. It all fit together, Greg continued. It was biodynamic. And he was interbreeding in the hope of producing a bird that was leaner than a Pekin, but still with a richly flavorful breast. Stocker nodded. He noted that Jen looked away when Greg talked about slaughter, his preference for stunning over cones, his belief you could do the killing humanely if the flock was small enough, you didn't terrify the birds beforehand, and you killed them individually, one by one. Jen had referred to the ducks as her girls, and Stocker wondered if she and Greg really had the toughness to make a go of farming. He'd give them a try at least. Stocker was keeping a cohort of small farmers in business: when he found a supplier he liked, he stayed loyal, unswayed by the winds of fashion.

Sometimes he missed the small farm where he'd grown up—barely a farm really, a vegetable garden, chickens, a single cow, Cherry. He had given her the name because of the red in her coat and because he loved cherries. She lumbered around the family's one field, always alone, grazing, ruminating, staring into space. He liked to run his hand along her rough hide—she was huge to him, and powerful. She could have knocked him down in a second if she'd wanted to, and her docility always seemed a gift. He liked to lead her into the barn and take her teats between his fingers, rubbery, surprisingly warm, and pull on them slowly and rhythmically, the first two, the second, thin streams of milk sloshing into the bucket, his head hard-pressed against her side, just him and Cherry, standing with her head down, turning now and then to look at him with her liquid unreadable eyes. How did it feel to be her, he wondered. What kind of dim slow consciousness moved beneath the hard ridge of her forehead? She saw him. She knew him. But what did he mean to her? In what language did she understand him? She shifted her hindquarters now and then as he milked, stilled obediently when he patted her. When they were done, he'd throw his head back and tilt the bucket straight into his mouth, letting the hot, foamy milk splash over his chin and down his throat in great jolts of funky cow richness.

Despite his own periodic transgressions—instant coffee, cheap candies—Stocker hated industrial food with a passion, and something in him rose in fury-spitting rage when he thought about cows hock-deep in shit, sows in pens so small they couldn't turn around, chickens crammed into cages. It wasn't anything shallowly sentimental, his anger. It was rooted in the profound wrongness of these practices, the terrible disrespect for food and eating.

Angela was coming toward him negotiating the cracked asphalt in ridiculous fluorescent pink heels, black raincoat flapping open. He watched, sucking on his cigarette. It felt different seeing her not in close-up but as he had the very first time; distance made the sight of her new. He loved her ungainliness and jutting bones; he wanted to press himself against her front to tame the jolting of her walk. She reached him and, without saying a word, took the cigarette from his unresisting fingers and inhaled. Her chest rose slightly as she did, and he thought of the breasts beneath her blouse, like domed silver buttons. She handed back the smoke, he put his lips where hers had been on the filter, and both of them looked outwards together. He was okay with silence, it was good just knowing they were experiencing the same sights and sounds at the same moment. Ready to eat? he asked.

Not yet. She was quiet again. Then, I like this alley.

Her upper arm pressed against his, and he reached over to grope her. She intercepted his hand. Not now, Stocker.

The cat crept from behind a trashcan, a thickened shadow among shadows. It paused a few feet in front of them and let out a miaow so loud and unexpected that they both laughed.

Skanky thing, said Stocker. It comes here all the time.

Angela bent down, and the cat approached, put her nose briefly to the inviting fingers and began a creaking purr, treading circles, rubbing her head and curved neck against air.

Stocker cackled. She's your friend now.

Shut up. You're scaring her off.

And indeed the cat had retreated a little, still purring, her eyes huge and otherworldly. Angela coaxed her, Hey, old girl. Poor old girl. Hey, Stocker, look at her stomach. She's pregnant. Let's get her something to eat. Her backbone's sharp as a razorblade.

She's an alley cat. She knows how to get by.

Angela stayed crouched, her fingers moving behind a triangular ear and the cat receiving her touch in that time-honored way of cats—a louder purr, mouth curved into that perpetual cat smile, a regal bending of the head. Starved and hopeless, the creature still knew how to thank an admirer.

I'm not going to set up a feeding station, said Stocker. You can't feed every stray cat in the city.

You can feed this cat.

She came with him into the kitchen, walked from place to place, lifted the lid from a pot and sniffed. The cooks looked up—neither women nor outsiders had ever been welcome in this kitchen. Stocker glared, and everyone returned to work. Harold tipped onions into a sauté pan. Yeah, yeah, he yelled into his phone. You'll meet the girl when I'm good and ready, ma. We're not there yet. I said, We're not there yet. Her and me aren't. Yeah, I know I'm thirty-one. No I've got nothing against you. I don't hate children. I said, I don't fucking hate children. Well, okay, maybe I do. No, I don't hate my nieces, I just can't be around them because they drive me crazy. What do you want me to say, ma? Look, I gotta go.

Angela scooped a spoonful of liquid and some pieces of meat into a bowl, cool as if she owned the place, and headed for the door. Stocker followed her back to the alley.

The cat squatted before the offering, back arched, taking in the fragments of meat, in a series of fast violent hiccups.

"Enjoy, you mangy beast," Stocker said. "That's a sixty dollar entree you're getting."

Fifteen minutes later, Angela was seated at the basement table alone, feet up, reading her newspaper when Sean sidled in, holding plates. She hauled herself a little more upright, yawned loudly without covering her mouth, focused, Hey, you're Sean, right?

Uh-huh. He said to bring you this.

Okay. She set her newspaper aside to make space on the table. He'll be down?

Sean nodded and placed the deep plate in front of her, a little gravy slipping over the edge as he did so.

You're staring, Sean.

He colored, put his thumb in his mouth to suck off the gravy, realized that was wrong—there was no greater sin at Stocker's than smudging the rim of a customer's plate—and glanced quickly away. She pretended not to notice, though she'd heard his breath quicken a shade and seen him flush. His discomfort was so strong, it was almost as if he wanted to be invisible. Now he was sliding away toward the door; he would have gone backwards if he could. Angela slid her feet off the table and let them thump to the floor. Why don't you sit down? she said. He flinched, and took another step backwards. Come on. Come keep me company. Sean glanced toward the door. He can spare you for a minute, Angela said. The boy shook his head. Please, Sean. You'll be doing me a favor. I don't want to eat alone.

He moved closer.

What was wrong with him, Angela wondered. Was he actually slow? Stocker called him Fuzzy Bunny and it made sense. He was like a little huddled bunny. Or a mouse. Something small and quivering. Perhaps he was actually slow witted, perhaps it was just that he was weighing everything he heard, pondering the right response. Perhaps he wasn't really present at all, but attuned to some completely different reality or set of rhythms, hearing voices she couldn't, voices in other rooms, bits of melody. Ever since she'd first seen Sean working away in a shadowy corner of the kitchen, Angela had wanted to figure him out because he roused feelings in her that she wasn't used to and had trouble pinning down. She wanted to shield him from the casual violence of Stocker's kitchen, the flying obscenities, the cuts and burns, to try and fathom whatever was confounding and confusing him so deeply. She motioned to the chair beside hers and nodded once, imperious.

He looked around again and sat down.

What's this he's feeding me today?

Rabbit.

She wanted to laugh, but she didn't. Do you know how he prepared it?

There's ... some kind of brown sauce.

She nodded gravely as if he'd given her significant information, kept her eyes on his until he felt obliged to amplify. Rabbit with ... beer. No, ale. He put in a pod ... vanilla. A vanilla pod.

Angela felt a core-deep flush of empathy for the silent pulsating human animal beside her. Okay, she said. Sounds interesting. He half rose. No, she said. Please, Sean. She carefully cut some of the meat away from the bone, took the bread off her bread plate and placed the sliver there, spooned on sauce. You taste it. Tell me what you think. He began shaking his head furiously. Do it, Sean. You can. I'll tell Stocker I forced you. It was like coaxing the feral cat, watching it inch forward, tantalized but terrified. He took up the meat in his thin-skinned red fingers and put it to his mouth. He smelled fusty—not unpleasant, Angela thought, but the way a child smells when you first wake him up in the morning, the warmth of skin and hair, a whisper of staleness on his breath.

When she was very little—four or five perhaps—Angela had fantasized about her brother—her baby brother, as she thought of him, though Kim had explained over and over again that Jeffrey, wherever he was now, was older than Angela. She had faint memories of placing a pudgy baby doll in its cradle every night just before going to bed herself, smoothing a blanket over it, crooning songs with made-up words, pretending it was Jeffrey and she was singing in Vietnamese. And there was the morning when she found the doll on the floor beside the cradle, its head twisted at an angle, one arm broken off from the shoulder, and realized—though she didn't want to—that she had done this thing herself, snatched up the smiling plastic creature, tossed it down and stomped on its head—though she had no memory of the deed.

Sean was shifting uncomfortably under her gaze, so she looked away. The front page of the fashion section caught her eye, a model in an outfit suitable for a moon walk staring haughtily at the camera. Look at this, Sean. He looked, chewing slowly; he clearly didn't know how she expected him to react. I love this stuff, she said. It's a joke, a cosmic joke. That's what people don't get. They're making fun of us, the designers. It's like this little isolated, completely nutty inworld they live in where everyone's just playing everyone else. Nothing to do with the things you actually put on your back. Nothing to do with rain or warmth or practicality. Is this making any sense at all to you, Sean? How's the meat.

Good. He swallowed effortfully.

I love this stuff because it's like a finger in everyone's eye. That's how I see it. If you do put these things on ... Okay, it's like you're the Christmas tree, just this poor scraggly little Christmas tree, maybe the last one on the lot. She was starting to enjoy herself now, warming to her own metaphor. His silence wasn't vacant, it throbbed with a kind of underwater curiosity. So there you are on your Christmas tree lot, Angela continued, with your arms outspread—she held out her hand toward Sean, a forgotten rabbit bone in her fingers—and you're just this pathetic spindly thing, but once you've been taken home and draped with color and glitter and candies and tinkling things, everyone's entranced, not with you but with the ... the ... adornment. She stopped and laughed. I've no idea what I'm saying, Sean. Is it crazy? Oh, yes, it's to take the focus off what isn't there—you—and fix it on the externals, the stuff you can play and have fun with. That's fashion. That's my job, Sean, that's what I do for a living, work in a high-end fashion store. Regular people look at this stuff—Angela gestured to the hollow-eyed, grim-mouthed model—and they say, who'd want to wear that? Those designers are nuts. But that's not the point. It's meant to be nuts.

What if they're not playing?

She felt a small flash of delight. He'd been following her train of thought, and he'd spoken, and those few words were a gift.

I guess half of them don't think they're playing. But if they're not, they have to be psycho. Or crazy shallow.

He finally smiled. Then he said, Stocker's food ...

Right, she conceded. That's play, too, sort of, and just as in your face. You're gonna eat what Stocker gives you or nothing. But the difference is, it's deadly serious, and he's deadly serious about it. It goes deep, Stocker's food. Here, take some bread and sop up some of my gravy.

He did as she told him. She watched as he registered the taste. They were eating together when Stocker came in. He opened his mouth to roar at Sean, but Angela held up a hand: I wanted him to taste your cooking. I made him sit down.

Stocker nodded, forced out a grudging Okay as Sean stood up, and moved aside so Sean could sidle past him through the doorway. Just outside, Sean looked back. Ignoring Stocker, Angela smiled at him: Come share dinner with me again, Sean. I'm here every Thursday.

The boy gone, Stocker sat down opposite her. The rabbit?

Good. But you know that.

Good how?

I'm kinda tired, Stocker.

But good how.

Not sure the vanilla was right.

Me neither. Vanilla's tricky in a savory dish. He stuck his finger in a leftover smear of sauce on her plate, sampled, shook his head. Then: You oughta fuck that boy. He's always staring at you.

Sure, Angela said, I'd love to. Sean's sweet. She laughed, and after a moment, Stocker did too.

At midnight, Stocker stood in Angela's bathroom, naked, watching as she took off her clothes, then turned to bend over the tub and feel the water temperature, her heavy hair sliding across her shoulder blades. No occidental woman had hair anywhere near that texture or color, he reflected, black as eggplant, but with none of an eggplant's luscious roundedness, hair that absorbed light, held it, and gave it back in a cold blue-black sheen like a blackbird's wing. He was obsessed with her Oriental girl hair, liked to lift the slippery strands and kiss her scalp underneath, take the hairbrush with the hard little plastic knobs and pull it slowly through. He'd poke his fat forefinger in her ear—her ears were so small—prodding at the cartilage until she said, Ow. That hurts, and then he'd slow and become gentle. "Come on," Angela said. She'd stepped into the bath and immersed herself up to the chin. "Wait. I have an idea," he responded, and ran into her tiny kitchen, returning with his hand closed around something. He slipped into the water. She barely had time to say, What? when he cracked the egg he was holding directly against the top of her head, watched the yolk begin sliding down her waterfall of hair, the white thinning around it like semen and—even as she yelled Hey!—dunked her head backwards into the water. "That's for the cat. That's for wasting my food. And for wasting my commis's time." Angela expostulated and waved her hands at him, but he swished the egg off with his palm and placed his mouth over hers, felt her laughter sputtering against his lips.

Stocker learned about Angela, the pinched circumstances of her early life, slowly over time, from the first few grudging hints she let escape, usually while they were in bed together, to the freer descriptions she used once she'd come to trust him. He could visualize the gray dead sidewalks outside her family's working-class suburban home, the grass and weeds pushing through. He sensed her father's bullying narrow-mindedness and her confused contempt for her mother. But where had she acquired her power, that unshakeable sense of who she was? Her mother lashed out sometimes, she told him, pulled her hair or bruised her shoulders with bony fingers. But Stocker wasn't under the impression there were beatings or that Angela feared Kim. She used to laugh at the rages, she said, particularly once she'd reached her teens. She provoked them. She knew what her mother was in this expansive, jiggling, object-crammed American world: A refugee. A noncitizen. A small crawling, negligible thing, angry and charmless, complaining all day long at the sewing machine in a low bitter mutter, unable to pick up enough words of English to fill in official forms or talk comfortably on the phone, so that, growing up, Angela had been forced to mediate constantly between her and the world.

But if Angela despised her family, it wasn't because she craved entry into the dominant culture, the acceptance of athletes, goths, cheerleaders, or arty types at school. She liked to stay at the edge of things. The boys didn't know what to make of me, she told Stocker. They'd see the Gook hair and eyes and think, Oh, exotic, but then I talked like any other California girl. I dressed differently though, and wore tons of makeup. I liked to draw those fat black retro Elizabeth Taylor lines round my eyes and wear lipstick the color of a stop sign.

You still do.

Uh-uh. It's magenta now.

She laughed, sitting straight up in the bed. Lonely, half-admired and half-despised, she'd drawn attention, courted it with eccentric clothes, constantly-changing hairstyles, the arrogant tilt of her chin, those teetering heels. She didn't care that everyone else wore running shoes or flip-flops and that stilettos made walking difficult. Difficulty was the point. Life should be difficult as far as she was concerned. It was her vocation to overcome difficulties, even those as stupid and unnecessary as aching feet.

You sleep with those boys?

Of course.

But she'd given nothing of herself, and her emotional inaccessibility made them want her more. Stocker sensed that. They got obsessive craving her, the way you crave a food that doesn't even taste very good.

It was no big deal getting me into bed, Stocker. At thirteen, I'd open my legs for any pimply-assed adolescent who bought me a bag of chips.

Seriously?

Feed me and I was yours. You had my number when you saw me in the alley that first night and offered me dinner.

He snorted. I could have had you for a bag of chips?

Chips. A cinnamon roll or corn dog. Soft pretzels. Pizza.

He raised himself on his elbow and pushed his hand between her thighs, and she drew in her breath. Tell me about the pimply kids, he urged. Tell me about your first time.

She shook her head. I don't do confession, Stocker.

He found her clitoris and stroked it between finger and thumb. You were hungry at home? That's why you came so cheap?

She said No. Yes. Well, there was food at home. Keep doing that. Don't stop.

Tell me. She didn't say anything. Her eyes were closed.

The truth was—as she eventually admitted to him—Angela had been famished, despite the meals her mother dutifully put on the table; hunger gnawed at her sides, waking and sleeping. When she was older and went to the mall with her friends, she was thrilled at the array of food she found there: dishes from Vietnam—spring rolls with mint, clear sauce flecked with red heat—that she loved all the more because Kim complained they didn't

taste right; Korean and Chinese; sloppy, cheesy Mexican; fries faintly rancid from the suet in which they'd been cooked.

He repeated, Tell me what you ate at home.

Oh, for God's sake, Stocker, I can't think when you do that. Her
hips began a rhythmic undulation, he felt her vaginal walls contract and
pull on his fingers, relax, contract again. He stopped stroking. Tell me.

Hamburgers, meat loaf, spaghetti, canned stuff, that's what she
cooked. Angela paused, but he didn't resume his labors. I know she made
Vietnamese when they were first married—she told me—stuff she grew up
on, but my dad wouldn't have it. Said it was dirty. Gook food; he wasn't
eating frogs and puppy dogs and rotten fish. You're in America now, he
said. Cook American.

So she was bitter? Stocker began moving his fingers again, and
Angela writhed like a soul in torment. She was bitter? he repeated.

Angela sighed and pulled a little away from him. In so many ways.
Her food was like a punishment, tasteless stuff, like she was saying, This is
what you want? Have it then.

At seventeen, Angela moved out. Bored with her classmates, disgusted by their easy sense of privilege, she'd taken up with the owner of the
local dry cleaner, a sad, drooping man of forty-two, and moved in with him.
He took her to the movies and bought her clothes and earrings, and she
could manipulate him. The house was grimy, the living room filled with
piles of magazines and newspapers so high you had to thread your way
through narrow pathways between them. Mice rustled in the corners. Almost every evening, they ate take-out food together in front of the television and in an odd way she became attached to him, found comfort in his
large soft body and the grubby warmth of his place. She didn't move out
until she was almost nineteen, when she got a scholarship to the fashion
institute.

So you see, Stocker, my standards weren't high.

Stocker grinned and resumed his stroking. Angela began turning her head from side to side. Please, she said, stop torturing me, and he relented, slid slowly downward, and pushed his bullet head between her legs.

CHAPTER ELEVEN

Stocker hated the idea of hiring a pastry chef; he'd thought of doing without. It wasn't that he didn't like sweet things. He'd nip a brown sugar cube off a table sometimes as they closed up the restaurant and suck it between his teeth. He liked Hershey's for the same reason he liked Folger's, he supposed, his palate having been irretrievably ruined by his upbringing. And he yearned sometimes for the kind of lemon meringue pie with cardboard meringue and a gluey Jell-O-like interior that Violet used to put in front of him. Still, he thought of desserts as fiddly, unnecessary things, antithetical to his idea of serious eating. He knew however that he couldn't get away without them—despite the trendiness of his place and the customary sycophancy of reviewers. So there was Jon sitting opposite him at the staff-room table in his red sneakers, impossibly thin and tall, faintly foreign-looking—Middle Eastern? Spanish? A British accent—his black hair moussed into short upstanding quills, and talking energetically about dessert chefs in Europe and London, his experiences in New York kitchens and why he wanted to work for Stocker—because he sensed Stocker needed him if he was to get his kitchen to the next level—and Stocker too taken aback by the sheer impudence of that remark to respond. He talked about the superiority of this brand of chocolate over that, threw around words like conching and couverture, extolled the joys of a trace of bitter in a sea of sweet, waxed eloquent about sugar. He said dessert represented a natural home for molecular gastronomy—or avant garde—or whatever they were calling it these days—because baking was all about chemistry, but he wasn't interested in putting corn kernels into cakes or covering bacon with chocolate. Vulgar, he said, lip curling. Clunky. Not that he was against fusing disparate elements. But he wanted them to come together and create a taste as clean as glass. Classic combinations were unbeatable. There's a reason people have been coupling milk chocolate with hazelnuts forever, Jon said, and dark chocolate with mint, lemons and lavender, honey with pistachios—and his eyes closed slightly at the word honey, as if he tasted sweetness at that very moment. But then I want to build on that, he went on, make the classics new, add something beautiful and unexpected—and that's where the excitement comes in.

Before Stocker could comment, Jon fanned out a sheaf of photographs: bits of things in spoons, foams of various thicknesses—big, transparent bubbles, bubbles so tiny you could barely see they were there—patterns of sauce on white plates, foodstuffs in electric blues, greens, and purples.

Stocker stabbed his finger at one of the pictures. What's the red?

Beets. They candy beautifully, and they have this gorgeous ruby color. People think they're eating plums or grapes, and ... surprise. It takes most people a while to pin down the flavor.

The display ended with two photographs: a dress comprised of hundreds of dark chocolate sequins and molded to a dressmaker's form—A bit of a pointless show-off, this dress, Jon said wryly, but most people want to see a showpiece—and a series of rising silver spirals on a mirrored base.

Sugar, he said reverently. There's nothing you can't do with it.

How about lemon meringue pie? Do you have a clue how to make that?

Obviously. Jon thought a moment. We could deconstruct it. Come up with some kind of interesting shape for the base. A quenelle of buttermilk ice cream at the side. Cassis coulis. Or—hey—serve the whole thing in a glass.

No. No. No. No glass. And no fucking beets.

Okay.

Once Jon was hired, he did almost exactly as he pleased, playing with molds and paintbrushes; carefully covering his mousses with cling wrap; creating thin-stretched webs of caramel; hovering over each dessert plate before it was sent out while Crystal or whoever was serving shifted from foot to foot; turning rigid with silent fury when one of his creations smeared or refused to hold its consistency, complaining endlessly about the dirt and anarchy of the kitchen. I can't deal with all this heat and damp, he declared. Chocolate is sensitive. I need a dedicated space. What he needed, Stocker fumed inwardly, was a good, swift kick in the butt. But he held his tongue because there were benefits to having Jon around. He added a particular kind of humor, wiry and laconic to the kitchen and also—in an odd, off-kilter way—to the food. He'd hum songs from The Wizard of Oz as he worked, and a small plastic pair of glittering red shoes hung above his station. The staff tested him for a while—his flamboyance demanded it—but they soon realized that if they crossed him they'd get the worst of it, even though he never raised his voice. Uh-oh, he's me-e-e-lting, Jon would murmur, as his opponent turned away in defeat. Unexpectedly, Stocker began to enjoy the alchemical mix of flavors and textures Jon created, tidbits so cold they burned your lips, hard surfaces that melted into nothingness, the way the boundary between sweet and savory got blurred time and again: Lemongrass ice cream, curried cake, chocolate spiked with thyme.

CHAPTER TWELVE

When she'd learned she was pregnant again all those years ago Kim was almost happy. Ron appeared proud. He stopped the incessant low-key complaining that served as background to her days, and sometimes took her out for pizza or bought her a beer. Her belly began to curve outwards, and the mix of fear and hope grew so strong it was all she could do to hold her sides together—imperative because otherwise everything she was would spill out, including the place at her core where Tuan lay, curled and tranced. He wasn't dead, Tuan, but as inaccessible to her as if he were. To bring his spirit close, she kept an altar on a shelf behind her machine, an altar Ron knew was there but never bothered to challenge. On this altar were a half-burned stick of incense lying across a saucer, a photograph of Tuan in her arms—the only one she had of him—and the wrapper from a candy bar he'd once been given by an American soldier, softened by sea water, sweat, and humidity and saved and re-dried again and again until it was nothing but a tight tiny disintegrating ball preserved in a plastic bag. Also a bowl of rice grains, replenished regularly so that Tuan would never be hungry or unhappy. Sometimes, in the gray hours before dawn, the sharp smell of his birth still invaded her nose, or she heard clearly among the muted sounds of the street outside his first sweet staccato attempts at shaping words, but most of what she remembered—Tuan crouched intently over a worm stranded at the side of the road, Tuan floating a bamboo boat in a puddle—was soft-edged and distorted, as if she were seeing him through rippling water. Now there was life inside her again, life that could re-connect her with her ancestors and awaken a tenderness she thought she'd lost forever. She moved her hands again and again across her swollen stomach.

Congratulations, said the doctor, as Kim and Ron stared baffled at the gray shadows of an ultrasound. It's a little girl.

She nodded and forced her lips into the expected smile. Then she went to the bathroom outside in the corridor with its blank surfaces and faintly antiseptic smell, locked the door and sat down on the floor. Over. Empty. He wasn't coming back, Tuan, her missing boy, the boy the foster mother called Jeffrey and wrote her cheerful letters about three times a year. Jeffrey was growing so tall, this woman wrote. He'd soon have the biggest feet in the family. What family was that? Kim thought bitterly. She was his family. They were taking him to Vietnamese restaurants, the American woman continued, reading him books about Vietnam so he'd know his own culture. I am his culture, Kim wrote back. The letters stopped, and the terrible silence began.

He was four when the regime began its agonizing fall. There was panic in the village, all over the country, and everyone said she had to get Tuan out because otherwise the communists would douse him with gasoline and burn him alive. Someone gave her the address of an orphanage, and afterwards there was a long thirsty walk along roads clogged with panicked people carrying everything they could hold or drag, Tuan trotting beside her or, when he became too tired to walk, heavy in her arms. An American woman met her at the orphanage doorway and gave her a paper written in English to sign. There wasn't time to translate, the woman said, but she could promise Kim that Tuan would be well taken care of by rich Americans. He'd have opportunities he could never have in Vietnam. Where will he be? Kim asked. When could she join him? Would they give her something—please—a form, an address, a scrap of paper that acknowledged her rights as a mother and would help her find him when the war was over? Sorry, there wasn't anything official they could give her. When she placed Tuan in the American woman's arms, she knew instantly she'd made a mistake. He began to scream and she snatched him back, walked outside, and sank down with him in the dust. I'll come back soon, she promised, kissing the tears from his cheeks, kissing the tips of his fingers, rocking desperately back and forth. Be a good boy, Tuan. Do what they tell you. You'll see me again soon. The memory of that never-fulfilled promise, his red, wet, scrunched-up face and reaching hands, still twisted her intestines to the point of nausea.

It was Ron who picked the name Angela. It didn't sound right to her, but she didn't particularly care either. The quiet skinny baby who arrived after a few hours of labor wasn't really hers. She got the child started on a bottle while they were still at the hospital, and resisted all the urgings of the nurses to hold and rock her more. Once home, she let Angela cry herself to sleep every night. Angela learned fast. After a few nights of frantic bawling, fading into desolate hiccups and eventual silence, she made no sound at all. Even when Kim inched the door open, Angela didn't look toward her or the light spill, just stared up at the ceiling with her small, dark eyes. The baby isn't thriving, the doctor said when Kim took her for a wellness check. Are you feeding her enough? Is she sleeping at night? His questions became insistent and Kim decided to stop seeing him. Her daughter was fine. She was Vietnamese, that was all. Not all noise and blubber like those big soft American babies.

CHAPTER THIRTEEN

Jon nudged the man sleeping beside him: You need to go. I have work to do. The man turned, sleepy, grunting, smelling of hair and skin and sex, and reached blindly for Jon. You kidding? he said into Jon's neck. It's not even daylight.

Jon detached himself from the embrace. This is when I work.

You're serious?

I'm serious.

In the wee small hours?

I have to get to the restaurant. I need to concentrate.

There was some muttering, a shuffling of blankets, and the man leaned over the side of the bed and began feeling on the floor for his clothes. Can I have a little light at least? Jon clicked on the bedside lamp, and watched in silence as the man stood up and dressed. I won't be back, he muttered, pulling on his shirt, fumbling with buttons.

I know, said Jon. It's okay.

Jon liked his lovers occasional. He also liked them to have big warm hands and broad thumbs like hammers. For no particular reason, muscle-roped arms reminded him of the amber twisted sticks of barley sugar his grandfather used to find for him when he was six at a special chemist shop in a forgotten corner of London. Making love to such a man, he sometimes imagined himself as brittle as one of those sticks, his body breaking into splinters of light-filled glass at the moment of climax and then shivering into translucent dust. This man, though, was a large teddy bear, pale-skinned and blurry around the edges.

They had met the day before. It was gray, drizzly, warm and airless, and Jon had been walking the streets, light on the balls of his feet, his head back, occasionally tasting the rain. He liked rain. He liked it when the sky was the color of pumice or the paving stones near the Tower of London, stones that had been trodden for so many centuries that they looked soft as suede. He liked the way the mist blurred his vision so that he could imagine himself home in England, surrounded by dripping mackintoshes and black umbrellas. New York was a great city, but it lacked something essential: that sense of bones under the earth, the lurid history of plagues, fire, political intrigue and public execution—and here he remembered stories he used to shiver at as a kid about men immured in wire cages and left dangling over public streets to die of thirst and hunger, to shrivel and rot while people passed below, jeering, fleetingly sympathetic, indifferent. A tourist guide told him once that even the most hardened criminals wept and shook as they were led to those cages.

That phrase of Dr. Johnson's about the man who was tired of London being tired of life was a truism because it was true, Jon reflected. The city was a crossroads for the entire world, a place of constant immigration and fertilization, a locus where past and present merged. Underneath all the contemporary churning slept those bones, and you could still be surprised, turning a corner, to come across a centuries-old church, or a green, daisy-dotted park with a memorial to someone important at the center. Londoners didn't carry the air of nervous tension he saw in New Yorkers, that need to simultaneously impress others and shield their inner lives, and he thought it was precisely because of the worn gray stones and the constant, sobering presence of the dead.

His grandfather, a Hungarian, had come with his wife to London after the abortive revolution of 1956. A watchmaker in the old country, skilled at dealing with rare and precious timepieces, he was soon in high demand among the wealthy. As a boy, Jon loved visiting his grandfather's workshop, the watches laid out on counters, along with the tiny intricate wheels and springs that allowed them to keep time. He thought of the old man as a figure out of a fairy tale, tap-tap-tapping at his bench, hunched over and tinkering, even as he aged and his hands slowly thickened with arthritis. The family said Jon had inherited the old man's meticulousness, and he knew that his propensity for working in the pre-dawn hours came from his Nagypapi, who used to talk to him as he worked about watches so old they could no longer remember their function and had to be reminded of it, or open for him the wooden drawers holding his stock of ancient parts and special tools, along with the bits and pieces he'd collected to create parts that didn't exist any more. Working at night was crucial, Nagypapi had explained, because it was only in absolute silence that he could hear the voice of the watch's maker. Sometimes when he was in his teens, Jon sneaked out to the workshop after midnight and sat in the breathing silence, still as stone, watching his grandfather work in his circle of lamplight.

His grandmother, Marika, couldn't have been more different, and he had adored her too, her thick warm body, lustrous brown hair and melodious voice. Eastern European women had the most melodious voices in the world, he reflected, walking through the misty New York rain. He loved the rhythms of her speech and the way she took care of his grandfather, serving him but without servility, taking off his shoes when he came home from his workshop and sliding slippers onto his feet, keeping his dinner warm—and doing all this with queenly poise, gentle and smooth as cream. In the early days, when she and his grandfather were still struggling, fine pastry shops were rare in London, so she'd begun a small business making Hungarian desserts—cream horns, nut cakes, apricot tarts, crescents made of crisp, light puff pastry. She refused to give up her business even when they no longer needed the money, though his grandfather—a traditional Eastern European patriarch—fumed a little. His grandparents were able to ensure a first-rate education for Jon's father, and this, combined with his father's combination of old-world courtliness and British modernity and his fluency in several languages, eventually won him a place in the diplomatic corps. And also the love of Jon's mother, a fair-haired country-blooming English rose. The family traveled widely as Jon was growing up, and everywhere they went, he and his brother Theo investigated the food: Moroccan spices, Parisian chocolates, rose-scented Turkish lamb stews. He arrived at Oxford wreathed in an aura of mystery and otherness he knew very well how to exploit.

It was at Oxford that he developed a passion for Elizabethan literature, loving the way the poets condensed a world of complex emotion into a single transparent and vibrating lyric, with everything extraneous—corruption, self-regard, sentimentality—burned away. Rose-cheeked Laura, come, he murmured, as the rain dampened his face, and he wondered if he could create a sweet that would somehow express—visually and in terms of taste—the lyricism of the poem, "Sing thou softly with thy beauty's silent music, either other sweetly gracing." So hard to scan those lines, so intuitively musical.

The drizzle intensified, and he decided to take the bus home. There was only one other person standing at the stop, a man, and Jon gave him his usual swift, appraising glance. Nope. Not his type. About his age, but appearing older and more solid, a broad face with sandy eyebrows, hair somewhere between dark blond and brown. Neither good- looking nor unattractive. Just ordinary. The rain began to pelt, Jon opened his umbrella, and at that moment the world turned to water, pouring over the sides of the umbrella with such force that the drops bounced back up from the sidewalk staccato. Within seconds, the man's skin gleamed with wetness, as if he were wrapped in cling film. On impulse, Jon held out his umbrella—and the second he'd done it wished he hadn't. The man scuttled under with a quick "Hey, thanks," and they stood awkwardly side-by-side. The stranger was clearly trying to give Jon as much room as possible, and also to take up as little space as possible himself—which meant exposing his entire right side to the rain. But they were still standing far closer together than Jon found comfortable, and he was annoyed with himself. Why had he crafted this small, idiotic predicament? He checked his watch, meaning the gesture to be seen, intending to convey something along the lines of, Hey, don't make any assumptions; I'm just being a good neighbor. Minutes passed. He gazed down the street in the direction from which the bus would eventually arrive. And finally—there seemed no help for it—Jon looked at the man directly: I'm Jon.

Keith. The man held out a wet hand.

They stood in silence, and Jon became increasingly aware of the warmth of the stranger's arm against his. It had been a long time since he'd been with anyone. He realized he was horny, and also—as he'd known instinctively all along, his gaydar being in good working order—that Keith was gay. He stole another glance. Keith really didn't look too bad. Not beyond the pale, anyway. There couldn't be any harm in inviting him back to the apartment for a glass of wine, and eventually—after the requisite minuet of advance and retreat—allowing himself to be serviced. Keith seemed like someone who'd be willing to do it.

Now Keith was standing by his bed, fully dressed. Are you sure you want me to go? he said. I thought we had a good time.

We did. We had a good time. And now I need to work.

Silently, Keith walked out of the room.

Half an hour later, Jon was in Stocker's kitchen. It felt odd to be there alone. The place was all shadow and outline, but even in the dim half-light, Stocker's sins were apparent—crumbs breaking up the long metal gleam of the counters, implements left out of place, the lingering smell of grease. Jon knew there were things in cracks and corners, blobs disintegrating or furred with dust, that he didn't want to think about. But still, he found something touching in this space, Stocker's sanctum sanctorum, silent for the moment and emptied of the creator's angry restless spirit.

Jon pulled a wooden box containing pick-up sticks from his pocket; lying beside Keith, he'd come up with the notion that this favorite childhood game would jog his imagination. He seated himself at the end of one of the counters, held the cluster of sticks loosely in his hand, and allowed them to fall. He and Theo used to spend hours playing with pick-up sticks when they were boys, arguing about whether the game went better on carpet, linoleum or a wooden floor, creating more and more absurd challenges for each other: drop the sticks from high in the air, try picking up with your left hand, or while lying on your stomach over a chair, feet waving in the air. Jon usually won, but he took his sweet time doing it, ignoring Theo's urgent requests to for heaven's sake hurry up. He liked thinking about the unpredictable ways the sticks fell, the chance permutations of color that resulted, the shapes they made on the floor.

He planned to put something like this on a plate, to resurrect the childhood pleasure of holding those thin sticks in your fingers and have it followed by a moment of surprise as the sticks broke in the mouth, brittle and sweet. Every flavor needed to be different, strong and clear, familiar and also unexpected. Yellow sticks? He'd make them from summer squash. Or honey, truffled or—no—tinted red-gold with saffron. Did sunflower petals taste like the seeds? He'd have to check. Red? That was easy. Cherries with a hint of almond. Purple? Bitter little damson plums. The orange-colored sticks would taste of nothing but orange, popping in the mouth. Green? Asparagus. No. Too distinctive and too strangely out of context. Fresh spring peas then. He closed his eyes for a moment, imagining these living, luscious ingredients translated into straight and rigid lines. Then he began balancing the pick-up sticks against one other, letting them drop, picking them up again. Walter Pater had written about the ecstasies experienced through the senses, the need to burn always with a hard gemlike flame, and though it was an absurd comparison, that was how Jon was thinking about the elements of his dessert. He wanted each stick to appear lit by an inner flame, to glow with its own essence. Ding an sich. Whatever that meant. He thought of Theo, now a philosopher teaching at Oxford and mildly contemptuous of his brother's vocation. Theo would understand the phrase ding an sich in all its permutations and ramifications. You're asking a lot of those pick up sticks, he'd say dryly. Theo had limited patience for anything that couldn't be clearly articulated; his philosophy might be abstract but he liked his definitions precise.

Jon sighed and stood up. He paced the kitchen a time or two, then took the pot he used for caramel down from its hook and placed it on the stove, poured a small cascade of sugar into it, turned on the flame. The process of melting sugar always calmed and mesmerized him, the pure whiteness thinning into transparency and beginning to change color, from palest amber through honey to a deep bronze gold. With a pastry brush, he cleaned off any crystals that might be trying to form on the side of the pot. But something was wrong. There was a change of color around the tiny bubbles at the edge, a white granular hardening, and he knew his caramel was finished. There was no use tilting the pot or stirring because nothing could prevent the ugly color—like the belly of a dead fish—from taking over. He snatched the pot from the stove and slammed it down into the sink. A few days earlier, a cockroach had fallen onto his hand-made fondant. He'd raced over to complain to Stocker, and heard someone laughing behind his back. One of the cooks, perhaps the dishwasher.

He had marked his tools and utensils clearly—they were supposed to be for his dessert work only, and if he didn't mark them some idiot would be sure to use a pastry brush to baste meat, or leave a grungy ridge inside a saucepan. Which was obviously what had happened here.

There was a movement at the door, footsteps, and Stocker progressed along the corridor sideways, huffing under the weight of a large box of onions. It was a point of pride with him to visit the early morning market himself rather than sending a staffer so that he could personally discover any interesting new ingredients: a fruit or vegetable that had just come into season, the first catch of the local fisherman who traveled to Alaska annually for salmon, springtime ramps and snap peas, early-summer plums, treasures that would remain on a vendor's stall for no longer than an hour before some eagle-eyed chef or savvy shopper snatched them up.

Stocker dumped his box on the counter. Where's Sean? Truck's in the alley. Well, I guess you can help me unload.

Jon didn't move. I can't work under these conditions.

What? You don't carry?

I can't work in this kitchen. I need a dedicated space for sugar and chocolate, somewhere clean where I can keep the temperature steady.

Hey. You don't like it here you know where you can go.

I'm not going anywhere. I'm staying with Stocker's Kitchen. And I want a dedicated space for desserts. It's not that hard.

Jon had worked out the logistics, paced and measured the kitchen, found a corner that could be extended outward into the alley without too much disruption: We could do it. It'd just take some planning, he said. We just need to knock out part of that wall over there.

You nuts? You heard of building codes?

The city can be negotiated. And then we'd erect a bit of a barrier. I have a friend who does all kinds of walls. He'd give me a break on materials, we could design it together, and I could do a lot of the carpentry and construction. It'd just be a cubbyhole, but it could work.

Stocker had begun vibrating with anger. Who the fuck do you think you are? If my kitchen's not good enough, you can get the hell out of it.

Jon took in a deep breath. This wasn't his first fight with Stocker. Their arguments over the last few weeks had been a reliable source of amusement for the rest of the kitchen crew. Stocker would hurl insults—queer, cornholer, bumsucker, faggot—while Jon maintained the calm dignity he knew drove Stocker wild and that was his strongest weapon. It was like watching someone tormenting the hippo at the zoo, Angela had commented once to Jon: There he is in his cage—Stocker—impotent, huge, roaring with fury, and you're standing outside, just out of reach, like a Victorian dandy with a silk pocket handkerchief and an ebony cane.

It made him smile, Angela's image, and he held onto it because it would help him maintain control, and this was a fight he intended to win.

I belong here.

Oh, yeah? Pardon me, but we were doing just fine before you graced us with your fabulous faggot self.

I belong here at Stocker's Kitchen. Your food's amazing, brilliant, but I can take it to the next level. I can add something. I can add the finishing touch.

What I send out is finished. There's no next level. You got nothing to add except maybe some dumb finicky frill that oughta be in a museum not on a plate.

My desserts don't belong in a museum. They're food, not art.

They ain't food. Food is what you put in your mouth when you're hungry. Food fills your belly.

Hippopotamus, Jon thought. Roaring.

Right. But when you're not so hungry maybe food can be art as well as sustenance. Or play even. Ever seen a toddler with a pile of mashed potatoes?

People eat because they're hungry. Stocker had found his certainty now; he was on firm ground. You eat because if you don't, you're gonna die. No one ever died because they didn't have art. Jon started to speak, but Stocker bulled forward unstoppable. Hey, maybe where you should work is that Spanish place where they make raindrops out of potatoes and kale into candy and serve teeny-tiny glass tubes of smells and colored air and you can't even eat till somebody tells you how.

That chef's an artist. Jon walked to the sink, ran water into his pot of ruined sugar, then plunked it on the stove and turned the gas up under it. He didn't look at Stocker. You're saying you don't want any kind of art in your kitchen?

That's right. Fuck art.

At that moment Jon knew he'd won, even though it would take Stocker a while to realize it. He said, My sugar crystallized because someone used this pot and didn't clean it out.

And fuck you, Stocker yelled.

Okay. If that's it, we can talk about the space later. I have some plans I'd like to share with you.

Nothing to talk about.

Jon took his pot off the stove and rinsed it out slowly and deliberately. Then he boxed his pick-up sticks, nodded at Stocker, and turned toward the door. Want me to help with the onions?

Nope. Wouldn't want you to dirty your hands.

Jon began pushing through the boxes in the corridor. Your food's no different from mine, Stocker yelled toward his retreating back. It all comes out as shit in the end.

Once outside, Jon decided to walk home: he was too aroused, angry and exhilarated for the subway or a bus. The world was fresh and clear after the rainstorm. He had withstood Stocker's storm of vitriol, and he knew, though nothing of the kind had been said, that he would get his space. A piece of melody, jazzy and syncopated, started zizzing through his head; he adjusted the rhythm of his walking to it. He was tired, sexually sated from the previous evening, proud of having bent the world to his will. Jon was developing a reputation, and there were many places other than Stocker's where he could work. But there was something compelling about the place—perhaps in part that Stocker's crudeness and the chaos he created were so strong a counter to Jon's obsessive need for order. On seeing his room at Oxford, a lover had once teased him with a Beckett quote: "I love order. It's my dream. A world where all would be silent and still, and each thing in its last place, under the last dust."

Sounds restful, Jon had retorted. And what about Yeats: Where there is nothing there is God?

But there was something about the way Stocker fished cleanness out of muck that intrigued him, and he imagined his own dedicated space as both rebuttal and balance. He had ideas for that space. He had already made sketches, and begun anatomizing the myriad problems he would need to solve. Everything would be stracked. Everything would have its rightful place. He knew exactly where he would keep his spoons and spatulas, his sieves, where he'd place the pegboard for pots and sauté pans. There'd be a drawer filled with tools for candy making and chocolate dipping, a machine to temper chocolate—though he wasn't sure what size it needed to be because he was still assessing the number of chocolate desserts ordered each night. He'd find a cool, aerated home for fruits and vegetables, and provide bins for flour and sugar, a fridge for cream, milk and butter. The problem remained of how he'd filter out steam, grease and infiltrating smells, but he'd work on that. And though he planned to push Stocker into covering as much of the cost as could be squeezed out of him, he was also willing to spend his own money if he had to. Stocker's insults still sounded in his ears as he walked, but the jazzy music was bouncing through his mind as well and quickening his feet. He would have his kitchen. He could see it now: the row of pots hanging on the pegboard, gleaming and ordered by size.

Jon stopped a couple of times: for a newspaper, a brioche from his favorite bakery. He'd make a good strong cup of coffee when he got home to keep himself going for the rest of the day because he knew from experience that if he napped he'd be too tired to get through his restaurant shift later. He had some pills that would help, and he'd shower away the day's grime, the scent and effluence of sex from his groin. He flashed momentarily on the image of the top of Keith's sandy-brown head between his knees, himself lying back on a pile of pillows. Keith's tongue had been supple. You make me feel like a pasha, Jon had said, and Keith had raised his head: A what?

Never mind. Don't stop.

Jon rounded the corner of his block, and saw that Keith was sitting on the stoop of his apartment building wearing a dark blue tracksuit and reading the *Times*. He'd been home—obviously—changed and come back. As Jon approached, he folded the newspaper and stood up. They faced each other in silence and Jon caught the clean whiff of aftershave.

A few seconds passed, and then Keith smiled his broad calm smile. I thought I'd give you a chance to know me better, he said.

What makes you think I want to know you better?

You do.

A brief pause.

You said you wouldn't be back.

Guess I lied.

Jon took that in and started to laugh and his laughter, driven by tiredness, the intense pitch of his quarrel with Stocker and the absurdity of this new confrontation rose helplessly higher and higher. He couldn't even tell after a while if he was laughing at Keith, with him—and by now Keith was laughing too—or just for the pure convulsive relief of laughter. Finally he caught his breath and said, Okay. You'd better come in.

That first conversation with Keith at the kitchen table—Jon had made coffee and split his brioche in half, provided butter and jam—was halting and tentative. How had the work gone, Keith wanted to know. Why did desserts need planning, and how was making them different from any other kind of cooking?

You can experiment with regular food, Jon explained, add this or that, taste and adjust as you go along. But with cake and candy, you have to be precise. Mismeasure by a fraction, miscalculate the temperature, and everything flops. Plus they need visual appeal. And maybe some surprise.

Keith nodded and buttered his brioche.

So what do you do?

I'm a dentist. I work mostly with kids.

You must deal with a lot of crying.

Keith laughed. I invent things to keep them calm. I tell them to sing to me—they've got their tongues stuck at the bottom of their mouths because I'm poking and prodding at their teeth, and they're tensing up. I sing a little song—Baa baa black sheep or whatever—and ask if they'll please hum it back to me. Then I say to sing louder because I can't hear the words. Of course the louder they try to sing, the goofier the words come out, and then they start to giggle.

Jon smiled. When Keith stood up a little later and said he had to go to work, Jon hesitated. Then he said: Why don't you give me your number? I'll be in touch.

CHAPTER FOURTEEN

"You know they's a kind of bird that don't have legs so it can't light on nothing but has to stay all its life on its wings in the sky?"

Megan recognized the speech from Tennessee Williams's *Orpheus Descending*. The man speaking it on the studio stage was dark-haired, dark-eyed and slight. "You can't tell these birds from the sky," he continued—he had just a hint of an accent that she couldn't quite place—"and that's why the hawks don't catch them ... they live their whole lives on the wing, and they sleep on the wind ... and never light on this earth but one time when they die ... They's lot of people would like to be one of those birds and never be corrupted."

She was mesmerized. The speaker spoke so quietly, his voice expressive, but not lushly so, his low-key approach working against the heated romanticism of the script so that you heard it new. She was learning. In this class emotion—real emotion within the artificial medium of theatre—was prized above all else, and Megan herself always strove for it in her acting. But it was hard. Sometimes, performing, she did feel genuine anger or joy or grief, but when that happened she'd become a double self, evaluating her feelings even as they arose, awash in self-doubt. So tears might spring to her eyes just as she intended but instantly she'd question whether they were real. Or real enough. And what was real anyway? Was she—Megan—even capable of real, let alone truth? Her voice rose in uncontrollable anger—but was it in fact uncontrollable? Didn't she just sound shrill and melodramatic? This new student was delivering a lesson she couldn't quite parse, managing to sound cool and warm simultaneously—a warmth that was doubly powerful for being damped down. And it didn't hurt that he was beautiful.

She wasn't the only one who'd noticed. After the blue period and some strong praise from Fritz, after a handful of other monologues and scenes that she had trouble focusing on, she watched a group of classmates clustering around the new student as he stood to leave, asking what he planned to work on next and whether he'd be interested in a scene they themselves were contemplating. Lauren pushed to the front and invited him to the Liffy for the in-group's after-class beer. Sure, he said, and Megan's heart sank. At the door, Lauren turned unexpectedly: Hey, she said, Megan. Tracy. Why don't you two join us?

Ten minutes later, they were all sitting at the Liffy's large central table with its dark, aged wood and scatter of discolored white rings. Megan liked it here, the yellow gleam of lights, the sawdust on the floor, the overwhelming smell of beer, and the garrulous Irish middle-aged waiters, one of whom, Megan saw, was winking at her. The place was stuck in time, she thought, unregenerate and full of unseen presences. Orpheus was sitting across from her between Lauren and Tracy, and she kept stealing covert glances at him while phrases from her romance novels drifted through her mind: fathomless dark eyes, chiseled features, sensual lips. Sometimes clichés were clichés because they worked, she thought. The Liffy was loud and she had to strain to keep up with the conversations at the table. We've been wondering where you're from—this was yelled above the noise by Jojo, loud, large, irrepressible and proudly gay—Latin America? Greece or Italy?

The Middle East, he responded. I'm Nabil.

The conversation drifted as glass after glass of beer was poured from bottomless pitchers and everyone shared baskets of fries. Lauren's favorite waiter asked her to marry him, as he apparently did—judging by the knowing laughter—every time she came in: Sure, I'll be taking you to Kilkenny, he said. You'll love it in Ireland. Head bent, Nabil talked quietly to Tracy. In the forgiving dim light, her eyes fixed on Nabil's face, Tracy looked almost pretty, and her green fingernails gleamed, exotic and Bohemian. Megan forced her attention away from them. Lauren was talking about her beauty routine, which involved several products, and how important it was to keep up your appearance at all times if you were an actor. She could see a clear difference in her complexion when she forgot to use her facial mask every week, she said, and she wished she could afford to get her hair styled more often. Not to sound shallow, Lauren continued—and Megan saw Doug smirk at Jojo—but they were in a profession where looking good was a requirement. Your body is your instrument, she said sententiously. You have to keep it in top condition. On the other side of the table, Maria was suggesting naturopathic remedies to Phil, who had a cold, and someone else was saying she'd tried homeopathy once and it hadn't done her any good.

Now Lauren turned the bright spotlight of her attention on Nabil: We were all knocked out by your scene, she said.

He nodded his thanks.

Tell us a bit about yourself. You're from the Middle East?

My mother's French and my father's family's from Palestine. I'm a mongrel.

You're Israeli?

No. Gently, as if explaining to a child. Palestinian.

Lauren looked puzzled, but kept smiling.

Megan wanted to say something, but she didn't want to reveal her ignorance as she sensed Lauren had hers. So it was a relief when Jojo said, Palestine. Is that really a place? I mean, a country?

It's complicated, but I assure you it's a place. My father was born in Jerusalem.

The capital of Israel?

No. Jerusalem is an international city.

You know—Jojo again—there've gotta be a lot of roles around for someone with your background. All those CIA and homeland security shows. Movies. You could play a spy or a terrorist.

Nabil smiled. I'd rather play a lover.

Several people chimed in with suggestions for scenes he might want to work on—preferably with them: Sarah Ruhl, Annie Baker, "that British guy who's making waves right now."

Megan gathered up her courage. Are you interested in Shakespeare? she said. As he turned to her she faltered. I mean ... I've been wanting to tackle Shakespeare for a while. The verse scares me ...

I grew up with Shakespeare, Nabil said. He's big in the Arab world.

Seriously? said Doug. Shakespeare?

He was translated into Arabic in the nineteenth century, and now they do all kinds of versions. Everywhere, every country almost. Hamlet. Richard III. Othello. The Merchant of Venice. Think about it. Who understands all those crazy political currents better than us? What do you think Richard III means to an Egyptian? They did a version of Romeo and Juliet in Jerusalem once in Hebrew and Arabic, with Jewish actors playing the Capulets and Palestinians the Montagues.

Wow. Lauren leaned forward, but Nabil was still looking at Megan. I'm kind of liking the idea of a comedy, he told her. There's so much darkness in the world right now and I keep trying not to think about it. I want to do something frivolous.

A Midsummer Night's Dream, said Tracy, as Megan struggled to remember the titles of the comedies.

Perfect.

There's some great stuff when the lovers are in the forest, Tracy said. You and I could do one of those scenes with maybe—she looked around—Doug. You interested, Doug? Doug nodded.

Damn her.

I'll be Helena, she continued. And Megan could be Hermia.

And bless her.

CHAPTER FIFTEEN

Stocker was wandering Angela's bedroom while she boiled water for tea in the kitchen, and he noticed a pair of earrings on her dresser. They were shaped like feathers, so artful and delicately tendrilled that it seemed they could actually trap air, create loft and enable flight. But when he picked one up, instead of the expected softness, his fingers encountered hard enameled wire. Stocker was interested in feathers, the hollow shaft and tight orderly rows of vanes, the unbelievable lightness, the link they represented between earth and air. He'd heard that a white pigeon landing on a roof symbolized death in the house, and pigeons carried away the souls of dying people. But folklore also said that pigeon feathers stuffed in a pillow created a cosmic discordance and unease that kept death away. Every now and then, working in his restaurant kitchen, Stocker wondered how he could translate the meaning of feathers into something edible. He imagined a soft fluttering in the mouth, a rush, an evanescence.

Angela came in holding two cups of tea, and he turned. The French eat songbirds, he said, glancing at the earring in his hand. They're a delicacy.

Feathers are back in fashion big-time. In all the department stores as well as the couture houses, she said. Though the ones in the department stores are dyed these flat ugly colors—green, pink, purple. People used to kill birds by the thousands once for hats, feather boas, fans. She set down the teacups. Hey, you ever tasted it? Songbird?

He had, or something like it. Many years back, he'd read about Francois Mitterrand's last meal. The French president had requested ortolan. When the birds were served, he ceremonially draped a spotless white napkin over his head—to intensify the flavor or to hide his sin from God, people said. Or both. Reading the news articles, Stocker had found himself almost trembling with curiosity. There weren't any ortolans in America as far as he knew, so he went into the countryside and netted a goldfinch, placed it in a box and fattened it on fruit and millet for a month. After that, he drowned the tiny creature in Armagnac, and plucked it—a far messier and more difficult process than he'd anticipated. Stripped of feathers, the bird was pitifully small. But he cut off the feet and roasted it for a few minutes. Then, like the dying Mitterand, he covered his head and ate.

Intestines and everything? Angela asked.

Even the beak.

Did you like it?

He had. It had been delicious, a small hot mouthful, full of fat, tasting of hazelnut and Cognac, the bones cracking lightly between his teeth. But he was wishing now that he hadn't mentioned any of this to Angela. He didn't like remembering. He didn't like thinking about the trapped bird twittering in the dark box—two calling notes, and a trill, two notes and a trill, sweet and clean, over and over again until it lost the heart to make any sound at all.

But confession bred confession, and over their tea, Angela began talking about her schooldays. This girl lost her hair to chemo, and half the school—teachers, principal, everyone—shaved their heads too, she told Stocker.

You all did that in sympathy?

Well, not me. I didn't get the point. Why would seeing a bunch of bald people all around make a cancer patient feel better?

But a year later, after the girl had died and everyone else's hair grown back, Angela found herself staring, mesmerized, into the bathroom mirror one morning, and eventually, she picked up a pair of scissors and began cutting. Soon fat coils of black hair—the black hair that linked her so tightly to her mother—littered the sink. Still she didn't stop, pulling her head down hard with her left hand and stabbing with her right. When almost all the hair was gone, she stopped and contemplated her patchy head. She looked like a cancer patient herself, a concentration camp survivor, someone old and dying. She picked up a razor, slid it over the hollow at the base of her skull and the shelf of bone above, over the crown of her head, up to her hairline and then back down, working in slow, steady strokes until she could see her naked skull and the clear contour of bone beneath it. She touched her head. The skin felt perfectly smooth. She wasn't a cancer patient now. She was an abstraction, a marble bust, a spar of wood, a stone smoothed by millennia under water.

What you do? Crazy girl, what you do? You want be ugly? You ugly enough before. Her mother had burst through the bathroom door, and Angela mimicked her scolding for Stocker.

Angela turned her naked head slowly. She said nothing. Her mother was a mosquito—no, not even as substantial as that—a whine, a disturbance in the air. She caught her mother's wrists as Kim approached with clawed fingers, and felt a surge of power. She was too big to be controlled now. Too big to be hurt. She wanted to throw back her head and crow like a great bird as her mother's fingers curled harmlessly in the air, and her wrists grew slippery under Angela's hands. After a few minutes she let go—her mother staggered with the suddenness of the release—and walked out of the bathroom, leaving a string of complaints to blur into nothingness behind her: You leave for me? I clean up your filthy hair? You block up my sink and walk away? Angela? You walk away and leave your filthy hair for me?

She left the house and swung down the street, the air cold against her naked head. Her forehead stung a little, and reaching up to touch it she realized her mother had managed to inflict one long deep scratch after all. She walked until she reached her friend Sara's house, pudgy, plain Sara, always content to be in Angela's shadow. She rang the bell, and immediately, without waiting for an answer, began banging the bell-shaped knocker. Moments later, Sara stood in front of her in the baggy khaki shorts that made her legs look even whiter and stubbier than they were. Oh, my God, she squeaked. Angela. What happened to your head?

I want to go to the mall.

The mall? Like that?

Uh-huh. Ask your mom to take us.

Sara's eyes bulged as resistance, repulsion, and excitement competed in them. Mom's making dinner.

It won't take ten minutes. We can eat there. Ask her.

Sara turned obediently back into the house. Her mom didn't particularly like her, Angela knew, but she was Sara's first real friend, and Mrs. Perry was grateful for that. Muffled voices rose and fell, and then Mrs. Perry was in the doorway and Angela had to submit to her exclamations of distress and concern. She allowed herself to be led into the kitchen and have the scratch on her forehead washed—it was bleeding fairly copiously now—and soothed with ointment: It's nothing, she kept repeating. I don't even feel it. Please. I want to go to the mall.

She rather liked it though, the feel of the warm, damp washcloth against her skin. Her own mother's touch was never gentle. Maybe it had been once, long ago when Angela was little, but if so, she couldn't remember. Does that sting? asked Sara's mom, and Angela shook her head.

Mrs. Perry rummaged in a hallway drawer for a scarf and insisted Angela put it over her head. Then she drove them to the mall.

The minute we were inside and on the escalator, I pulled off the scarf, Angela said.

Stocker imagined her rising slowly through the unforgiving artificial light, her naked forehead like the prow of a ship.

People stare? he asked.

She shrugged. Maybe.

At the head of the escalator was a pretzel stand, and a group of boys from school were clustered in front of it. They turned and gaped. Hey, Angela, one of them asked eventually, you want a pretzel? The others snickered.

She ignored the snickers. Long as you're buying.

He said he was.

Angela turned to Sara. Take off, she said. I'll find you at the earring place in an hour.

But we were going to look at tops together. You were going to help me pick out something. My mom'll be here in an hour.

Forty-five minutes then.

Sara didn't protest further, just gave a little whimper—no boy had ever offered to buy her a pretzel—and turned away.

Later that night, Stocker and Angela sat huddled together on the sofa watching a reality show: a group of fat people competing to lose weight. Angela liked seeing the transformations, commenting on exactly what kind of outfit she'd have picked out to emphasize the newly-trim bodies; Stocker was more interested in the opening episodes, the contestants' incomprehensible blubberiness, the waves of fat spilling over waistbands. It was halfway through the season now, and he half dozed as a man called Frank talked weepily to a muscular trainer about his withholding mother and unhappy childhood.

You love me, Angela said suddenly.

He jerked away and stared at her.

You love me, she repeated, as if she knew to the core of her sharp little bones it was true.

Stocker shrugged, said, Maybe, got up and went to the fridge for a beer. He needed a few seconds. Love wasn't the name he'd have put to the coiling in his guts whenever he saw her, the way her name repeated over and over in his mind—Angela, Angela—in the shower, in his clattering kitchen, outside in the alley as he watched the little cat feed, or to the way the scent of her skin and hair lingered always in his nostrils, the thought of her tongue circling her lips as she sought out the last vestige of grease from his cooking.

He stood by the fridge irresolute. He didn't believe in love. He didn't believe in anything you couldn't eat, and as far as he knew, you couldn't eat love. Well, he'd eat out Angela of course, rooting and snouting in that sweet little crotch, and she sometimes returned the favor—"Eat me," he'd snicker, honking with laughter because he wanted it so much and didn't want her to realize it, and then he would let the air out of his lungs in a loud whistling breath as he felt the agonizingly slow descent of her tongue from the hollow of his neck, over his chest to the indent between hipbone and the swell of his belly. When her lips finally brushed the tip of his penis, he'd jolt into action, seize her by the hair and press downwards. Hungry? he'd shout. That's right, baby. Grab on and keep eating.

But love? He didn't want to go there. He hoped his mother had loved him once, regretted having to abandon him, held him in her arms for a moment before leaving him howling on top of that overflowing garbage can, but deep down he envisioned it differently, saw her grabbing his squirming, vernix-greased body the minute he'd popped out, exhausted as she was, shoving him into a car, then stopping in that alley behind Yen Ching. It was a stifling, smelly summer night, and love was nowhere around.

He came back into the living room. So I love you? he said. Angela's lips tightened into her customary half-vicious little grin. Does that mean you love me?

Love's a big word.

The truth was, Angela didn't know if she loved Stocker. He could keep her off-balance. That was his power, as hers was the pretense that she was never off-balance, never nonplussed. She liked the relationship, the warmth and dishevelment, the coarseness, crudeness, appetite, and raw physicality of it: Stocker padding from their bed in the middle of the night to fry sausages with eggs, which they'd eat under the sheets together, and sometimes smear on each other's bodies. She enjoyed prodding playfully at his belly button, tossing him sections of the newspaper over breakfast, laughing with him at dopey television shows like this one. She liked the Sundays when they'd walk from one end of Manhattan almost to the other, while he made her try every kind of food they encountered on the way. She liked the orgasms. It wasn't the kinky stuff that did it for her, the ice cube shivering against her clitoris, the vulnerable opened-up feeling when he sucked a raw egg from her belly—those things were okay, they jolted her, kept her electrified and hyper-awake—but it was the way his fingers knew exactly when to prod and when to stroke so softly they felt like feathers, the tiny experimental bites in odd places, the edge he walked between hurting and soothing, and the way he sent her effortlessly, time after time, out of her body and into a deep black spiraling fall.

Sometimes she played with the idea of marrying him. She had no desire for children and as far as she knew he didn't either. But there were things she planned to have eventually. Stability. A nice house. Leisure. And all the clothes and jewelry she could play with. She was tired of serving rich customers while she herself scraped by month to month in her box of an apartment. Stocker had money. But he was short and fat and vulgar, and there was no peace or order to his life.

I know you love me, she whispered now, taunting. She nipped his earlobe hard and, as he yelped, jumped up and started running circles around the apartment, her robe sliding to the floor, the knobs of her spine appearing, disappearing, re-appearing as her hair swung from side to side like a horse's tail. You do. You do. You do. You love me. Stocker jumped up. The image came to him of a lion stalking a zebra, head low, tail twitching, separating it from the herd, predator and prey, eater and eaten—and the game took off. He ran at her and she circled back sharply, foiling him, brushing past his fingers, and round and round they went in the tiny living room, through the kitchen where he grabbed an apple to toss at her and she evaded it, as fast and lithe as he was clumsy and cursing—Watch out, she said, you'll churn yourself into butter—until finally he grabbed her wrists, held them behind her back, and nudged himself against her front. They struggled their way back to the sofa, and he soon felt her thin hard legs clamped around his hips, heard her hoarse breathing under him, his furious pumping met by an equally furious receiving. Even emptied, he kept grinding against her until they were both exhausted, and then they lay in silence, easing their bodies slowly apart. He could hear voices outside on the dark street, two women in some kind of argument.

You love me, Angela said.

CHAPTER SIXTEEN

Stocker walked out into the alley, Marlboro already between his fingers, matches in his other hand, making the familiar transition from the clangorous kitchen through the doorway into the hot, damp, river-scented air. He lit the cigarette and inhaled greedily, sucking in the mix of Marlboro smoke and steamy stink from his kitchen's exhaust fans, a stink comprised of cooking oil, beef suet, the essence of the dozen chicken carcasses he boiled down daily for stock and glace. He checked briefly for the cat, both in the pool of light thrown by the door and along the partially lit shadows beyond the doorway's light, but there was no sign of her. He felt the reassuring hardness of brick against the knobs of his spine, and leaned back, exhaling. This was his place, the sound of traffic mingling with that of the not-too-faraway river—a sound he may have been imagining rather than hearing; the shabby spikes of grass; the broken bottle with the pattern of shards around it, streetlight shine shifting on them kaleidoscopically as he moved his head a little; the shapes of trees, stripped of light and color, leaning toward him like druidical figures, simultaneously protective and threatening, too ancient to be only one thing or another.

There was something white protruding from behind the trashcans, a hand, Stocker realized once he'd focused more closely, seeing it first only as an irritating intrusion into his aloneness. He sucked at his smoke, then tossed it aside. He'd awakened sleeping bums often enough, cursed and told them to take their pathetic, melted-down selves out of his alley. Once in a while, he'd hand a poor sod a buck as he shambled off, bent-kneed. Now he walked toward the trashcans and peered around them. The man was lying on one side, his head on his thrust-out arm, a bottle in the other hand. He smelled of pee. Stocker kicked the bum's foot, and his leg doubled limply. Hey, you, wake up. The moment he made contact, Stocker realized the man was dead. But he kicked a couple more times anyway, then paused for a long breath before making his way around the prone form and staring at the face, closed eyes, gray bristles blurring the outline of cheek and chin. There it was, behind those closed eyes, the heart of the mystery, the absence of ... everything: trees, river, cigarettes, brick wall, spiky grass, everything. No consciousness there, no thought, none of the constant fluxy comings and goings of images, impulses and sensory response that make up a human mind. Nothing to remember or look forward to, nothing to look forward with. No booze. No bread. No movies. No tight little cunts. Stocker swayed. He felt he was standing at the edge of a vortex.

It wasn't that he was squeamish. He had seen the light fade from the eyes of hundreds of living things, heard the breath leaving. He knew the feel of just vacated flesh on his fingers, the sight and smell of meat deliberately aged, and also the scent of decay. The borderline between life and death was a quotidian place for him, the place where he made his living. And it wasn't really that this was different, this corpse, because it was that of a man. Why should the transformation from man to meat be more exalted or significant than the transformation of steer or sheep? It was just that he'd been somewhere else at that moment, peaceful, sated, and poised between kitchen and alley, the two worlds that belonged to him, and now there was this icy wind around his heart, the soul-withering vortex at his feet. He kicked at the corpse again, but without energy, and then he pulled out his cell phone and dialed 911. This man had once been somebody's loved child. Now he was refuse. He would be buried in the polluted soil of potter's field, and no one would ever ask where he had gone.

CHAPTER SEVENTEEN

The first rehearsal left lacunae in Megan's memory, though images of it kept bobbing up later like tapioca pearls in bubble tea. Wow, you live in the city, Tracy had said as she and Megan walked into Nabil's apartment on the Upper West Side. How can you afford it? Nabil had texted the two of them to say Doug couldn't come, but he still thought they should get together and talk about the scene they were planning for class.

My dad teaches at Columbia, Nabil said. He and my mom have the apartment below this. The whole building's rent controlled.

It made sense. The apartment didn't have the provisional, unfinished quality of Megan's own place and the places of her friends. It looked settled. The furnishings were a mix of the kind of things relatives gave you when you first moved out on your own, furniture you found at flea markets or garage sales, and objects you picked out for yourself after painstaking deliberation, but somehow it all fit together and spelled out a specific personal history. There was a shiny, efficient kitchen; in the living room a jewel-shaded lamp cast colored light on a worn carpet. A large silver-gray cat sprawled in sleep on the sofa. Megan's eye was caught by a poster showing a series of doors: a gray wood door half-rotted away, two doors painted in fresh bright colors, one blue, one red, a pock-marked stone entryway, and an arch with the standing figure of a woman holding up a vase on each side of it. The caption read, Doors of Jerusalem.

Nabil had come up behind her. Who knows who lives behind those doors, he said, startling her, or what kind of lives go on there. Cities never stand still; they're always in flux. And they're not just physical places. Cities are people, cops, musicians, vendors, dogs and dog shit, kids playing, people fucking and people dying. Pigeons. Buses and cars. The physical structure—streets and buildings—they're like the city's brain. Its mind gets created and re-created over and over again. And the things that go on in the city—all the coming and going—those are its thoughts.

The city thinks? said Tracy.

Sure. New York thinks. Haven't you both noticed?

Nabil was an attentive host. Having seen them settled, he went into the kitchen and came back with a tray holding three glasses, some green leaves, and a pitcher of pale, cherry colored liquid. The leaves went into the glasses first and Nabil crushed them a little, ceremonially, with a spoon before pouring in the liquid. Megan was on the sofa, running her hand along the cat's soft back; he stretched languidly in response to her touch. He's Hali, Nabil told her. Short for Halim. It means gentle.

So did you grow up in ... in Palestine? Tracy asked.

No. Here. I feel a bit of a fake sometimes, claiming Palestine. My mom's from Paris—very cultured and upper class. All the time I was growing up we'd go to France for vacations. My dad teaches the history of the Middle East, but I don't know as much about it as I should. I know way more about Europe. We're all mongrels in my family, polyglot. Growing up, I resented it. All I wanted was to be a regular American kid and eat regular American things.

I learned to cook from my mom though—she loves cooking, straight-up French stuff—and then I started incorporating dishes from Gaza and the West Bank. I learned them out of cookbooks and also I wrote to my aunts and cousins for recipes. How do you like the tea, by the way?

The mint's great, but I can't figure out the other flavor, Tracy said.

Hibiscus.

Megan struggled to find something to contribute to the conversation: Her background seemed flat and ordinary compared to Nabil's.

Sometimes it feels like a pose almost, Nabil went on. I don't even speak Arabic. Well, maybe a few words. When we decided to visit Jerusalem and the West Bank ... I was seventeen; my dad wasn't even sure he could go there. The last time he tried flying to Israel was when I was little and me and my mom weren't with him. The authorities detained him. They let him in after a while but they said they knew the kind of stuff he was writing and they'd be watching him. It freaked him out.

The kind of stuff ... ?

Then we went together. I wonder sometimes if there's such a thing as ancestral memory because Jerusalem ... the minute we got there, I felt like I recognized it. There was this sense of familiarity, like, Hey, I'm home. I've spent all this time with my mom's family in Paris and I love it, but Jerusalem is different. It's completely different from a European city—you know with a river running through the middle and trees along the banks and a medieval castle up on a hilltop? Jerusalem is on a rocky plateau; everything's dry and bright. It grew in a whole different way—and everyone fights about exactly how that was.

Tracy nodded. Did she really understand what Nabil was talking about, Megan wondered. Because to her it was all new.

There's this thing called epigenetics, Nabil went on. They say the parents' traumas, grandparents' traumas, can be in the kids' bodies—something to do with genes and how they interact with their environment. It means we retain some physical trace of what our families went through. Like if you're Jewish and your people lived through the Holocaust, it's in your bones, the suffering. When we entered Jerusalem—maybe it's just because it's so old or my dad talked about it so much, but I was so happy as I walked along the streets; I felt I was where I was supposed to be. You could see all the things that were wrong though: clean white neighborhoods and rows of chain stores where the Israelis live, and trash and graffiti all over in the Palestinian neighborhoods.

He laughed. Maybe it's self-important wanting to be rooted in some significant historical event. Maybe I thought being an Arab made me more interesting than being a regular New York teen. From Jerusalem, we visited family on the West Bank and that made me crazy. Waiting all the time at checkpoints, seeing my dad pushed around by Israeli soldiers the same age as me.

That trip sort of freed me though, opened up my mind to start identifying as Palestinian. My folks wanted me to be an engineer, but I decided to be an actor and I found a group of kids who were all poets and musicians—black, Puerto Rican, Asian, Jews and Arabs, mongrels like me. I wasn't any kind of musician or poet, so I started doing comedy, and I still do that some. I'm pretty terrible, but it's practice for acting, and it lets me say things I want to say. Well, I've talked enough. How about you two?

Still tongue-tied, Megan shook her head.

Nothing worth telling. Tracy's voice was tight.

There was a silence. Okay, Nabil said. We met to rehearse. Let's see what we can do without Doug here. He went to his crammed bookshelf, searched a moment, and pulled down a paperback copy of *A Midsummer Night's Dream*. I've just got one, he said, so we're going to have to share, and he plunked himself on the sofa between the two women. Megan felt the warmth of his body against hers. Okay, he said, let's go.

They found the scene they wanted. You be Hermia, Tracy said to Megan. She's the pretty one. Momentarily flattered, Megan ran the few of Hermia's lines she remembered over in her head. Wasn't Hermia the vapid cheerleaderish one? And wasn't it Helena who had the terrific speech about Hermia betraying their friendship—something about twin cherries on one stem? Or was it blossoms? I'd rather be Helena, she said.

Helena has to be tall, Nabil responded. They're both great roles. Okay? And I'll be both guys for now.

They began reading, Tracy in a deliberate monotone, Megan intensely self-conscious.

After a few lines, Nabil stood. This'll loosen us up, he said. It's always hard getting started. He opened a drawer and pulled out a box of neatly rolled joints. Re-seating himself, he lit one, inhaled, then passed it to Tracy. Megan had never smoked pot before but she tried to look casual and unfazed as she watched. Apparently she was transparent. Just sip at it, Nabil said, handing her the joint. It'll make you cough, but that's okay. And don't hold the smoke in for more than a couple seconds. Seriously, Megan. This is strong stuff.

The joint was damp from his lips as she put it tentatively to hers. She drew in her breath. And then she was coughing furiously and pushing the joint away, toward Tracy, who said, Just relax, Megan. Hold onto it and try again. Choking, sputtering, tears in her eyes, she tried to calm herself down, took a small tentative mouthful of smoke and held it in briefly, felt the heat trickling down her throat. Soon she was coughing again and she passed the joint on as soon as she gracefully could.

After a while, they went back to reading, but Megan was having trouble concentrating. The words entered her mind, but their meanings kept slipping around so that sometimes they felt deep and significant and sometimes nonsensical. "You speak not as you think. It cannot be," she said, and sudden bubbles of mirth jolted her diaphragm. She hiccupped and the other two dissolved into laughter. Now her attention was drawn to the inside of her mouth where it felt as if her cheeks were being sucked together in a sensation she knew intimately but couldn't find a word for. Finally, it came to her: I'm thirsty, she said, and was startled when their laughter redoubled. I'll get you something, Nabil said, unmoving. Seconds later he asked, What did I say? You said you'd get Megan something to drink, Tracy told him, and he nodded and poured some of the hibiscus tea into Megan's glass. She picked it up. The color, she said, the transparency, and she saw that Nabil and Tracy were laughing again. Did you forget how to take a sip? asked Tracy.

Nabil tapped a finger on the script. Okay, he said. We're in the woods.

Sort of a wild and scary place for Shakespeare, Tracy said. Scary and freeing all at the same time. Civilization dissolves in the woods and anything can happen. She always sounded as if hers were the final and authoritative judgment, thought Megan, and she was daring anyone else to contradict her.

Hey, said Nabil. Let's go experience some trees. It'll help us get into it.

Soon they were outside, walking south on Broadway and after several blocks turning East at 96th Street. Tracy and Nabil were ahead of Megan, bending toward each other and suddenly it seemed to her they were talking about her, mocking her, ganging up. She thought of turning a corner and vanishing, just vanishing and leaving them to their communion, but instead she quickened her steps and caught up.

Here's Megan, Tracy said with what seemed unaffected pleasure.

It was dusk as they entered the park, walking past a few late runners and an occasional whizzing bicyclist. For Megan, feeling the air cooling against her face and taking in the scent of grass and trees, it felt as if time had stopped. Here, said Nabil.

Megan looked up to see a massive bronze statue of a woman—or perhaps a girl— surrounded by other strangely-shaped forms. It was hard to make out the outlines in the dropping darkness, but the girl seemed to be sitting on a large mushroom. Oh, she said, It's Alice. Nabil was settling onto the stone step at the statue's base and Tracy sank down beside him. Megan walked slowly round the bronze monstrosity by herself and touched a smaller mushroom to the side with a rearing caterpillar on top of it. There was a rushing in her ears, as if the park were flying past her, along with everything in it, and now Alice had noticed her and was leering.

You can hardly get near that statue in the daytime, Nabil said, as Megan rejoined him and Tracy. Kids climbing all over her, parents taking pictures. He rolled a joint, slowly and meticulously, inhaled, and gestured for Megan to sit down. This time it was Tracy who put her lips to the damp paper where Nabil's had been, but Megan was too full of feelings she couldn't name—fear, excitement, wonder, profound absorption in each and every physical sensation—to feel jealousy. They had food with them, she saw now, M&Ms and barbecue-flavored chips, and she strained to remember when and how the food had happened. Oh yes, there was a newsstand where they'd stopped to stock up, and where Tracy and Nabil had had a long, animated discussion about exactly what candy to buy while the owner rolled his eyes. A package of small square tablets that smelled strongly of violets appeared in her palm and it took her a second to realize Tracy had placed it there. Oh, Megan exclaimed, putting the silver-violet roll to her nostrils and inhaling. What is this?

You've never had violet pastilles? said Nabil. You're a New York virgin, Megan. You have to eat one right now—you'll never belong till you do. Taste good? Okay. Let's get down to business. Here's an acting exercise. Close your eyes and think about the woods. What comes up for you?

There was a silence. Megan sucked on her pastille. Okay, Nabil said after a while: Images, thoughts, ideas.

Fairies. Magic. Transformation. Like with Bottom's head, and how the lovers don't even remember who they love when they're in the woods,

Tracy said.

Or who they are, Megan added.

Ravens, exclaimed Tracy unexpectedly. Cawing and kek-kek-keking and—ugh—tearing at road kill. Forest fires. The treetops catching fire and then the fire roaring and racing along the treetops and all the living things in there trying to get away ...

What is it with you and fire? said Megan. That thing you recited in class the other week: "The men caught fire. The women caught fire. The fire caught fire" ...

I love fire. I love the way it burns away dirt and irrelevant stuff and leaves things clean. Cauterizes. And it's beautiful. The colors and the way the air wavers and distorts around the flames. I used to set all kinds of things on fire when I was a kid. Nothing drastic. No arson. I'd just make a ring of stones in the yard and burn leaves, paper, cloth, plastic even, and watch the way different stuff burns. Plastic melts into black blobs. It's evil. Newsprint whooshes up suddenly and blooms. And then it's ash.

Was she crazy, Megan wondered. Or was this what creativity sounded like? I had a dream about fire once, she said. The whole city was on fire and a man on a motorbike saved me.

The hero. Tracy's voice was mocking. Haven't we had enough of him? In case no one's noticed, we women are saving ourselves now.

Megan said, It wasn't like that, but so quietly the others didn't hear. Okay. Nabil said, let's focus.

I saw this movie once where a girl was raped by three men in the woods. Tracy, normally so reserved, was unstoppable now. An old movie. Afterwards she stood up and moved around like ... like one of those blind, white underwater things that don't need eyes because they live in ocean caves so deep that light can't penetrate. She was moving, this girl, but she wasn't conscious; it was like she was already dead. One of the men came up behind and hit her with a tree branch—there was this horrible crack—one blow and she went down.

I was afraid to walk in the woods after seeing that.

That's what the woods mean to you? Nabil said after a silence. Gothic horror? No picnics? No hikers. Nothing to do with leaves, insects, birds, fertility?

How about those whirly seeds that twirl like helicopters all the way down from the tree? Megan said. I used to love playing with them when I was a kid.

I mean, there are real scary woods in say, Macbeth, Nabil continued, but in Dream the woods are all about love and kisses, play and silly quarrels.

Tracy didn't seem to have heard. Before I saw the movie, I used to walk through this wooded area on the way to school. Her eyes were closed. I didn't want anyone to see me. I couldn't go out on the sidewalk to the bus stop because the other kids hated me. What you said about never feeling at home, Nabil? I know how that is.

Everyone hated you? Megan repeated.

I was this sad, sick creature skulking at the edges of their world, always in shadow. And they were in sunlight. It was so natural to them. I couldn't figure out how to be like them. It was like I was cursed, like I was that blind dead thing in the movie.

The land of exile, said Nabil.

My parents sent me to a shrink, but she was no help.

Everyone feels like an outsider in school, Megan said.

No. Tracy shook her head emphatically. Not like this. I was so weird even the freaks didn't like me. If you guys had been my friends in school no one would have liked you either.

Well, Nabil said, at least no one called you a terrorist.

Tracy raised her head and looked at him steadily. I want another of those violet things, Megan said to break the tension, and Tracy started slightly, then handed over a pastille. But the sweet dissolving in Megan's mouth didn't help. The air was rapidly cooling, the shadows were lengthening and the circling trees seemed to creep closer every time she glanced toward them, menacing and claustrophobic. Tracy's description of the dying girl wept in her bones. Still seated between them, Nabil put his arms around the two women. Let's not talk any more, he said. Let's just sit for a while. Tracy stiffened at his touch, hesitated, and then placed her head against his shoulder as quietly and easily as if it belonged there.

That speech you did in class? she said. About the bird? I loved it.

Trees rustled, a blue jay called out harshly once, twice and then fell silent. The self-important hustle of the city felt a long way away. "I seen one once," Nabil said softly. "It had died and fallen to earth and it was light— blue colored and its body was tiny as your little finger, that's the truth, it had a body as tiny as your little finger and so light on the palm of your hand it didn't weigh more than a feather, but its wings spread out this wide but they was transparent, the color of the sky and you could see through them. That's what they call protection coloring."

Megan glanced over her shoulder to see if Alice was still leering, but it was too dark to make out her face.

Hey, Nabil, Tracy said, startling her. You must feel like Alice between the Red and the White Queen right now.

I do.

Go on, said Megan.

"But those little birds, they don't have no legs at all and they live their whole lives on the wing, and they sleep on the wind, that's how they sleep at night, they just spread their wings and go to sleep on the wind like other birds fold their wings and go to sleep on a tree ...

"They sleep on the wind and never light on this earth but one time when they die ... They's lots of people would like to be one of those birds and never be ... corrupted."

CHAPTER EIGHTEEN

Jon seldom allowed lovers to linger in his apartment, stay for dinner, listen to his music, or sprawl in front of the television set with him: they were expected to spend the night when invited and leave expeditiously in the morning. That's how it began with Keith. But somehow, visit by visit, Keith moved further into Jon's life. He brought over his shaving things and a change of clothing, left a book he was reading on the bedside table, placed a box of the breakfast cereal he liked in the cupboard. Going into the bathroom one morning, Jon inhaled the warm steaminess from Keith's shower, the scent of Keith's shaving cream, and stood irresolute, trying to figure out if what he was feeling was pleasure or annoyance. Even once it was clear that Keith had moved in, neither of them acknowledged it in words, or broached the topic of whether or not he would give up his own apartment. Keith was a cozy presence—no other word for it, Jon thought—a cozy, cocoa kind of guy and somehow grounding, particularly given his own wired, vibrating sensibility, the daily conceptual tightrope he trod with food, the screaming stress of Stocker's kitchen. It was nice—he had to acknowledge it—coming home to this big calm quiet man who kept his own work life tactfully in the background, didn't ask for anything much, and could put Jon in a light ecstatic trance just by rubbing his feet.

Keith took their clothes regularly to the dry cleaner, knocked around the place in jeans and white T-shirts that smelled of laundry soap, a bit soft in the belly, but nothing obtrusive—though he'd probably run to fat eventually, Jon thought—and didn't mind retreating from the living room to the study to watch television when Jon, who found Keith's liking for sports inexplicable, wanted things quiet. He chatted easily and freely with other people: within days he knew, for instance, that their doorman—about whom Jon knew nothing—had a grandson in college, the first in their family, and the kid hadn't yet decided on a major. He picked up cleaning supplies; he had a weakness for doughnuts, and always kept a couple of boxes on the kitchen counter; he enjoyed cooking—hamburgers, pancakes, meatloaf, barbecue—and remained placidly unselfconscious about doing so for Jon, though he did occasionally ask how much of a particular ingredient to add or how hot the oven should be. Which was all just fine with Jon. Keith's meatloaf was a decent one, moistened with milk-soaked bread, and it reminded him of the food he'd had at boarding school—stodge was what he and his friends called it because using Billy Bunterish slang like tuck box, jam roll and tiffin was one of their affectations, along with toasting crumpets in front of the fire and then slathering them with butter. Perhaps it was the sense of outsiderdom his immigrant family had never managed to fully throw off or perhaps the gypsy blood his grandfather insisted they possessed that made the smug, rooted self-assurance of Victorian England so appealing.

I like bread and butter, he hummed after dinner, standing to clear the meatloaf plates. I like toast and jam ...

At breakfast, Jon read the international news, commenting now and then on what was happening in the Middle East, poverty in India or Latin American drug cartels. You don't know what I'm talking about, right? he said.

Keith was flipping through the sports section. Go ahead and explain, he said. I'm interested.

If you were interested, you'd read the paper.

What? And deny you the chance to feel superior?

Jon grinned.

When Jon had a cold, Keith would stop at the deli to pick up chicken soup, or make hot tea with whiskey, lemon and honey. He'd rub ointment on Jon's chest, resisting when Jon seized his hand and attempted to guide it further down his body. No, he'd say. You're sick. You need to rest. We can fuck any time. Jon would have liked to return these favors when Keith was ailing, but sickness repelled him, all the wheezing and gurgling, the throat-rattling phlegm and dirty tissues, and he usually asked if Keith would mind spending the night on the couch because he—Jon—needed his sleep. Keith never took offense. He was so peacefully American, Jon reflected, so at home in his own skin. For a large man, he moved so quietly, as if he were friends with the air, slow, ambling and easy.

Jon knew Keith had grown up with three brothers and two sisters in a pleasant Midwestern town with two banks, a few restaurants, and three churches, and he assumed it was because of this large family that Keith knew so well how to rub along with other people. His father was a dentist like him, and his mother had worked in the same lawyer's office since Keith was six. Even coming out hadn't been hard. His sisters voiced their support immediately; his parents took no more than a week or two; only his oldest brother had reservations, and this was not because he had anything against homosexuality, he'd told Keith, but because of what it would mean for Keith's life. Plus he wanted to be an uncle sometime. There were a few gay people in the town, a couple of men who strolled along the street with a well-groomed afghan hound morning and evening and came to his father every six months to have their teeth cleaned and whitened. There was even a gay student group at the high school. But dating possibilities were limited, Keith told Jon, the nearest gay bar was in Chicago, two hours' drive away, and he didn't like the bar scene anyway.

Jon had had his first sexual encounter at the age of fourteen, initiated by a seventeen-year-old friend with a taste for pornographic websites and wine from his parent's expensive collection. Jon could see now how ridiculously affected this boy was, but at the time he'd thought him the height of sophistication. Once in New York, Jon had gone crazy. Feasted on flesh. Explained to lovers he was Hungarian, with family in Transylvania, and they had better watch out for their necks. Growing up in London, I never even had to think about being gay, he said to Keith. I don't remember ever not knowing I was.

That's how it is here in New York. No one cares, and you can just settle in and live your life. I love this town.

Right. But you've still never been to MoMA.

No.

Or tasted a bialy or a pig's blood sausage.

Maybe you can initiate me.

I'm not playing Pygmalion. Initiate yourself.

Keith laughed. Sounds dirty.

Sometimes Jon fretted about sharing his life and fantasized about how it would be if he could persuade Keith to move out, pondered redecorating and thought about not having to deal with hairs in the bathroom sink, the niggling voices of sportscasters coming through the study door, the morning newspaper carelessly refolded with the page edges not flush.

####

On the screen, a camel was being led toward a beautiful white and gold hotel by a man holding a long knife. They're going to kill it for a banquet, Jon said. The Emperor of Ethiopia is putting on the banquet for the most powerful men in Prague. He and Keith were watching I Served the King of England.

A camel? Keith dug into a bowl of buttered popcorn. They're going to eat it?

Stuffed with antelope, the antelope stuffed with turkeys, the turkeys stuffed with fish. And eggs.

Poor camel.

Hands scattered spices, steam rose from cooking pots. And then the scene shifted to a long, formal dining room. At the table black faces alternated with white, and the emperor sat at the head of the table. At a signal from him, dozens of waiters poured wine into dozens of lifted glasses, tilting the bottles one at a time in a flawless choreography. Seconds later, a Czech diner, short, plump and self-important, lifted the silver cover from his dish, and took a bite of the contents. A strange expression crossed his face, and then he rose and very slowly began dancing with his plate. With their African hosts looking on and laughing, diner after diner, spotless napkins at their necks, rose and joined the dance.

I just don't get this stuff, Jon.

I know it's weird. It's satire. Just hang with it.

What are they satirizing?

I suppose the fatuous blindness of pre-war Europe, the wealth and formal manners, everything stately and untroubled like some kind of fairy-tale—just before the cataclysm. And there's the waiter, the short one, who's just as oblivious, and takes advantage of everyone's weakness and greed to get rich.

I think it's also about the way those Czechs in that land-bound gray city imagined the outside world, the warm, exotic places. They'd never have tasted those spices.

And I really like the idea of food so delicious that the only possible response is to dance with it.

Jon loved Czech film, but it was a chore trying to communicate the reasons for this love to Keith. He loved the women, the way they reminded him of Marika, his grandmother, with her thick, shining hair and voice like rich cream. Most people don't think of Eastern European women as sexy, he told Keith now. They make jokes about steroids and hairy legs. But that's because Americans mostly don't know any Czech or Slovak women.

Uh-huh.

And look at the way Jiri Menzel—the director—uses light.

You're gonna have to shut up, Jon, if you want me to watch.

Right.

Anyway, I thought you were Hungarian, not Slovak.

Yeah. We're a colder, more arrogant lot.

Keith snorted softly. I've noticed.

But I spent a lot of time in Prague. It's the Czechs who had this amazing cinematic revival.

They watched for several minutes in silence before Keith's breath began to deepen. His hand was still in the popcorn bowl on his lap, but his head lolled against the back of the sofa. At any moment, he'd begin to snore. It was stupid, Jon reflected, trying to get Keith to see the movie—or anything else—as he himself did. Keith had no mind for the inexplicable or transcendent, no sense of metaphor, and most of the time that was fine with Jon. But now he wondered, Was this man, so blind to so many things he himself cared about, the partner he wanted for life? Earlier that day, he'd glanced over Keith's shoulder as Keith sat at his computer and seen that he was reading an article about gay marriage: when it would be universally accepted now that it was legal. Keith talked about wanting to marry someday, and how when he did, it would be for keeps: Just one person, Keith always said. No tomcatting around. He'd describe his dreams for his life, his longing for children, how he wanted to live away from the city—not too far because he loved New York—but not right in the middle of things either. He needed green around him, he'd say, a garden, a place to grow vegetables.

It sounds like a commercial, Jon always responded, and Keith always laughed. But he hadn't laughed that morning when he realized Jon was looking at the article about marriage.

I know people wonder what you're doing with a shlub like me, he'd said. I know other guys are always checking you out. I've seen them. But you'd better watch out, Jon. Someday you won't be tight-muscled and glossy and a major player on the restaurant scene. You'll be old and alone, a lonely fastidious old fart who fusses with his hair in front of the mirror every morning to cover his bald spot and irons his jeans. Now Keith was laughing. Yeah. You'll wipe the chair seat before you set your precious butt down and cut your toast into little skinny fingers.

I'll be a fine old fart, Jon said. And I already cut my toast into fingers.

In fact, the thought of old age didn't bother him, and he had no fear of being alone. He thought of himself as a point, a moment, in the great continuum between past and present—Theo's philosophical influence, no doubt. He didn't matter, not really, and ultimately nor did anyone else. One day he would flicker out quietly, and that wouldn't matter either. Except to himself—and he wouldn't be there to grieve the loss of himself. But part of him knew Keith was right and if he wasn't careful, he'd become peevish and shrunken, focused on minutiae, wincing if anyone sneezed near him.

The movie was nothing now but background sound. Keith was snoring lightly and Jon watched him sleep. There was a little spittle in the corner of his mouth. He had come to bed after a session on the john the previous night with a bright red toilet seat ring imprinted on his white backside and it repelled Jon—or maybe he just thought it should, he wasn't sure, because when Keith slid into bed, he found himself nudging up against that absurd cold backside and putting his face to the hollow between Keith's shoulder-blades breathing him in and then relaxing, muscle by muscle, like a contented cat. Clamped together, their bodies grew damp and hot, and eventually Jon moved away into the cool of the sheets on his side of the bed and stretched himself out. Coolness and warmth. Intimacy and separation. This was normalcy, Jon thought, this was the mucky, cluttery way normal people lived, and maybe it was enough.

He took the popcorn bowl from Keith's lap, shook his shoulder gently and murmured, You need to get to bed. Without moving, Keith opened his eyes and after a second smiled: We're getting domesticated.

No. Jon moved away abruptly. We're not.

CHAPTER NINETEEN

Angela was sitting at the kitchen table with a cup of coffee riffling through the pages of a fashion magazine. She stopped to run her finger along the line of a dress, dove-gray, with soft drapey lines, clinging to the model's body. Unforgiving, that amount of cling, Angela thought, and the dress as fragile and evanescent seeming as the early morning sky. It would show every imperfection, and you wouldn't be able to wear even the lightest and thinnest of panties under it. She shivered as she imagined the soft material sliding along her own hips. Everything in her life was sexualized; since Stocker she lived in a state of permanent arousal.

The phone rang.

Angela. This is your father. Your mother's in the hospital. She's dying.

Kim had kept the lump, the pain along her breastbone secret for a long time, but eventually her joints and lower back had begun hurting so fiercely that she couldn't ignore what was happening. She bought every painkiller at the pharmacy, but the pills helped only a little or not at all. The Chinese doctor she consulted used acupuncture, prescribed herbs—and advised her emphatically to see a Western specialist, which she wouldn't do. But she couldn't lie comfortably in bed at night, and started sleeping upright on a chair in the living room, keeping the television on because the voices, colors, snatches of music, and flickering images were a hedge against fear and thought, a partial distraction from pain. Day by day she was coming to understand, past denial and every dogged attempt to carry on with normal life, that something was terribly wrong: her bones were disintegrating within her. It was all she could do to drag herself from place to place in that stuffy little house, bent almost double, fighting a fatigue so profound it felt like moving against high water or being slowly smothered by a heavy, dark blanket. The despised meatloaf burned itself black in the oven. Dishes piled up and crusted. Sometimes, when Ron was safely away, she lay writhing on the floor and wept. Wept for the pain, for all her losses, for the bitter life ineluctably ebbing away. Finally she told him she needed medicine, strong medicine from a real doctor, and once he'd made the appointment, everything was out of her control.

Angela's first response to her father's words was irritation. She didn't want to know about her mother. It was Sunday. She'd planned a leisurely morning, Stocker coming over with lunch, a walk in the park, and a long afternoon of play, laughter, and sex. Now Kim had intruded, demanding sorrow and guilt from her, and the muddy waters that had almost drowned her childhood were rising to claim her again. Her father would expect her to come to California and baby him through the crisis, clean house and make sure there was food in the refrigerator; she'd have to fight tooth and nail not to become her mother, not to get trapped and lose everything she loved about her life: the cheeky, brightly-colored, finger-in-the-world's-eye fashions at the shop, Stocker's Kitchen and the dim alley behind it, his food and his grabbing sweaty hands—suddenly all inestimably precious.

It's crazy at the shop, she told her father. Spring's our busiest season. I'll try to come out in summer.

Your mother has two weeks, they're saying. Maybe three.

Okay, Angela said. I'll get there.

When she walked into the Long Beach hospital room two days later, her father was sitting in a chair in a corner by the window, a magazine with a bright red car on the cover slipping from his knees, his head back and his mouth slightly open. He snapped to attention when Angela came in, though he didn't stand up, and without hesitating began talking about Kim's condition, the long hours he'd spent alone with her while no one else cared enough to visit and Angela was running around New York, all this in a grumble that seemed almost disassociated from thought, a burble like thick porridge bubbling rhythmically in a pot or forming a gray dribble down a toddler's front. He didn't know how long it would take for Kim to die, Ron told Angela, but he couldn't stay away from his job much longer, and now that she was here maybe he could get home once in a while, put a few things in order. His talk rambled on while her mother's silent presence on the bed dominated the room. Angela thought she ought to go over and kiss her, touch her cheek, look her in the face, but she couldn't bring herself to do it. She sat down slowly, still at a safe distance from her mother, and took in the tubes piercing her body, the way her chest rose and fell, the beep-suck of machines, and a faint scent that might have been a cleaning agent or antiseptic powder used to mask the scent of illness.

I need to go home and take a shower, her father said. You might as well put on the television. Or read. She's pretty much gone.

Angela nodded.

And now she was alone with this thing, this person-corpse, neither her mother nor not her mother, and a coldness shivering along her bones. She forced herself to stand up and walk to the bed, look down at Kim. The hospital room was quiet except for the machines. The thin curled form on the bed was like a dried up insect, or a husk left behind as the creature went through some kind of transmogrification; so dry and desiccated now, the body that had never emanated joy or nurturance, as if it were preparing to blow away altogether. In her deep coma, Kim had slipped away from everything: the poky house, Angela and her father, the faraway country where she grew up and that Angela had never asked her about. For Angela, Vietnam was a cliché, inextricably bound up with war movies and images of people in conical hats, feet painted red by the mud of rice paddies.

Kim's hands lay still on the blanket. They kept them clean, dying people, Angela reflected. The hospital personnel wouldn't allow any obvious smells of urine, diarrhea, vomit or the cancer that was rotting Kim from within to come through, though you sensed all these behind the faint dry-leaf scent of powder, body-saturating drugs, chemical antiseptics. Deliberately, she pulled her chair to the head of the bed and sat. She didn't touch her mother. And she worried. What if Kim were seized suddenly with uncontrollable pain or suffered a foaming fit while Angela was alone with her? What if she died? Angela listened to the click and gasp of the machines, saw lines moving across a screen and flickering numbers that meant nothing to her. Every now and then there was a beep that sounded like a warning, but no one came running through the door to check. Though twice during the long afternoon, a scrubs-clad figure appeared: a bearded doctor who, after nodding to Angela, lifted Kim's hand and examined the ends of her fingers with detached interest, then a nurse to check Kim's pulse and record the amount of urine in the catheter bag. They were looking for signs of shutdown—Angela understood that much—and she wondered why they bothered, since there was no useful intervention left to be done.

Here's how you get us to come if you need to, said the nurse, showing her the button. Do you have any questions about your mother that you want answered? Angela shook her head. She's quite a fighter, the nurse said. We had to restrain her on the bed for a couple of nights because she kept getting up and wandering around the corridors. We found her on the floor by the bed one morning because she'd tried to get up and go to the bathroom. She doesn't need to. She has a catheter. She struggled against those straps like you wouldn't believe; it took everything we had on hand to sedate her.

Well, said Angela, she's quiet now.

After the nurse left, she finally leaned over the bed, breathed in deeply, and took up her mother's hand. It was cool. She put her fingers to the wrist and felt a quick, weak fluttering, ephemeral as the half-glimpsed flight of a bird, then set the hand down again. She'd heard somewhere that as death approached, blood drained from the extremities, pooling at the body's core in an attempt to maintain life.

Her father returned and picked up his magazine. She settled back in her chair. Time stopped. The days began blurring into each other. Now and then, gazing at Kim's closed face, Angela expected words: Why you dress like that? You look like monkey. But Kim remained silent, stubborn as ever. They call this a deathwatch, Angela thought, nothing real in the world outside this silent room. She began to find a certain comfort in the hospital routine, the buzzing television, her father's sitting, standing to stretch, sitting again, their alternating visits to the cafeteria, the coming and going of the staff. Routine was like a swaying bridge across a bottomless crevasse, a skin of normalcy over the vast emptiness and darkness yawning beneath. Angela prided herself on being a sophisticate in the world, but here she was a naif, lost, wandering without a map. By the time she was Angela's age, she reflected, her mother had been an old hand at death. As a toddler, she'd watched the Vietcong drag a local teacher from his house while his wife shrieked for mercy behind him, and she had clustered with her friends around the body a few days later when the man was found with the top of his head blown off. She had crouched in her home while American bombs exploded. Why had she, Angela, never wanted to know about these things, Angela wondered now. Why had she so passionately resisted understanding the world that had shaped her mother and that was now reaching insistently forward through time to claim her too?

She fidgeted. She grew bored, angry, and restless. She bickered with her father, and raged inwardly at his loud conspicuous sighs, the sullen set of his shoulders. Everything that was wrong between herself and her parents was thrown into relief and magnified in this room. What would Stocker do, she wondered, if she were in her mother's place, if the comatose figure on the bed was Angela herself? She half smiled at the thought. He'd curse her, no doubt, grab and shake her, shock the nurses with scatological jokes, and then, alone with her again, howl at her not to leave him.

She went down to the basement cafeteria again and again for coffee she didn't really want, up and down the stairs, walking the corridors and passing closed doors with warning signs not to enter, partly open rooms where she glimpsed a still form on a bed, or a cluster of people, or someone sitting up reading. With the constant artificial light and the clatter of television, the commercials for Viagra and beer and investment groups, she almost forgot that sunlight and the scent of fresh air existed. But it was good, this plastic jiggling normalcy, nonetheless. It was something you could hold onto, something to keep down the rising sea of ice that threatened to freeze her heart and still the warm air in her lungs. So she stayed seated in the cafeteria reading as long as she could, momentarily caught by the shape of a skirt in a magazine or a spiky ornament on a lapel, sipping bitter coffee. And then, reluctantly, she trod the stairs up to her mother's floor because the elevator got there too fast, and she needed time for the transition, stopping at the sixth floor to catch her breath and slip off the torturous shoes.

She called Stocker every night, and his loud voice provided a welcome jolt. Is she in pain, he asked. Does she have long? Does she know you're there? Angela hadn't been framing these questions so straightforwardly, and when she hesitated, he jumped in with stories about the restaurant. Harold had finally been home to see his mother, he said, but it hadn't gone well, and afterwards there was one of the loudest craziest phone conversations so far. Sean asked about her almost every day: You ought to fuck him when you get back, Stocker said. The kid gets a hard-on every time he looks at you. His Adam's apple goes up and he can't force it back down. Angela laughed and said Maybe I will, and for a blessed moment she was herself again.

Kenneth was leaving at the end of the year, Stocker went on. He'd been putting it off, but he was getting too old for the restaurant game; he'd move in with his daughter and her family, help take care of the kids. Maybe George would leave too once his father did. That'd be a loss, both of them so hard working and steady.

He paused. She didn't want the conversation to stop. What'll you cook for me when I get back? she asked.

Whatever you want.

I want noodles, thick cheesy noodles ...

And off he went as she'd counted on him to do, riffing on the different kinds of noodles—had they originated in China or Italy? No one really knew, but they'd colonized the world—and the way it was decay that made cheese taste so delicious. The minute she walked in, he said, he'd sit her down at the table and bring her a bowl of soup as green as new grass and filled with swimming, fantastical creatures, brightly colored little jellyfish. No, she said, I don't want to swallow living things, and he laughed. They won't be living. They'll die the second they're in your mouth. They'll die of happiness because the only reason they exist is to feed you. They're like the shmoos in L'il Abner.

What?

And then he had to explain how the shmoos laid eggs and gave milk and were so anxious to succor humankind that they lay down and died in ecstasy whenever a hungry person looked at them.

By the next day, Kim's breathing had changed. Her expression was inward and withdrawn, her face looked fallen in, she was using all the energy she had to pull air into her lungs, fighting the uncaring universe for every breath. Her chest rose; there was a long pause during which Angela's own heart seemed to stop; Kim's chest fell; and the struggle began all over again. On and on, desperate and mechanical, her mouth a yawning cavern of darkness. Angela sat down beside the bed, reached for Kim's hand, and tried gently to uncurl the hooked fingers, but it was impossible. She gave up and picked up her book. Minutes later, her wrist was encircled suddenly by what felt like a bracelet of bone. Kim, who hadn't moved for hours, whose entire life force had seemed concentrated only in the erratic rise and fall of her chest, had reached through the bars at the side of the bed and claimed her daughter.

Can you hear me, mom? Angela asked. Are you there?

Nothing but the jagged breathing, the closed and distant face.

She sat with her heart beating fast, her wrist in her mother's grasp, afraid to move. Time passed. She heard the machines buzzing and Kim's rattling breath, saw sunlight outside the window, a bright universe away. They were alone together, she and her mother, in a vast void, and there was a current pulsing between them, something primitive, wordless, and powerful that she couldn't have broken even if she'd wanted to. So, she thought, that was all there was to it after all. The bond she had raged against all her life was only this.

Her arm began to cramp; there was a deep ache starting low in her back. She tried cautiously to loosen her mother's grip—It's okay, she said, I'm not leaving you, mom—but Kim's hand was an iron manacle, and with every movement Angela made, the grip tightened. She gave up; she stayed bent uncomfortably over her mother, the ache in her back deepening, easing, and deepening again as the sky beyond the window darkened.

The next morning, Angela and her father were at home preparing to leave for the hospital when the phone rang. Kim had died just a few minutes earlier, a voice said. She had slipped away quietly while the nurses were washing her face.

The days after Kim's death, spent at her parents' house marking time until she could get back to New York, had the quality of damp gray felt. The very walls seemed to sweat gray tears. There was a noisy old air conditioning system, but the relief it provided was spotty. Angela would have preferred to leave the doors and windows open despite the outside heat, but her father wouldn't hear of it, and so she kept fidgeting, positioning and re-positioning herself at the kitchen table, shifting on the sofa in front of the television in the evening, seeking out a cool breath.

The funeral arrangements kept them occupied for a few days: They sat in the generic conference room of the funeral parlor, drank coffee out of Styrofoam cups, and discussed arrangements with a blandly inoffensive young man in a suit. The cheapest casket possible, said her father, and closed—so no need for all that makeup and nail polish. No, he didn't want red roses draped over the top of the coffin—ridiculous at the cost; a bouquet of lilies in a vase would suffice.

On the day of the funeral, her mother's coffin stood on a dais in the mortuary chapel, and Angela was surprised to see a few guests enter the room and file past it, some of them obviously Vietnamese. Absurdly, it had never occurred to her that Kim might have had friends or acquaintances that she knew nothing about, a life separate from her own. For the service, a young woman sang a song about going into the sunset, her voice so sharp and shaky on the high notes that it was all Angela could do not to laugh. Perhaps the singer came at a cut-rate price too. And then her father stood on the dais beside the coffin and said that Kim was a loving and faithful wife, and a wonderful mother to their daughter, Angela. He was clearly enjoying being the focus of attention, exuding unctuous self-pity and extending his thoughts for long, long minutes, past all communication of sense or feeling, until she noticed the mourners starting to shift discreetly in their seats. She felt her loathing for him thicken in her blood. Afterwards, people left, murmuring condolences, but an elderly couple stopped to speak; the man took her hand and pressed it with unexpected emotion. You look like her, he said. And then: She was one of the last of us. Angela was startled to see tears in his eyes. Her own had been dry all week.

After the funeral, Angela helped her father as he silently and methodically organized Kim's things. The image came to her again of a dried-up insect, something you'd sweep out with the trash. Kim's clothes, those drab, self-effacing things she wore until they fell apart, weren't worth donating, and Ron put them in black plastic bags and set them on the curb. The sewing machine went to a thrift shop. Once it was gone, Angela prepared to dust the shelf behind it, which she was dimly aware had served her mother as a kind of altar. She tossed out a burned-down stick of incense, and a brown flower stalk stiffened in a vase, briefly examined a plastic sandwich bag holding a blob of tightly folded paper, attempted to unfold the blob, which began disintegrating in her hands, then threw it into the wastepaper basket with everything else. She stopped at the photograph of Kim with a baby in her arms, mesmerized by the roundness and softness of her mother's face, the grave questioning gaze she leveled at the camera. It wasn't that she'd never seen this photograph before, it was just that she'd never really looked at it. How had this clear-eyed young woman turned into her mother? Angela knew her brother had been stolen by the Americans; that was part of family lore. But she knew little more than that, and she wondered again at her own lack of curiosity. What was his Vietnamese name, this legendary half brother?

Rummaging in a drawer, she found an accounts book: rows of small inky figures with dollar signs in front of them, tracking down through page after page. She tried to puzzle out what they meant, what her mother could possibly have been paying for. The book didn't seem intended for her father's scrutiny, so she slipped it into her purse. In another drawer was a thin sheaf of letters, each bearing the same return address: Land of Hope Adoption Agency. Angela sank to the floor, eased off the rubber band holding the letters together, and began to read the enclosed pages:

"Jeffrey is so cute. He'd never even seen a fork before he came to us, so we're teaching him to eat American style ..."

Another letter said, "I'm sure it was hard to give him up, but of course it was in his best interests. Who knows what those godless Communists would have done to him? Anyway, we're just tickled to death to have him with us."

And another: "He was very naughty yesterday. He kept screaming and throwing his food on the floor. It's hard because we don't know what he's saying, and of course he doesn't understand us either."

She tried briefly to imagine what an infant raised in rural Vietnam would have made of the affluence and plenty of an American household, the heaping portions of food, the magical machines that provided sound and pictures at the touch of a button, light, or instant running water, but she couldn't do it. And how did this lost baffled child understand his mother's absence?

She shuffled past a few more envelopes. Opened one dated 1978: Jeffrey loves to visit the zoo, especially the monkey yard. We went last week and we bought him a stuffed Carol the Elephant, though he's a bit big for stuffed animals now.

At the bottom of the stack, a typed letter from a lawyer: I have instructed my clients to have no further correspondence with you, and I would advise you not to try and contact them.

That was all. It felt as if all the empty leavings of Kim's life, all her lost hopes and desiccated realities, were in those papers Angela's held. She felt an immense pity for her mother; she wished she could feel love.

She remembered then that her brother's name was Tuan.

She thought of trying to find him and tell him Kim had died, but she didn't know how, and anyway, she wasn't sure he'd want to know. He'd be a mature man now, with a life of his own, and he could have sought out Kim any time after turning eighteen and hadn't. That baby boy in the photograph, held safely in his mother's arms and squinting happily into the sun was gone, and anyway, he was nothing to her.

On the floor of Kim's closet was a large flat white box, and in it, carefully folded in tissue paper, Angela found a blue dress Kim had made for her when she was fourteen. She remembered Kim on her knees pinning up the hem, and how she'd hated the entire fitting process, standing still, obediently lifting and lowering her arms, her mother mumbling through a mouthful of pins. It was revolting and disconcerting to have her mother beside her in an attitude of abasement that fit perfectly with the unspoken contempt Angela felt for her. But even on her knees, Kim retained the power to humiliate, to sap Angela's confidence. Angela remembered the slightly sour scent of her mother's breath, how much she had disliked the thought of Kim's saliva on the pins she pushed into the skirt, and the way Kim had muttered all the while about her daughter's physical deficiencies: Shouldn't hang like this; you too bony. You like starving person. Stand straight, girl.

Angela saw now that it was a beautiful dress, noticed the way it changed color in the light and shadow of the room. She held the glimmering blue material—a color her fourteen-year-old self would never in a thousand years have worn—against her skin, looked in the mirror, noted the way it contrasted with her black hair and dark eyes. Who or what had her mother seen in her that she'd made a garment so lyrically pretty? Had she sewn hope into this dress, hope that Angela might have the life of freedom and joy that Kim herself had never experienced? After she'd finished it, Kim asked Angela again and again where the dress was and why she never wore it—You go out tonight? You wear dress. Why you not wear dress? In answer, Angela had screwed the thing into a tight ball and tossed it onto her closet floor to stiffen with dust and grime. Kim must have found it after she left home. She could imagine her mother angrily shaking out the folds, sending the dress off to be cleaned, and then folding it carefully into the tissue-paper-lined box, a coffined emblem of the daughter she had always wanted and could never have.

CHAPTER TWENTY

A mild summer evening and Megan, Tracy, and Nabil were swinging along the street, hands linked. We should be singing, said Nabil. We're like a trio in a musical. He looked up at a billboard looming ahead of them and started singing Johnnie Walker, Johnnie Walker, Johnnie Walker, his voice rising on each first syllable, dropping to a bass on the second. Tracy joined in with a fast counterpoint: Manipedi. Manipedi. They paused at a crosswalk: Walk, Stop. Walk. Stop Walk. Stop. Walk. Stop, Megan ventured, imitating the sound of Big Ben's chimes. Soon they were riffing on every passing sign, synthesizing their rhythms, scatting and bopping, using any musical form or snatch of melody that came to mind: Armani. Armani. Armani in an operatic trill; an ululating Lion King—Not fair, said Tracy. Lion King's already a musical. But the title's not a song, retorted Nabil. Aquatic zumba, chimed in Megan. Pineapple Design. Hot yoga. Watch Galaxy. Donuts.

They were bonded, the three of them. They shared a private world that encompassed and welcomed their individual eccentricities: Tracy's sarcasm and how hard you had to work to win her laugh, not to mention her serious attention, as well as how rewarded you felt when these things were forthcoming; Nabil's political passion and the way he seemed to have experienced and evaluated all the big things, the things that mattered; and her own—Megan's—fears and hesitations along with the dreamy, ecstatic romanticism underlying them, a romanticism they all shared, despite the way they teased each other. There was nothing overtly sexual about the relationship, no sense that Nabil was romantically interested in either Tracy or Megan—though they were both more than half in love with him—just a continuing sense of exploration and play. With Nabil and Tracy as her friends, the city opened up for Megan. It was as if her life had been spooling along in black and white and suddenly everything was in color, vivid and lush.

Nabil had artist friends, he moved in a circle of writers, musicians, comics, painters, people living in Queens, Brooklyn or New Jersey, scraping a living, reading poetry in coffee shops, exhibiting photos or sculptures wherever they could. Nabil knew the city intimately. He pointed out odd anomalies, hidden streets and alleys. Churches. The small shops tucked behind an ordinary crowded sidewalk, statues like the one of Joan of Arc on her horse on a Broadway median, holding her sword aloft to receive heaven's blessing. There was a fluidity to his choices. He was unpredictable. He liked kitsch and high art, experimental dance, ballet and street dancing, all kinds of music. And they haunted the TKTS booth in Times Square, grabbing up cheap tickets and going to plays as often as they could.

Some nights they still rehearsed, though Doug seldom showed up and they all knew the rehearsals were just a kind of framework for their developing relationship. Afterwards, they hung out at Nabil's and watched movies on television, analyzing the actors' interpretations, trying to figure out whether a particular emotional effect stemmed from the acting, the direction, the cinematography, the script. They agreed on actors they admired and tried to analyze why they admired them, as well as others they considered overrated. Could you be famous without selling out, they wondered. They had intense discussions about the idea that artists had to suffer for their art, the mythical starving artist in the garret, Gauguin, who gave up wife and children for his art (but then, how much had he ever really cared about them?). Van Gogh's madness. John Belushi and Kurt Cobain. They lamented the commodification of art, the way rising rents were driving artists from the cities that were their natural habitat so that all the theatre companies that had once flourished in lofts, bars and warehouses were gone and only big safe institutions and dumb Broadway musicals remained.

They shared secret things, they were a secret society, they had their own language. They adopted song lyrics and lines from plays and poems for this language, phrases that had detached themselves from their contexts to stand alone, flush with meaning and a significance that couldn't be put into words but that all three of them believed they—and only they—understood. We're the geniuses, they said, we're the future of theater, mocking themselves into half believing it. Their amazingness as a trio was encapsulated in the way they fell automatically into step as they walked the streets, the coconut bubble tea they all craved, violet pastilles, and the statue of Alice, majestic, wondrous and threatening, an emissary from another time and place plunked down in the middle of contemporary New York.

But seriously, one of them would say, were they themselves artists? Could they call themselves that? And if they were, what made them so? Dedication? Hard work? Inherent talent? What was artistry anyway? Tracy thought it was a way of experiencing the world and becoming larger than before in expressing that experience, more capacious and human. Megan, who agreed, wanted to confess her dreams about dead people, but when the others' attention turned to her, became too self-conscious to do it.

The task of the actor was to get inside someone else's skin, said Nabil, adding that he sometimes followed strangers down the street as an exercise.

Creepy, said Tracy.

Not like that. He explained that he'd maintain a slight distance, copying the walk—not looking for anything dramatic like a hump or a limp—though these too sometimes—but something smaller and more ordinary, one shoulder held a little higher than the other, a chin lowered too close to the neck, a sideways tilt of the head. When he did this, he felt within himself not the specifics of what that person was thinking, but a wordless understanding of his or her inner landscape.

Megan liked the idea of trying to enter into another person's reality. She wondered sometimes how a dentist felt putting his gloved hands into a decay-ridden mouth, a soldier under fire, a man on a swaying platform washing windows high on the side of a building. It distracted her from the persistent sense that she herself wasn't quite real, at some point she might dissolve, molecule by molecule into her surroundings. Any certainty she felt on any topic could easily be overridden by another's certainty—and certainty was something both Nabil and Tracy had in spades. Nabil's felt experiential though. His ideas could change. Tracy was different. Her ideas flowed from some deep underground place, solidifying into granite as they emerged into the air. It would be dangerous, Megan sensed, if one of those beliefs ever cracked. Perhaps she, Megan, after all was Alice between the two queens, the White Queen gentle, the Red dictatorial. They guarded and preserved her contour, and in their clear strong sense of who they were, she glimpsed a hope of fully inhabiting herself.

It helped that her status in class had shifted. She was part of an elite group now, a trio of outsiders who had chosen to be outside and whose talent made them formidable.

Megan's string of temporary office jobs were supplemented by a monthly infusion of cash from home and she often wondered how long it would be before her parents insisted she make a living. When she'd first moved to the city, her mother had said they'd give her a year and then evaluate; they couldn't support her indefinitely. She wondered if that deadline still stood—it had been six months already and she hadn't made any money acting—but during the weekly Facetime sessions with her family she was afraid to ask. Acting classes cost a lot and every week she finessed her mother's suggestion that she take a break from them and save some money. She seldom went to Stocker's Kitchen these days—she couldn't afford it, even when she confined herself to an appetizer or two—but sometimes she thought wistfully about Crystal whose matter of fact kindness had sustained her during through the lonely early weeks.

More and more Nabil occupied her mind. Her life became clearly divided between the days when she saw him and the dreary ordinary days when she didn't. She checked his Facebook page obsessively, disappointed if he hadn't posted anything, swift to like everything he did: videos, political articles, jokes or photos. She tried to think of reasons to text him—just often enough, but not too frequently. When he texted her and Tracy about an idea or event—anything at all—her heart sang. She stored up anecdotes, snippets of poetry, things she'd observed or overheard to share in return, hoping they'd make her interesting to him. At night, lying in bed, she called up his image, the timbre of his voice, the way he moved, things he'd said— like the time Lauren called pigeons rats with wings and he responded, But look at the shape of their wings when they're in flight, the way they curve like a scimitar. Scimitar, Megan repeated to herself in the darkness. She'd had to look it up. She dwelled on the clean planes of his face, the outline of his eyebrows, the color of his skin. He was glorious to her, an Arab prince. It wasn't possible to compete with Tracy's distinct gravelly voice and far-seeing blue-gray eyes, but perhaps it didn't matter because Megan sometimes felt she was half in love with Tracy too, or at least in love with the entity the three of them comprised together.

One night, she and Tracy went to see Nabil perform at an Upper West Side comedy club called Still Standing. Nabil led them to a table he'd reserved at the front, whispering Wish me luck as they seated themselves. This was a night of Arab comedy. Looking around, Megan was relieved to see that at least half the audience was white, and promptly felt ashamed of her relief. For the first time she could imagine how it must feel to be a lone person of color in a place filled with Caucasians. The conversation around her was loud and animated, accompanied by bursts of laughter. They sat through a couple of performances: someone from Lebanon, a woman who said her parents were Irish and Yemeni. Some of the jokes struck her as lame, others she simply didn't get. Chin high as always, Tracy seemed absorbed in the routines, periodically laughing her hoarse, loud laugh.

Now Nabil was onstage. You're wondering if I'm a terrorist, he said. Sure I am. Just look at me. And as everyone did, Uh-oh. Let's keep it between ourselves.

But here's how you know. I have a sly look, as you can plainly see. He gazed meaningfully at the audience, and a little laughter rippled among the tables. I've been heard using the word "scum," especially when I'm cleaning the bathroom. More laughter. Yesterday I got a box of olive oil from Palestine and couldn't get it open so I had to use a box cutter. Also, there's a pressure cooker in my kitchen. Sometimes you can feel the pressure building and building, and then watch out ...

He paused dramatically.

Rice all over the floor.

Now the laughter was full-throated.

Observe my cunning disguise: I don't wear a kafiyeh. No beard. I wear jeans like all good Americans. After I went through airport security a couple times, I made up a rhyme all Arab travelers need to memorize: Dress white. Make your flight.

Say it with me.

Dress white. Make your flight, the audience chorused obediently.

But if you're sitting next to someone like me on a plane and you're afraid he might be a terrorist, there's an easy way to find out: Start eating a pulled pork sandwich.

Actually I'm worse than a terrorist. I'm a Palestinian. Yes, that is a country, folks, though it's getting smaller by the minute. He moved backwards a step. It's getting a little crowded on this stage, don't you think? Oh—addressing someone imaginary—you need more room? You want me to stand here? He took two more steps back. Okay? Further back? Okay. Fine. Flailing his arms frantically, he mimed falling off the stage.

There was more laughter, but it was scattered and uncertain.

Nabil took a breath, surveyed the room and changed his tack. See those women at the table in the front? He gestured toward Megan and Tracy. Aren't they beautiful? Megan ducked her head, embarrassed and delighted, while Tracy shifted and sat a little straighter. They're not virgins though, so I don't have to wait to get to heaven to be with them. Tracy snorted with laughter. Like all Arab men, I have several wives—dozens—and of course I don't let any of them drive. But these two—they're stubborn. They insist. They rented a car behind my back one time and got to the Washington turnpike in New Jersey. You remember that traffic pile-up that lasted for days and days? You heard maybe that was something to do with the governor? Nope. It was me. I had to stop these girls somehow. Don't piss me off again, ladies.

After his act, several people came to their table to pat Nabil on the shoulder and congratulate him. You nailed it, dude, said a tall, skinny black guy. But, hey—wasn't some of that stuff kinda risky?

CHAPTER TWENTY-ONE

Stocker was in the walk-in freezer, struggling to get a huge marlin off its hook and peering out periodically to check on the cooks in the kitchen, when he saw heads beginning to turn, Sean standing up in his corner, a shucked ear of corn tumbling from his lap and the blotchy color rising in his face, and knew with a sudden jolt that Angela was back. She was walking down the hallway toward the staff room and would pass his kitchen in seconds. He stood immobile, wanting to go to her, unable to move. It felt as if he'd been holding his breath the entire time she was gone, and now the air was whooshing in so hard it was threatening to explode his chest. He had to prepare a face to greet her with; he had to wash the smell and slipperiness of fish off his hands. She'd reached the kitchen, and everyone was moving toward her—they liked her, he realized, liked her as a person independent of himself, not just Stocker's girlfriend and someone who put him in a reliably good mood, but Angela, Angela herself. The Scotsmen were coming forward to shake her hand, smile, and offer condolences for her mother's death in their pleasant, low-key brogues. How's the girlfriend, Angela asked Harold, who grinned sheepishly and told her the affair hadn't ever been right and was over. Again? she said, teasing. Already? Sean was still standing, and Angela went to him and took his face between her hands as if he were a child. Sean, she said, Is everything okay? How's he treating you? and kissed him lightly on the cheek. It was more than Stocker could bear, the unaccustomed gentleness of her voice, and he burst from his hiding place in the freezer, and clamped her to him, stroking that Oriental girl hair with fishy fingers, and hearing behind him, vaguely, spurts of laughter and someone clapping.

You came back, he said.

You knew I was coming back.

Did he? He hadn't been sure. She wriggled in his arms and laughed, and said, You look like a hungry hyena.

It was a familiar riff.

Yup. And you're a bone.

He loosed her from his grip, led her to the staff room—calling over his shoulder that the spectacle was over and everyone should get back to work, and then kissed her hard, urged her into the chair, and stood back: What would you like me to get you?

But something was off. She was feverish that first evening back, a little strident, drinking too much. He had never seen Angela lose her essential aloofness before, her absolute and enameled self-possession, and now she was gorging on the expensive wine he'd fetched for her, glass after glass—not even tasting it—he might just as well have brought water or juice—gesticulating with the bottle and laughing with her mouth wide open. He had given her squid cooked in its own ink, and he wanted to tell her about the dish, to ground her and bring her back to him. Come on, Stocker, she said, waving the bottle. You have some. But he seldom drank. He never wanted to be stupid or caught at a disadvantage. Squid have three hearts, he told Angela. Spatial intelligence. They can learn to navigate mazes. People have seen them pick up coconut shells to use for shelter, like a snail has its shell. There was a dribble of wine on her chin, and he wished with all his heart that she'd stop laughing.

That night at her apartment, he asked about California and her mother. She said, I don't want to talk about it. I'm tired. On the bed later he drove into her until they were both damp with sweat, their skin making slapping-sucking sounds as their chests came together and separated, Angela breathing hard, her head turning from side to side, and finally the low saliva-y growl she emitted just before orgasm, like an angry little terrier with a rat between its teeth. Even then she wasn't his, though afterwards she lay with her head on his shoulder. The sheet covering them was damp and hot, and he pushed it off, and felt the cooling rotation of the ceiling fan on his skin. He was uncomfortable. There was a band of sweat where her arm circled him, and he wanted to move away and was afraid to. You gonna lose this watermelon sometime, Stocker? She stroked the hard dome of his belly.

Nope. You'll have to take me the way I am.

Which is what?

Someone in a neighboring apartment laughed loudly, and other voices joined in. The neighbors must have got hold of some really good dope, Stocker thought. Perhaps they'd share. He could use something. At his side, Angela's quiet listening breath. What you see is what you get, he said.

She stopped her stroking. It can't all be just sex, Stocker.

He snorted Why not? and started jabbing at her body, the shadowed concavity at the side of her hip bone, but she pulled away. It seemed to him that this was a danger point, and he had no idea how to navigate it. There was nothing to say, and also far too much. How could Angela say she didn't know him? She had eaten his food, week after week, she'd ingested him. The space between them was no more than a few inches, the fan whispered, and he felt utterly alone. What did she want from him now? Sob stories? The crap customers laid nightly on his barkeep? Did she want to know how he'd gone to school in mismatched clothes, smelling bad, and had gotten into fights every day? What it was like when his father turned on his mother at home—not his father, not his mother, but those loathsome imposters—and she, weak and afraid, tried to use him as a barrier. A barrier. When he couldn't even protect himself. How he'd sat by the pond later, bruised and shivering, taking in the twilight glimmer of the yellow narcissi and the incessant croaking of the frogs, and finally understood that there was no one he could turn to for warmth or comfort; survival meant holding himself tightly together every second of his life, and never ever showing weakness.

Stocker, Angela said. It's all right. And she put her arm around him again, pressed up close so that her breath tickled the hairs on his chest. But it wasn't all right. He could hold and envelop her, but he could never know what was happening in that small, hard-skulled head. He could eat her out and make her wail with pleasure, but he couldn't eat her up. He would never possess her.

Something inside her was shifting, and if his food wasn't enough to keep her, he didn't know what else he had to offer.

Her breathing deepened into sleep, and Stocker drifted too, entered the discord and clangor of that long-ago kitchen, his father yelling at his mother, his mother yelling back. She knew what would happen if she lashed out, but she was a stupid, mulish woman, and she did it now, struck his father full across the face with the oven mitt she was holding. She'd be screaming for help soon, but Stocker was at the end of his rope that night, too hungry to sleep, too tired to fear his father or fear for his mother, and he sidled out and crept up the stairs to the bedroom, slid out of the bedroom window and thumped down onto the ground outside. It was cold, ash-gray moonlight lying over the rusted tractor parts and trash in the yard, and he shivered in his t-shirt and underpants and walked barefoot toward the barn, ignoring stones and thistles. Cherry was lying on her side. He stopped in the doorway to take in her hulk, the barnyard smell of her—he'd never understood, given the size and strength of cows, why they acceded to the daily humiliations they endured, never attacked or broke free. Only a week earlier, the men had taken Cherry's calf from her. He was male, he was no use to anyone, and there was no point in letting him drink her milk. Stocker was only nine; he half understood that the living creature, desperately struggling, calling for its mother as it was dragged away, would be killed for veal, but he didn't want to understand. For three days and nights, Cherry had stood in the place where she had seen her calf being loaded onto the truck, her head raised, bellowing to the indifferent air, constant, monotonous, louder than he'd ever have thought possible, shifting her forelegs but otherwise unmoving, and all of Stocker's attempts at comfort and caress had made no difference. But now she lay quiet. He sank down in the straw beside her, moving closer until her ridged back pressed against his front, his arm, raised high to encircle her, rising and falling with her breath.

He couldn't remember now, lying beside Angela, the words he'd murmured into Cherry's hairy flicking ear, or if there had been any words at all, but he remembered pushing the hurt parts of his body up against her. He thought of a Christmas card he'd seen in the classroom with a picture on the front of animals in the manger. He was eight and still couldn't read, but his teacher had quoted the words from the card to the class: So hallowed and so gracious is the time.

There were sighings and creakings outside in the darkness, a brief quietly surprised cackle from the henhouse, and then thinking stopped and there was only darkness and a kind of slow circling in his brain as he coordinated his breathing with Cherry's, in, out, slow and primal. Somewhere far away his parents went through their jerky, convulsive rituals, but here he and Cherry breathed together and the darkness cradled him, soft as feathers and deep as his woods.

He wanted to tell Angela about the oldest guilt he carried. It wasn't really his fault, he wanted to explain. He'd had this ferocious relationship with eating since he was a child, flavors exploding in his mouth, filling his mind and body, and he had to consume what he loved—milk from Cherry's udder, for example, or objects he needed to understand—in huge self-annihilating gulps. When he came across a dead bird at the side of the road once, a sparrow with maggots crawling over it, it was all he could do not to put the thing in his mouth.

He was eleven, and his father had told him to fetch Cherry. He knew there'd been grumbling in the house that she was tapped out, but he still didn't understand why he was to bring her. She came with him trustingly as always. And then his father cut her throat. Ineptly, as he did everything. The death took a long time. Stocker still had trouble erasing the memory of her rolling, white-rimmed eyes and bellows of pain from his mind when he fell into sleep at night. And yet he had put his mouth to her bleeding neck and sucked, sucked frantically in the midst of all the noise and confusion, sucked in the essence of this large warm being who had given milk and trust and comfort, even as she bucked and bellowed and his father clung to her as if in an embrace, digging his knife deeper and deeper into her neck. Drinking her blood was a disgrace and a betrayal, but it was also the only way he knew to honor her, to take in her essence and her dying and make her part of himself forever. Then came a deep awful sound that vibrated along his bones and lodged permanently in his brain, neither a groan nor a bellow but a tortured, despairing acquiescence, a long slow seeping away of life and spirit. He fell back, wiping his mouth. Cherry's knees buckled and she toppled onto her side.

He pressed closer to Angela and felt the warmth of her buttocks against his groin. She was still here. Despite everything, she was still his. At least for now.

CHAPTER TWENTY-TWO

A week later, Angela was awake, alone in the pre-dawn silence, having banished Stocker earlier because she wanted time alone. Now she almost longed for his fleshy presence in the bed beside her, the grunting, sighing noises he made in his sleep. What had woken her was a jolt of fear. A dream lingered in her mind, elusive, dissolving, having to do with Kim's ragged agonal breathing, the image of a skeletal hand reaching toward her. At that moment, forcing herself into consciousness, she fully understood the power of that hackneyed movie trope, saw how it encapsulated the rage and envy the dead must feel toward the living and the terror of the living in the presence of the dead. She had put a continent between herself and Kim and now she realized that a continent wasn't enough.

There had been a pulse throbbing in her mother's wrist as she reached for Angela's arm on the day before she died, and something palpable had moved between them. Something she couldn't put into words and that had nothing to do with fear. Afterwards, her father slipped the thin, worn wedding band from Kim's finger and offered it to her. She refused with a shudder. Later, after he'd taken the ring to a pawnshop, she wished she'd accepted it.

When Angela was little, they'd had a neighbor she called Aunt Tollie. Aunt Tollie had taken her to the toy store once, and the piles of stuffed animals—lions and tigers, quizzical monkeys, soulful looking dogs of every breed—had amazed her with their softness and plenty. Suspended in the air, a fat black and yellow bee flew straight toward her face.

Aunt Tollie was cheerful and large. She took care of Angela after school sometimes, setting her to help in the kitchen, asking what she thought about this and that. Angela was only six, but she was highly opinionated, and this amused Aunt Tollie no end. You won't believe what she said, she'd tell her husband when he came home tired from work. He always listened intently. They had no children of their own, and they loved fussing over her. She remembered that Aunt Tollie used to make a meatloaf with a row of hard-boiled eggs down the middle, so that when the loaf was cut there'd be a clean circle of egg in the center of every slice. Angela was always entrusted with setting those eggs in a neat line, standing next to Aunt Tollie on a chair at the kitchen counter and basking in her praise: You're doing great. I've never seen them straighter. And it didn't stop there. Aunt Tollie's husband regarded the dish as a small miracle, and he remarked on Angela and Aunt Tollie's cleverness every single time it appeared in front of him at the dinner table. Afterwards, the three of them would sit in front of the television eating snacks and dropping crumbs that nobody bothered to whisk away until Kim scrabbled at the door and demanded Angela come home.

What would you like? said Aunt Tollie, indicating the shelves of toys, and Angela didn't even have to think. The minute she'd seen that dopily-smiling bee with his bright stripes and the tiny gauze wings that could never under any circumstances sustain flight, she'd known she wanted it. She couldn't remember exactly when Aunt Tollie and her quiet little husband left the neighborhood, or if she'd even had a chance to say goodbye, but she had slept with that bee on her pillow for years.

She wanted to weep now for Aunt Tollie's cheerful kindness, and she strained to remember a single moment of tenderness she had shared with Kim—it seemed she used to put her arms around her mother's neck when she was little, resting her head against Kim's bony chest. But the strongest image was of Kim tending dead brown things on the altar behind the sewing machine, oblivious to Angela's living needs. When she was seven, Angela brought home a puppy that had run up to her on the street in that confiding, waggling puppy way, an ugly little white thing with brown spots, and had begged to keep him—though she hadn't really allowed herself to hope, and anyway she half wanted Kim to refuse. Taking care of that puppy, giving it the love and care it needed would be painful. So she didn't object when Kim opened the door to push the dog out into the street again, even though its pathetic yelps twisted her insides. Part of her even admired her mother's ruthlessness.

She clicked on the light and threw off the covers, went to the fridge and pulled out an apple, carried it to the table with a knife and plate, and started skimming a magazine on her iPad. The apple piece wouldn't go down; her throat felt bruised. And she couldn't force herself to focus on the glossy images. Outside the window the city pulsed, night workers went about their business, cars moved along the streets. She pictured Stocker sleeping alone in his apartment, arms wrapped tightly around a pillow. This, her own place, felt like a fragile lighted craft pitching on an infinite black sea. She put down her apple and stood up. She began walking in circles from the kitchen to the living room to the bedroom, round and round, until she found herself leaning over the kitchen table, sobbing. It was stupid. It made no sense. She had never loved Kim. And yet here she was, bent double over the table, shaken with sobs.

Since coming back to New York from California, Angela had been hungry all the time, irritable with Stocker, unconcerned about what she wore and unable sometimes to find enough energy even to wash her hair. She felt so tired at work that she wanted to sink to the floor while the customers walked around her, holding earrings to their faces, clicking hangers along racks, exchanging platitudes: It looks great on you. It's cute. No, it's absolutely not too tight.

The shop owner was a retired ballerina married to a hedge fund manager. She had befriended Angela one afternoon as she browsed in the shop, excited by New York, in love with the inventory but entirely broke, and they'd talked clothes for over an hour. Elizaveta offered her a job on the spot, and when Angela said she didn't have a place to live yet, secured her the cramped apartment in a building her husband owned—though Angela knew the arrangement was short-term and the building would eventually be profitably converted. The shop was called Piqué, and as Elizaveta saw it, this referred both to the stabbing little ballet step and the idea of piqued interest—but these days Angela brooded more on its sour negative meaning. A couple of days earlier, Elizaveta had invited her out for coffee, and probed a little, trying to be friendly, her voice a touch too bright: You're our best advertisement, Angela. Everything looks great on you and you have this amazing eye for advising customers. Could you just maybe—you know— not wear the same outfit tomorrow? And I found this great new stylist on Fifth Avenue. I bet he could do wonders with your hair.

Angela had contacted the people whose addresses she'd found in Kim's densely written accounting book and almost immediately calls, letters, and texts had begun arriving from Vietnam: We have nothing. We are poor. Please send us money. She studied the incomprehensible signatures on the letters. She had no idea who these people were.

She blew her nose and decided to take a shower, went into the bathroom and turned on the water. Her mind was running in crazed circles and she felt frantic for the sound of another human voice. Stocker was her best and perhaps only friend, but she couldn't call him, and she couldn't think of anyone else. She had seen a Victorian doll in a museum once, its white porcelain face so webbed with cracks it seemed held together only by the abstract idea of a face. Now her own face felt as if it were disintegrating in the same way. Looking into the mirror, she was relieved to find herself pale but intact; her cheek, when she put her hand to it, was warm. She was alive. She was going crazy.

Jon. He had told her often that he liked to work at night, and there was a song he used to hum in the kitchen, accompanied by the thumping beat of the stand mixer: "My time of day is the dark time, a couple of deals before dawn. When the street belongs to the cop, and the janitor with the mop, and the grocery clerks are all gone." Perhaps Jon was at work now. And if he wasn't ... Well, it was a short walk and the darkness outside was inviting. She decided against showering, turned off the water, tossed on some clothes and fled the apartment.

A little later, she stood in the doorway of Jon's new workspace, taking it in. It was small but he'd made the best of it. On the walls were black and white prints of feathers and leaves, a couple of Frank Lloyd Wright sketches, and directly opposite the door, a large, glowing image of a red and bronze pot-bellied vase. His mobile stood on a dock sided by large speakers and piano notes fell into the silence separately, like drops of water. Seated at the table, shoulder blades drawn together, absorbed in what he was doing, Jon didn't notice her. Angela smiled slightly, remembering his fights with Stocker over this space, Stocker bouncing on the balls of his feet, incandescent with fury and chuffing like an overheated little engine, while Jon bent toward him in a posture of ostentatious courtesy. She must have made a sound because Jon raised his head.

Angela? he said, without turning.

She stayed by the door. How'd you know?

Your scent. It's got that dry quality. Almost astringent. Like you.

That pleased her.

Can I come in?

Of course.

He shifted to make room, and she came and sat down at the table beside him, noting his sense of style, even now, at four in the morning, the clean outline of his body, the well fitting jeans and white shirt with one button open at the neck, everything subdued and understated except for a small diamond in one ear flashing darts of red, yellow, and silver—and even this felt more like an ironic comment on gayness—or what gayness was perceived to be—than flamboyance. They said in the kitchen that there was a trace of gypsy in Jon, and she thought that fit: he had warm clear olive skin, and hair almost as black as her own. There was something about Jon's Englishness that intrigued her too. It felt—not like an act exactly, more like a private joke, a cloak he wore to cover his foreignness and the darkly mocking gypsy soul within. Jon had told her once that it was funny the way Americans reacted to a British accent: They're either indignant—who the hell do you think you are, talking like that?—or almost servile, laughing at the most mundane comment as if it were a Wildean epigram, he'd said. That was the kind of guy Jon was, Angela thought, as faint memories of high school lit classes hovered. The kind who said Wildean.

What was he sketching?

It's a design for a dessert. Just the basis, the architecture.

I didn't know desserts had architecture?

Mine do. I make spires. I build cathedrals. He laughed. It's my religion.

The piano music grew louder and faster as if preparing to build to a crescendo, then fell unexpectedly into a minor key.

You and Stocker still arguing about food and art?

We do that a lot. It's a hard one. I tell him they're both elemental, but he doesn't buy it, and in a way he's right. His stuff is elemental. My desserts don't make blood cells or lay down bone; there's nothing necessary about them; they're something to play with when daily life is safe and no one's hungry. Well, I guess they are real in a way. I can encapsulate a whole melon in a little mound of melon caviar and the process is synthetic, but the taste—that's truer than true, the essence of melon, the melon platonic.

Sounds like you sort of admire Stocker.

Don't ever tell him.

She watched him in silence for a moment. Can I draw?

He pushed a piece of paper toward her, and she began sketching. A hand. A face. A fish. Nothing worked. She pushed the paper away. I'm so fucked up.

He set down his pencil and turned to her.

I can't sleep. Food sticks in my throat. And Stocker drives me nuts. I can't eat what he gives me. I don't even like the way he smells any more. I want to hurt him. I want to hurt him all the time.

She stopped.

I imagine it's easy for you. Hurting him.

Oh yes. She laughed. It's like stomping a stranded jellyfish and watching it squirm. Or ... I saw a raven once that had snatched a baby robin. It had it on the ground and the parent robins were hopping around, helpless, and it kept ... striking, and that naked, half-dead thing on the ground writhed with every strike. Every fucking time. I wanted it to die, but it wouldn't, it just kept writhing. And then it went limp after a while and the raven flew away with it.

That's me, that raven. That's how it feels wanting to strike at Stocker and see him squirm. I hate myself, and it's disgusting but it makes me ... It turns me on.

Your mother died recently, didn't she? Jon said. I'd guess you're grieving.

Angela was surprised. I don't think so. I didn't even like my mother.

Kim bent at the sewing machine. Kim who hated her for who she was and for who she wasn't. Kim's hand encircling her wrist like a bracelet of bone.

That makes the grieving harder.

It was a new thought. A couple of seconds went by, and suddenly she found herself talking about her mother as she never had to Stocker, the journey Kim had undergone, the son left in Vietnam. Tuan. A baby tossed into the sea. Or who might as well have been. She had finally Googled the words Vietnam, orphan, babylift a few nights earlier—seated on her sofa, feet up, drinking coffee she'd already re-heated twice in the microwave—and hundreds of hits had popped up. She read without discrimination, abandoned the task, went back to it. She found a video that showed dozens of infants in cardboard boxes on the floor of a giant aircraft, another where they rolled loose on the floor, a single harassed woman trying to take care of all of them. She imagined the incessant wailing, the thick smells of shit and vomit. Tuan had endured all that. And then the video showed a child in the arms of a beaming adoptive mother, flashbulbs going off in front of his dazed eyes. She understood in that moment, speaking to Jon, why she had spent so little time thinking about her brother before: the idea of him carried too much guilt. Guilt because she was born safely American while his whole life must have seemed provisional, his Americanness always in question. Tuan wasn't a baby when he left Vietnam. He'd been four. He must have had memories. She flashed on the photograph of him in her mother's—their mother's—arms, the expression on Kim's face—one she, Angela, had never seen in all their years together, the softness around the mouth that she remembered as always pinched around dressmaking pins. She pitied Tuan, but she envied him too because Kim had loved him as she, Angela, had never been loved. Well, there was Stocker's love of course, his hot smothering love, and she had opened herself to it and loved him in return. But at this moment he repulsed her. She didn't want messiness, heaviness, expectation; she wanted something clean, clear and cold. In the end Tuan was lucky, she reflected bitterly, to have been spared Kim's toxic love.

I see.

Jon's voice was so calm that she wanted to put her head on the table and weep with relief. It was as if he'd opened a clear empty space between the two of them into which she could hurl her inchoate anger and confusion and watch it acquire coherence and shape.

Jon pulled a silver cigarette case out of his pocket, and opened it to reveal a row of neatly rolled joints. How about it?

He lit a joint, handed it to her, and she inhaled deeply. The sky beyond the high narrow window was beginning to lighten, there were sounds of the city coming to life. The invisible pianist in the room tossed off a series of light-fingered runs and then became meditative again. My time of day is the nighttime, Angela said, and giggled. Jon nodded. Exactly. A couple of deals before dawn.

I love this kitchen. I love the way you've kind of emptied things out. It feels like there's room to think in here.

That's the idea. That's how ideas come. He breathed in smoke, exhaled, and passed the joint to her. Where there is nothing there is God.

What?

It's a quote. Yeats.

God?

Okay. Maybe not God. The maker. The ur creator. The mathematician in the sky with his book of elegant and ultimate proofs. That's the reason I work at night. So everything's quiet—or as quiet as it ever gets in New York—and I can hear him.

What does he say?

Like I said. Nothing. Or maybe, time to eat. Are you hungry?

She realized she was starved.

He went to the refrigerator and returned with a board and several cheeses, which he sliced into thin slivers and told her to sample, talking as she did about provenance, grass, cows and goats and sheep, vine leaves and ash, morning and evening milk. There was a fruit paste on the board, and he told her to try it with some of the cheeses, and there was also a bulbous piece of ham, and she started laughing at his uncharacteristic garrulousness and the shapes his moving hands made in the air, the clean edges of his cuffs, the odd grace of his bony wrists. Jamon iberico, he said, and the words struck her as so absurdly funny that she made him repeat them again and again—jamon iberico jamon iberico jamon iberico—until she was breathless with laughter, and he was laughing too, watching her. And all the while, she tried to analyze his accent, those traces of something not-quite-English, the broadened 'a's and thickened 's's of Eastern Europe pushing against the smartly tapped British consonants.

Her eye fell on the cigarette case, and she looked at it more closely. It was battered and slightly tarnished, with a swirly pattern like leaves and flowers vining along the sides.

It used to be my grandfather's, Jon told her. He said it was a gift from a Hungarian baroness.

Oh, come on. Angela laughed harder.

That's what he said.

She sobered a little. Your folks were Hungarian? Have you been there?

Of course, Jon said. He began describing Budapest, the church spires and domes, the cobbled streets of the old town, and something about an uprising: My father talks about when he was a little boy seeing Russian tanks burning on Andrassy Street—one of the main streets—and corpses hanging from trees by their feet. He said there's been so much sadness in Budapest that the buildings are still black with tears.

Okay. Enough of that. He leaned forward, put his forefinger beneath her chin to look into her eyes, then kissed her lightly on the lips.

Shame you're not a man, he said, moving away.

Angela laughed and stood up. Thanks Jon. I think I can sleep now. And I'm also thinking—well, it's crazy, but I'm thinking I need to find my brother.

CHAPTER TWENTY-THREE

Sunday. Jon was skimming the art section of the paper over a breakfast of waffles and bacon. The San Francisco Ballet's coming in two weeks, he told Keith. I'd like to go.

Great. I'll come with you.

You don't like ballet.

I like being out with you.

Jon hesitated. I used to date one of the dancers. I'll probably want to talk to him afterwards.

That's okay. I'll come home afterwards.

They were both quiet for a few moments, reading. Then Keith's voice: Were you in love with him? His need to know had overridden his reluctance to ask.

It was purely physical.

What does that mean? You loved his body?

Yes.

And more. Saul was difficult, prickly, and beautiful, and Jon had been in love with him, in love for the first time in his life. It had been a long-term relationship, at least for Jon—which meant it lasted almost two years, during which time they'd been free to see other people on occasion, the only stipulation being that they'd never have unprotected sex and would both be tested regularly for AIDS. A host of images intruded as he sat across the breakfast table from Keith: Saul seated on the floor sorting photographs, his legs scissored into an almost-split on either side of a large cardboard box. Saul, naked, standing on one foot while he brushed his teeth, the other leg slung up onto the bathroom counter in one of those casual, unselfconscious dancer stretches—Saul had no compunction at all about walking into the bathroom when Jon was in the shower, shaving or on the toilet. The notion of privacy was foreign to him. Saul waking tousled in the morning, the sheets tangled around his limbs. Saul seated in front of the television at night, brushing his fluffy white cat, Isabelle, in long smooth strokes while she melted bonelessly across his knees.

Saul was a classical dancer, what they called a danseur noble. Jon imagined him as a child, being taken by a doting single mother to classes where he was praised and cosseted by the teacher as only a talented boy in a room full of little girls in pink tights could be praised. When he got to the American Ballet School, he was soon noticed, Saul had told Jon, moving upwards in the annual Nutcracker role by role and given small but significant parts in the big ballets. Though it was an adjustment. He had learned old-fashioned Russian style in his small-town studio, the exaggerated arms, the look-at-me pause whenever he assumed a pose. But in New York they wanted something swifter, less about the dancer and more about the choreography. He eventually came to a combination of styles all his own, and a perfect fit for certain roles—and he still colluded with the conductor to gain an extra fraction of a second at certain moments so the audience could take in his lines. It was life's blood to him, performing, it was mother's milk; he greedily absorbed all the attention in the auditorium. But he was also generous in his dancing. He gave himself whole-heartedly to every moment, and the women in the company sought him out as a partner because his strength and sense of balance made them look so graceful and light. Though he'd mock his partner later to Jon, say she was getting fat and lazy and needed to retire.

But always that unconscious, core-deep grace, the kind that only years of ballet can give. With toothpaste foaming from his mouth, Saul was beautiful. Clipping his toenails, he was beautiful. And he was most beautiful just walking down the street, skimming along the sidewalk as if he had no weight. When Saul came into a room, all Jon's senses alerted and excitement prickled along his nerves. Saul was olive-skinned like him, tightly muscled like him—a kind of doppelganger, a princely Jewish alter ego, as devoted to his craft as Jon was to his and, beneath the flood of whining and complaint he regularly unleashed, just as impermeable.

And Keith, rising now to take the dishes into the kitchen, well, Keith was just Keith, kind and self-effacing. Love didn't enter the picture. Their relationship was like an old broken-in pair of shoes or one of those thick wool cardigans you pull over your shoulders on a cold night.

Saul's regular partner did retire, and another dancer who was bright and quick as a skittish little horse took her roles, and Saul couldn't find a way to make their rhythms mesh. After a season, the company found her another partner. Saul read the cards and put out feelers. When he was offered a contract in San Francisco, Jon knew their time together was over.

California's too new for me, he told Saul. Too sunny. I need my ghosts.

That was true. But he also knew the two of them couldn't go on forever. During those few clear-eyed moments when he emerged from the fog of sensuality that enveloped them, he could see how narcissistic Saul was, how impossible to live with. He generated a constant mini-whirlwind of drama and stress. He dropped, broke and lost objects, and was constantly on the search for his car keys, scarf, mobile phone, ballet bag. He stayed out late at night, went to the studio hung over every morning, complained bitterly of fatigue, and kept himself going with amphetamines. He took offense easily and had to be pacified with large dollops of reassurance and attention. Saul's conversation was a droning monologue about roles he should have been given and wasn't, roles he was hoping to get, roles he was currently dancing, the venality of the company's artistic staff, and the limitations of the other male dancers.

They don't love me enough to keep me in here in New York, he said. He was lying on his stomach while Jon ran his hands along his long smooth back and circled the knobs of his backbone. Anyway, Saul continued, I take comfort in knowing you'll miss me desperately and I've ruined you for anyone normal.

You have, Jon assured him. You're a demi-god.

Saul rolled over and caught Jon's hands between his. Just a demi?

Oh, God, you are such a faggot, Jon said affectionately. And such a cliché: a gay ballet dancer.

Spoken by a gay pastry chef.

Exactly. Touché.

CHAPTER TWENTY-FOUR

It was early afternoon, and Piqué was empty. Walking into one of the dressing rooms, Angela saw a skirt on the floor, a lacy diaphanous thing tossed there by someone obviously used to having other people clean up for her. Angela thought of her mother squatting at a customer's feet, pins in her mouth, silently absorbing criticism and constant new demands. Then she picked up the skirt and checked for rips, missing buttons, lipstick stains. The thing cost well over a thousand dollars, but her customers were above worrying about price—or even such small niceties as politeness and consideration. Though they almost always did ask her opinion once they were in front of the mirror: Did she think the trousers fit? What about the color of the blouse? Were they so stupid they didn't know it was her job to insist that whatever they had on their bodies at that particular moment looked fabulous? Just fabulous.

She was hanging up the skirt when Nancy came in. Nancy was a regular, a plump little soul, with purple-streaked hair held back by a pink plastic barrette and butterfly clips, and she babbled nonstop: about where she'd had lunch, and what she'd eaten, what the friends she was with thought about a new reality show, a cute litter of kittens she'd seen in a pet store window, her last visit to the dentist where she'd had her teeth whitened because her husband wanted her to look more sophisticated, but she didn't know how to do it, and anyway her freshness—that's how he'd put it—freshness—was what he'd liked about her in the first place. And now he seemed to want her to be someone else. She needed shoes. Could Angela help her choose shoes?

Angela nodded. She knew Nancy was idling away the afternoon because she had nothing else to do, and would try on every shoe in the place. She didn't really mind. Nancy was amusing and, unlike most of her other customers, rather sweetly self-deprecating, and you didn't actually have to listen to the endless stream of giggle-babble-babble-giggle she produced. She watched as Nancy crammed her pudgy feet into the first pair of high heels she brought out, pale flesh bulging through the straps.

Angela had told Stocker she wanted to look for her brother, and he had asked if he could help. She didn't want help, she said. Would she leave town? How long would she be gone? She didn't know. She didn't know anything about her brother except that his name was Jeffrey, and she had to do this on her own. She was finding herself more and more fretful in the relationship, wanting some kind of experience that she couldn't get with Stocker, filled with an unfocused longing having to do with Jeffrey and her constant sense of being the wrong person in the wrong place at the wrong time, deracinated, unmoored. She imagined taking off for somewhere she'd never seen, working in a smart little boutique in Paris, Milan, or the Budapest Jon had described to her. She had no idea what she wanted, only that it wasn't what she had.

Perhaps it was marriage after all. Perhaps she should become a rich man's wife, like poor Nancy, live in a big house in upstate New York, accumulate closets full of clothes. She wondered what it would be like to do nothing all day but gossip, lounge by a pool, shop, make appointments to get her hair and nails done. She'd go mad with boredom. But there was something about extreme wealth that aroused yearning nonetheless, the way it provided safety and power, proved your worth and elevated you effortlessly above everyone else. She was tired of serving the rich, pushing shoes that cost hundreds of dollars onto buniony and sometimes dirty feet. She hated the smell of feet. She wanted those shoes. Stocker had money, but their life together was chaotic and his skin felt greasy to the touch.

Angela knew the pain her growing coolness was inflicting on Stocker and it filled her with a kind of sick pleasure. Before, the hurting had been a game. She'd tease him to the edge of madness, and Stocker would give as good as he got, though his sallies were blunt and frontal, where hers were pointed or elliptical. She enjoyed these games: Stocker as predator and herself as prey, his just-on-the-edge-of-hurting pokes and bites, the crescents her teeth sometimes left on his shoulder. She had tested him constantly for vulnerability, and he had always remained impermeable. Until now. Angela had seen photographs of birds rescued after an oil spill and read that they rarely survived even after being rescued: the process of cleaning their feathers removed the natural layer of oil that enabled them to repel water, and then they were defenseless and bedraggled even in their own element. That was Stocker.

Nancy stood up, teetering in a pair of spike-heeled silver sandals: I can't walk in these.

Keep trying, Angela said. It takes practice.

She wouldn't let herself be trapped. She wouldn't be Kim. She'd figure out what was hers, and force the world to give it to her.

A middle-aged man walked in, perhaps in his mid-forties, and Angela left Nancy to the boxes of shoes that had accumulated around her chair. He was tall, a little thick around the waist, wearing a meticulously cut gray suit, clearly a man who had his life under control. I'm looking for something for my wife, he said, a ring maybe, or a pin. As they examined the jewelry together, he offered that Cheryl was a photographer—not one that she, Angela, would have heard of probably—but very good, and with excellent taste. He held up a pair of earrings shaped like enameled fish, a bracelet made of hand-painted medallions of porcelain that Angela loved and had fastened onto her own wrist several times when she was alone in the shop. It's so hard to tell what's hip and and what's just, well, silly, he murmured.

Angela had thought about this a lot. She wanted to tell him that it's the way you see an object that makes it beautiful or ordinary, the value inheres in the story rather than the thing itself. Who had designed this bracelet, and what had that person been thinking? What was in fashion right now, and did the piece jibe with the places where it would be shown off? More importantly, how would it make his wife feel, and what associations would it raise for her? Did she love him? Perceive his gifts as heartfelt or dutiful? But of course she said none of this. Instead, she asked whether Cheryl usually wore big bold pieces or small, intricate ones, about her skin tone and the color of her hair. Did she gesture a lot, and if she did, would the porcelain shards make her gestures look graceful or just tinkle irritatingly whenever she raised her arm?

He was intrigued. I've never thought much about it. I've never thought about whether she gestures but, yes, she does, all the time.

I need these in a six, Nancy called out plaintively across the shop.

By the time Angela returned to the jewelry display, the man had decided on a necklace. At the counter, his fingers touched hers for just a second as he handed over his credit card. So she wasn't surprised when he returned a couple of days later to say he wanted to exchange the necklace, and then again after a week to search for another gift, this time for his sister. And by the time he asked if he could see her outside the shop sometime, perhaps for dinner, Angela was expecting it.

I know just the place, she said, and her smile was tight and mean.

CHAPTER TWENTY-FIVE

A ripple that felt like a sigh moved along the line of corps dancers, the principal ballerina turned, her entire body expressive of graceful welcome, and Saul was on the stage.

Jon felt Keith's elbow at his side—That him?—moved away slightly and nodded.

Saul paused a second, chest raised, and the music paused with him. Then he took a few steps forward and unleashed a sequence of high, scissored leaps, seeming momentarily suspended in air with each one. This was the thing about ballet that always fascinated Jon: the contrast between the dancer's imperial mien and his doomed, endless and quixotic struggle to achieve weightlessness, a struggle to which—as Jon knew from having watched Saul's classes—hundreds of sweaty and self-abasing hours had been devoted. The piece was that old warhorse, "Paquita," and Saul was turning and turning in his gold-braided top and white tights.

Jon's obsession with beauty, his usual state of mind when he assessed a sketch or contemplated the shapes and colors of his sugarwork, tended to be cool and detached, and it was in this state that he took in the moving lines of his ex-lover's body, the way Saul curved his neck or beveled a foot, his intimate relationship with the music. But he also knew Saul's nakedness beneath the tights, the way his penis canted very slightly to the right; the scent of his skin after exertion. So he found himself watching in a divided state, mesmerized and suspended in time, contrasting the formal beauty of the dance with a thousand raunchy images of their time together. Connecting the two responses was like bringing the ends of electrical cords together—a sharp spitting sound, a spark darting from one to the other. By the final piece of the evening, a long-drawn-out slithery pas de deux, full of twists and turns, the woman sliding again and again across Saul's body, Jon had given up all attempt at purely aesthetic appreciation. He must have let out a low-voiced exhalation because Keith turned his head to look at him.

Afterwards, they went to the backstage door, gave their names and waited, Jon wishing he had come alone. In a few minutes, Saul was walking toward them in all his glossy sweeping theatricality, hands outstretched. Hey, he said, it's the Hungarian prince, the man of sweets. He was still in his tights with his makeup on, and he was naked to the waist. Jon was shaken by the familiar scent, and keenly aware of Keith's efforts to keep his eyes from the dancer's chest and crotch. This is Keith, he said. He didn't add, my lover, and he knew Keith noticed.

Saul nodded without interest.

You were great, said Keith.

Now Saul looked at him. The tempo was too slow for the "Paquita" pas. I've told the maestro again and again.

Still, Jon said, You were beautiful.

Come in. I have to get this stuff off my face.

Jon watched Saul's buttocks as he moved ahead of them down the corridor to the dressing room. Either other, he thought, sweetly gracing.

Saul plunked himself down at the dressing table and ran a moistened cotton pad over his face, swift and professional. We're all going out for a drink, he said. You guys want to join us?

Keith said he was tired and had to get to work in the morning. Then he turned to Jon. Why don't you go?

I'm tired. I need to get home too.

Saul shrugged. Okay. We still need to catch up while I'm in town.

Walking home through the cooling night, Jon could sense Keith's gratitude, but it felt obtrusive and unwelcome, and when Keith reached for his arm, he hunched his shoulders and pulled away.

Why didn't you go for a drink with him? It'd have been fine with me.

He knew what Keith hoped to hear: I wanted to be with you. But he said, I'm just tired. They're here for a couple of weeks. I'll call him to-morrow.

Later, in bed, Keith began stroking his body, but Jon clenched him-self tight: Not now. Keith turned on his side, his back to Jon, and pulled the blanket over his shoulders, waiting, Jon knew, for a penitent word or touch. Jon gave the large solid flank in front of him a swift businesslike ca-ress. It felt loose on the bone, flaccid. He murmured good night and settled on his back, staring through the semi-dark at the ceiling, and letting the evening's images move through his mind—Saul's muscled thighs and the flowing movement of his arms, those magnificent, weightless, turning leaps. He deepened his breathing, consciously courting sleep, but his penis was painfully hard. He hesitated, then closed his hand around it. Two or three strokes—careful to keep the rest of his body still so as not to jiggle the bed and disturb Keith—and he stopped. It was useless. It was Saul he wanted. He turned onto his side, bunched the pillow up under his head, smoothed it out, and finally, giving up the struggle, sat upright. Keith was either asleep or faking sleep. Jon slid out of bed and pulled on his t-shirt and jeans. Turn-ing at the door, he saw that Keith had opened his eyes.

I'm going to the restaurant, Jon said. I had an idea for something. He didn't care if Keith believed him or not.

Keith said Uh-huh, sighed, and buried himself deeper in the bed-clothes. In the hallway, Jon closed the door quietly behind him, and then abandoning all restraint raced out of the building.

He knew where the ballet company was staying, in a hotel roughly twenty blocks downtown, and he began walking there, too driven to grab a cab or wait for the bus. Lighted shop windows flowed past him—a meditating Buddha in the middle of an empty window, a display of green and yellow Crocs, a huge red fish on a slab of ice, its jellied eye following his steps. The hotel doorman was asleep, his head on his chest, and the lobby was shadowed and empty. Someone should have asked who he was and what he wanted, but no one did. Saul had given him his room number, and he couldn't bring himself to wait for the elevator, so he flew up the stairs, down along a corridor in what turned out to be the wrong direction, reversed himself, and finally stood outside room 517, shaking. And now he hesitated. It was two in the morning. He ought to go home and call Saul later. He beat a rapid drumbeat on the door.

After a few minutes, he heard movement inside the room, and voices. Saul was with someone. Jon hadn't allowed for that. Once again he turned to go, but before he could move, the door opened, and there was Saul in his underwear. He didn't seem surprised by Jon's presence—Well, look at this. The candy man's here—and he stepped forward and half closed the door behind him: My roommate will be wanting to get back to sleep. Oh, Saul added, seeing Jon's expression, don't worry. He's straight as a die. The company just doubles us up because they're cheap.

Jon wasn't sure who moved forward first or if a few more sentences got exchanged, but he felt Saul's body pressing against his and they were embracing, groping, kissing, murmuring inanities like Oh, there you are again, and, God, I missed you. He had forgotten how fierce desire could be.

Where? Saul breathed.

The park.

Is it safe?

Who cares?

Give me a second.

Saul disappeared into the dark recesses of room 517, said something to someone, and emerged again buttoning his shirt.

It felt like being twenty-two again, walking the streets of New York with Saul beside him, noticing how easily they swung into step together and recaptured the accustomed rhythm of their walking. Like arriving here for the first time and finding all the riches of the city, the discoveries and surprises, the pulse and excitement, available to him. My time of day is the nighttime, he sang aloud, and Saul joined in, A couple of deals before the dawn. They had gone to dozens of musicals together. Jon felt light, weightless, filled with fizzing energy. Stocker's kitchen was a world away with all its darkness and complexity, the leaping flames illuminating the sweat-streaked faces of the cooks like a scene out of Dickens, and his own daily struggle to maintain the sanctity of his alcove. Goodbye to all that—at least for the moment. And goodbye too to the late-night returns to the apartment where Keith waited in their stodgy, porridgey bed. He wasn't going to think about Keith right now, or the irresponsibility of what he was doing, not with this fine dark stallion beside him. He'd never made a commitment to Keith, never said he loved him; he owed Keith nothing. Figures moved along the street, curses and laughter issued from windows. He smelled coffee and bread baking; the trees on the edge of the sidewalk held up sooty hands to the sky; a streetlight glinted on the jagged bottom of a smashed wine bottle. The air was thick with breathing humanity, and every nerve in his body was awake and yearning. They made stupid jokes. They stopped for a lemon ice, and focused lewdly on each other's licking tongues. And then they walked on, arms linked, Jon's hand sliding downward now and then over Saul's princely ass.

They wandered into Central Park and moved off the path into the tree line, sank to the grass behind the trees, and made love in all the ways Jon remembered. Afterwards, he lay on his back, feeling the sweat cooling on his body. Opening his eyes, he saw Saul, propped on an elbow, studying his face: Good?

More than good. I'm emptied out. Turned inside out.

Can that other guy—Keith—do that for you?

No one can do it but you.

Tomorrow night? Our disgusting cunty bar?

I'll be there late, after work.

Me too.

Saul moved away abruptly, turned onto his belly, and slid his pants down. Let's go again.

Dawn was breaking when Jon arrived home. The place was quiet. He went into the bathroom and turned on the shower. Keith's voice came from the bedroom, muffled by the door and the sound of running water. Hey.

Was the word weighted? Did it carry any special significance? Jon couldn't tell. Hey, he called back.

You get what you needed at the restaurant?

It took him a second to remember what Keith was talking about. He wanted to laugh. I got a couple of ideas. They're still rough.

CHAPTER TWENTY-SIX

Megan, Nabil and Tracy tried to rehearse now and then, but the rehearsals had become sporadic. Doug often canceled, came late, or said he'd be there but failed to show up—though when they asked if he was still interested in doing the scene for class, he insisted that he was. But the idea of rehearsing still seemed important to them, even if they half knew they'd never take their Midsummer Night's Dream to class, and all of them had presented some other scene for Mort over the last couple of months. Meeting to rehearse was part of the glue that held them together—the snacks Nabil prepared, the movies they watched, the music they shared, the long evenings of joking, confession, and mutual exploration. Sometimes they sobered and tried different tactics to bring a scene they were all a little tired of to life. They'd say the words with an exaggerated English accent, or do the whole thing lying down on the carpet staring at the ceiling, unmoving, or improvise, performing the characters' actions but replacing Shakespeare's words with their own. Sometimes Doug was there; sometimes he wasn't and they discussed ways they might do bits of the play, a sort of experimental collage, without him. Let's rehearse this way, Nabil suggested one night. I'll read both male parts, and we'll say the words as written but without any expression. Just flat. We'll only be expressive if the feeling gets so strong it overwhelms us and we have to let it out. That might bring things alive.

It was amusing, speaking in mumbles—Nabil on the sofa, Megan on a folding chair by the table, Tracy lying on her back on the floor, carefully not looking at each other, suppressing grins at the monotony of their own voices. Her eyes closed, Megan began hearing the words she spoke differently, found them yielding new shades of meaning. It was safe within the confines of these rigid rules Nabil had set to think about him and let her longing for him bloom until it filled her mind and forced its way out of her mouth and Hermia stopped being a figure in a story and became her, Megan, contemporary her playing Hermia, nothing between the two Hermias except a meaningless accident of time and place. "Since night you loved me," she said, "Yet since night you left me." She became aware that Tracy had stood up and she half-slitted her eyes to look at her. "Lo, she is one of this confederacy!" Tracy said, her voice suddenly vibrating with passion. "Now I perceive they have conjoined all three/ To fashion this false sport, in spite of me." A brief astonished silence followed and then, with no warning Tracy launched herself at Megan. Hey, said Nabil, standing—Megan was aware of him, but she could focus on nothing but Tracy's bent fingers with their long fingernails coming straight toward her face. She lost her balance, the folding chair gave way under her, and she was on the floor, starting to laugh helplessly with the shock and unexpectedness of the assault. But Tracy was on top of her now, her face inches away, her forehead damp and mouth twisted, and Megan realized this wasn't a time for laughter. She seized Tracy's wrists, but Tracy was unexpectedly strong and Megan began to feel actual fear. She was aware that Nabil was pulling at Tracy's arm saying something—Hey. Stop. Tracy—what are you ...?—but Tracy was laughing, ignoring him, saying, Come on, Megan. Fight me. This is the woods. This is the wild place, the place where the demons come out to play. You want Nabil, right? Well, I want him too. So have some guts. Fight for him. That's what this whole fucking scene's about, isn't it?

Megan's heart seemed to stop momentarily.

Fight back, Tracy said. That's what Mort would say. Fight me for Nabil. Make it real.

Megan could barely gather breath to whisper, This isn't acting.

It's all acting. Tracy's tone was exultant. It's practice. Fight back, Megan, and then remember how it feels for when we do it in class. Scratch out my eyes. You know you want to.

I don't.

Nabil succeeded in loosening Tracy's grip and Megan rolled sideways, her face turned away. Slowly, she stood up. The three of them faced each other, breathing hard, and the buzzer from downstairs sounded.

I was just acting, for Chrissake, said Tracy. I'm done. It's okay. You can answer the fucking door, Nabil.

The buzzer rang again. After a wary, admonitory glance at the two women, Nabil nodded. It'll be Doug.

I can't do this, said Megan.

Doug's here. We'll talk about it later. Nabil placed a hand on her shoulder. Let's calm down and try to act normal.

I don't want to do this. Megan moved away from his hand, too shaken to cry. She reached for her purse, keeping as far as possible from the two others and walked fast toward the door just as Nabil opened it. Hey Megan, said Doug as she brushed past him.

Let me know when you're ready to do some serious work, Tracy called after her.

Outside, Megan leaned against the side of the building, her head throbbing with emotions she couldn't sort out—rage, defeat, shame, sadness, fear. She was afraid to be alone and half thinking of going back to Nabil's apartment—maybe it really was an acting exercise after all and it was she who was crazily over-reacting. Perhaps she'd made a fool of herself. But Tracy's words had exposed all her confused feelings about Nabil and she didn't feel she could ever face him again. Or Tracy, now that she understood that Tracy loved Nabil too. Which meant that what she'd seen as a friendship that transcended ordinary definition was nothing but a dumb cliché after all: two women wanting the same man.

She was still trembling from the shock of Tracy's rage, but an answering rage was rising in her. She wanted to drive her fingers into Tracy's eyes as Tracy had threatened to do to her. She could imagine it, could feel the revolting jelly beneath her nails—and there was wild pleasure in the image. She put her hands protectively over her own eyes to block out the thought. For a few seconds, the pulsing darkness beneath her fingers soothed, but then memories of the struggle on the floor of Nabil's apartment swarmed in and the anger returned. There was some ugly power in Tracy that called up rage, a desolate black nihilism like a black hole. In a few chaotic moments she had destroyed the Three Musketeers, the beautiful and extraordinary balance that existed between the three of them. And then she had laughed.

Megan began walking, lecturing herself as she walked: Breathe, she told herself. You're being melodramatic. Breathe long and slow ... She lost track of time, walking aimlessly along street after street, until she realized she was in Chelsea, a few blocks from Stocker's Kitchen. Her wallet was at home, and all she had in her purse was a single twenty-dollar bill, not even enough for an appetizer. But she kept walking until she stood in front of the half-hidden door at the side of the restaurant building. I don't have a reservation, she told the maitre d', and he nodded: We always have room for you.

Minutes later, she sat at the familiar table in the corner by the river and saw Crystal approaching with the menu: Hey, stranger. What can I get for you?

Megan hesitated. I forgot my credit card.

I'll cover you for soup at least; you can pay me back next time.

Megan nodded her thanks.

Crystal looked at her closely. A glass of wine, hon?

Now Megan was crying.

I'll get you one.

Soon the soup was in front of Megan—a creamy white puree with a cluster of pink pearl-sized eggs in the center. She circled her spoon in the warm, buttery depths, watching the eggs disperse and feeling stupefied and empty. What had just happened that her friends were no longer her friends: Nabil lost to her; Tracy seeming to have lost herself? In that desolate moment, the second loss was as shattering as the first.

CHAPTER TWENTY-SEVEN

Stocker wasn't one of those chefs who worked the dining room glad-handing customers, flattering, bringing out little extra tastes of this and that or recommending special wines or beers to go with a particular dish, but he did hover fairly often at the top of the narrow stairs just out of sight behind the doorway so that the waitstaff had to push past him with their trays. Only Crystal dared to josh him as she did so: Come on, Stocker, I can't get my fat ass past yours, and he always responded mechanically that her ass was just fine, delicious in fact, and sometimes patted it absent-mindedly, never taking his eyes from the dining room where his customers ate: The man staring pensively at the calf's liver on the plate in front of him—Stocker's jokey play on pate, served with caramelized onion and a sweet-sour pomegranate reduction; the dish was a tribute to Cherry and her weeping calf in some perverse way Stocker could never verbalize. A woman texting under the table while her date, oblivious, kept talking. Someone salting the food—which Stocker never minded, though he knew a lot of chefs who did. He liked plenty of salt himself. What he was looking for was appetite, gusto, a napkin spread over a fat stomach, a man licking his fingers, a woman sopping up sauce with bread. Go on, he'd always urge Angela. Go on. Lick the plate. And she would, while he watched.

But then he saw her. His eye flickered over her, and he had to look back to be sure. Unmistakably Angela, seated at a shadowed corner table, smiling, the lamp above her head casting a glow on her skin, a glass of red wine in her hand. A man sat opposite her. Stocker couldn't see his face, but he took in the meticulous haircut and expensive gray suit, the stylish black and silver watch on the arm held up to summon the waiter. Angela's smile was seductive, though her eyes darted about the room. Looking for him, Stocker thought. She was playing this man. And she was playing him.

Crystal was beside him in the doorway now. Her eyes followed his. Stocker, she said very quietly, sympathy in her voice, and affection, but also a warning, Let me by. He teetered on the balls of his feet. A few swift steps would take him across the room. He could swipe the food from their table making a rain of everything on it, crockery, wineglasses, bread. One more swing of his hand—he knew how it was done, he'd seen it done plenty—and she'd be on the floor, blood bubbling from her mouth, and the man standing up, fist bunched ... Oh, he could deal with the man. It'd be a pleasure. Crystal touched his arm. Let me by, she repeated, and he turned away and began stumbling down the stairs.

He went out into the alley, leaned against the wall and lit a cigarette. The cat approached and he called to her, but she circled warily away. Smart. He himself didn't know if he intended a kick or a caress. He lit a second cigarette from the stub of the first, consciously willed his breathing to slow down.

Ten minutes later he was in the kitchen, as usual a blur of activity. He stalked along the line of cooks at the stove, peered over a shoulder, snatched the wooden spoon from someone's hand and yelled, Clockwise, take it off the heat and stir it clockwise. Idiot. Baboon. To the next linesman: That's done. Caramelized. You want bitter? You want it to taste of nothing but bitter? And hovering over a sauce: I don't want it strained. I want those bits in it. No, strain it. Strain it. They can guess. Fuck them. Look at that—now he was staring into another pot. It's broken. The hollandaise is broken. What are you, a cretin, a retard? Hollandaise is ABC. Hollandaise is nothing. You should be able to make hollandaise in your sleep. Oh, you, Juan, Pedro, whatever your name is—the teenager scraping dishes at the sink looked up startled—Yes, you. Move faster or you'll get sent back to whatever godforsaken place you came from. He paused in the center of the kitchen. Why is everyone staring? Why are you all lolling around? Work, damn you.

Harold chopped like fury, keeping his back to the commotion, the knife in his right hand rocking ceaselessly, steadily, the Bluetooth at his ear. Stocker walked up behind him. There's nothing wrong with your lasagna, ma, Harold was saying, sotto voce. I'm just saying I could bring a bit of basil from here to give it some ooomph, a bit of fresh, you know? I'm not suggesting yours is tasteless. I say, I'm not suggesting yours ... I know you've been making the stuff since before I was born. He paused, allowing the agitated gabble on the other end of the line to build to a crescendo, then interrupted, Hey, it's lasagna, ma. That's what it tastes like. Fucking lasagna.

Stocker reached up. He pulled the Bluetooth from Harold's ear, and the knife blade slid through the top of the prep cook's forefinger, dissecting the nail with a thin, clean line of blood. Harold dropped the knife, put his finger in his mouth, his other hand groping at his suddenly naked ear, his long, goony face a study in stupefaction. He said, Ma? questioningly to the air, and Stocker hurled the Bluetooth across the kitchen. I pay you to work, he yelled, not to blab all day to your mother—he ejected the word mother from his mouth as though it were bitter, his spittle landing on Harold's cheek and Harold too frozen to wipe it off, though his hand moved mechanically toward his face. I pay you to work, to chop things. It's not much to ask. Look at this. Stocker picked up a silver-green, perfectly transparent wafer of cucumber. You expect me to use an ugly great chunk like this in my food?

The staff was used to Stocker's rants, but none of them had ever seen anything like this before. Sean seemed to be trying to vanish into his customary corner, hunched over, mechanically shelling and de-veining one shrimp after another. And now Kenneth was making his way toward Harold and Stocker. Now then, Kenneth said, take it easy, chef.

Stocker was incandescent with fury, a whirling dervish spinning off fingers of darkness and sucking everything around him into the inferno of his burning, black and despairing rage. He flung off Kenneth's hand,

and turned back to Harold. I'm sick of your jabber. Every day, all day long, jabber jabber jabber. Awww, did you hurt your finger? Why don't you take it home to mommy? Take your owie home and mommy'll kiss it better. Harold turned away, his bleeding finger in his mouth, and dropped to his knees to locate the Bluetooth, and without warning Stocker's foot flashed out and sent him face forward onto the slickly malodorous floor. Get out, he said. Get out of my kitchen. You're fired.

Kenneth tried again. Now, now, he said, in the pleasant Scottish burr he'd maintained through all his years in the States. You don't want to do that, chef. We can't get by without Harold.

Really? When I want your bloody limey wisdom I'll ask for it. Now George stepped up and stood behind his father, a squatly muscular young man, one fist bunched, and Stocker stared at both of them a moment before turning to the line cooks. Why have you all stopped? What are you thinking? We have customers upstairs, people waiting for food. You've heard of food? That's what we serve here. Harold struggled to his feet, and Stocker rounded on him. Get out. I mean it. You're fired.

Even after Harold had walked slowly to the door, turned, with his injured finger still in his mouth to stare around him, and then staggered down the corridor to the alley, Stocker didn't relent. He caught sight of Sean in his corner. You, he ordered, finish those cucumbers. Sean looked at the others as if seeking help, sidled forward, picked up Harold's knife and began slicing. Faster, roared Stocker. Get going. You can take your fingers off for all I care. A little blood won't hurt the food.

He was filled with righteousness, almost joyful. He was on top of his form. He harangued; he criticized; he snatched implements from suddenly nerveless hands and tossed them down; he tasted, wrinkled his face, pursed his lips, spat food into the sink and conspicuously wiped his mouth with the back of his hand. Lovely. Perfect. Have you morons all forgotten how to cook? He was in hell and he was giving them hell, and they deserved it, they were all in this with him, and at the end of the service when everyone had left, one by one, silent except for the occasional muffled goodnight to one another—not to him—faces averted, resolutely neutral—he knew they'd be leaving, half of them, as soon as they could find other jobs. He also knew he couldn't blame them, and, as his breath began to even out, that he couldn't afford to lose them, not Kenneth, the resident wise man, or Harold with his swift, sure hands. Sean shuffled past him, a protective Scot on either side, and then he was alone. He felt dizzy for a moment, caught his balance, staggered into the staff room, and saw that Crystal's coat was gone from its hook—well, of course it was. The time was well past midnight. Suddenly, he wanted desperately to talk to her. Crystal knew what he had seen; she'd served Angela and her gray-suited date. He wanted to know what they'd ordered, if Angela was smiling or serious, listening or talking. And if talking, about what. He wanted Crystal to tell him that she'd listened and discovered the man was Angela's father, an uncle, a cousin—though he knew enough about Angela's family to know that this ostentatiously wealthy man couldn't possibly be a part of it—or, failing that, to say that the man was an idiot, a cretin, and then to make a scurrilous joke or two about him the way she did about her ex-husband, whose tiny dingle made Stocker laugh every time she described it. He needed with all his being to hear Crystal's voice with its broad Southern accent and the dark, gleaming undertones like the notes of a cello, to be enveloped by her, rescued from the place where he found himself now and given absolution.

He went into the deserted kitchen. Now that he thought about it, Angela had been laughing. He was pretty sure she'd been laughing.

The rage welled up again. The cleanup had been cursory, soiled damp cloths skidding over surfaces. He sloshed water round in the sink, slammed shut a drawer that had been left half open, and kicked viciously at one of the metal legs of the prep table, but the satisfying spurt of pleasure and then pain rapidly fell away to emptiness. His mind kept touching on the helter-skelter moments of the service, Kenneth looking over at him, his eyes dark and giving away nothing, the wrinkles around the corners and the gray hair peaking at his forehead, greasy, like everything else in that place. Kenneth would be too old to work there soon. He would leave the city, but he was dreading living with his daughter, he'd told Stocker once in an uncharacteristically confiding moment, because she lived someplace— Wyoming, Montana—one of those empty off the map places, and he had no idea what he'd do with himself there. Maybe open a coffee shop. Now Stocker was fighting to keep the rage going because if it drained away he'd see Harold's blubber- stained cheeks and stricken expression as he held his bleeding forefinger to his mouth.

He grabbed his coat and darted out of the door, down the alley and onto the street, forcing his way through the night, brushing hard and deliberately against the few people walking past him along the sidewalk un- til he heard, Hey, you, whataya doin'? and turned, adrenalin rising, spoiling for a fight. But the man, a tall skinny black guy, shrugged and kept moving. Funny phrase, spoiling for a fight, Stocker thought. True, he was percolat- ing with anger. But he was also spoiling in another way, decaying, disinte- grating, ugly maggots of jealousy squirming in his stomach. Angela laugh- ing, touching the man's hand; the attentive way the man leaned toward her.

He'd been walking along Broadway, and now he found himself turning at her street, past the curtained windows and flickering blue tele- vision screens, the people moving invisibly behind walls, and there was the building, a tall, narrow row house pressed between two similar row houses, the blank exterior. Craning his neck, he saw a light at her window—not the living room light, but far inside, the kitchen, perhaps, or the light in the bathroom. He strained upwards, hoping to see her moving shadow, dread- ing a glimpse of the tall man but there was only the retreating light, which seemed to get smaller and further away while he gazed. Were they on the mattress in the alcove on the floor? His guts clenched at the thought. He couldn't put together a coherent sequence of thought, just images and bits of sound and roaring in his head: Harold's face, the unexpectedly squishy feel of Harold's butt against the ball of his foot—something about that, the squishiness, the contact, made him shiver with revulsion—and Harold pitching forward, the flush of power he'd felt, raw, mean, and angry, and then the shame, and now here he was, helpless and stupid, short, fat, and vulgar where his rival was elegant, hovering under her window full of emotion he couldn't find words for. Kenneth's voice and his steadying hand: Now then, chef, now then, and later the row of white coated backs turned toward him as every man in the kitchen returned to his task and he realized he'd become a pariah. Which was fine, just fucking fine. He was the energy, the soul, the heart of Stocker's Kitchen, and they could all get the hell out if they didn't like it. They could be replaced. New York was crawling with jobless people. Chinks and spics. Blacks. Hajis. All kinds. But there he stood in the warm late-summer evening at the blind building door, Angela behind it upstairs in her apartment, Angela whose cunt was his, Angela of the thick slippery heavy black hair, and he wanted to kick at the door and press his finger to the bell for as long as it took for her to come out to him, forever if necessary, and when she did, he'd push her forcefully backwards onto the elevator, up, up, and into the almost-bare apartment with its square cheap brown fridge and single armchair and the mattress where he'd had her groaning under him, his fingers pressing into her flesh hard enough to leave bruises while she squirmed—in answering lust, in protest, at this moment he didn't care which, he only needed to feel her pressed up against him again, his Angela, whose clitoris he'd had between his teeth, dear God, how was he to live without her and why couldn't he bring himself to bang on the door? and then he dropped onto the step and sat with his head between his knees. He was done for, finished. He could smell himself, the sweaty folds between his belly and his thighs and see between his legs the cracked grayness of the sidewalk, glints of mica, nothing living on that dead gray surface, not a weed or a scuttling ant. After a long time, perhaps an hour, perhaps a couple, he stood up and began walking slowly down the street. He needed a drink.

The place was called the Den. He'd passed it daily, but never gone in. Stocker walked through the door to heat, a babble of voices and raucous laughter, the smell of cigarettes, sweat, and beer, the pounding of the sound system—no melody that he could ascertain, just a steady hard thumping that rose through the soles of his shoes and vibrated up his body, a dark angry lyric squalling out over it. There were people up against the bar, walking through the space, seated, leaning toward each other, the outline of their bodies blurring in the dim light, the haze of smoke. He sensed an intimacy here within which he was invisible. He didn't exist—no Stocker, no Stocker's kitchen, no Angela, no gray-suited man—fuck him, fuck him a thousand times. In this world no one cared. There was a rawness here very different from the rawness of his kitchen, a rawness connected to the kind of sex that came uncoupled from tenderness or meaning—he'd understood that immediately—and it was a relief; he liked it. He waddled toward the bar through a mess of elbows and shoulders, pushing a bit, muttering excuse me's that no one heard or cared to answer, ending up with his stomach pressed against the wooden bar, at his elbow thick square glass jars holding cheap green olives and drying spirals of lemon peel. The bartender wore gleaming black leather pants and a leather vest over a white shirt, the sleeves pushed up high to emphasize the bulging muscles of his upper arms. Slut, Stocker thought, faggot, but he was too tired, too emptied out to even murmur an insult. He asked for a beer. The place smelled of sex. There was probably a back room where people did it. Glancing toward the shadows at the back of the bar, he thought he glimpsed a closed door that wasn't the john. Semen, penises in rectums, dirty brown holes. Why would anyone want to do that? And then he thought of Angela, and knew he would do that with her if she'd let him, have her penetrate him that way too, with a finger, an object, do anything that would let him grab and hold and possess her, and he pulled himself onto a barstool and sat hunched over his beer. No one paid any attention to him. He could lose himself in the sounds and smells and general slipperinesses; he imagined the floor of the back room slippery with semen, men lined up behind each other, men bending over, and he shuddered, seized with a spasm of what could have been excitement, could have been rage.

Time passed. He almost never drank and the beer was making him slightly woozy. He asked for a shot with it, then another beer and a shot, kept his shoulders defensively high, watched the bartender, his bulging biceps, his small moving ass, tossed down the shots, swallowed, wiped his lips, asked for more. He'd drink till he fell from his barstool onto the floor, he decided. He'd drink till everything melded together and nothing individual mattered or stood apart in the great stream of filth and decay swirling round him. The world was presenting him with its filthy brown asshole and he'd show it, jam in his fist, ream it out. Enter and be lost. He was already lost. Lost and in hell. A face floated into his line of vision like a dim early evening moon, a young man with puffy cheeks and glasses. He heard, Can I buy you a drink, and had no time even to frame a thought before he felt the raw shock of his fist connecting and the jarring along his arm, bone breaking, blood on the white moonface, and the creature falling backwards among tumbling stools. The bartender leapt the bar; even in his stupor Stocker could see the theatrical grace of the leaping, and hands were pulling him back, fists coming at his face. He squirmed on the floor, pulled his leg up to shield his groin—he'd had plenty of opportunities to practice this kind of self-defense through his grim and endless boyhood. He grunted with each hit, turned his face from side to side to avoid the fists, saw at eye level a wash of beer and blood that might have been his or the moonfaced boy's. Everything collapsed into shouts, blows, roiling, noise and broken glass grinding against his cheek, and it was fitting. He deserved it. Harold falling face forward onto the floor, Angela's hand in the crook of someone else's arm, Cherry's eye rolling, frantically rolling, the exposed whites, her bellows of pain and terror and then the thick blood filling his throat. His fault. His sin, and his penance.

They dragged him along the floor, through the room at the end— he'd been right, he saw men pausing in their activities as he was pulled past them, the punches still coming, but with less force now—and then he was outside, curled in a fetal position, lying among the trashcans. Consciousness ebbed like a black tide, receding and returning, receding and returning, carrying the flotsam of his miserable smashed up life. There was pain, but it was dull and distant. It would manifest in force later. He was alone and far away now, lost in the blackness inside his own skull.

His head was on someone's lap; there was a hand stroking his hair. Angela he thought, turning to nuzzle at her, but the thighs supporting him were bony and unmistakably male; a face leaned toward him, thin, beak nosed, a fashionable blur of dark stubble in the hollow cheeks. Jon. That was all he needed. He closed his eyes against the humiliation of it, his head on his pastry chef's lap, opened them and tried to raise himself, fell back. Relax, said Jon. Wait it out a minute. His voice was gentle. Stocker's eyes drifted closed again and the image he'd tried so often to rub out of his consciousness returned: himself, newborn, red and angry, howling in a trashcan behind a Chinese restaurant. He used to imagine his mother returning to take him from that trashcan and hold him, if only for a moment before kissing him goodbye.

Someone was hovering near them. Someone was saying questioningly, Jon?

Hold on, Jon said, and then turned his attention back to Stocker: You poor fat little fuck, he said. What in hell were you thinking starting a fight in there? Listen, I'll find you a cab. Can you get yourself home?

CHAPTER TWENTY-EIGHT

Angela sat down at the computer, called up Google and typed in Vietnam Babylift. There were hundreds of hits and she settled down to read: People sharing their experiences. People now in their thirties going back to Vietnam in search of their birth mothers. Tips on how to search. But how would she even start to look for Jeffrey with only the pitiful bits and pieces of information she had? And why had he never tried to find his mother—her mother? Or had he?

It's funny, she thought, how there can be a shift in your reality, a different way of looking at something you already know and then you realize there's a universe of understanding shared by hundreds of people you've never met and whose experience you can't begin to fathom—and yet to whom your life is linked. Sometimes the strange world she'd fallen into seemed as familiar as the poky little house where she grew up, sometimes altogether other. Here on the screen was the bond linking her to her brother, this magical boy like a bird flashing through forest branches and vanishing. This boy, she now realized, was an actual solid human being in his thirties like all the unknown people whose messages she was reading.

Now they were advising each other about what to expect if they chose to return to Vietnam and finally meet their relatives:

It wasn't the way I thought it would be. Be prepared to be disappointed.

Finding my birth mother changed my life; it made everything come together. She's funny. Who knew? I've always been a joker, class clown and all that—and turns out my mother loves to laugh. My mother. Sounds so weird just saying that.

She bought books about Vietnam, found movies—travelogues,

political films from the nineteen-sixties. And suddenly saw images of homecoming, of mothers and children everywhere. She cried at a Netflix movie about a cat and two dogs making a long trek home, at a commercial showing a woman diapering a chuckling baby. She stopped dead when an elderly Asian man caught her eye in the supermarket, struck by something in his face and eyes, convinced he was from Vietnam and somehow related to her. Seated on a playground bench, she watched the hands of other women, mothers and nannies, as they dealt with children: wiping a toddler's chin, handing a child a half sandwich, zipping a jacket. She saw a woman chatting with a friend in a coffee shop while nursing her baby beneath a protective cover from which only his wiggling legs protruded, and one starfish hand opening and closing on air. The mother cradled him in the curve of one arm, while with the other hand she smoothed the cover over both her own body and his small, cherished one as if there were nowhere she ended and he began.

She watched a film about an adoptee brought over on the Babylift who decided as an adult to go to Vietnam and visit her birth mother. She'd been raised in a racist small Southern town where her cold religious mother curled her straight hair every night because, like her slant eyes, it was a badge of shame. But when this young woman arrived in Vietnam, she found herself, after a brief period of joy and discovery, repelled by what she saw, the food and the pungent smells, the poverty-stricken relatives whose pleas for help she could only understand as greedy and grasping. Once she'd returned to the States, pleading letters with Vietnamese stamps began arriving, but she refused to open them. Like me, Angela thought, simultaneously relieved and guilt-ridden. She had closed the dozens of letters she received after Kim's death in a drawer, along with her mother's book of names and dollar amounts. Money was desperately needed in Vietnam, she knew, but she didn't have enough to give. Or—she told herself repeatedly—any obligation to give. And she was sure that whatever she could scrape together to send, these unknown relatives would demand more and their clutching hands would pull her into something dark and unknowable. The woman in the film was profoundly relieved to return to her husband and children, her life in the United States. Except that now she understood she was an outsider: uneasy in the country where she'd grown up, a stranger in the place where she'd been born, a citizen of nowhere.

There were books about the Babylift; it had been controversial. Some writers talked about how the lives of the children had been renewed, others said many of the children had been stolen from their biological mothers. She saw photographs of crying little ones, others of weeping women, a mother running along a runway after a taxiing plane, shrieking, her hands outstretched. Had Kim ever mentioned the name of the orphanage where she'd left Tuan or explained exactly what the circumstances were and what she had signed? Angela didn't think so. All she remembered of Kim's story was the image she'd described so often of a wet-faced little boy, his chin quivering, desperately holding out his arms to her. But the name of the place? The organization that took him in? In videos she had seen children packed onto planes, rolling on the floor, crying, many of them ill, a few volunteers trying frantically to take care of so many babies shitting, peeing, throwing up, wailing and hungry. She read about the identification difficulties caused by the chaotic process, the missing papers, the older children who, when they were finally able to speak to Vietnamese interpreters in San Francisco said they were not orphans at all and they wanted to go home.

Angela had never thought much about the chaos her mother must have endured. She had never understood how profoundly wars affect those who live through them, and the way those effects move forward through time, distorting lives. The bond between mother and child cracked. History set askew.

Many of the Babylift adoptions turned out badly, Angela learned, but the lives of Amerasian children left behind were no better—and often worse. They were jeered at and ostracized, most grew up in the streets begging for food. Here was a story about an Amerasian, now thirty, who hadn't made the Babylift and was stranded in Vietnam. This man made his living collecting mud and shaping it into tiles to sell, and he continued to dream, despite everything, that his American father would one day come and rescue him. When he did receive some money from a relative in the States, he gave it all away in one drunken evening and the next day killed himself. That was something about Vietnamese culture she would never be able to grasp, the idea that money was meant to be shared with family like food or water, and not hoarded to oneself. This man had given everything to relatives who disliked and were ashamed of him while she, Angela, jealously guarded every morsel she possessed from her unknown kin.

She set down the book and went back to the drawer where her relatives' letters were stored, took out her mother's list and stared at the names. Kim's ceaseless grumbling—You not respect your own mother. You bad daughter—was taking on new meaning. She had been a bad daughter, mean-spirited and withholding. She thought of the baffled rage and longing on Stocker's face as he stood at the head of the stairs watching her eat dinner with Mark and rapidly pushed the image out of her mind.

It seemed the Vietnamese had a belief that any profound wrong would eventually be righted by the inexorable turning of time's wheel. If that was Kim's belief, she must have expected that any day she would look up from her sewing machine to see Tuan standing in her doorway.

She was going to find him. She was Angela. She knew how to get what she wanted. She pulled off the frayed rubber band holding together the letters her mother had saved and began reading:

Dear Mrs. Packer: They suggested I write and let you know that our son Jeffie is well and happy. He has been with us for three years now. I'll always remember picking Jeffie up at the airport. He didn't speak a word of English, so we couldn't explain anything to him. He didn't want us to touch him. We told him he was safe in America now, but he just stared. No smiles, nothing. On the way home we stopped for a bite—I don't think I'd ever seen a child as skinny as Jeffie before. We tried to show him how to eat his burger, but he wouldn't touch it. All he did was stare. After a while he picked up a French fry, ate it and made a bit of a face, but then he ate a couple more. We told him he was safe and we loved him but of course he didn't understand.

These days you can't stop him talking. He has a little sister Lucy, two, and he's always wanting to pick her up and carry her around. We have to stay real close when he does, because she's too heavy for him though he won't admit it. You can't keep him away from the fries and hamburgers now, and he has lots of Legos, Power Rangers, Transformers, Bayblades, all the usual.

Well, I just wanted to let you to know Jeffie has become a real little American boy, and you don't have anything to worry about. Warmly, Pat.

Angela set the letter down. That was her brother this woman Pat was talking about. The shell-shocked four-year-old who didn't know how to eat a burger, the seven- year-old with his sibling and a room full of toys. There was something about the existential loneliness of his life that pierced her to the core, something about what it meant to be an outsider in a far more bitter and absolute way than she herself had experienced, a slit-eyed, black-haired kid in a world of blue-eyed people.

She called her father.

Hello? That flannelly voice that absorbed energy instead of transmitting it.

I've been wondering about my half brother, kinda thinking I'd like to find him. Do you have any idea where he is?

I don't know anything about that. When are you coming home? I could use you here.

His lack of curiosity, his absolute self-absorption, drove her wild. Kim hadn't even been a separate being to him, she reflected, just an incontrovertible fact of life, an automaton who provided dinner every night, washed and ironed his clothes, and—Angela was sure of this—lay stiffly apart from him through their long nights together. You couldn't even call what they felt for each other hatred. Hatred was too strong a word for anything Angela had ever known in that house.

I have a life in New York, she said to her father. I have a career in retail.

You work in a shop.

She mumbled something and hung up.

She returned to Google. Babylift. Vietnam. Reunion. Endless articles, nothing concrete. She sank onto the floor, spread the letters out and began riffling through them again. She remembered something about a zoo, an elephant. Oh, there it was: He loves to visit the zoo, especially the monkey yard and we bought him a stuffed Carol the Elephant, though he's really too big for stuffed animals now. She turned back to the computer. The words monkey yard brought up articles on lawn care and yoga. She added zoo, and three words appeared linked by dashes: San-Diego-Zoo. She got up and circled the room, sat down again and began reading. The San Diego Zoo had a famous attraction called the Monkey Trail. It had originally been called the Monkey Yard. Her breathing quickened. She tried Carol the elephant. Lots of irrelevant hits. She typed: Carol elephant zoo. And there it was, halfway down the page. Carol was a famous resident of the San Diego Zoo, an elephant who supposedly painted pictures and had appeared with her trainer on The Tonight Show. She lived to be forty and then had to be euthanized because of a degenerative joint disease.

San Diego made sense. It was a navy town, and a lot of Babylift children were adopted by military families. But it made a mockery, almost, of Kim's grief: if her son had grown up in San Diego, a two-hour bus ride could have reunited them.

One of the posts by a Babylift adoptee talked about the local newspaper in St. Paul where her adoptive parents lived when she came, the fuss the media made over the Vietnamese children. Angela remembered the news photograph she'd seen somewhere of a bewildered Asian baby in the arms of a beaming white mother. She called the San Diego Union-Tribune wondering if they had had similar coverage. They no longer kept paper archives, she was told by a human being after a fair amount of listening to canned music interrupted periodically by a robotic voice assuring her that her call was important, and then being shuffled from desk to desk. And there was nothing online from before 1990, the voice continued. Try the historical society. She called the historical society. No answer. Not even a machine. She called again, close to tears, thinking, What if I pack up and go to San Diego—ask for a two-week leave from Piqué and just go there, visit the zoo, look around? But what would she do then? She slammed the phone down and got up to put on a hot dog for dinner. The next morning she called the San Diego historical society again, and this time heard a human voice, a woman on the other end saying, Good morning. San Diego Historical Society. Angela said, I called yesterday. No one answered.

The woman kept her equanimity. I'm sorry. We only staff the office a couple days a week.

Do you ever think people might need help at other times?

I'm sorry. That's all the funding we get these days.

Angela knew she was being ridiculous; there was no reason to be angry with this woman. As she fought down her rage and searched for words to explain what she wanted, the urgency of her quest suddenly overwhelmed her and she began to cry. She tried to steady her voice, furious with herself. This wasn't her, Angela, this pathetic creature choking on her own speech. But her distress accomplished something efficiency might not have: the woman from the historical society turned gentle. Oh, yes, she said. I remember those babies. I'm old enough to remember when they came, can you imagine? There was a lot of carry-on about those Vietnam orphans. One of them was your brother? And his name's Jeffrey? Okay, I'll see what I can find out.

Angela set the phone down. She had done it, made contact. It might come to nothing or, like the butterfly wing flutter in the Amazon with the power to stir up a hurricane, it might create a tempest.

Ten days later, a fat brown envelope arrived in the mail. Angela tore at it, heart hammering, snagged a nail, cursed, thought about using her teeth, then went into the kitchen for a knife. The thing was maddeningly hard to open. But finally the contents were in her lap. The woman from the historical society had copied several pages of ancient microfiche and folded in a personal note: I hope this helps you find your brother Jeffrey. I'll be praying for both of you. Best wishes, Gretchen. She sank onto the floor and began reading. Five San Diego families had adopted children through the Babylift, and one of those children, a little boy, was four years old. The father was in the navy. His last name was Connor, and he and his wife planned to name the child Jeffrey. Her hands began to shake and she had to stop reading for a moment. Next came an article with a blurry photograph of a blond woman and a crew-cut man with an Asian child seated between them. Angela tried to make out the child's expression, but the photo was small and blurry. The accompanying article was a chirpy piece about how Jeffrey was adjusting to his new life. The Connors had always longed for a son, the reporter said. They had prayed for him every night, and now here he was.

And now here he is, Angela thought, in the rustling sheets between her hands. Thanks to microfiche and the kindness of a stranger named Gretchen.

CHAPTER TWENTY-NINE

Saul walked into the living room, dropped his case on the floor, and immediately began complaining about the taxi ride from the airport, the crowded flight, the fat man sitting next to him and oozing onto his seat, the struggle over the armrest, the attendant who'd ignored his repeated requests for a drink. Keith was away at his convention, the San Francisco Ballet was on hiatus, and Saul had come to New York to spend a few days with Jon. He paused, and Jon came forward to kiss him. After a couple of minutes in Jon's arms, Saul pulled back and proclaimed, I need a shower. I stink. He headed for the bathroom, shrugging off his clothes as he went, looking back at Jon over his shoulder. Before he'd reached the door, Jon was after him, stripping off his own clothes as he came. They grappled their way into the shower together, ran soapy hands over each others' bodies and slowed to explore more deeply.

A little later, Saul sat at the table in the kitchen naked while Jon, a towel round his waist, scrambled eggs and made toast. They ate, laughing, legs touching under the table, their talk broken and nonsensical.

Your boyfriend's at a convention? Saul asked finally.

Keith.

Dentists have conventions? What do they convene about?

A moment of guilt as Jon remembered asking Keith the same question. Career opportunities, Keith had said. Health care reform. Changes in practice. New and better ways of imaging. And Jon had responded, All mechanics then. Nothing conceptual. For the first time since he'd known him, Keith looked visibly hurt.

Now he stood up abruptly to get coffee. Sleeping with other people—with Saul—was nothing. That was his right. But joining with Saul to mock Keith was something different entirely.

They spent the afternoon on the bed, making love, dozing, making love again as the room darkened and evening shadows crept across the floor. Propped on his elbow, Jon considered Saul's body, the flat muscled belly and jutting hipbones. He slid downward, sat cross-legged, took hold of Saul's feet and placed them in his lap. They were broad and almost brutal in their strength, coarse peasant feet with bent toes, bruises both new and fading, wrecked black toenails. Ouch, said Saul, as Jon's fingers grazed a bunion. Jon remembered the drill. He got out of bed, went to the bathroom, and returned with supplies. Then he began gently rubbing cream onto the rough soles and heels, caressing the twisted toes and separating them with cotton balls.

I have lamb's wool in my case.

Later.

That feels so good. Saul lay back and allowed himself to be tended to. After a few seconds, he sighed. I'm thirty-five. What am I gonna do when my body gives out? What am I gonna do when I'm done with dance?

Maybe you'll teach.

Don't want to teach. Don't want anyone to be as good as me. Ever. Besides, ballet teachers don't make squat.

So you'll marry some rich guy.

You?

Jon shook his head. Someone old and lonely. And a lot richer than me. Hey, he tried to lighten the mood, No one really cares about ballet. We're all just there for the tights and the bulges.

And the ballerinas' knickers.

Not so much the knickers.

Shut up. Saul pulled his feet away and leapt from the bed. I need more food.

When they'd lived together, Jon had been fascinated by the culture and language of ballet. It was a small, hermetic world, he learned, populated almost exclusively by young, white, middle-class people. The dancers talked about dieting and who was in or out of favor, they partied and screwed each other and gossiped. But in the classroom, they were heroic beings, selfless and focused. The contrast between their physical power and mental endurance and the powerlessness and insecurity of their professional lives fascinated Jon. No wonder Saul clung so fervently to the glory of his premier danseur position. He had developed only one way of existing in the world, and he couldn't relinquish it without losing himself. We give ourselves over to the director body and soul, he'd told Jon once. We're nothing but servants really.

Magnificent servants.

Maybe.

Three days into the visit Jon began to remember acutely why he and Saul had broken up. Saul was high maintenance. He was on a ridiculous and incoherent diet that shifted day to day. He said he couldn't eat bread, dairy or anything with sugar, and he'd brought with him an array of sawdust-tasting health bars. For breakfast he ate one egg scrambled in olive oil, for lunch a gluten-free bagel with an apple. Dinner was a small steak, trimmed of fat, with frozen broccoli on the side, no butter. You're a chef's nightmare, Jon complained. But later in the evening, he'd find Saul in front of the television, stuffing himself with ravioli out of a can or scrabbling the last crumbs from the bottom of a bag of chips. He strewed his clothes all over the apartment and Jon, coming home tired from his hours in the kitchen, found himself walking from place to place picking up socks and underwear. In the bathroom, he'd wipe slicks of lotion from the counter and try to set the squeezed and battered tube of toothpaste to rights. Then he'd walk out into the living room, and forgive everything as Saul rose and floated toward him like a djinn.

Who cleans up after you in San Francisco? he asked one evening.

Things get a bit ripe. That's why my roommate moved out.

There was a question waiting to be asked in that statement, but Jon didn't ask it.

More than anything, Saul swept anyone who came near him into his emotionally cramped and self-pitying reality. As he described it, sales clerks ignored him, and the stinging putdowns he needed only came to him too late. San Franciscans were way more ignorant about ballet than New Yorkers, and the choreographer kept giving him moves that didn't suit his style. And why was Jon away at work all day? He, Saul, had nothing to do when Jon was gone.

Saul had always been like this. But there was a new tone to his complaints now, something sad, ugly and defeated where once there'd have been a touch of humor, a certain self-aware charm. Jon knew that a dancer's life was risky and short, but that had never seemed to apply to Saul, who could bend the world to his will through whining and pouting and the sheer beauty of his moving. Jon thought of Oscar Wilde's petulant lover Bosie, who inveigled Wilde into the lawsuit against his hated father and in the process destroyed Wilde's life. That was the power of beauty, Jon mused: there was nothing you wouldn't forgive the truly beautiful.

Saul's beauty was still there though there were faint lines circling his neck. What he'd lost was something less specific: the glossy hormonal energy, the breathless sense of possibility and transience that animates the young. Now he was just a man, handsome and lithe but also—in the sober light of midday—ordinary. Saul had never learned to fill his time usefully or to structure his days beyond the rigors of daily classes and rehearsals. Now he drifted around the apartment bored and disengaged, listening to music and switching from one song to another, demanding Jon take a walk with him or slumping in front of the television to gobble chips and switch channels. Afterwards he'd complain about feeling stuffed.

You don't love me, he said to Jon one evening.

You know I don't. We've never been about love.

Well, you don't appreciate me then. Saul curled a loose thread from the sofa cover around his finger. Who's going to love me now that I'm old and fat?

The old guy you'll marry. The rich one.

Fuck you.

Any time.

Sulky silence.

Saul, you're still strong and young. You've got years of dancing left.

Character roles maybe. Courtiers. Carabosse.

A little later, his tongue loosened by wine, Saul told Jon that he and his lover had broken up because the kid was jealous and eyeing his place in the company. He'd prance into class, Saul said, like a prize pony, all look at me, look at me, look at me, and suck up to the artistic director and gossip with the other dancers while he, Saul, became more and more invisible. Jon could imagine how the young man's initial admiration had soured as he cleaned up their apartment and dealt with Saul's routine infidelities—when Jon and he were together, Saul had fucked whomever he wanted whenever he wanted, becoming wasp vicious, however, when he thought Jon might be unfaithful. Saul sucked down another glass of wine and then came out with his deepest and most heartfelt complaint. In a review of the company's last production the critic for the San Francisco Chronicle had given him, Saul, the usual respectful mention and then waxed rhapsodic about Saul's lover, praising the way he combined driving energy with technical precision, calling him a daredevil, a virtuoso and—worst of all—the future of the San Francisco Ballet.

Bitch musta fucked that reviewer, Saul said, his tongue thick.

This man, now so terribly diminished, had once lived for the sheer instinctual joy of movement. Jon had seen mature dancers whose work had taken on a transcendence, a glow that held its own against the fire of youth, but this was a gift Saul would never receive.

More and more we grow into who we are, Jon thought. Our essential weaknesses don't manifest much when we're young and full of juice. Certainly, Saul's hadn't as he climbed the company ranks in New York. Behind all his complaints then was an intense sense of triumph, a sureness about who and what he was. But those weaknesses, like cracks in a vase, deepen over time and web inexorably outwards. Jon could feel it in himself, that hardening, the way the sense of irony he'd so assiduously cultivated all his life threatened to transform into too-easy cynicism. He could see it in Stocker too, passion ebbing, a slow settling into anger and loss.

But making art, that was something you could protect. Jon knew his work was becoming richer with the passing years. He had acquired knowledge and dexterity, a satisfying level of skill, and he was still capable of joy—not the unthinking joy he'd known as a boy, those transports the Romantics wrote about—and still not the deep quiet pleasure he imagined as the province of old age and had seen in his grandfather as the old man tinkered with his watches in the pre-dawn silence, although he believed that would come. It was more that he understood so much now that he hadn't understood before and, at the same time, he was shedding self doubt, seeing it more and more as childish, unnecessary and self-absorbed. He still worked in the spirit of play, but now it was serious play, play on which everything depended.

Jon had been infatuated with Saul when they were young, and the infatuation had lasted two years during which he'd found himself constantly in service, coaxing and soothing, and then Saul had left and after a few days, Jon realized he wasn't missing him at all, not even the sex, that he was loving the quiet evenings spent reading and listening to music or playing with images on the internet, summoning up the work of architects and designers. He'd developed a fascination with certain architects—Libeskind, for instance. What Libeskind wrote about his work struck Jon as cloudy and incomprehensible, but the work itself soared. Architects like Libeskind didn't worry about their forms being practical and people actually using the buildings they made; their creations were theoretical, abstract. They could create vertigo and move the ground beneath your feet. Their work expressed the mind at play freed from all grubby, earthly restraints. They painted with light and shadow and bent forms in ways that could never have been possible when stone, wood, brick, and concrete were the only building materials, before plastics, durable fabrics, and metallic glass stronger than steel. These men—and they were almost all men—experimented with the contradiction between permanence and ephemerality, and the scale of their thinking, their self-indulgence, elegance, and pure ego fascinated Jon.

His own creations, his spirals on plates, his abstractions in sugar, were tiny and puny by comparison, but they had the same spirit, and while even the most ethereal buildings needed to be solidly engineered, his edifices, being dispensable, didn't. It didn't cost millions to create little pearls of various substances; they could be eaten or swept aside and that was that. He could mimic the architect-sculptor's shapes, but his desserts had no function other than to please the palate and the eye and perhaps re-organize the brainwaves a little. With buildings, you could explore with your hands and try to creep into the mind of the maker, but his art was even more intimate because you smelled it and put it into your mouth and it became you.

With the ending of that first affair with Saul, he realized how distracted he'd been, and dived deeper and deeper into his own process. He worked at a couple of restaurants to establish his credentials, then found a hole in the wall, almost literally—a window in the side of a building that he rented for a small fortune. He sold his confections there to a growing crowd, and as he perfected his technique and word spread, more and more people came to ask for his macarons for parties, his miraculous light crisp macarons with the softly chewy exteriors and the tastes of wine and exotic fruits in the cream at their centers. After a while, some of the top restaurants courted him, but by then he had his eye on Stocker's Kitchen where he'd eaten several times, drawn by the contrast between his concept of dessert and Stocker's funky, down-home entrees. Once at Stocker's, he had settled in, focused on his work and lived like a monk with only occasional sorties into the world of quick easy sex—the world of the Den—feeling no need for steady companionship until one afternoon Keith appeared, a heavyset, ordinary-looking man standing at a bus stop in the rain.

When Saul's visit came to an end, Jon offered to go with him to the airport. The taxi stopped outside the drop-off curb and Saul tossed out his suitcase and slid out after it. Jon followed. They hugged. Saul extricated himself, turned to walk away, hesitated, then came back running with his arms open. One more, he said. Jon was surprised to find himself fighting back tears as they held each other. He ran a finger lightly along Saul's smooth neck and bent to kiss the hollow at the clavicle, thinking this was almost certainly the last time he'd feel the warmth of Saul's skin against his lips. You were the love of my life, he said thickly, surprising himself. Saul's eyes were bright: Me too. You were mine. He disengaged himself, and walked swiftly away through the sliding doors and into the terminal—that easy grace, those tight moving buttocks. Either other, Jon thought. Sweetly gracing.

The cab was still waiting at the curb, and he got into it. The Den, he said to the driver. You know where it is? I'll direct you.

Half an hour later, he sat with a beer between his palms taking in the unspooling performance in front of him, the carnival of pairings and separations, the bodies that jiggled and strutted like walking sex organs, the whiff of easy sex. He could imagine smirking Hieronymus Bosch faces in the dusky corners of the place, peering under tables or around the customers' legs. Decadence this ripe went beyond decadence, he thought, and became an aesthetic. It was pleasant sitting at the bar on his own, inhaling a sense of possibility. He hadn't cruised in years, and this hot, smoky moment felt like an exhilarating hiatus, a pause in his rightful life, Saul gone, Keith not yet returned. He could do whatever he wanted.

A man sat down at the bar beside him, a man with crisp curly black hair, healthy clear skin and bright blue eyes. He introduced himself as Gerry, laughed and said he was a cop but not to worry. He wasn't on duty tonight. Could he buy Jon a drink? Perhaps Gerry was a cop, perhaps he was just a fantasist, but his thigh was solid and muscled against Jon's, and Jon felt his desire rising. He couldn't help thinking about how easy and uncomplicated it would be to have sex with Gerry. They could go into the back room or out to the alley, grope each other, get sweaty. After a moment's hesitation, he shook his head. I have to go, he told Gerry. Sorry. I'll see you around.

He slept deeply that night, sprawled in an X across the cool sheets. The next morning was Monday and Stocker's Kitchen was closed. Jon showered, ate a quick breakfast and began cleaning the apartment. Keith was due back that evening, and Saul's presence lingered in every crevice, his scent was on the couch pillows, on the bedding. Jon wiped surfaces, washed dishes, vacuumed, pulled the linens from the bed and laundered them and made up the bed again, tight and square from corner to corner, checking as he worked for any too-long, light-brown hair that might have become caught in the frame or the mattress. He searched the bathroom to make sure the mangled tube of toothpaste wouldn't give him away—it was a different brand from the one Keith insisted on—or Saul's foot cream, or a tossed rubber that had somehow missed the trashcan. He emptied the trashcan and scrubbed it out in the bath. Then he paused. He had read a story once—was it by Poe?—which described a murderer cleaning up obsessively after his crime, believing that no matter how much he scrubbed and wiped he could still see traces of his victim's blood everywhere—on the walls, the furniture, the floor. He worked, this killer, hour after hour until the police arrived and arrested him. And here he himself was, Jon, circling the place like a haunted man, peering under furniture, opening and closing drawers and closets, wiping, rinsing out the cloth, wiping again. He forced himself to stop, grabbed his jacket from the closet and prepared to leave. Then he paused in the doorway to inspect his work. The apartment looked innocent and orderly. Too orderly. He walked back into the living room and shuffled the magazines on the coffee table so that the edges no longer lined up perfectly. Better. Then he lined them up square again. Re-shuffled. And finally forced himself out the door, down the stairs and onto the street. Once outside, he breathed in deeply for a few moments before walking the three blocks to the corner grocery store where he picked up two boxes of doughnuts, the kind with the tender interior and brittle flaking glaze Keith liked.

CHAPTER THIRTY

Let me in, Megan.

Tracy's flat, inexpressive voice followed the sound of the buzzer. Megan hesitated, then pressed to admit Tracy and stood irresolute, wishing she hadn't and mentally timing how long it would take Tracy to climb the three flights of stairs to her apartment. The place was still very bare, no pictures on the walls, nothing colorful or ornamental anywhere. The suitcase she'd never finished unpacking was still under the bed; she kept her underwear in it, rummaging through for something clean to wear every morning, and every morning telling herself she really needed to get organized. It was too late to tidy up now. Tracy was on her way up and there on the windowsill was the coffee press with yesterday's grounds still in it; her cereal bowl from the morning with its souring milk sat in the sink. Her place, visual proof of her unsavory, unsanitary, lonely life, offered no support for this first meeting since Tracy's attack on her at Nabil's a month earlier. She had seen Nabil a few times since—in class, for coffee—his warm matter-of-factness melting away her stiff embarrassment. But the old easy intimacy was gone, and if he was still in touch with Tracy, he kept it to himself.

Her mother had visited a week before, and Megan had done some hasty clean-up beforehand, but she had no knack for it, and her mother had actually teared up when she saw the grimy sink, had gone out to purchase cleaning supplies, and spent a couple of hours furiously scrubbing. You could rent a house with a yard in Newark for what you're paying for this place, she'd commented. Megan shook her head. There was no way of explaining what it meant to be an artist living in New York to her mother, this sheltered and conventional woman with her hovering, anxious kindness, the woman who, at home, put dinner on the table every evening promptly at six—recipes she'd found in women's magazines or on a blog she liked called Neighbor's Kitchen. No way of explaining the exhilaration of finally being in the place where real theatre happens. They had eaten at Stocker's, slept uneasily together in Megan's small bed and, before leaving in the morning, her mother had hidden a fifty dollar bill in the book Megan was reading.

There was a fumbling outside the door, and she went to it. Tracy's eye appeared through the peephole, fishlike, and then she was walking into the apartment. Megan felt a sudden unexpected impulse to hug her, but Tracy's hunched shoulders repelled intimacy, and dislike rose in Megan's throat. She didn't want Tracy in her apartment, or anywhere near her. Tracy's presence had the power to unbalance her already confused life. She nodded toward the table, pushed aside a clutter of mail and notes to herself, and sat down, gesturing toward the chair across from her. Ignoring the gesture, Tracy began walking around the perimeter of the room like a soldier on a mission. She stopped and Megan swiveled her neck to see her face. Still, Tracy hadn't spoken.

What? Megan said when the silence became unbearable.

Tracy shook her head slightly.

Megan's second What? was louder. No answer. Why are you here, Tracy?

A tight resigned smile: The sickness unto death.

Megan stared.

Kierkegaard.

It was too much. The green nails. The absurdly pretentious quote. The sense that something was required of her, Megan—What? Compassion? Wisdom? Understanding?

You're depressed? Megan said.

Tracy smiled faintly again, and again silence followed; in that silence, the passing of time felt almost palpable, a maddening tick-tick-tick, gray wavelets sliding inexorably along the floor beneath their feet and into a gray infinity. She wanted to say, I can't handle this, Tracy. I'm not a therapist. Please go away, but she couldn't speak. Something deeper and darker than she had any way of understanding was happening.

I shouldn't have come, Tracy said at last. I'm sorry I bothered you.

It was Megan's cue. She was supposed to say, No. Stay. Or, Look, it's okay, do you want to talk? Can I make us some coffee? She was supposed to say ... well ... something. But her voice stayed frozen in her throat. Tracy turned, walked back out through the door, and closed it gently: a soft click, silence blooming like darkness in her wake. Megan went back to the table and sat staring at her phone. She should call someone. The sickness unto death, Tracy had said. She should call Nabil. She picked up the phone, and pressed the screen. Within seconds, Nabil's face appeared: Hey, Megan. It's been a while. I've been missing you.

I'm missing you too. Listen, Tracy's just been here. I don't know what it means, but she was acting weird and I'm worried about her.

Weird how?

She came in and just stood there without saying anything and then quoted something about the sickness unto death. I'm just worried about her. I don't know if she's being dramatic or if there's something really wrong.

Okay, Nabil said. I'll come right over. We'll go find her together, okay?

Megan hesitated. I'm not sure she wants ...

She has problems, Megan. Can't you see that? It's like she's got no skin. It hurts her sometimes to talk to other people—even us—to breathe almost, to walk across a room. She's that fragile. But that's where her power comes from too.

She hadn't realized any of this, but when he said it, it felt true, and she wondered at her own obtuseness. Nabil had been watching Tracy closely. Perhaps he loved her, even in her craziness. Because of her craziness.

We're her friends, Megan.

Yes, she said. I know we are. We'll look for her.

CHAPTER THIRTY-ONE

Angela sat at the round table of her motel room, a bottle of Merlot in front of her, no plastic glass. She had checked the directory before leaving New York and found eight Jeffrey Connors in the San Diego area and several more J. Connors, but she hadn't begun making her calls. Somehow she couldn't imagine trying to contact her brother from the stifling metropolis across the continent where she lived, the place where everything in her life felt landlocked and dead, and Stocker seemed to lurk around every corner. He had tried to contact her several times since she'd visited the restaurant with Mark, sometimes drunk and angry, sometimes through conciliatory, pleading texts, but she'd ignored his messages. She didn't know what she felt for him any more, or what she wanted to say. And she liked the idea of her relationship with Jeffrey—if there was to be one—starting under the clean-washed skies of California.

It was evening now, and she'd closed the curtains against the gathering darkness. She extracted her mobile from her purse and set it down on the table, took a long pull from the wine bottle, contemplated the phone. She needed a shower. Maybe she should take one now. Or finish unpacking. She pulled the phone toward herself and checked her e-mail. Downloaded and read an article on fall fashion trends Elizaveta had sent. She had better read it closely, she knew, and be prepared to comment when she got back to Piqué. The leave she'd taken was dangerous. Elizaveta liked her but Angela hadn't exactly been an ideal employee lately, and work was much harder to come by now than when she'd first arrived in New York.

She cradled the phone in her palm. The motel room felt airless and plastic. On the wall opposite her was a square painting of scarlet poppies with dead flat black centers. She heard cars sliding by outside. She was hungry. It might be early evening here in California, but it was long past dinnertime according to her inner clock. She slipped the phone into her purse again and hurried out, pausing to inhale the salt-laden sea air and realize how much she'd missed it. There was a McDonald's across the vast black parking lot from the motel, next to a featureless box store with a sign that said Huge Shoe Sale. Just how huge were those shoes, she wondered, trying to lighten her own mood. But she hesitated as she passed the store's open door thinking it might be fun to go in and play with those cheap, brightly-colored shoes, figure out ways to combine them with the chic, expensive—and highly discounted—stuff she brought home from Piqué. She walked on to the McDonald's window.

Ten minutes later, she set down her greasy paper bag on the table in her room, inhaled the warm smell of meat, and decided that—despite the squirm of hunger in her gut—she wouldn't let herself take a single bite until she'd made her calls.

It was easier than she'd feared. She got a couple of answering machines, and left messages: I guess this is a bit strange, but I'm looking for my half brother who was adopted from Vietnam. He has the same name as you, and I wondered if you might be the same person. If a human being answered, she ran off a second spiel: I don't quite know how to ask, but are you by any chance adopted? A couple of people hung up on her. One man was friendly and said he wished he could help; another wanted to settle in for a conversation and listen to her entire story. Far too many lonely people in the world, she thought, hanging up as soon as she politely could. Another man:

Is this Jeffrey?

Yes. His tone was guarded. He must think she was selling something.

I was wondering if you might be adopted. I think I might be your half sister.

He didn't say anything.

I mean, I'm looking for someone. My brother. My mother Kim came to America after the war and she'd left a baby in Vietnam.

I'm American, he said.

Yes. I'm not trying to ... I mean, I'm an American too. My name's Angela. Kim had me here in the States ...

He hung up.

She had done all she could for the moment, and she had no idea what to do next. It was stupid of her to have come. She sat down at the table and started playing with her iPad. It was completely dark outside now, she only had one bedside lamp lit, and a neon light from somewhere across the street was flashing on and off across the ceiling. She heard the voices of people splashing in the small pool outside the window. On the screen, the heads of hair models silently rotated. Finally, she clicked off the iPad, unwrapped her burger and begin eating rapidly, gulping wine between bites. She needed to hear a human voice, someone saying her name. Perhaps she should call Mark. He could be relied on for pleasant and mildly distracting conversations that skated along the top of things. In New York, he took her to places she could never have afforded on her own, restaurants where the food was interesting in a tip of the tongue sort of way, though it didn't fill your belly. He got tickets for cheeky little off-Broadway musicals that would eventually catch the attention of the *Times* reviewer, move to Broadway and lose their souls. She had no problem with their lovemaking: Mark was skilled and in reasonably good shape. But there was no exhilaration in it. Moving beneath him, head turned to the side, she'd try not to think about the rocking oceanic swells she and Stocker created so effortlessly together.

Mark had no intention of leaving his wife, and that was fine with Angela. Cheryl was smart, charming and undemanding, it seemed. What he wanted from Angela—though he was far too cool to let it show direct-ly—was her urchin appeal and vivid clothes, her Orientalness, her life at the margins of the comfortable world he'd lived in all his life. Stocker was different. Stocker got her. But it was fun to play to Mark's conception of her. It made her feel sexy and interesting. And there were tangible rewards. After their first night together, he had bought her the bracelet with the hand-painted porcelain panels she had shown him that first day at Piqué. The thing was fragile and bright, and so hard to fasten that it must have been created for a woman who had a maid to help her dress. Struggling to put it on, Angela always imagined a Saudi royal.

Her phone buzzed. Stocker. She'd been feeling a little ashamed of taking Mark to Stocker's restaurant, but she didn't want to talk to him now or bear the brunt of his passions and rages. It was a sign of how lonely she felt that she found herself pressing talk.

Angela?

Yeah.

A silence; his breathing was hoarse. He was drunk. Stocker who when she first met him rarely drank. She imagined him like a bullfrog squatting in the middle of his murky kitchen, exuding malice. She said, I can't talk to you right now.

I saw you with that guy.

I said I don't want to talk.

Who was he?

It's none of your business.

Another silence. She could still hear the breathing.

Oh, for God's sake, you sound like a stalker. I was on a date, okay?

You were on a date and you came to my restaurant?

It's a public place.

Angela.

She heard the pleading in his voice. It tore at her and at the same time her irritation began building toward rage. I really can't deal with this, she said.

His voice thickened. You bitch. You goddamn bitch. She couldn't make out most of the words in the guttural stream of obscenities that followed. She knew there was pain behind them, but he was frightening like this. He was saying things like, came to my restaurant, in front of my staff, ate my food with him, ate my food, what were you thinking? And then: What are you trying to do to me?

Stocker, she said, surprising herself, We're done.

Why? It was a howl almost.

We just are. I don't know why. I don't want to see you.

Ever?

I told you I don't know. Sometime maybe. I don't know. Not now. She clicked off the phone.

It rang again almost instantly and she tossed it across the room.

Then she was lying on the motel room bed on her stomach, crying. I need help, she thought. A hand on her hair. A kindly voice. Aunt Tollie had let her stay on the sofa at her house once when she was sick. Why had Kim agreed to that and where had she been? Angela couldn't remember. Aunt Tollie had settled her down, made a thick pea soup with bits of ham in it out of a can, and served it with slices of buttered toast. They'd eaten together on the sofa and then sat side by side, shoulders touching, watching sitcoms on television late into the evening, Aunt Tollie's quiet husband reading his newspaper in an armchair nearby, until Angela's eyes drifted shut. It seemed to her that her head was on Aunt Tollie's cushiony front and then, with no transition, Aunt Tollie was gone and she was alone under a blanket, floating in the peaceful dark. She was seven years old when she came home after school one afternoon to find Aunt Tollie and Uncle Sy had left town. No one had told her they were leaving.

The next morning, she called the front desk to let them know she'd be vacating early and began packing her belongings. It didn't take long; she'd brought nothing but a change of underwear, a dress, tight jeans, trainers, makeup and two pairs of heels. She slammed the suitcase shut and carried it to the door. She was half inside the room and half out when her cell phone buzzed. She realized it was still lying on the carpet and bent to pick it up.

You called me last night. You asked if I was adopted. You took me by surprise. I am. Adopted.

She took in a shaky breath. From Vietnam?

Yes. I was four.

She searched for words.

You said I might be your brother.

Half.

What?

My half brother. My mother was Vietnamese. She had a son with an American GI and he came to the US through the Babylift and was adopted by the Connors in San Diego.

A long pause. She was afraid he might hang up again. Then he said: Your name's Angela?

Uh-huh.

Your mother's name is Kim?

Yes.

I think we'd better meet.

The address Jeffrey Connor had given her was in one of those quiet in-between neighborhoods, shabby but not entirely impoverished—tricycles and toys in some of the yards, a lone and lonely dog barking on the end of a chain, clipped, trash-free front lawns, a plastic wading pool or two and a scatter of kids' toys. Small houses and old cars. Working people, Angela thought, maintaining stable lives but probably only with difficulty. She clicked open the metal gate and walked up the pebbled path to the front door. Before she could knock, it opened. Oh, she thought, it's you.

It wasn't that she knew Jeffrey Connor, just that he seemed oddly familiar, as if she'd known him once before but had somehow forgotten him: a short slim guy in jeans, tight-bodied and powerfully muscled. Dark hair, of course, and a slight slant to his eyes. He might have been handsome if his expression were less guarded and distant. She said, Hi, I'm Angela.

She held out her hand and after a moment's hesitation, he took it. His palm was warm. Flesh of my flesh, she thought. Blood of my blood. She felt a momentary dizziness and wanted to laugh at herself, at the melodrama of the moment. He motioned her inside and gestured toward the living room sofa.

Can I get you something? My wife said to be sure and offer you iced tea.

Iced tea sounds great.

While he was in the kitchen, she looked around the room. The furniture was a mix of the kinds of things you'd pick up at a yard sale or be given by friends or family. There was a large, old television. Everything was clean, preternaturally tidy. Glimpsing the bedroom through an open door, she was relieved to see the bed still rumpled and unmade.

He came in, slid a coaster with a beer logo onto the coffee table in front of her, and placed her glass of tea on it. Then he sat down across from her on a straight-backed chair.

How did you find me?

It was a safe question, she thought, far safer than the one he hadn't asked, What made you want to? Now? After so many years?

She knew how to be entertaining, though she usually preferred being entertained herself. She made a story out of the tedious process, the blind alleys, the frustrations, and the more his silence lengthened, the more animated she became. Meet Angela, she concluded. Girl detective.

He smiled politely. What kind of work do you do?

I'm in fashion. You?

He worked at a supermarket, he said, as a manager. But he was taking online courses in criminal justice.

You want to be a cop?

I want to do something in corrections, maybe work with kids.

She had no idea what to say. After a pause, he asked, Where is our mother?

She's gone. She lived just a couple of hours from here, but she died a few months back. I'm sorry, Jeffrey.

He nodded. His expression gave nothing away.

Here. She handed him the photograph Kim had kept on her altar and he took it and looked at it for a long time. Meanwhile, she studied him, marveling. She was sitting in the presence of her brother, someone she'd always imagined insubstantial as the beings in fairy stories: dwarves and wizards, talking moles and river rats, hissing creatures half-snake, half-human, princes who had been transformed into swans or spirited away by a Snow Queen. Searching for him had seemed absurd, fantastical. Yet here he was, a compact dark-haired man intently studying a photograph. Was his hand shaking or was she imagining it?

Finally, he looked up. Why did you want to find me?

I don't know.

His eyes stayed on her face. She went back to describing the search. She told him about the internet search, the historical society and Gretchen who had sent the package of newspaper clippings, and when she got to the part about the monkeys and the panda bear, he smiled and it felt as if a tightly-closed door had opened just a crack. I was always wanting to see the monkeys, he said. And Caroline the elephant.

Yes. I found her on Google.

They stared at each other. Angela took a sip of the iced tea, sweet and cinnamony with a hint of oranges.

She makes it herself, Kathryn. My wife. He picked up the photograph again. This is my mother? With me?

She knew what he was seeing, and her sense of the gulf between the gentle young woman on the photograph and the crabbed, bitter mother she had grown up with yawned so wide it left her almost speechless. She wanted to protect Jeffrey from the real Kim and give him a mother he could love. She thought of saying, She cried for you. She never got over losing you. But he was still a stranger.

This is me she's holding?

Yes.

She hoped he might say something that would cue her on how to continue, but at that moment a woman walked in. She was flushed, slow moving, very pregnant and lugging a bag of groceries, saying something about how she always forgot to take the canvas shopping bags into the store, that she meant to be virtuous and ended up paying ten cents for paper anyway. Angela saw her brother's face change perceptibly—not that he smiled exactly, but there was a lightening of his previous dark aloofness. He stood to take the bag out of his wife's arms—I carried this to the car, she protested, I think I can get the stuff into my own kitchen—but he took it from her anyway and set it on the counter. Kathy, he said, this is Angela. She turned her thrusting belly toward Angela, came forward with her arms open and, ignoring Angela's hesitation, wrapped her in a hug. Sorry, she said as she stepped back. I'm a bit sweaty. She pushed a strand of fair, flyaway hair away from her face: Wow. You're Jeffrey's sister. You found him. That must be so amazing. Angela smiled because you simply couldn't help smiling at this woman. It seemed Jeffrey had been genuinely lucky.

In the kitchen, Kathy sank onto a chair by the table. Gotta get off my feet. You'll stay for dinner, Angela? It's just frozen pizza. And I'll open some wine for the two of you. We have to celebrate.

Sure, Angela said.

Jeff, would you stick the box in the oven? She turned to Angela: Every time I pull the oven door open, it hits me in the stomach.

A cheerful fount of information, Kathy talked as freely as Jeffrey didn't. The baby was due within the month she said later, sipping a Diet Coke as Jeffrey set the pizza on the table. Which was good because she felt like she was spilling. Or splitting. Couldn't really afford any new clothes, but these she was wearing were coming apart. She was basically a big sack of heavy and sometimes she wondered if the baby was ever coming out. But then she was kind of afraid of its coming out too.

You know, like they say—it's like you're building a great big beautiful sailboat in the basement and you suddenly realize you'll never get it back out through that little door. It'll never fit. She laughed. I was looking at women with kids in the supermarket this afternoon and thinking, hey, those women got those kids out somehow. It's weird to see a six-year-old running around, so big and with those solid legs and arms and all that energy and realize that's what's inside me. That kid was curled up in his mom's tummy once, tiny just like mine is now.

She went on to explain that they had set up a room for their baby; they'd show it to Angela after dinner. They thought they had everything ready but who knows for sure they hadn't forgotten something—We must have, mustn't we, Jeffie?—Oh, yes, it was a girl and she didn't want to be sexist or whatever but she did like pink and she had found the cutest little pink curtains and she couldn't help picking up those frilly dresses to admire everywhere she went even though they couldn't afford them. But she wasn't going to treat their daughter like a doll. She'd kind of hoped for a boy originally ... Well, she herself didn't care either way, but she thought Jeffrey wanted a boy—You did really, didn't you, Jeffie?

I'm good with what we got.

She had three little sisters, Kathy said, so she knew all about diapers and colic, bathtime and mess and babyness and the smell of talcum powder and though they hadn't planned for this one ...

Jeffrey's face tightened. His wife was giving too much away.

... and she had no idea how they'd manage she knew they would. Lucky they both had jobs and she had a month off from hers—but then she wasn't being paid for that month and after that there'd be daycare which was so expensive it'd pretty much eat up her entire paycheck.

Had they decided on a name, Angela asked.

Kathy looked at her husband. Not yet. You know, so as not to jinx anything.

She took a second slice of pizza. Jeffrey's silence was making Angela uncomfortable. She kept glancing at Kathy's stomach, trying to be unobtrusive, but Kathy caught her and laughed. Want to feel the baby? Angela shook her head. You sure? It's your niece. Go on. Let her know her auntie's here. Kathy got up and stood beside Angela's chair, and Angela put a hand tentatively to her stomach, startled by its hardness because everything else about this woman was so yielding and soft. You'll never feel anything that way, Kathy said. She took Angela's hand and pressed it firmly to her front. Wait, she said. Wait. And then, Ah, feel that? Angela didn't and then she did; it reminded her of a bubble bumping up against the glass wall of an aquarium. In her fluid, lightless world, the baby was turning.

Angela stayed a week, spending long days in the motel room and late afternoons and evenings with Jeffrey and Kathy, watching them singly and together. Kathy was openly curious about her and her life: What's New York like? I don't think I could handle the big city. Tell me about fashion. How do they decide what's in and what's out? Once, when they were alone together, Kathy told Angela Jeffrey hadn't gotten along with his adoptive family and she was trying to get them reconciled now there was a baby on the way, but there was a lot of ... you know ... well, water under the bridge ... family history, that kind of stuff. What history? said Angela. Oh, said Kathy, I'm talking too much. And she clammed up.

Then there was Jeffrey. Being alone with him was strange and awkward; he'd simply ignore her, sitting quietly and gazing into space—just thinking, she supposed, or observing something she herself couldn't see. One evening, the two of them were in the living room after Kathy had gone to bed. Angela commented on the weather. He nodded. She asked about work. He said it was fine. His silence was so profound she felt she could drown in it. It seemed supernatural almost, as if his tongue had been stolen by a malignant fairy at birth. She began to fidget. Time was passing and she wasn't any closer to understanding her brother or forming a relationship with him. She might as well give up, go back to the motel and leave for New York in the morning. But she'd put too much effort into finding this man to let it go at that. She tried a couple more polite questions and got a couple more monosyllabic responses. He wasn't going to let her in. Perhaps she scared him because he saw some of his own hardness in her, and also the essential unrootedness. Or maybe he just didn't like her. Eventually, irritated and bored, she pulled out her phone and began sifting through e-mail as if she were alone. A few minutes later, she was startled by the sound of his voice: You want to see the crib I'm making for the baby?

She said she did.

He led her to the back of the house. The crib was on the narrow concrete porch of the house sheltered by the roof's overhang. He pulled off the tarp covering it.

You made this yourself? She didn't know anything about carpentry, but she could see how precisely the crib was put together, the graceful shape, the perfect way the pieces fit. A row of cutout bunnies marched around the base.

It's beautiful.

It needs to be finished.

He picked up a piece of sandpaper and began rubbing it over the wood, and she sank to the ground, her back against the wall of the house to watch. He was still silent, but the atmosphere had changed in some significant but indefinable way. He was sharing something important with her, perhaps the most important thing in his life, and his hands as he sanded, paused, ran a palm against the surface of the crib and sanded again, were sure and precise, as if he and the wood were familiars. She began to understand that his habitual silence wasn't angry or judgmental, but simply the element he needed to exist in to survive. Watching his work with the crib, she remembered children's stories she'd once read—Frog and Toad, Alice, The Little Prince. What was it the Fox had said to the Little Prince about how they could become friends? She pulled out her phone, found the text on Google, and skimmed: "You must be very patient. First you will sit down at a little distance from me—like that—in the grass. I shall look at you out of the corner of my eye, and you will say nothing. Words are the source of misunderstandings. But you will sit a little closer to me, every day … " Angela smiled as she clicked off the phone.

For the next three nights, Angela followed Jeffrey out to the porch after dinner. Sometimes it got boring, watching him work, and she thought about checking Facebook, pulling up a video or just how pleasant it would be to go back to the motel, shower, and relax on the bed with a bottle of wine and something meaningless clattering on the television. It was tiring, waiting for him to speak, wondering if there was something she could or should say. But she schooled herself in stillness.

How long did it take you to make this crib? she asked finally.

A month, mostly on weekends. Want to feel? She stood up and ran her hand across the wood. It was warm and smooth as satin.

This is fantastic, Jeffrey. What a lucky baby.

There's a lot to do besides this. Stuff in her room, and I have to clean up so she can play outside. Angela looked past the roof overhang to the dusty, junk-strewn yard and imagined it like the others on the street: a green patch with a plastic pool and a swing set. She could imagine the child, too, lying on her back in Jeffrey's beautiful crib, swatting with boneless, ineffectual hands at a mobile of the moon and the stars.

Okay. Jeffrey sat down on the floor beside her, pulled a pack of cigarettes from his pocket and held it out. She took a cigarette and he lit it, his face illuminated briefly by the match. Then he settled back against the wall and inhaled deeply. Do you remember anything about Vietnam? she asked eventually.

He shook his head. Just her leaving. A bunch of kids bawling. They told me I tried to climb out the window of the plane when it was taxiing for take-off and it took three people to haul me back into my seat.

It must have been hard.

It was a long time ago.

He drew on his cigarette. Angela stayed still. Time passed.

My adoptive mother and me, we didn't get along, he said, just as Angela was thinking yet again about a warm shower at the motel. There was yelling at our house all the time. It wasn't all her fault. She tried, I guess, but I was wild. And everything was so rigid; rules on top of rules. When I first got here from Vietnam ... there were woods behind the house—not open fields like I was used to with patches of trees at the edge here and there, but dark woods that smelled moldy with all the trees crowding up together. She was always telling me to go play outside, but those woods frightened me and I wouldn't. They smelled like corpses. She wanted me to be an American kid. That's how she dressed me and cut my hair. But I never looked right no matter what she did. When I hit thirteen I blew her off. Started hanging with some messed-up people, did drugs, skipped school, got in fights. One fight was with this fucking asshole—oh, sorry.

No problem. Angela had never heard Jeffrey put so many words together at once before and she didn't want him to stop.

This kid said my real mother was a hooker in Vietnam and I went after him with a brick and opened up his head. He needed twenty stitches. I had a real bad reputation at that school and I liked it. I wanted those stupid white-faced kids to be afraid of me. I got beat up a lot when I was little but not after I worked out and got bigger and got a couple tattoos. She said I was out of control and wanted to throw me out of the house. If she told me come home by ten, I stayed out till midnight; if she said midnight, I was gone two days.

Angela laughed. I thought I was rebellious.

I had a bad drug habit and it cost money so I broke into houses and stole things. Neighbors' houses, people they knew. I stole jewelry, liquor for me and my friends. One time we stole someone's TV. I was so fucking dumb—and so fucking out of it. The thing was heavy and huge and the police caught me trying to climb out a window with it.

She wasn't sure she wanted to hear more about this. Did you think about looking for Kim? she asked.

Kind of. When I was little, I fantasized about how she'd be, like those pretty Asian ladies on television. After a while I was just pissed. What kind of mother would abandon her child? Now it's too late.

He turned to her and studied her face. She said, I don't look a whole lot like her, Jeffrey.

But some?

Yes, some. He nodded and stood up, then poured a rich mahogany stain onto a cloth and began stroking it onto the crib. I'm not sure I'm ready for this, he muttered.

For a baby?

He didn't say anything, just kept working. The smell of the stain was making her faintly sick, and the conversation seemed to be over. She wondered again if she should leave, stubbed out her cigarette and palmed the butt. His voice again, his back still to her, his hands moving slowly across the wood: My American mom made a cake on my birthday every year from when I was a kid. It was a layer of chocolate cookies and a layer of whip cream on top, and more cookies and more cream, and she'd leave it on the counter and after a while the cream would soak into the cookies and they'd look and taste like chocolate cake, regular chocolate cake. I thought it was a miracle, the way the cookies turned into real cake. I used to sit in the kitchen and watch her set them down on the plate, one by one, so precise. Even when we were fighting the whole time, she made that cake on my birthday every year. On my fifteenth birthday ... He stopped, poured out more stain, resumed his long, smooth strokes. Things were terrible, he said after a few moments. We hadn't talked for ... I dunno. A month. Maybe six weeks. I remember walking home from school that day and I was going real slow because I was afraid to go in the house. I knew if my mom didn't make that cake it meant everything was over between her and me for real. I slid open the glass door at back and there was no one in the kitchen, nothing on the counter or the table, everything wiped clean. And a note on the fridge saying there was stuff to microwave if I was hungry. So I took off.

Where'd you go?

Stayed at a friend's house. Bummed around. Did a load more drugs. Took an odd job here and there.

Did you see your parents after that?

A couple times. My dad came looking for me once. He found me in an alley passed out, got me up and took me to a diner for a burger. He tried. They both did. I tried even. But we had nothing to say to each other. And then I went to prison when I was seventeen and they pretty much washed their hands of me.

You were in prison?

What I didn't tell you—somebody died in that robbery with the television.

You killed someone?

Not me. The guy I was with.

She digested that for a few seconds. How long?

What?

How long were you in prison?

Five years. I got a plea. I spent most of it in solitary.

You went to an adult prison?

Yeah. I got in fights. That's why they put me in ice. I attacked a guy in the shower one time.

Why?

He disrespected me.

He ...

You can't let anyone disrespect you.

Angela hesitated, but she had to ask: Being in solitary ... How did you handle that?

I told myself I wouldn't let them break me.

I've heard people in solitary ...

He flashed back: I told you, I wasn't going to let them make me crazy. And then more calmly, Okay. I tried to structure the time. Wash my face at a certain time every day. Do push-ups at a certain time. I read stuff. I watched the History Channel on TV. Sports. I had a lot of time to think. I decided that when I got out, I wanted a real life. I'd had enough. I wanted a life. They put me in a halfway house and I got a job and hung onto it, and kept with it once I was done with that place. I found an apartment. It was hard. I didn't know how to open a bank account. I burned my socks trying to dry them over the gas burner on the stove. After a while I got on an on-line dating service and that's how I found Kathy. She'd posted her picture. I didn't lie to her. We went out for coffee and she knew everything after the first night. Any other girl would have run.

Kathy seems great.

Uh-huh. He stopped working and came to sit by her again. A brief silence. Then: Tell me about our mother.

Angela was torn. She owed him truth—truth was the least she could give him—but truth seemed too heavy a burden to place on this man's shoulders. Kim talked about you a lot, she said. You were the one she loved. I felt I could never live up to you. There was an altar behind the sewing machine where she worked ...

An altar? He was looking out into the dark patch of garden, a second cigarette unlit between his fingers. She addressed his profile: It's something Vietnamese people do when a family member dies or is away. She kept that photo on it—the one I showed you of you and her. And some rice and stuff so you'd never be hungry.

He said nothing.

You were her treasure, Angela said. She wasn't happy with her life or being married to my dad. It was the memory of you kept her going all those years.

He drew in a deep breath that sounded like a sigh. Okay, he said. Thanks.

Later that night, she parked and walked across the asphalt parking lot to the motel, passing the Huge Shoe Sale sign and the people yelling and drinking in the pool. In her room, she made a cup of tea, took a sip, abandoned it for a plastic glass of wine, lay back on the bed and turned on the television. The show was a sitcom in which a teenage girl tried out clumsily for the cheerleading squad and the other girls laughed at her. After she'd talked to her mother, the girl went back and did so well she shamed the snooty, mean girls. Angela watched to the end and then watched a second episode of the same show, and a third. The voices began melding together. Behind her eyelids, she saw her brother's profile, still as stone. She'd wanted to hug him before leaving, but he was too stiff and seated too far away. Still, something important had happened. She opened her eyes. Now the teenage girl was arguing with the head cheerleader right before the game and you could tell she was right. Angela's vision blurred. She dozed, jolted into wakefulness, set her dangerously tilting wineglass down on the bedside table, dozed again. She felt the warmth of Aunt Tollie's cushiony front against her cheek for a fleeting moment and slipped into sleep.

CHAPTER THIRTY-TWO

Jon could smell the sickness when he walked into the apartment after his shift. In the bedroom, Keith was asleep, rolled up in blankets, the pillow clutched in his arms. His breath gurgled; the atmosphere was fuggy with the smell of perspiration. Jon leaned over and touched Keith's side. It felt warm. Heavy and flabby and warm. Keith responded to his touch, shifted, turned slowly, struggled into consciousness and held out his arms. Hi, Jon, he said. Horrible cold. Probably got it from one of the kids at work. I've been getting a lot of colds lately. He started to slip into sleep again, heavy against Jon's front and within seconds the gurgling, phlegm-laden deep breathing began again. Jon hadn't bargained for this. He thought of taking off his clothes and slipping in beside his partner, but the thought wasn't pleasant: The mucusy exhalations, the damp warmth of the bed. He said, I think I'll sleep on the sofa. Keith just flung up his arm to burrow his nose in the crook of his elbow and moved deeper into sleep.

On the sofa, Jon lay staring at the dim ceiling. Saul gone just three weeks, Keith in the bedroom: The place was full of presences. Over several breakfasts, Keith had told Jon about the convention, ideas he had for his own practice, how kids' dentistry was a thing apart and you had to modify everything you'd learned to be effective with kids. He'd joked about a good-looking man he'd seen at the hotel. Safe joking, just to remind Jon that he too had options though he had no intention of exploring them.

And Saul. Jon heard from him more now: periodic calls that reminded him of the gossipy sprawled-across-the-bed chats they'd had in the early days before they'd broken up. And then during Saul's first few months in San Francisco when he'd still call several times a day, walking across a parking lot, waiting for his order in a coffee shop, just wanting to affirm himself, denigrate his rivals, or bitch about his day. Jon had been a sympathetic listener at first—he knew locating to a new city was hard—but after a while he'd put his foot down.

Jon rolled onto his side. The sofa was narrow and he kept one knee out to balance himself; when that got uncomfortable, he turned his face to the sofa back, a hand to his forehead so he wouldn't stick to the expensive leather. He pulled the blanket over him, dozed and woke again to find it had slipped to the floor. He was cold, and the sofa had become intolerably cramped. But he didn't want to face the fug in the bedroom, so he stretched out again, sighing.

CHAPTER THIRTY-THREE

Angela walked into the place as if nothing had happened. Stocker saw her from the kitchen, armored in a slick repellent raincoat, tapping her way along the corridor to the staff room, and all rage and sorrow lifted instantly. He wanted to forget her dinner in his restaurant with a date, the ten days she'd been away, the terrible phone call. He wanted to find her victuals, watch her pull chicken bones apart with her savage quick little fingers, suck at bone marrow, lick thick sweet soup from a spoon. And he also wanted to toss boiling oil at her smug pointed face, that face he could never read. She waved into the kitchen as she passed. Sean saw her and brightened, the Scots smiled, everyone looked at Stocker. He'd been hell to deal with for weeks, not the usual blustering windy hell but viperish and mean-spirited. He'd fired a dishwasher who had a wife and kid to support and left close to tears, and wouldn't reconsider even after both Kenneth and Crystal spoke to him. He didn't respond to Angela's wave, instead turning away and minutely inspecting a row of plates bound for the dining room. There was a thumbprint on one of them, he said. No, said Crystal, coming up behind him, calm and slow. The plate's fine, Stocker. But he called over a commis to wipe the rim.

When he could stand it no longer, he went into the staff room. Angela had settled herself at the table with her back to the door. She wasn't leaning back in the chair and she hadn't pushed off her shoes. Her hands were folded, and she looked demure, almost penitent. Any food for me, Stocker? she said, half turning, the feather earrings swinging in her ears.

The image came to him briefly of her chipped toenails, her leg tossed on the table with the calf slightly flattened. He didn't know how to play this. He imagined his foot connecting with her bony little butt the way it had with Harold's, and was filled with such sudden exhilaration that he almost laughed. But that wasn't what he really wanted. What he wanted was to clasp her shoulders, look into her eyes, and beg her to make it not have happened—her dinner with the gray-suited man in his restaurant, the terrible scene he'd caused in the kitchen, the sex-suffused nightmare of the Den, the fight on the phone while she was in California. He wanted to tell Angela she could do whatever she liked, spit in his face, walk on his back with her sharp high heels, put a dog leash round his neck and lead him through flame—anything but leave him alone in a world she had deserted.

I don't have anything, he said. Not for you.

Aww, come on, it's a restaurant. She was trying to lighten the atmosphere. You must have a few crumbs.

It was all he could do not to cry. Stocker, she began, I'm sorry about what I said on the phone, and he interrupted: You came in with that guy. You ate here with that guy.

Her chin tilted. Why shouldn't I? We're not going anywhere, you and me.

What was she talking about? Where were they supposed to be going? What they were together was nothing to do with sequence or progression. It was about his food in her mouth and Angela sprawling on the bed at night, or prancing naked beneath sliding fabric. The words I love you came into his mind but he hated their insipidity, and besides he didn't know if they were true. When his throat opened, it was a primitive child's cry that came out: Because you're mine.

Please stop it. I thought we could talk like adults.

You said we were done.

Stocker, I'm sorry. I don't know what I want anymore.

You came here to find out?

Oh, I can't stand this. She pushed away from the table, stood up, and walked past him toward the door, and the physical sensation of her passing—her warmth and scent, the movement of the air—made him dizzy.

Okay. We'll talk. Sit back down. He reached for her arm.

Head down, she pulled away from him and kept walking. Without thinking, he was after her. She half turned and he grabbed at the metal feather dangling from her ear and tugged. Angela stumbled backwards and caught her balance, hand to her injured ear, and he saw that the lobe was split cleanly in two. The earring was in his hand, the cursed pigeon feather, with a single drop of blood on the wire. He dropped the thing as if it burned, and Angela went down on her knees to retrieve it. She was at his feet, and when she looked up, he saw on her face the sudden awareness of his physical closeness and her own vulnerability. It was a look he knew to the marrow of his bones. He had seen it hundreds of times on the face of his cringing mother. Angela scootched backwards, hand to her chest. She was afraid of him. Of him, Stocker, her joker, her friend, her frenzied and inventive lover, the man over whom she had always had absolute power. The knowledge ran through his body like an electric shock. Angela was afraid. He had made her afraid. And that meant it was over between them. Finally and definitively. She scrambled to her feet and began lurching along the corridor, feeling blindly for the wall as she went, and he called after her, Angela, Angela, Angela. Please. The alley door opened to the night and closed behind her.

CHAPTER THIRTY-FOUR

Everyone had left the restaurant and the kitchen was deserted. Crystal walked heavily into the staff room to get her coat. Her feet hurt, and that morning she had been through another painful phone conversation with Jennifer about the children. Crystal had asked if she could to bring them to New York and take them to the zoo. She could take the older but not the younger, Jennifer said. Coral was too little to be away for a whole afternoon. Crystal's hand shook as she held the phone, but the important thing was not to raise her voice, to sound placid and reassuring. Sure thing, sugar, she said. But I think Coral wants to come too. I think she'd love it. Jennifer didn't answer. After a second, Crystal realized her daughter had momentarily abandoned the phone and now there was a child's voice at the other end: Hi Grandma. Hi, Crystal said, adjusting her tone. Madison? Maddie? I was just telling your mom I'd like to take you to the zoo here in New York. There's an elephant that you can feed peanuts. He'll just reach down his big old trunk and take that little peanut right off your hand. Maddie? The child said something incomprehensible, and Jennifer was back. You'd need to get her home by five, Jennifer said. Can you do that?

The thing is, Crystal said carefully, It's just ... I think Coral would want to come too.

Did you tell her about it?

No, but when she sees Maddie leaving ...

I won't have her away from me for a whole afternoon until she's at least five.

Okay, Jen. However you want it. You're her mom.

That's right.

It felt like a high-stakes negotiation at the United Nations, the maneuvers, the feints, the relinquishing of this thing in order to secure that other. Finally, they agreed on a plan, and Crystal hung up, happiness and sadness so mixed in her mind that she didn't know which predominated. Now, coming into the staff room, she felt a deep fatigue. Why was it always so hard talking to Jennifer? Would she be paying penance forever? Still, she'd have Maddie with her Sunday and with any luck they'd have a good time together and Maddie would want to see her again and little by little ... well, she didn't want to get ahead of herself or jinx anything.

Sean was sitting at the table. She saw his outline in the dim light, his slumped shoulders and the illuminated flyaway halo of his hair. She wanted to take those bent shoulders in her hands and gently straighten them. What was it about Sean that made everyone so protective toward him? Was it the permanently fuddled look? Or the sense of innocence he projected? Whatever it was, she'd noticed it affected even Stocker. Sean, she said softly, not wanting to startle him, Sean, I'm turning on the light.

He made a small sound of assent.

Can I make you a cup of something? Coffee? Tea? I'm having tea. I could dish up some of Stocker's stew.

He shook his head.

She sat down at the table, pulled out a cigarette and held the pack toward him. He shook his head again. She pulled smoke into her lungs, exhaled, said, It's good to sit down. My feet are killing me. So. Sean. What're your plans? What'll you do when you get out of here tonight?

He looked surprised. Watch television. Sleep.

No parties? No girls? Teasing.

He flushed. No.

She knew so little about him. She'd noticed that he'd adjusted to

Stocker's kitchen, found his pathways through the customary melee, and that when no one paid any visible attention to him, his hands stopped shaking and he could peel a potato in long, smooth, clean strokes. But what did he think about? The heavy, dark fall of Angela's hair perhaps; his feelings about Angela were transparent.

Crystal allowed several minutes of silence to go by. Eventually she said, There's a girl comes to the restaurant sometimes who wants to be an actress.

Sean nodded.

She's lonely, Crystal said. It's hard for her. This place eats people alive.

Stocker's?

The city.

I guess. His head drooped. He seemed to be intently contemplating his curled fingers.

Crystal could have been irritated but she wasn't. She didn't mind silence from Sean. She smoked, sipped her tea. This kind's supposed to relieve tension, she said. I could use a bit of relief. I talked with my daughter today.

He looked up.

She's thirty, married, lives in New Jersey and has two little kids.

She's lucky. You're a nice mom.

Crystal laughed. I'm afraid that's not how she sees it, Sean.

Now his eyes were on her, and she noticed the soft gray-blue of his irises.

I wasn't a very nice mom when she was growing up, Crystal said. I'm trying to make up for it now. His silence seemed to draw her thoughts out of her. It's like her husband thinks I'm the devil. When she hit her twenties we started getting along a little bit again, her and me. We did those mother-daughter things together—shopping, movies. She went to college and I bought her clothes and helped with money when I could. But then she married and her husband made it clear he didn't want me around, and now I guess she doesn't either. Crystal pulled out her phone to show Sean a couple of photographs: Madison holding up a tooth and grinning wide to show off the gap in her mouth, Coral at a table in a burger joint watching intently as Jennifer poured ketchup onto her plate.

They're pretty.

Crystal drew on her cigarette. You're missing Angela? It was just a hunch, but the minute she said it, she saw how true it was. Sean seemed to shrink into himself at the sound of the name. She reached over and stroked his arm and he started at her touch, then relaxed. These things are hard, she said, her hand still on his arm. You have a girlfriend in high school?

He shook his head. Angela ... He couldn't frame the words. His face was flushed. She's beautiful. He—Stocker—wasn't nice to her.

Crystal laughed. Sometimes she wasn't very nice to him either.

How lonely he must be, Sean, lonely in some profound existential way. And Stocker was grieving too. He had been mean and morose for a while now. The night before he'd sat with her at this table going over and over his last encounter with Angela, how he hadn't given her any food and he wished he had, how she'd walked out of the staff room before they could really talk about anything, and Crystal sensed there was more to the event than he was admitting. What should he do? Stocker asked her. He'd tried calling, but Angela never replied and now the number didn't even work. He had been to the fancy place where she worked, but when she'd seen him standing outside, she just mouthed the word No and turned her back.

This stuff is complicated, Crystal said to Sean now. People like Angela ... You can't get inside their heads. You can't lay claim to them. They exist independently. They make a sharp impression on the world but the world doesn't leave much impression on them. You'll find someone eventually, Sean, someone your own age—and as she spoke, she tried to see how that might happen. She imagined him with someone slow and sweet, perhaps a girl with a disability of some kind. A life spent entirely alone—a life like hers now—was too heavy a penance for Sean's small sins.

You will, I know, she said, convincing herself, stubbing out the cigarette decisively. This is a beautiful world, and God wants us to enjoy it together.

CHAPTER THIRTY-FIVE

Stocker stood by the alley wall, holding a plate of broken egg yolks, calling for the cat. He used to take Angela up against this wall, and he still got stiff thinking about it, sadness spreading from his groin to his belly. No more Angela. Someone else was probably flirting with her, maybe poking her, while he stood here like an idiot calling, Hey, kitty. Hey, kitty, the night alive around him, a hawk sailing the sky, circling, searching for prey. God help those tender kittens if they'd already ventured out into the world. The cat should have been sliding against the wall toward him by now, but she wasn't. She was used to coming to Angela. She didn't come to him.

Over the past week, he'd endured levels of misery he'd never known existed. His life was drained of color, his cooking lost its soul. Whatever impulse had kept him chopping, stirring and tasting all these years, cracking eggs and smooshing garlic under his thumb, the joy he'd taken in the sheer wetness of water and the slickness of grease, the sight of a sauce slowly thickening around a circling wooden spoon—all these things had deserted him.

His kitchen, the nexus of myriad threads—the Bluetooth that linked Harold to his mother; the mutual agreements and understandings among the cooks: you move against the wall and I'll squeeze through here, I'll open the oven door, you slide in the hotel pan; the hierarchy; the respect and the joshing; the Puerto Rican kid who manned the old dishwasher with its spurts of scalding hot water—the balance of his kitchen was out of phase and all its rhythms broken. He half smiled, thinking about Fuzzy Bunny's sad, mutilated bits of vegetables: With Harold gone, Kenneth and the others had redoubled their efforts to bail the kid out, chopping away behind Stocker's back as if they thought he wouldn't notice, when in reality he just couldn't bring himself to challenge them. Chopping, that humble, stupid, repetitive chore, was at the base of everything he accomplished in that kitchen.

And then, a couple of weeks ago, Harold had returned. He had simply walked into the kitchen, knife case in hand as if nothing had happened, and silently stationed himself in front of a cutting board. Without saying a word, Stocker had approached the bags and boxes of produce stacked against the back wall and toed a bag of onions over toward Harold's feet. Harold looked at him and placed the Bluetooth slowly and deliberately in his ear. Then he slid out his chef's knife, selected an onion and set it on the board. Within seconds the onion had been reduced to a pile of small, translucent squares. Remembering, Stocker almost laughed aloud, and for a brief moment his despair lifted.

Angela. His mind kept returning to her. He couldn't get the memory of her clitoris out of his mind, the way it felt between his fingers. And the way she bit his shoulder when he was inside her, the smell of her saliva on his flesh, the way she jerked against him like a skinny, electrified monkey—it had taken him a few sessions to realize that the electrified jerking and the visceral sounds she made, pulling him closer and closer, represented pleasure. Before Angela, he'd liked being with fat women, the sheen of sweat over a large curved flank, the vastness and undulation. A fat woman was a heaving sea in which you could lose yourself. But Angela with her heartbreaking child's body and small hard breasts, the hollow between her hipbones where he lapped like a ravenous creature at a pool of bright clean water, she was something else. And nothing in that image of gentleness and cleansing could prepare him for the jolting fury of her response when she became fully aroused, the hoarse, angry cries as if she were killing something or being killed, the fierce energy of her flailing limbs. At those times, she was all hunger, all wanting: Come into me. Lose yourself in me. And he did, and when he did, he returned again and again to the road that separated his bitter childhood from the life he lived now, the road he'd walked after killing his father.

After a few minutes of calling and searching, he began exploring the alley. He found the cat lying on her side on the grass at the verge, stiff, her starved mouth open in a soundless meow. Perhaps she'd been hit by a car—or a person—and staggered here to die. Perhaps it was hunger and disease that got her. Stocker wasn't usually squeamish, but he didn't want to touch her. He remembered a rusted old spade leaning against the building, went and got it, stared down at the stiffened body, the once jet-black fur now brown and dulled with dirt. He thought about how he used to run his hand along the cat's side while she was alive, sunken with hunger but warm and soft, and images came crowding in from documentaries about famine and drought: cracked earth and stunted crops, cattle dead in the fields. Cherry, oh, Cherry. The peacefulness and darkness of the barn where she slept. Children with potbellies, huge eyes, teeth protruding from fallen-away faces. Food crammed in by the tiny fistful at feeding stations in Somalia, in Ethiopia, in Afghanistan, because of the child's raw terror that the food might be snatched away and there would never be more to follow.

He raised the cat on the spade awkwardly, the body slipping, unexpectedly heavy. Her head rolled over to the side, inanimate, clunking like a piece of wood. Obscene the transformation from life to death. No words he could summon up could do it justice. He carried the corpse to the side of the alley, and shoved it into the tangle of weeds and overgrown grass there. The river flowed by within earshot, filthy, rotten with chemicals, condoms and shit. The long grass swayed and bent over the cat. Ants scuttled. The maggots were already at work on her, he guessed, on the side that had been on the ground. He hadn't wanted to turn her over and look. He remembered how Angela had insisted he feed the cat when they were first together, how they'd bickered and flirted over the idea, and the way the cat had wolfed the food down, sucking it into her body in convulsive gulps, hunching her back to make space above her ribs. He turned away and began walking to the door, then turned back. It wasn't enough that the cat was hidden by tall grasses. There should be earth over her too, she should dissolve into earth. That transmutation would represent the only possibility for—not salvation, that was too grandiose a word for this poor scraggly creature, but something having to do with salvation, with gentleness and caring. He started to dig, but the soil was flinty. He wedged in the tip of his spade, couldn't make it penetrate, stomped on the top with his full weight and finally stood on the spade and rocked back and forth. He managed to dislodge some pebbles and cindery soil, and he tossed this scant spadeful over the cat, and then a second. She'd disappear eventually as if she'd never existed, this hungry little ghost, this creature who had never been anything more than a shadow among shadows. Her hidden kittens would cry themselves into famished silence and eventually their brittle skeletons—like hers—would dissolve into dirt.

He stood over the makeshift grave, head bent, for several minutes, wiping his nose with the back of his hand, remembering.

He was fifteen, coming home from school, and as he traversed the back path to the kitchen, he found himself already clenching his fists. Once in the doorway, his eye was caught by the plastic plates and cups jiggling on the table, and he felt his father's loud voice grating against his skin. His father was leaning over the table like a looming comic book villain shaking with rage and making the cups jiggle while his mother cowered by the side of the stove, whimpering, No, no, no, Henry. His father moved fast and sudden—No—and Stocker heard the thud of his fist connecting.

Stocker didn't love his mother, or if he did that love wasn't available to him. Once he reached his teens, he thought of her with nothing but hard contempt. She was weak, but she was vicious too. She never protected him from his father: he'd thought for a long time that she was just afraid but finally realized that she just didn't care enough. The woman was utterly self-obsessed and endlessly sorry for herself—with reason, he thought now, dear God, with reason—but her self-pity created a force field that repelled pity from others. When he'd been beaten, she'd kneel beside him sobbing and put damp, warm cloths on the bloody places—but it was clear it was herself and not him she was sobbing for. There was a time when he'd responded gratefully to her touch, tried to nestle his head against her front, whispered mama, but as he got older, things changed. He was only ten when she started looking to him for help, expecting him to place his own body between herself and harm. He was small but stocky, and already beginning to feel the power in his bunched-up fists—but it was a power he hated, an ability to inflict hurt he associated with his father. Still, for many years he did as expected when she was threatened—so afraid the first few times that he peed on the floor—and even felt a tiny curl of pride in his role as protector. Once she'd escaped and locked herself in the bedroom, he'd take the beating himself.

Now, standing in the alley over the nameless cat's grave, he saw how small and pathetic they were, these once all-powerful people who had stolen his life and turned it into a haze of sadness, confusion, and bitter aloneness.

But that day, in that chaotic, banging kitchen, he took in the scent of the bacon his mother had been frying in the heavy black skillet. He didn't want to rescue her. He wanted nothing to do with her. He hated her servility, the theatrical way she knelt on the floor and clasped her hands. He was sick of the way the ordinary horror of their ordinary days repeated and repeated, like a punishment being slowly etched onto his skin, endurable at first, but penetrating further and further, inexorable, inescapable, through skin, through flesh, until it pierced bone and entered marrow. He was sick of being the poor abused kid other people whispered about without ever intervening. Over the years, a teacher or two had asked about his home life, but while he recognized the impulse to help, he'd never dared take advantage of it. He imagined that if he opened his mouth to tell anyone about the rottenness at his family's core, he would vomit out the years of rage and hurt in an unstoppable flood of green-black bile. The kind teacher would turn away, disgusted. But this stinking bile was him, his very self. Emptied of it, he'd shrivel into nothing. So he held his body together, pinched in his sides and made himself impermeable.

His mother fell against the stove, and Stocker placed his hand on the handle of the skillet. It was hot, but he didn't react to that, just lifted the thing, bracing his wrist against the weight, and stood motionless for a long moment before bringing it down against the back of his father's head. There was a hollow thumping sound and his father fell forward to his knees then, slowly, face-first onto the floor. His mother, his treacherous mother, crawled over to her husband who managed to raise his head an inch or two from the floor and sputter out a string of strangely-gurgled, half-swallowed epithets. She began to pray, fast and frantic: Holy Mary, mother of God, pray for us sinners now ...

Stocker put the skillet back on the stove, centering it carefully on the burner, and turned off the gas. Ignoring his gibbering mother, he left the kitchen. It was quiet in his parents' bedroom and the noise of their struggle seemed a long way away. He slid the wallet from his father's jacket pocket and extracted the money it held—a twenty, three tens, a five, some ones—then tossed it to the floor and went downstairs. Walking through the kitchen to get his own jacket from its peg by the door, skirting the tableau his parents now made—his mother holding, or attempting to hold, his father's slippery head on her lap while he still gurgled curses—he picked up a piece of bacon that had fallen to the floor and shoved it into his mouth.

The air outside was a blessing against his face as he breathed a goodbye to the chickens pecking on the grass and the rows of new green lettuce his mother had set out earlier. He walked past the shed where Cherry had kept him quiet company over so many bitter nights, steadily, as if he knew where he was going. When he got to his pond, he sat down on a large smooth stone at the rim, put his head between his legs and vomited into the dirt. Eventually, he looked up, wiping his mouth with his forearm, and took in the bright yellow narcissi marching toward the water, the cerulean sky and the frogs' pulsing and eternal serenade. The image came to him of his father's head—he had avoided looking at it directly as he stood in the kitchen, yet now he saw it vividly, the jet-black hair, the blood throbbing up at the roots. He began to laugh. He stayed where he was for a while, sitting on the stone, still laughing, before finally pulling himself up, brushing off the mud as best he could, and walking on.

He had wanted to hit his father again. After that first blow, his mother had ceased to register in his mind as anything more than a crawling, moaning nuisance, an injured bug creeping along the floor toward her broken husband. To this day, the image visited him whenever someone dropped a lobster to the floor of his kitchen and he watched the thing scuttling from side to side in a frantic search for safety. He felt a vague, disinterested desire to kick her, but his focus was riveted on his father. He thought fleetingly of the fat, kindly cook behind the counter at Skeeter's, the eggs and sausage sizzling in his frying pan, and the gnawing hunger the smell always roused in him. He wanted to grab the skillet, raise his arm and bring it down again on his father's skull, again and again until he'd hammered the raging, drunken brain inside into mash.

Why didn't he? It wasn't any compunction that stopped him, not the slightest wisp of tenderness or love. Nothing he could remember coming from that prostrate furious wriggling form invited such a feeling. It wasn't fear either. It was that his breathing had started to even out and his body was taking over, telling him the spasm had passed and he should leave.

And besides, he was pretty sure his father was dying.

Walking along the road away from his childhood home he'd pulled the head off a stalk of wheat and put the grains in his mouth, chewed them to a sweetish paste. That road, he realized years later, was his River Lethe, the passage dividing past from present and life from death—only he had crossed from death to life, a journey granted to very few. Life meant going forward; if he looked back, he'd become dust. He didn't know it then, but he knew now, standing over the cat's grave in his alley, that he was walking toward freedom, toward his life's work, toward his kitchen. And also toward Angela, in whose body he reliably found the terror and exultation of that long-ago road. But Angela was lost to him now, and he couldn't stop himself from doing the dangerous, the forbidden thing: he was looking back.

He wished he had a prayer for the cat, but he had no one to pray to. He set the spade down in its place by the wall and went inside.

CHAPTER THIRTY-SIX

One evening, Megan's phone rang. She answered to an unfamiliar voice. I'm Grace Price, the voice said. I'm sorry to trouble you, but I've been so worried. It took Megan a minute. Oh, she said, You're Tracy's mom. Yes. Sorry. I should have said first off. I'm Grace Price, Tracy's mom. She talked a lot about you and Nabil. I haven't heard from her in a month. Her phone isn't working. Me and her dad came to the city last week and went to her place and she wasn't there. The super said she was gone. I understand you're her best friend.

Her best friend. The phrase felt like a weight on Megan's chest—and also it wasn't true: she had known Tracy no more than a few months. But Tracy had come to her apartment four weeks ago needing something from her, and she had remained silent, leaving Tracy to walk out alone into the cool fall day. It was true she and Nabil had tried to contact Tracy almost immediately afterwards, tried for several more days, had called and called again until they found the phone was disconnected, walked the streets near Tracy's vacated apartment, eaten at the burger joint she liked, gone to the Cloisters because she sometimes spent a Sunday afternoon there. But her best friend? Megan didn't even particularly like Tracy, except that, yes, despite everything there had been a kind of troubling kinship between them. It wasn't just that she and Tracy were passionate about theatre and both loved Nabil, it was that Tracy had become an essential part of her reality and everything about her was etched deeply into Megan's consciousness: the faint brown hairs on her arms that embarrassed her so much she wore long sleeves even on stifling days, her pallor, the scent of her shampoo. In her absence, Tracy had haunted Megan's dreams—Megan never remembered the substance of those dreams but she'd awake to a sense of Tracy's presence, heavy as a life-and-breath-sucking succubus.

Grace Price was still talking. Always, she was saying, since she was a little girl ... We tried so hard to help her. She was angry all the time and she'd lash out at me—me mostly. She was nicer to her brother and her dad. We tried everything, me and Bruce. Therapy. Drugs. The doctors told us she was struggling with depression, but we knew that. Tracy has always struggled with depression ... The light voice ran on and on, desperate and confiding. Depression was such a pat and ordinary word, Megan was thinking. It had no meaning in the face of Tracy's strange otherness, the unease she habitually created and inhabited, the persistent sense that there was something dark and icy at her core. Meaningless also because of the uninhibited joy Tracy was sometimes capable of—the word "joy" surprised Megan even as it surfaced in her mind, but the minute it did she saw how fitting it was. No one else she'd ever known could be as joyful as Tracy, as lost in the ecstatic moment. She saw Tracy putting a spoonful of coffee ice cream to her lips, her entire being focused on the tip of the spoon, closing her eyes to savor the taste. Tracy skittering along the ice on the afternoon they'd all visited a skating rink and falling, and then laughing so hard—that rough-edged, full-throated laugh—that she fell back helplessly every time Nabil and Megan tugged her upright. Was that a sickness, the sickness unto death? Tracy's intensity and sheer aliveness? The way she expatiated on topics she obviously knew little about, laying down her opinion as if self-doubt were impossible even as her hands shook? Tracy didn't bend with events. There was no suppleness or fluidity to her. But she went deep. Megan saw her absorbed in a movie, tears leaking as if she were melting into the scene. Sitting motionless for long minutes after listening to a favorite piece of music and shushing furiously if Megan or Nabil seemed about to break the spell by speaking. Megan thought about the girl in the film Tracy had described, moving through a dark forest like some blind underwater creature, the crack of a tree branch against the side of her head and then the silent sliding fall. I don't want to bother you, Grace Price was saying—the voice had been buzzing in Megan's ear for quite a while now without pause like the hum of a hovering mosquito—but we haven't been able to reach her and Tracy has these episodes ...

We've been looking, Mrs. Price. Megan said, and I promise we'll keep looking. And keep you posted. I'm sure Tracy's fine.

Thank you. Mrs. Price was crying now. Thank you, Megan. I know if anyone can help it's you and Nabil. She talked about you two so much.

A few days after the phone call, Megan was walking along Broadway when she saw Tracy sitting in a corner coffee shop. It took her a few seconds to take in the fact that it was Tracy—she had already walked past the shop—but when she returned and peered in through the window, she saw it was indisputably Tracy, wearing a long-sleeved, high-necked black sweater and sitting at a table with her coffee and a book. She looked up as Megan pushed through the door, her expression remote and unchanging. We've been looking for you, me and Nabil, Megan said. We miss you, and we were worried. So's your mom—she called.

She hovered by the table, unsure if she ought to sit down.

No need to worry. I'm a big girl. Tracy's voice was as flat as ever. She was pale, though her eyes were bright, and that small habitual smile— contemptuous and self-protective—played on her lips. I just needed to be by myself. I needed time to think.

You're okay?

I'm going home tomorrow. My parents found me and they're taking me home. Her hand shook slightly as she picked up her cup. No need to stay and talk, Megan. No need for you and Nabil to worry any more. I'm done here. I'm leaving. My New York adventure is over.

CHAPTER THIRTY-SEVEN

They were going out to dinner, a place near Keith's practice with a dessert menu Jon had been wanting to check out, and Jon was sitting in Keith's waiting room. A young woman was filing her nails, and through the door, which was slightly ajar, Jon could see Keith bent over his dentist's chair, solid and reassuring in his white coat, and also the top of a child's head. He's terrified, the woman said, looking up, but Dr. Asher is so good with him. Jon nodded, then pulled out his worn paperback copy of The Power and the Glory. He was on a Grahame Greene kick: "He had the kind of dwarfed dignity Mr. Tench was accustomed to," he read, "the dignity of people afraid of a little pain and yet sitting down with some firmness in his chair." An odd coincidence to be on this exact passage here, seated in Keith's waiting room. He'd have to read it to Keith over dinner. Keith's jovial voice came through the door. He was telling the boy that his teeth left their assigned places every night, tumbled out, and rushed to meet elsewhere in his mouth and play with each other. Then they rushed right back to where they were supposed to be before the boy could wake up in the morning. Try fooling them, Keith said. Try lying very still and pretending to be asleep and you might feel them playing. No, said the child in a big surprised way that indicated he knew bullshit perfectly well when he heard it but still wanted to believe. Really, said Keith. The voices stopped and the drill began whining. Uh-oh, said Keith. I think I see something in the back of your mouth. Right there. Oh, wait. It's a tiny stegosaurus. How did that get in there? Look, I'll hold up the mirror so you can watch it while I'm drilling. Can you see it? No? Look closer. The kid giggled.

He told him to hum real loud last time, said the mother to Jon. He said the vibration from the humming made the drill work better. It's amazing how good he is with kids.

Jon smiled. I've heard about the singing trick.

That's why we decided to keep coming to him, despite, you know.

Despite?

You know, despite the HIV thing. Jon stared at her. Oh, you didn't know? I thought it was okay to mention since he wrote all his patients a couple weeks ago. He said he thought we should know, but it's safe with the precautions he takes. He even invited us to check out his status with his doctor if we had concerns. I know some people left—and we thought about it—but Patrick loves him.

Keith came out sliding his white jacket off his shoulders, a solid picture of health and stability. The mother smiled at Jon—a sort of muted smile—he could tell she was afraid she'd said too much—collected her son and turned to leave with him. Could there really be a stegosaurus? the boy was asking as they walked out into the hallway. I mean really, could there be? Jon stepped back as Keith moved to embrace him, but Keith didn't seem to notice. I'm starving, he said. Jon nodded. They left the building together and fell into step on the street outside, Keith apparently oblivious to Jon's silence. Sweet funny kid, he said. I want one of those someday. It was a relief when they reached the restaurant and were shown to their table.

Keith perused the menu, mused aloud about what to order, and finally said, You're very quiet tonight, Jon.

I didn't know you were so whimsical.

A waiter in a maroon shirt and slim tie approached the table and Jon waved him off. Give us a minute.

Keith laughed. You mean with the kid? There's a lot about me you don't know.

Like that you have AIDS.

The smile froze on Keith's face. Seconds passed. Okay. Keith took a long audible breath. I don't have AIDS. I'm HIV positive. It may never progress to AIDS. You know you're not at risk, right? We've been careful. And the thing isn't active, might not be for years. My virus load is almost non-existent. I could live to be eighty.

He paused. I just found out last month. I asked about the regulations when I was at the convention and then checked with the state board when I got back and it's okay for me to keep my practice as long as I take all the precautions. I've been trying to figure out how to tell you, I wanted to tell you. I'm on the drug—there's just one pill you have to take now; it's amazing how far they've come with treatment—and we can make sure you're protected. Jon. We've always used protection.

How do you know it's not active? You had that cold that wouldn't go away and lasted weeks.

I told you—the numbers. Really. We're okay.

We're not okay. Not if you can lie to me about something like this.

I didn't lie.

Jon stood up. Your silence was a lie. There was a tall gray-silver cunningly twisted candleholder in the middle of the table. Jon seized the thing, held it for a moment assessing its weight, then sent it crashing into the thick glass tabletop where a zigzag crack began slowly spreading. He said, You can pay for that. He was half aware of Keith's white face and frozen immobility, the waiter running over, but he couldn't let that into his consciousness. Shaking with rage and revulsion, he walked out of the restaurant.

Minutes later, Keith was running after him. Breathing heavily, he seized Jon's arm. Jon. Don't. Please.

You've got AIDS? You've got fucking AIDS? Talk about a cliché.

It's not a cliché. It's an illness. It's an illness that could take my life.

Jon pulled his arm from Keith's grip. Go back inside and tell them we'll pay. I'll pay. Then you can come round to the apartment and pack.

This is ridiculous. We need to talk. We haven't even talked.

One hour to pack. The voice emanating from Jon's throat wasn't his own. He felt like a character in a play—Angelo, perhaps, in Measure for Measure, stiff, self-righteous, black-clad, upright. And hypocritical. He didn't want to be Angelo, but he couldn't stop. He felt possessed.

Jon, I wanted to tell you. I was afraid. I was afraid you'd leave me.

How right you were.

Jon pulled free, walked away fast, then began running. Block after block, stumbling forward over his own pounding feet, breath coming hard, trying to outrun thought. Keith had AIDS. Sickness and dying had invaded his life in the shape of Keith's comfortable, familiar person and he wasn't prepared. He had no idea how to cope. He tried frantically to remember when they'd last made love. It was true they'd always used protection. But there was kissing; sometimes they went down on each other. Was any of that dangerous? Was Keith going to die? Was he? For all his air of world-weary, seen-it-all sophistication, Jon hadn't seen much dying in his life. When he was sixteen his grandfather—by then very old—had collapsed at his bench in the middle of the night, and a few days later there had been a funeral. Jon had been afraid to enter the church. He had stood outside the doorway for several seconds, trying to reason with himself. He desperately wanted to see his nagypapi's face again, to say goodbye, and with equal desperation he didn't want to see him dead. He pushed open the ancient wooden door, passed under the thick stone arch and into the cool shadow of the interior, feeling the uneven flagstones under his feet. When he reached the dais holding the coffin and looked down into it, he was filled with relief. This wasn't his nagypapi, his odd, bent, obsessive, funny, wise little nagypapi. This was bone and skin, leavings and dust, an empty carapace harmless as a Halloween joke. His nagypapi was gone. Elsewhere. That was all that had happened. Nothing huge and earth shattering, just an absence where there had for so long been a presence. Later, he asked his grandmother, almost overnight shrunken and diminished, her chestnut hair dulled into gray, for his grandfather's cigarette case, the one from the Hungarian baroness. She searched it out and gave it to him, weeping and showering kisses onto his face as she did so. Now he slowed his run, slid his hand into his pocket and felt the worn smooth sides.

Another frightening and portentous doorway came to mind as he ran, feet thudding on the sidewalk, rain dampening his forehead, the doorway to the hospital room of a friend's lover. Come and see Leon with me, Ted had urged. He gets such a kick out of visits from you. You can always make him smile. The hospital corridors were cold and bright, the walls an institutional cream color. But stepping into Leon's room, Jon found himself in another reality. Ted had transformed the place with ornamental screens, a couple of elegant curved-legged chairs, a dock on which an iPhone played Mozart. Photographs edged each other on every ledge: Ted and Leon on a beach, playing in the waves, Leon mockingly showing off a bicep, their curly-haired black spaniel with his head cocked, the two of them at the center of a group of friends, all holding up celebratory wine glasses. Ted crossed the room and kissed his lover on the forehead. Leon had always been a sensual little beast, Jon remembered, perky and funny, quick with lewd observations that only he could get away with, but now his face was grotesquely swollen and disfigured, too large and heavy for his bony body.

When he saw Jon, Leon hauled himself as upright as possible. Well, he said, a visit from the Prince of Wales.

Jon approached the bed and asked Leon how he felt, trying to make his voice warm and empathetic. He was holding a box of hand-tempered molded chocolates, but he wasn't sure he should offer them. Leon couldn't eat, Ted had told him on the way up in the elevator. Eating hurt because there were sores all along his alimentary canal from mouth to anus.

But Leon glimpsed Jon's present and opened his mouth like a greedy baby robin, so Jon slipped out a disc of chocolate and placed it on his tongue. Leon closed his eyes. Is it okay? Ted asked. Can you taste it?

Leon shook his head. Not really. But I can remember the taste.

Rain was drizzling down Jon's face as he ran or perhaps he was crying. His breath sounded loud in his ears and he could feel the blood pulsing against his forehead. He was remembering what Leon had said to him: This is it, Jon. This is dying. The big scary thing everyone's so afraid of. And it isn't so bad. Well, I mean, it is. Very bad sometimes, night sweats, pain, the feeling my whole body's out of control. But they keep me comfortable and give me pills for panic and depression, and most of the time I'm okay. I can't say how it'll be at the end, but day-to-day this is all there is to it. Just lying on this bed and Ted talking or reading to me, drifting in and out and wearing this gorgeous robe he bought and knowing he'll be around to see me through. Hey, Jon, don't look so solemn. I've got some games here— Scrabble? Monopoly?

Scrabble.

And next time you come, bring champagne to go with the chocolate.

There was no next time. Leon died three days later.

But this wasn't someone else's lover who was sick, it was Keith, and where only this morning Jon's path had been clear and specific, filled with pleasure and potency, now he couldn't see through the gathering murk. Keith, big, solid, cozy Keith shitting uncontrollably or spitting blood or breaking out in pustules, and when that happened how would he, Jon, protect the cleanliness and sanctity of his own body? He stopped and leaned against a wall to catch his breath. That stupid, pretentious, nonfunctioning candlestick at the restaurant, the handsome healthy waiter, they belonged in a different universe altogether than the one he had fallen into now. If

Keith stayed at the flat ... But he wouldn't, he mustn't stay. AIDS devoured you from the inside out, corrupted the blood, rushed through every vein in your body, took a sledgehammer to the immune system. It had to do with vomit, bad smells, daily infusions, pills, injections, nausea. It was completely unpredictable. AIDS could take your eyesight. Your sanity. Or both at once. It hath made me mad, said a voice in his head. I say we will have no more marriages.

Ted had been living with Leon for a year before Leon's diagnosis and he'd been thinking about ending the relationship. Ted was a corporate lawyer, focused and ambitious, Leon a drifting playboy who drank and smoked dope, stayed out till all hours of the night and slept around, and had no idea how to shape a stable life, getting by on his little-boy charm, elfin sex appeal and a wheedling dependency. But once Leon had received his diagnosis, Ted felt he couldn't leave, and over time he became a conscientious and unfaltering nurse. He studied the disease, kept up with therapies on the internet, went with Leon to support groups, and learned all the little tricks, physical and psychological, that might ease his lover's distress—even as his billable hours dwindled and his own life became little more than round-the-clock caretaking. The funny thing was that as Ted rose to the challenge, so did Leon. The closer death approached, the more gentle, peaceful, grateful and loving he became. Nothing in his life became him like the leaving it, Jon thought. And then a host more quotes flooded in: "Thou knowest 'tis common, all who live must die" and "The living and the dead are but as pictures. It is the eye of childhood fears the painted devil." They comforted, these fragments. They were like spars of wood you could cling to in a vast and heaving sea. You are not alone in this emptiness and horror, dead voices whispered. Someone has been here before you.

Jon could see how Ted had changed in the lovingly decorated hospital room, in the quiet tenderness with which he wiped chocolaty drool from Leon's chin. But when he said something about this at Leon's memorial service later, Ted grimaced. I guess. But mostly it was one long gray un-differentiated slog. Time just stopped. You can't imagine how tired you get, how you lose everything you treasure about normal life—just things like a quiet, uninterrupted cup of coffee. I never want to go through anything like that again as long as I live. It was a relief when he died. He paused. But I miss the little shit.

Jon was outside his building now, looking up at the window of his own apartment. There was a light on. He took a deep breath and entered the lobby.

Only a bastard would leave his lover because of an AIDS diagnosis. But Keith wasn't his lover, and he hadn't signed up for caretaking. Besides, Keith's dishonesty excused him. Keith would have to go. Now, while he was still healthy enough to make decisions and take care of himself. Maybe he'd go back to his family or find someone else to love him. He deserved better than anything Jon had to give.

Keith was moving about in the bedroom when he got inside. Neither man called out the usual greeting. He heard the thunk of a suitcase on the floor and Keith came to the bedroom door.

Do you really want me to move out?

Yes.

I squared with the restaurant.

Good.

A pause and Keith went back into the bedroom. Jon stared dully at the wall in front of him. The words kept marching through his brain. Nothing in his life became him like ... He got up and paced. Turned on some music and turned it off. Keith walked past leaving a good distance between them, the dance of avoidance, and set his case on the table. He went into the kitchen and collected some items: his coffee mug. A bottle of the hot sauce he used to spice up everything from eggs to his homey meatloaf. Jon stood aside, observing wordlessly the things Keith had accumulated, milestone by milestone during the time of slowly moving in, slowly becoming ... whatever it was he had become to Jon. And had been until this afternoon. Back and forth, room to room, toothbrush and shaving kit. Underwear. His handful of history books and biographies of famous Americans—those books he started reading and always seemed to fall asleep in the middle of, Jon taking the book from his nerveless hands and saying Time for bed, I think. Cross trainers—Keith was a sporadic exerciser, always making resolutions, breaking them and laughing at himself as he broke them. Polished professional shoes and the worn-down plaid slippers that Jon—who walked barefoot every chance he got—liked to mock: old man's slippers, he called them. Comfortable old man slippers, Keith would retort. Keith began folding his sweatpants, and Jon caught that familiar whiff of him, funky and comforting. Piece by piece their time together was disappearing into the suitcase. Keith's back was eloquent. He knew Jon was watching. He held his silence. Jon heard himself say, Okay. Maybe we should talk.

Still holding his sweatpants, Keith turned.

I shouldn't have blown up like that.

Keith folded the sweatpants and placed them carefully in the case. When he spoke, his voice was quiet as if he were reassuring one of his frightened young patients. I can't stay here and have you afraid to touch me, shuddering when I want to touch you. I can't deal with it. I should have told you, and I'm sorry I didn't, but it's bad enough having this ... this thing without dealing with someone who can't cope. Knowing you're worrying about whether the cutlery's been washed well enough or might still have my spit on it. Whether the rim of a glass is clean. I won't be dirty in your eyes, Jon. I've got this virus in my blood, but I'm still who I am. Keith. Your friend who lives with you.

He'd wanted to say who loves you.

Jon stared at his own hands. Keith went to the bathroom, returned, put his comb and hairbrush into the case, started folding a shirt. We could see how it goes, Jon said. Why don't you unpack?

Keith didn't answer, just kept folding. The silence lengthened. It seemed to Jon an eternity passed. Keith, he said. Seriously. We should at least talk.

Keith stopped what he was doing and sat down heavily. I've been so alone, he said. He put his head in his hands and started to cry.

CHAPTER THIRTY-EIGHT

At seven in the morning, the phone rang and Angela heard Jeffrey's voice. The baby's here. She came last night, but I didn't want to wake you up at three your time. You should come out and see her.

By late afternoon Angela was walking into the hospital room where Kathy dozed against pillows, a tiny red sleeping baby pressed against her formless white breasts. Angela had gone online for airline reservations immediately after Jeffrey's call, paid far too much for a ticket, and phoned Elizaveta to tell her she wouldn't be coming in. I'm sorry, Elizaveta had said, but you were gone last month for two weeks; please understand I need someone reliable. I know, Angela responded. I do understand.

Now she kissed her sister-in-law's forehead and touched the top of the baby's head with a tentative curled finger, then seated herself beside the bed. She had underestimated this woman, she was thinking, been fooled by her softness and slowness, her quiet pleasant manner and breathy chattiness. Now, holding the small, warm, precious creature in her arms, Kathy was in her element, a queen ruling over her domain. And the baby, that scrap of a thing curled like a walnut in its shell, contained multitudes: Angela's life, and Jeffrey's, a long-ago war in another country, a host of clutching, begging relatives, and the unknown GI who was tall and big and powerful and gave Kim and her family rice and candy—what was his name? Angela strained to remember. Chip? Chuck? Chuck had sent a ribbon of DNA blindly into the universe and the result was this child sleeping in Kathy's arms.

Could you? said Kathy. She was reaching for a glass of water, her nightgown sliding down on her shoulder, awkward, not wanting to disturb the baby. Angela swiftly brought the glass to her reaching hand and stood over the pair of them for a second or two. She could feel the warmth of Kathryn's body, see the slight sheen of sweat on her forehead. I'm thirsty all the time, Kathy said. She looked down at the child. I wouldn't let them take her last night. They said I'd sleep better by myself, I'd worked hard and needed my strength, but I couldn't sleep at all when she was in the nursery. I'd close my eyes and see her face—you know how they make these funny clowny little faces, newborns? Angela didn't, but she could imagine. They squint up their eyes, Kathy continued. They yawn with their whole bodies and their heads loll to the side because there's no strength in their necks and they look like little drunks. You do, she cooed to the baby. Don't you? You look like a little drunk. She smiled at Angela.

Aren't you tired?

I've never been so awake. Jeff went home for a quick nap. He's going to be a great daddy.

I know. A brief silence. He says you met him ...

Online. I did. I'd been trying for a year. You wouldn't believe the losers I picked up. They'd hurt my feelings, not call, not be interested, and I'd be upset when I hadn't even liked them or wanted to see them again anyway.

Angela considered that some people might have classified her silent ex-con brother as the worst sort of loser.

Jeffrey hardly said a word that first time. Like he didn't think it was even worth getting to know me. We met in this coffee shop and he just sat. I asked him things. I talked about the weather and said I worked for Walmart which I did then. I was hungry—I'd just gotten off work—and I wanted a croissant or something, but you know, I'm a bit heavy, and I didn't want him to think I was greedy. I wanted to impress him even though I figured nothing was happening between us."

The baby stirred. Do you want to hold her? Kathryn said.

Angela nodded, though she didn't want to interrupt the story, and Kathryn handed the baby over. Angela wasn't prepared for what she felt as the sleeping creature settled against her front, heavy and warm yet at the same time inconceivably light. She held her breath, not wanting to move, staring at the comically pursed-up little face, feeling the silkiness of the baby's few strands of hair with a finger. Dark hair, like her brother's.

Go on, she said to Kathryn.

About the date? Kathryn laughed. Well, you know Jeffrey. I thought he was very handsome but he was so quiet and still and I was chalking the whole thing up as just another shitty experience, wondering what was wrong with me and why I'd even signed on for this dumb dating site, and he said, There's something you need to know—right out. Just like that. I've been in prison.

That didn't turn you off?

I hate to tell you, but my first thought was, Oh, good, it's not that he doesn't like me. It's just that he's been in prison. She laughed. Insecure a bit? I guess you could say I should have run, but I don't know, I guess I was intrigued in that dumb way—here was a genuine tough guy, the kind of sexy badass who scared and fascinated me when I was in high school, a tough guy who liked me—but when I look back I think I was seeing something else in him as well, something I still can't quite get at. You don't get too close to Jeffie—you know that, Angela. At the beginning I'd keep asking what are you thinking, or is everything okay and he wouldn't say anything. He doesn't even like answering when I ask what he wants for dinner. Even now I don't know what goes on in his head. And there's a kind of ... I'm not sure what to call it. Just that you can tell when you're getting too close and need to back off.

Were you thinking he was dangerous?

No, no, no. Not that, even with the prison thing. I don't like violent men—and he doesn't like violence either. He's been plenty violent in his life I know. He was a bad crazy kid. And in prison he had to fight because he went in there so young. But he hates it. It's not what he wants. He just wants peacefulness and maybe some dignity. It's just, you know, you can sense something inside him. Heat. No not heat, more like ashes, cold, gray, dead ashes where heat used to be—and you feel—I kept feeling—that if I loved him enough I could get those ashes to flicker to life again and there'd be warmth. But it had to be the right way or they'd flame up and be out of control. Does that make sense?

Angela nodded. She could see how those early months must have been between the two of them, how the less Kathryn pushed for answers, the more Jeffrey started to love her.

I finally figured it wasn't me talking that bothered him. He liked it. Still does. He didn't ask questions, but he'd listen so intently to just lame, everyday things. I'd talk about how much I liked a kind of soap you can't find any more, or tell him I'd watched a TV show about hoarders and how they got that way, and go on and describe the entire episode just to keep things going, even if all that was going was my own talking, and he'd listen.

Because, Angela thought, what mattered to him was the running on of your voice and the accepting warmth of your presence.

At the beginning, he didn't know how to balance a checkbook or how to dress. He'd only had on prison blues for such a long time and he was awkward in the stores and would buy these baggy, ugly things. I told him he needed jeans that fit because he had a cute butt and he didn't know how to take that. It was a while before I heard him laugh. Just laugh, Angela. Even walking down the street, I'd notice him glancing around like someone might come up behind him; if we went out to eat, he always wanted to sit with his back to the wall so he could see the door.

You know, I think he still loves just being able to walk down the street without anyone asking where he's going. She laughed. And sheets on the bed, and our john having a seat so he doesn't have to sit on cold porcelain first thing in the morning.

How's he feel about being a dad?

He was afraid to hold her at first, but then he did. He held her and said, I never had any relatives before, no medical records, no papers. Now I have her. Blood of my blood. He was in love.

The baby started to mutter and move, and Kathy held out her arms. With some reluctance, Angela handed the child back.

That's your aunt, Kathy crooned as she re-settled the baby on her breast. Your auntie Angela.

CHAPTER THIRTY-NINE

The place was a mistake, Megan realized as soon as she and Nabil walked into the crowded restaurant and heard the clatter of plates, the loud laughter, the multitude of voices—all rising toward a low, metallic ceiling that amplified sound. Grace Price had called earlier in the week, suggesting she bring Tracy to New York for a dinner. I thought it might help her to see you, she'd said. And I want to buy you both a nice meal to thank you for everything you did for us.

Megan noticed someone waving, but it took her a second to recognize Tracy as one of the two large, soft women seated side by side against the back wall. Tracy's face was puffy and custard white, her body pillowy. Still waving, Grace Price rose and then enveloped each of them in turn in her arms. She's looking forward to seeing you, she said quietly. Tracy half rose too, very slowly, and then sighed and sank back into her chair, deflated. She remained silent while Nabil, Megan and her mother scanned menus, discussed options, talked in generalities, ordered food. Grace Price kept the conversation going, light and determinedly bright: How's the acting? Are you finding jobs? What do you guys do for a living if you don't mind me asking? They answered dutifully.

Megan tried not to notice as Tracy stabbed ineffectually at a piece of fish, misjudging the distance to her plate, finally speared a morsel, raised the fork to her lips and sat perfectly still as the fish began to flake apart and fall. Silent tears rolled down her face. And all the while Grace kept talking, desperately talking, creating a skin of conversational normalcy over a gaping wound. And you, Nabil, she said. I hear your father's a professor? What does he teach?

Tracy left the table to go to the bathroom, and Grace leaned toward them. I know it looks bad, but she's doing better, she said. I thought it might cheer her up to see you. It's the medications causing all that puffiness and slowing her down—it's just temporary—we're still trying to figure out the dosages. Everyone's hoping she'll be able to come back to New York next year. She still wants to act, and she's so talented. She is talented, isn't she?

Yes, said Nabil. She's phenomenal.

It was a relief to walk out into the street afterwards, feeling the autumn heat that had been held in all day by the buildings slowly fading and Nabil's hand resting gently between her shoulder blades. At the corner he paused. The moon's full tonight, he said, or almost. Megan started to move on, but Nabil seemed rooted in place. "And art thou pale with weariness," he murmured, still looking upward, "Of climbing heaven and gazing on the earth,/ Wandering companionless/ Among the stars that have a different birth/ And ever changing, like a joyless eye/ That finds no object worth its constancy?"

Though they communicated briefly and sporadically on Facebook afterwards, Megan never saw Tracy again. But when she closed her eyes, she could still clearly picture that last dinner together: Tracy sitting with a fork a few inches from her mouth, still as a statue while tears tracked silently to either side of her nose. Grace reaching into her purse for a tissue and wiping her daughter's face as if she were a toddler. Sharp, erudite, stick-thin Tracy. Mocking Tracy. Tracy whose talent had once made Megan crazy with envy. Tracy sharp as broken glass.

CHAPTER FORTY

Jon was walking toward the restaurant, thinking about nothing very much, a new dessert he might work on perhaps, the coolness in the air that indicated winter was on its way. Keith had moved out two weeks earlier. This time there was no second thought, no softening or repentance. They had both tried. After the initial terror, the long discussions and sleepless nights, Keith had begun to cope. He had done research, joined support groups and learned—he said—to live with his illness. Often he seemed to forget his HIV status himself, though Jon noticed the primal fear surged back with every headache, fever, or bout of fatigue—and particularly before Keith's regular three-monthly check-ups with his doctor. But most of the time the disease stayed lodged in the back of both their minds, like a guest in the spare bedroom who never comes out or asks for anything but every now and then stirs, demanding to be remembered.

Periodically, Jon was overcome with superstitious dread. How many times had Keith cooked for him? Kissed him? He knew they'd been protected during sex, he knew about the current wonder drugs, and he remembered older gays talking about the unfocused hysteria of the early days, when AIDS was first in the news and people worried about the virus living in sweat, in tear drops even. Back then, Keith would never have been able to continue his dental practice. But now the disease was tamed: chronic, long term, manageable like diabetes.

And besides, he, Jon, didn't have it.

But he'd never meant to be with Keith in the first place. Keith was just a stopgap lover. What was Jon doing with this big bland man whose body was beginning to rot inside, who had pushed his way into Jon's life so gently and matter of factly, refused to leave and then revealed he was sick.

How would he take care of Keith if they were fated to repeat Ted and Leon's story? Even if they had money between them for a nurse and all necessary care, he, Jon, wasn't ready for the array of possible symptoms or—if he was honest with himself—for the sheer inconvenience of care-taking. This man seated on the sofa, with his thighs apart and the warm stomach where he had often rested his head while they watched television—what Jon wanted now, more than anything, was to get him out of the apartment. It wasn't his fault. He hadn't invited Keith in in the first place. If t'were done, t'were best t'were done quickly. If Keith was doomed, he should die soon so that Jon could get on with his life. Or move out. He had family. He had money. He couldn't expect Jon to be his nurse.

On their final night together, Keith had reached for him in bed across the barriers of misunderstanding, fear and coldness. We can still make love, Jon, he said. People who are HIV positive do have sex lives. They hadn't made love since Jon learned of the diagnosis. It wasn't that he wanted to be repulsed; he couldn't help himself. This time he tried. He turned his head to the side and received Keith's kisses on his neck, kissed him in return, mechanically stroked Keith's sides. He felt Keith's hand sliding down between their bodies feeling for his penis and moved away abruptly.

It was Keith who said in the morning, This isn't working, is it?

Jon's life post-Keith was peaceful. In the evening he'd microwave something—Thai dumplings or leftovers from the freezer—and watch a news program he'd recorded earlier. Now and then he'd start to make a comment about the stupidity of a particular politician or Americans' obsession with guns, and remember Keith wasn't there to give his usual reply: Yeah, Jon. We're a primitive tribe. He thought about Keith rubbing his feet, stacking the dishwasher, arguing that it was his turn to choose a program, and that he wanted something funny, a sitcom—and how the two of them would finally agree on a pleasantly bloodless, old-fashioned English mystery. He listened to the music he loved—Schubert, Bach and Mozart—and read late into the night: Julian Barnes, Ian McEwan, John Lanchester, authors whose clean, strong prose lines and English sense of irony he enjoyed. And every now and then he'd remember the gibe of that long-ago lover: Everything in its final resting place, eh, Jon? And under its last dust.

When his solitude threatened to become oppressive, he'd call Saul and they'd talk dirty. Remember? he'd say, when you picked up that kid and he had that scabby thing on his penis and nobody had any condoms but you wanted him anyway? And I found you two together just in time and dragged you away?

A block from the restaurant, and his idea for dessert was firming up. It would be quivering and blancmange-ish, rose-scented in a brittle casing of chocolate. A young girl in a yellow raincoat was coming toward him. She must be from out of town, he thought, taking in the sunshine color of the coat and the girl's easy open walk. She hadn't yet assumed the hard-shelled, self-protective persona the city demanded. He turned the corner to Stocker's Kitchen, and stopped. Something was wrong with the air.

CHAPTER FORTY-ONE

Angela carried the peace of her time with Kathy, Jeff and the baby back with her to New York and her uncertain future. She had two weeks left at her job with Piqué—Elizaveta had been quite emotional about firing her and had repeated several times her desire not to seem heartless. She had also said Angela could stay at the apartment in her husband's building for as long as she needed—well, a couple of months at least—while she figured out her next move. Angela had left the store and was approaching Stocker's Kitchen when she noticed a bruise-colored smudge expanding slowly into the sky.

CHAPTER FORTY-TWO

Megan's third callback and she'd finally succeeded. She was in a company for the holiday season. It was just a little non-equity Shakespeare company tucked away in the woods somewhere in upstate New York, but it was a job, her first, and she'd be getting paid. Which meant she was an actress. For a week beforehand she had lain in bed every night imagining herself entering the audition room, pausing in front of the director, taking a breath, speaking her speech: "I dreamed there was an emperor, Antony. Oh, such another sleep that I might see but such another man." Through the night, she'd woken periodically to find the words still running through her mind like a persistent musical phrase: "His legs bestrid the ocean, his rear'd arm/ Crested the world, his voice was propertied/ As all the tuned spheres ..."

Cleopatra had been Nabil's suggestion. Well, he hadn't suggested the role straight out. Megan had gone to his apartment to discuss the audition and seek his advice and had tried out a couple of speeches for him: "Gallop apace, ye fiery-footed steeds," and "Oh, what a noble mind is here o'erthrown."

You're enjoying the language too much, Nabil had responded.

You shouldn't enjoy the language?

Yes, of course. But keep it to yourself. Don't caress the lines. And don't play for pathos. Say the words as if you'd just that moment thought them up. As if they were surprising you. And maybe these aren't the right speeches.

Mort says ingenues are right for me—Juliet—Ophelia.

Why don't you try someone who isn't right for you? Like Lady Macbeth?

Nothing in her responded to his suggestion at the time, but once home, flipping through the pages of her Complete Works, she came across Antony and Cleopatra, started reading, and continued, mesmerized, murmuring Cleopatra's speeches as she came across them. No one would ever cast her in the role. Cleopatra was larger than life, beautiful, magnetic. It would be a joke for her, Megan, to try and play Cleopatra. She sat with the book on her lap for a long time, thinking about the exoticism and otherness of the play, the love at its center that seemed too large for a puny human body to contain, the powerful, amoral queen her subjects thought of as mother of all Egypt. "The barge she sat in, like a burnished throne, Burned on the water." It was too much, too glorious. She couldn't do it. She had to do it. Perhaps she could find an image, a metaphor that would help. She closed her eyes and saw Nabil's cat Halim in repose on the sofa, the lazy entitled way he moved his body in response to caressing fingers. But Halim wouldn't do. Cleopatra may have been feline, but she was anything but gentle. A panther perhaps, whose claws were sheathed only in the presence of Marc Antony—and not always then. A panther. That was a cliché, but the word pantherine was sliding through her mind and evoking something she could use: the slow roll of powerful shoulders, the great head with its shining unreadable eyes.

It was evening, and she hadn't turned on the light. She lay down on her back on the floor, propping the heavy book on her breastbone. I dreamed ... she said.

I dreamed there was an emperor.

The words brimmed with significance. She felt a deep oceanic swell at the center of her body, between her hips where she imagined her womb to be.

I dreamed there was an emperor, Antony.

O such another sleep that I might see but such another man.

The panther moved toward her, slow and deliberate, a hallucinatory delay to its movement.

No. That wouldn't do. She couldn't see herself as frightening.

You can be anything you can imagine, Nabil had said. That's acting. That's the magic of it. Easy for him, she'd thought at the time, because he was a liminal being to begin with, neither here nor there, a polyglot and a mongrel. What else had he said? You just have to make a shape and flow into it like water.

His voice was in her head now. Think more about the sea, it said, the ceaseless movement, the little playful waves on the beach, all foam and glitter, and the great waves behind them, heaving up their backs like sea monsters. Think of the unplumbable, unfathomable mystery of the sea. It can destroy you—and it will. And then he told her about boats full of immigrants—from Africa, from the Middle East—desperately trying to get to European shores in overcrowded boats, hundreds of them drowning during the voyage, others enduring an eternity of hunger and thirst on the unforgiving ocean until, as one of the survivors told his rescuers, "We didn't even know who we were any more."

Cleopatra was as cruel as the sea. She had made her servants eat the poison she herself planned to use to see how quickly it killed and with how much pain. She had murdered her own brothers.

Megan sighed. It was too much. Juliet and Ophelia were inside her, but Cleopatra required an imaginative leap she didn't know how to make. Though she did understand the Egyptian queen's love for Marc Antony. She herself was swimming in love. But it seemed to her that Nabil had been pulling away since Tracy left. He was still warm and attentive, but he was also busy. He had a part in an off-Broadway play; his comedy act was getting some attention on YouTube; there was even talk of a television appearance. Nabil had always been honest with her; he had warned her once:

We're artists. We follow the work we're given. Don't romanticize me, Megan. But she had romanticized him. She couldn't help it.

# # # #

The waiting area outside the audition room was occupied by a dozen women—culled from the hundred or so she had seen the first time—a couple model-beautiful, some interestingly eccentric, a few beautifully plain, all of them her competition. They sat on folding chairs or cross-legged on the floor, texting, checking e-mail, or chatting with each other in that nervous, too-friendly way of strangers trying to impress each other while at the same time reaching out for comfort. Megan tamped down her trepidation, sat on one of the folding chairs, and attempted to relax her body, limb by limb, starting at her toes. Your feet are heavy, she told herself. After a few moments, she gave up, pulled out her paperback and read, though the print kept blurring. It was two hours before her name was called.

The light in the audition room, white and unforgiving, buzzed faintly. Behind a metal desk sat three people: two men, and a woman between them.

Megan, right? said the woman, looking up from her notes. What are you planning to do for us?

Her mind was a blank. She didn't know what to do with her hands. She said, I dreamed ... The power of the words alone got her through the first couple of lines, and then the images returned—first in fragments and then full force. The panther. The crawling sea, an oceanic swell between her hips. She straightened. Beneath her feet generations of the dead began to stir.

You can tell when you're acting well, when your listeners' silence is more than just polite. There was an energy in the air of that sterile room like the energy after a lightning strike and in that moment Megan understood that she was acting very well indeed. It felt almost anti-climactic to hear the woman say, after a brief consultation with the two men, Very nice. We'd like to work with you, Megan. You'll be hearing from us, because she was, after all, Cleopatra, and who would dare deny her anything?

Now walking down the street toward Stocker's Kitchen, still half herself and half not, the darkening sky above the city full of promise, her skirt swinging against her bare legs, she felt blessed and transported. It was going to be all right, she was going to make it. She was an actor. She would meet Nabil and tell him about her triumph and thank him for all his advice, and order whatever she wanted—the hell with cost—of Stocker's divine, delicious and spirit-thrilling food, and comfortable Crystal would be happy for her and bring her wine. She embodied power. She, Megan. She Cleopatra.

She turned the corner and a sound came at her, a roar like rushing water. Fragments of ash fell onto the front of her dusky, red-purple Cleopatra dress. There were people all over the sidewalk, standing singly and in clusters, exclaiming, holding up cell phones, and a voice was yelling at everyone to get back. She saw firemen in black and yellow. A thick canvas hose unreeling along the sidewalk. Holy shit, someone said. Holy fucking shit. Now ash was raining onto her dress and she saw the air was full of black specks, some hard-sided cinders, some floating, large, thin and powdery like black snowflakes. Flame leapt from the top of the building, illuminating the underside of leaves and she remembered Tracy's words about forest conflagrations—how once they'd reached the treetops they'd start racing and become unstoppable. They were almost gorgeous in their primal power, these flames, and she stared at them mesmerized, several seconds passing before she realized Stocker's Kitchen was on fire, and several more still before an urgent question took shape in her mind: Was there anyone still inside?

CHAPTER FORTY-THREE

Harold was half aware that he was in an ambulance, lying on his back and staring up at the roof of the vehicle, listening to the waaaaahh-hh-waaaahhh of the siren. There was a throbbing in his arms, his hands felt thick as baseball mitts, a blanket covered him and an IV protruded from the inside of his elbow. Beneath the sound of the sirens, he heard a moaning and thought for a second it was his own, then realized there was someone moaning in a bunk across from him, a figure he couldn't see through the backs of the people bending over it. Sean. It had to be Sean. He wanted to call out Hey buddy, how ya doin'? but couldn't summon the energy. Besides his throat hurt like hell. Through a growing torpor he heard disconnected words: something about a catheter, something about needing to get permission for morphine. A voice said loudly to someone not present, We'll need IV fluids and a crash cart open. Out of somewhere came the single word "shock." And then, Give him a blanket, dammit, he's shaking. We're just gonna focus on keeping him alive till we get there, said the voice. The point is to get him there alive.

I can't start the fucking IV, said someone else.

Harold closed his eyes and summoned up the image of his knife, the way it rocked in his hand. He loved the weight of that knife, though he wouldn't have used the word love; it was more that the knife was part of him. He hadn't gone back in for Sean, he knew. He wanted to think he had, but he hadn't. He'd gone back for his knife. The chef's knife that was so much part of his hand that he never thought about it, kept it honed, sharpened it at home on a stone, because he wouldn't trust anyone else to do it. He chopped sometimes in his dreams, steadily, endlessly, the rhythm in his bones, as if he were the knife, the knife wielding him rather than the other way round. Harold could do many things in the kitchen. He was good with sauces and strong-armed when it came to wrestling huge pots of boiling water or oil. He could fill in almost anywhere he was needed. But he preferred chopping. Cooking wasn't about taste with him, just the mechanical movements, the ballet of chopping. What went through his head when he chopped? Nothing. Nothing about the foodstuffs he was so precisely decimating. Only a wordless pleasure in his own skill. He didn't have to think about what he was doing, just look at an onion on his board and take up his knife and moments later the onion would be lying in tiny perfectly identical squares to be swept into a bowl. Next, a brief contemplation of, say, a pepper—not as symmetrical as an onion and less willing to fall into neat squares because of the inward-curling top, the tiny point at the end, the fact that you needed to split it and take out the seeds. Or perhaps he'd confront the fibrousy triangle of a carrot, or a potato—the calculations were different for a big russet, a rosy round red bliss, a fingerling. Each required a moment of contemplation and analysis before, mindless, barely conscious, he allowed his hands to resume their accustomed task. He'd had that knife since he began working in kitchens, learned to use it under the tutelage of the first chef he'd ever known, who'd talked about balance and weight, urged him to investigate the edge, the point, the feel of the bolster.

Standing in the cool air of the alley outside Stocker's Kitchen, he'd watched the lurid flames and dark oily smoke against the sky, heard the crackle of fire, and remembered that his knife was in the kitchen. He hadn't been using it. He'd been cleaning a rack of lamb—such a tiny creature, hardly worth killing for the meat on those small sharp bones—working his slender boning knife carefully between the ribs and along the side of the backbone while the chef's knife, his possession, his own hand, lay beside the board, beside the meat that would be burning now, curling up, the bones blackening into charcoal. He walked toward the door. The heat coming from it was like nothing he'd ever experienced or could have imagined, roaring, huge and angry, dwarfing him with its indifferent rage and power. In the face of that searing heat, the sheer rage of the air that seemed to be consuming itself, he was nothing. He'd be atomized by it, vaporized. He edged closer to the door, felt the fire lifting the hair at the top of his head, and knew he couldn't go back for the knife: The heat was a physical force, a ruthless hand pushing him back and himself half weeping for that knife, that stupid knife, and then he remembered: Sean. Sean reeling back from the stove his hands clawed in front of him. Something about his face. Something Harold didn't want to see. If he'd thought for a second, he might have wondered if someone else had hauled the boy out by now. If he'd thought for a second, he wouldn't have gone in for what would surely be a suicide mission. The knife. The boy. The boy's raw hands on that knife blade as Harold showed him how to turn the knife on its side and mash a clove of garlic—the only person aside from himself who'd ever been allowed to hold it. And now Sean reeling back from the range, a wildness of flame all about his face and head, other figures staggering about him in the burning kitchen and Harold burst through the door, forced himself through, hands in front of him as if those poor appendages of flesh could ward off the fire, plunged along the corridor through smoke and crackling heat and saw that Sean was still there in the kitchen, slumped on the floor in front of the stove. He grabbed anything and everything he could of the boy's limbs and clothes, stunned by the slipperiness of Sean's body—Sean's skin was peeling off in his hands, he realized with horror—and began dragging the boy along the floor, cursing, through the red and black diabolical dancing of flame and toward the doorway, the sound louder and louder, the heat overwhelming, as if the blood were boiling beneath his skin until he could finally dump the limp body on the ground outside in front of a fireman, one of a yellow and black suited group that had appeared at some point without his noticing. Then he collapsed himself.

CHAPTER FORTY-FOUR

Stocker was in the alley. Eyes half closed, an unlit cigarette between his fingers, he imagined he was with Angela again, that he was cooking for her in his kitchen and his restaurant was jolting along as in its heyday, full every night, with a long waiting list, himself bustling about self-importantly, inspecting the foods that had come from the market, a whole fish fresh caught and gleaming, the counter holding a cornucopia of vegetables—baby artichokes, new potatoes, broccolini and purple broccoli, sweet potatoes, huge garnet yams, figs. Harold, Sean, George and Kenneth would be converging in a circle around that glistening fish, wanting to know what he intended to do with it. But he wasn't there. He was outside by the wall, his familiar place, the place where the little black cat had sidled up to him so many times after so much initial fear and hesitation, and where she had given birth and died. The place where he had first seen Angela's pointed face and narrow, penetrating eyes, Angela turning when he called out to her, then slowly starting toward him. Angela. He didn't want to think about her now but she kept creeping back. Angela, who knew his shame. Behind him, the burned and blackened shell that had once been Stocker's Kitchen. He had no idea what he'd do with the place now, whether insurance would cover reconstruction, whether he wanted to reconstruct. He could hear the river, a slow curdled burbling like the bubbles on the surface of a pot of oatmeal. He'd had to step over wooden struts and through yellow tape to get to his alley. The cat. Angela's angular, jolting walk: all of it, everything, finished and done with, corpsed. Still, there was a dim unthinking comfort in the feel of the wall pressing against his spine. He reached into his pocket for a match, scraped it, stared at the triangle of flame, lit his cigarette, inhaled, dropped the thing and stomped it out. The alley had always been a grace note between the kitchen and the world outside—cool air on his forehead, a cigarette between his stubby, fish-smelling fingers. He closed his eyes briefly and the images returned: strands of pasta uncoiling in furiously bubbling water, Harold's unerring knife coming down on the head of a struggling lobster and administering a swift blow between the eyes. When Harold lowered his knife, the legs kept waving. Living thing. Dead thing. Which was it? Sean. Was he living or dead? Stocker wanted to weep. Sean, who had always been a presence in his kitchen rather than a full-fleshed person, a little soft creature huddled in a corner, Sean and his endless fumbling incompetence. How often had he yelled at the kid about the eyes he left in the potatoes, the clumsiness of his thin, red hands, yelled at him to hurry up for fuck's sake. And there was Angela's inexplicable kindness toward Sean, the way he'd seen her gently touch his face when she came back from California. Angela would be sitting beside Sean's hospital bed now. Sean had seen the fire on the stove, the small grease fire, before it leapt suddenly—Stocker turning, his heart in his chest leaping with it—leapt in a single unhinged, orange moment. No. That wasn't how it happened. There was no moment, no time, no sequence, just the blackened pan and the flame that shouldn't have been there, but no matter, he'd thought at the time, no big deal. Pans did flame now and then and the flame would soon subside of its own or under a shower of baking powder. The oil had been left a few seconds too long on a too-high burner, that was all. And then time shuddered and jolted, the seconds between one thing and another were obliterated, and the flame surged and licked the ceiling. He saw Sean running up to the stove, taking the initiative as he, Stocker, had always nagged him to do: He could hear it now, his own cold, hectoring voice, and he remembered Jon's response once when he'd used it on him: Don't you dare talk to me like that, spoken low and dangerous. But where would Fuzzy Bunny ever have gotten the spine to defend himself when Stocker raged at him: Why are you even in this kitchen? You're a slug. A creeping, crawling, useless slug. So Sean took the initiative. There was a large pot of water on the stove in which strands of spaghetti were lazily uncurling. Sean seized the hot handles with his bare hands and raised the pot, poised it over the burning oil. Then came a chorus of people shouting. He, Stocker was shouting too—wasn't he? his voice loud and hoarse. But not loud enough. There was a whoosh that sucked all the air out of the place. Then silence.

It wasn't really silence. It couldn't have been. There must have been noise. Screaming. The crackle of flame. But all he remembered was a pause, a hiatus, a tear in the fabric of time. The "No" he either had or hadn't yelled had died away or been obliterated by the huge hot wind. In the hush he had seen Sean reeling back from the stove, his hands over his face, Sean bent almost in two slumping onto the floor.

But he could still see the flames now, yearning upwards with forked tongues, wanting to breathe, as bright and pretty as precocious children and above them a cloud, a hovering umbrella of greasy black smoke. The flames rose toward the cloud, brightness and darkness met, and devils danced in the heart of the fire.

Grease was the basic and essential principle of his work. There was regenerative grease, white, pure and smooth as maternal love, as Cherry's tongue gently cleaning her newborn calf, and there was also grease that clung, rotting and corrupting. That was his grease. The fire wasn't caused by the filthiness of his kitchen, but it was the filthiness that enabled it to catch hold and flame so fast and bright. There had been a fire extinguisher by the stove, he knew, but Sean hadn't thought to use it.

He closed his eyes. Behind his lids, everything was on fire. The pegboard holding pots and pans, the clear containers of flour and sugar, the sugar itself, the meat on Harold's board—you could smell it roasting—the vegetables. Bottles of wine exploded. Plastic melted. Small blazes started on white-coated backs. There were screams and figures running outside and rolling on the asphalt. Everyone got out. Except Sean. And Harold, who turned back.

In the cool of the alley, the shame overwhelmed him. His kitchen. His grease. The thousands of small creature deaths that had occurred there. His kitchen had killed Sean. Or maybe worse. Sean lived on in his hospital bed, swathed in bandages like a Halloween mummy, hideous beneath them. No one knew better than Stocker the effect of flame: His own hands and arms were rough with scars. Burns were routine in the kitchen, but the depth and urgency of the pain surprised every time.

CHAPTER FORTY-FIVE

Crystal heard about the fire from Stocker: Don't bother coming in today, he'd said. It's gone. The whole place is burned down. He didn't know how long it would take to rebuild, or if rebuilding was even feasible. She tried to frame a question, but before she could speak he said, I gotta go. I don't know what'll happen. Crystal. I'm sorry. I gotta go.

She sat down at the kitchen table, dazed. What would she do now? Where would she get a job? She was in her fifties and had almost no savings. The Italian couple across the way had their blinds drawn. She'd always liked trying to map their lives, it was a kind of game with her, and now she put her hands over her eyes and imagined that the wife was doing laundry in the basement after a slow, stiff, arthritic descent, and the husband napping on his armchair, a newspaper slipping off his lap and the curly dog asleep beside his feet. It seemed so blissfully peaceful and settled, their life together. For five years now, her life had been the jolting energy of the restaurant, cooks jostling each other in the kitchen, her friends on the waitstaff, the dishes she placed in front of her customers with so much pleasure and authority, a web of relationships that had seemed fixed and inevitable and had now been torn apart as easily as a spider web. What was there for her now in this hot, dark little apartment she could barely afford: a cup of tea, a cigarette, her grandmother's flying geese quilt, an ancient television? Stocker would rebuild perhaps but Crystal couldn't wait for him. She was tired to the bone. She thought then about Alabama, the slowness and regularity of her childhood. After a while, she roused herself, set her laptop on the table, opened it and Googled rentals in Auburn. All she needed was a little flat, a couple of rooms maybe, but it seemed she could rent whole houses for a fraction of what she paid here in New York. Over the next few days she kept playing with the idea of return, unsure herself how serious the search was, but checking job listings, looking for school friends on Facebook, even contacting a real estate firm.

In the middle of the week, the phone rang. Jennifer's voice, tight and accusing: Madison said ...

Sorry, Jen. There's a lot on my mind right now. The restaurant burned down.

Did you hear what I said, mom? Madison said the F-word. There's nowhere around here she'd have heard that word. I let her visit you and that's how she comes home, that's what she says to her mother. I'm afraid I can't let you take her again. Dan says you can't even see her, but I convinced him ...

Crystal interrupted: I just wanted to let you know I won't be bothering you all any more, Jennifer. I'm going back to Auburn.

An audible intake of breath. There's nothing for you in Auburn.

I'm tired, hon. I'd like to come by and say goodbye to you and the kids before I go.

Okay, mom, there's no need for drama. We can work some of this out.

I'm getting everything together. I'll write you from Alabama. We'll do Facetime.

Jennifer was talking, expostulating, but Crystal couldn't find the words or spirit to respond. I'll call you when everything's set, she said, hung up and went into the kitchen. Leaving the light off, she stood at the sink looking out into the dusk. Snowflakes from an unexpected late storm were drifting across the now-lighted window across the way and Mr. and Mrs. Italian were back in their accustomed places, sitting side by side with the curly dog leaning against the woman. Crystal wished she were an artist and had some way of capturing this ordinary scene, the two old people watching television, eating from TV trays, the curly dog alert for any crumb that might fall, and taking it with her to Alabama. For years she hadn't bothered keeping in touch with relatives and old friends back there, but a cousin she barely knew had sent a welcome home message on Facebook and asked if she needed a temporary place to stay—an unexpected touch of kindness that had briefly moved Crystal to tears. She turned away from the window, went to her closet to pull out her clothes and start deciding what to get rid of and what to take with her, and the old song began running through her mind again on an ever-repeating loop: Jennifer. Juniper. Lives upon the hill. Jennifer Juniper sitting very still. Is she sleeping? I don't think so. Is she breathing? Yes, very low. Watcha doin' Jennifer, my love?

CHAPTER FORTY-SIX

Angela sat beside Sean's bed in the burn unit, wearing a paper hospital cap, gown, and booties against the risk of infection. Brown ooze seeped from the bandages encasing his still form. She was glad she couldn't see what was under those bandages, glad that he must be only half-conscious at best. His entire face was bandaged, his hands white clubs, his arms tied above his head. It was comical almost, the way he looked with only his toes, eyes and nostrils visible. Like a Halloween costume, a mummy.

She hadn't wanted to come, but she'd had to. Something in her obsidian heart had started cracking in California. She remembered the way her sister in law's hard, pregnant stomach had felt against her palm, the pulsing, living thing within. And then the heavy warmth of the child in her arms. She wasn't allowed to touch Sean, and she could visit him for only ten minutes at a time. She'd been told by a nurse that he'd had a tracheotomy for his burned throat and wouldn't be able to talk for a while, even once he'd woken. The same nurse had explained the brown ooze to her: Burns weep fluid.

It was fitting, this long sleep. There had always been something sleepy about Sean, he had always exuded the sweet, thick scent of a sleeping child, but the smell in this room was different.

Over the next two weeks, she came here again and again, the length of her visits increasing as no one seemed to notice her presence or come to hurry her out. One morning, approaching Sean's room, she heard singing and stopped outside the door. The farmer in the dell, sang a wheezy voice that she couldn't place for a moment as male or female. The farmer in the dell. Hey-ho the dairy-o, the farmer in the dell. She pushed open the door. A short, stocky nurse and a couple of orderlies were placing Sean's bandaged form carefully on the bed. It was a struggle, he was heavy and awkward to move, but the nurse was singing. There, she said, leaning toward Sean's bandaged-masked face. We're done, honey. The cheese stands alone.

She glanced up at Angela. We're just bringing him back from his treatment, she said. And then to the orderlies, We're good now. Thanks. They left, and the nurse turned to go too.

What's the treatment? Angela asked.

It's called debriding. Tubbing. We have to do it twice a day. We change the dressings and put this stuff called Silvadene on the burns. They're covered with pigskin until we can harvest enough of his own for grafts. They've got those bags they lay over the wounds—mesh bags—you know, like you get oranges in. The slits let the fluid out, and they help the skin stick to the wound.

Does debriding hurt?

The nurse hesitated. We give them drugs for pain, as much as we can. My name's Bonnie, by the way. You're ... ?

Angela.

Okay, Angela. Rest assured we're taking good care of him.

Angela found herself drawn back, day after day, to Sean's bedside. With her job at Piqué ended, there was nowhere else she had to be. She had let Jeffrey and Kathryn know she was delaying her move to California for a little while, but she texted daily with Kathryn, and checked Facebook frequently for baby photos. She longed to hold the baby in her arms again. But this was her place for now, her place and her penance, sitting in the creaking hospital room, adjusting her breathing to the steady sound of Sean's respirator, her hands folded in front of her. Her penance and expiation. Sometimes Sean moved a little, most of the time he stayed motionless and silent. She checked her messages. Sometimes she dozed. And when she did, two hospital rooms melded—Sean's and her mother's in California. There the scent had been antiseptic; here the smell was thick and heavy and so uncomfortably reminiscent of those in Stocker's kitchen that she could rarely eat when she got home at night.

She was paying penance for every selfishness she'd ever harbored, for her reluctance to touch or comfort her mother, for the despised blue dress. But she was here also because Sean had no one else. The people at the hospital had contacted family, but those members they found said they hadn't seen him for five years, not since he'd left home, and there was no one available to visit. There was an uncle in New York and the hospital left him a message, but he never called back.

Doesn't matter he's indigent, Bonnie told Angela when she asked. We'll give him the best of care. We do the best we can for everybody.

It's good to talk to him, Bonnie said one afternoon. Keep talking to him. Just because he's not answering don't mean he isn't there.

Can you tell me what to expect?

You his girlfriend?

No. Just a friend.

It's still touch and go. I'm gonna be straight with you. It's touch and go. Thing about burns is they're not like other injuries where you maybe go through a bad time and then every day things get a bit better. A bad burn's like an illness. It doesn't stop. It works its way in and through. There's the biological process of the body struggling to heal itself and sometimes the healing causes more damage. You can get contracture. People's hands claw up.

In and through?

It's progressive is what I'm trying to say.

Angela knew Harold lay in another room down the hall, but she hadn't had the heart to visit him. Bonnie had told her his burns were less severe than Sean's, but bad enough: he was burned over twenty-five percent of his body. He'd be in the hospital a month or two, it would take some time after that for his burns to heal and he'd have to keep coming back every day for treatment. And then to another place for rehab.

One afternoon, walking the corridor, Angela had heard Harold on the phone: No, mom, it wasn't stupid. Well, someone had to get him out. He was burning. Yes, it did have to be me, mom. I said, it did have to be me. Why? Because I was the one that was there, that's why. It lifted her heart, the familiar rhythm of the conversation and the fact that Harold still had enough energy for the ongoing battle with his mother.

She learned the ecology of the hospital. She read Sean snippets from the newspaper. Oh, this'll interest you. This woman wrote to Dear Abby about her husband. He hates her dog, but she loves it. Or: How about this paper gown I'm wearing, she asked the silent form on the bed. Very fashionable shade of blue, don't you think? A whole new look for me. She took her cue from Bonnie and sang to him. Twinkle twinkle little star, how I wonder what you are, numbers she'd heard on the radio, a song about a dragonfly that ran away, but she came back with a story to say and another about someone running toward a riptide. She clicked on the television high on the wall and commented on the programs. Too many nature programs, she said crankily. I'm tired of always watching some critter about to devour some other critter.

Bonnie had told her she could now touch Sean anywhere that he wasn't covered in sticky bandages. You can rub some cream into his feet if you're willing, she'd said. Here's the tube. It helps. After that, Angela worked on the task every evening, sitting at the end of the bed, her hands sliding over his poor scarred feet: Sean, Sean, Sean, she said. You should have known better. You should have known not to pour water on a grease fire. But I should have known better too. I should have reported the place. That kitchen was its own world and it lived by its own rules and you're the one who paid for it. Now she was too close to talking about Stocker and she didn't want to do that. Was Sean's suffering Stocker's fault? Did she think it was his fault? She couldn't go there either.

She used to see Stocker as a Maurice Sendak comic monster, fat-bellied with that sort of dopey grimacy look—puzzled more than anything—triangular white teeth sticking out of his closed smiley mouth and big round klutzy paws—paws that were soft and caressing rather than fearsome. But Stocker wasn't harmless and his hands didn't caress.

Between tasks, Bonnie sometimes came in and talked. It's a slow time, she said. Usually we're slammed. Hey, Angela, what do you do when you leave here?

Nothing much. Glass of wine. A movie maybe.

Bonnie said she liked to soak in the tub or sit in front of the television watching junky shows and eating leftovers or quick easy things like a tofu sausage and a microwaved potato. Nothing violent on the tube. Nothing with blood. Escapist stuff. Comedies. She'd seen too much to enjoy violence. Babies deliberately burned by their parents. Young people who seemed to be recovering slipping suddenly into death. People who recovered enough to leave coming back disfigured and depressed and cursing the staff that saved their lives. Burns are so disfiguring, Bonnie said. Fire can burn off the flanges of your nose, your ears, just melt your flesh. She hated administering the daily pain of debriding. She didn't eat meat, couldn't stand the smell of it cooking.

She told Angela the reason for her pronounced limp one day: her school took everyone out to a farm for a treat—they were all city kids—and they coaxed her into giving a horse a carrot. She was scared because the horse was so big, but she did, and another kid gave a carrot to another horse, and this other kid's horse startled, stepped backwards onto her foot and broke most of the small bones at the top. She'd had to wear a heavy brace for a long time. But her back was very strong, Bonnie told Angela. She had to be strong to help move comatose patients, hold them and turn them.

Angela understood—she'd seen Bonnie with Sean, cradling him, talking and singing nursery songs. They're sedated, but they feel the pain, Bonnie said, and they can hear your voice too. She turned to Sean. You can, right? Hear me? You doin' okay, sweetheart? You breathin' okay? You gonna wake up and talk to us one of these days? I wanna hear how you sound.

And she had to deal with relatives too, she told Angela during one of their long, evening chats. Parents, partners, siblings. No one's prepared for what they'll find in a burn unit. No one realizes how long and torturous the process is.

Over the weeks, Angela began to realize that Bonnie belonged to an elite team. They were like commandoes, she thought. Tough and highly skilled. Very close, and trusting each other like soldiers going into combat trust each other. She'd passed the lunch room a few times and seen the staff sharing pizza and joking about their work, their aching feet, their non-existent home lives. She saw, too, that the doctors relied on Bonnie. She heard the interns ask for her help—except for one young guy whose arrogance and vanity precluded it—as did even the older doctors, the ones who'd been around for years. Bonnie understood things that went beyond anything they'd learned in medical school. She could lay her hand on a patient and sense what was needed.

Bonnie had never married. It's hard to have a real life when your hours are so irregular, she told Angela. And your nights get interrupted all the time with crises—it's real slow right now, but sometimes this place just overflows because there's been a traffic pile up, an exploding gas tank, an industrial fire.

Besides, who'd want to date me? She laughed. I smell bad when I get out of here. Disease. Burned flesh. No matter how much I shower, the smell never goes away.

I don't know how you cope, said Angela. I'd be crying every day.

Bonnie shook her head. I never cry. I seen too much. If I started crying right now I'd never stop.

Perhaps, Angela thought, Bonnie had no interest in sex or love because she poured all her tenderness into her work. It was there in the jokes she cracked and her loud bursts of laughter, the skill in her broad hands. Patients knew that if they had to endure the steamy, hot, stinking torture room where debridement took place, Bonnie was the nurse they wanted with them. She worked meticulously and without hesitation; she sang as if dealing with a frightened child. When Bonnie walked into a room, Angela came to understand, every patient who was awake felt better.

It was a huge achievement to get through nursing school, Bonnie told Angela. No one in my family ever went beyond a bit of high school. It was so hard to study at home with all the noise and confusion and the TV on all the time, and my sister wanting us to go out and party. But I stuck to it and got the certificate. Ordered the uniform. I still remember how it felt standing in front of the mirror and seeing myself in that white uniform for the first time. She laughed. They don't stay white for long here.

Do you ever wish you'd chosen a different profession?

I do wonder if I can take it forever—how long my back will hold up for one thing. But I can't imagine doing anything else with my life. We're so needed here.

I'm jealous of you.

Me? Bonnie laughed. Whyever?

Angela had to think about that for a moment. You're so necessary.

I bet you never even think about why you do what you do.

That's where you're wrong. I do that every day, wonder why I do it. I don't know why some people get to run through the daisies all their lives—stay in kindergarten in terms of understanding anything about suffering—you know what I mean, right?—those people who've got everything easy?—while other folks go to graduate school for pain, so to speak. I don't know how some of our patients stand it. I don't know how they stand it afterwards when they're gone from here and realize their lives will never be the same, they'll never be themselves again, their old selves. And I don't know why I have to be in the middle of it, in the middle of the swamp struggling every single day and sometimes you feel there's so little you can do. So little. She stopped. But you can do something. That's what I tell myself. You can do something.

Angela saw the shop, her customers, sad little Nancy pushing her plump foot into a far too tight expensive shoe.

Why are you laughing? Bonnie's mood had changed and she wanted to laugh too.

Oh, Angela said, I've been doing something too. I've been selling high fashion clothes to very rich people.

Well, that's nice.

But Angela could tell her life was as incomprehensible to Bonnie as Bonnie's was to her. And then they both laughed louder, Bonnie chuckling, loud and hoarse, Angela rocking in her chair.

Maybe you should go home and get some sleep, said Bonnie, wiping her eyes. You're not even related to him, right?

Angela sobered fast. I just want to stay for a while.

Penance. Expiation.

Right then. Don't overtire yourself. It's gonna be a long haul. Bonnie stood up.

But you think he'll ...

I don't know. At this point, nobody knows. I wish I could tell you something for sure. This business of tending to burns, it's gotten way more sophisticated these days but there's still so much guesswork. People you think will live, easy, they die. People you know could never make it get up and walk out of here. She nodded towards Sean. I'm hoping that's him.

CHAPTER FORTY-SEVEN

We're going to rebuild the whole place. We'll get the kitchen up to code, and get you back to work, I promise. We'll get sprinklers.

It wasn't like Stocker to be hesitant about anything, but it had taken him long minutes of standing outside the door to walk into Harold's hospital room and say what he'd just said. He knew Angela was visiting Sean only a few doors down the hall, and he'd checked the corridor before exiting the elevator, making sure he wouldn't run into her. He wasn't ready to see her, didn't know if he'd ever be ready. And he was pretty sure she wouldn't speak to him anyway. A short, dark woman was sitting next to Harold's bed. Now she rose and came toward him.

How he work? How he work in your kitchen with his poor hands?

Harold said with difficulty, Let him come in and talk, ma.

Stocker addressed Harold: I'll need you back. He saw Harold's glance go to his own arms, strung pitifully above him. He went on, There's a lot to do in a kitchen besides slicing vegetables. We'll figure it out. Eh? Eh, Harold? Even if you have to use your elbows, we'll figure it out.

She approached. Small, round and dark, an intense troll, dandruff in the parting of her hair, her chin quivering with passion, her scent rich and full. This was what he had longed for all his life, Stocker thought. This was mother love embodied. You almost kill my boy, she said. And that other boy almost dead too. Your filthy kitchen. My boy he cut himself sometimes because of all the yelling. You kick him one time. Oh, yes, he tell me. I cook all my life—every day—and I ashamed to have a kitchen filthy as yours. Everything in my house spotless. That how Harold grew up, how he cook since he was little boy. Now see what happen to his hands, his poor hands. They gonna operate but even so maybe his fingers never bend again.

Ma. I told you I want to talk to this guy.

Harold save that boy, Sean. You lucky he save him.

Stocker didn't move. He stood still and let her rage buffet him. He knew how to absorb rage, he'd done it often enough in his life, and he knew this time he deserved it. I just wanted to see how he was doing, he said when she paused for breath.

You almost kill him. You and your dirty kitchen.

Please leave the man alone.

Stocker held out a cardboard container. I brought this for Harold.

You bring food? You think he can eat?

I can eat. The doctor said ...

You eat what I bring. This man he almost kill you, you and that young boy. I'm the one bring you food.

Stocker cradled his offering between his hands, felt the slick of grease at the container's side. It was the stew he usually made for himself alone: beef bones boiled for hours to give up their marrow and release their gelatin, chicken feet and necks, eggs, vegetable stalks, buds and leaves. It contained the vitality of everything that had died to make it up. This is good stuff, he told Harold's mother, my stew. It'll help him get back his strength.

Harold said, I want some of that, ma.

Her shoulders sagged; Stocker felt her deep fatigue in his own body. I no sleep, she told him. When I close my eyes I see him run into flame ... She shuddered and stopped. This was mother's love, Stocker was thinking, this fierce ugly angry frightened thing. Mother's love confronted him, stood between him and her child. He said, I'm so sorry about what happened. Harold was a champ.

You sorry? You sorry? But the energy had leaked out of her. Almost staggering, she allowed Stocker to lead her back to her chair.

She's been here the whole time, Harold whispered.

She looked up at Stocker: Yes, Harold was champ. But now what will happen with his poor hands? A brief silence, and she held out her own hand. Give me. Stocker passed her the stew. She put the container on Harold's tray, pulled her chair to the head of the bed and began feeding him with a plastic spoon. Stocker watched Harold eating, bite by slow, difficult bite. He took in the woman's anger and desperation, the bristling furious energy that would never let her quit.

He nodded and turned to leave the room, but paused with his hand on the door handle when he realized Harold was struggling to say something. Then came Harold's mother's voice, then Harold again, and finally she spoke directly to Stocker: He say this stew is very good. He say to tell you thank you.

CHAPTER FORTY-EIGHT

Angela saw that Jon was in the doorway of Sean's room. He greeted her, then came to stand beside the bed, looking down on Sean. After a few seconds' silence, he said, I brought chocolate, but I don't imagine he can eat it.

He can't.

Hi Sean, he said softly.

The nurses think he can hear what goes on, so it's good to talk to him, Angela said. And speaking of nurses—I bet they'd like those chocolates.

He laughed. They should. They're hand-dipped.

She and Jon weren't close, but they had always been companionable together, and after so many hours alone with Sean's silent form, she found his presence a comfort. I understand you visit most days, Jon said. I didn't realize you and Sean were tight.

We're not. He doesn't have anyone else. But that didn't sound right: it was too bald, and that wasn't the only reason she visited. And there's something about him, she added.

I know. He always had an effect on people.

There was a pause.

What will you do now? she asked.

I haven't figured it out. Nothing for a while.

God, Angela said suddenly, I hate hospitals. Then: Will you go back to the restaurant when Stocker rebuilds?

Maybe.

With Keith gone and the apartment still and quiet, Jon had given a lot of thought to where he wanted his life to go now—whether he wanted to continue exploring every aspect of sweetness or leave the restaurant business altogether and take up something new. He listened to music all day—putting on his clothes in the morning, eating breakfast alone, reading, sliding into sleep at night—the repeating yet ever-changing forms of Mozart and Bach, the lonely flute-like freedom of Satie, and the mesmeric transparent edifices of Philip Glass—never, he thought, was an artist more aptly named. He found himself obsessed with form, rhythm and harmony and he sometimes thought about going to architecture school. It wasn't too late. When he closed his eyes, he saw the beautiful lines of Saul's body and analyzed the physics of the way he moved through space. Saul, whom he'd had to call about Keith's status and who had responded with a white-hot rage that he, Jon, understood only too well. So far, he himself had tested negative for HIV, and in another two months, he could count himself safe.

Sean's struggling, Angela said, startling him. Hanging on for dear life. They keep him pretty doped up. She and Jon watched the muffled rise and fall of Sean's narrow chest under the bandages. I want to know what's going on in his head, Angela said with sudden emphasis. I never could figure that out. Even when he was okay at the restaurant and could talk, he was somewhere else. Partly with you but mostly somewhere else. I always hoped it was a nice place, away from all the yelling and confusion.

Fuzzy bunny, Jon said.

She nodded. That was cruel.

But Stocker had him pegged with that; also he took care of him.

She was surprised. Stocker?

He didn't protect Sean exactly but he made a space where he could function.

You mean that corner where he worked?

Well that. But not just a physical space. He made everyone understand that Fuzzy Bunny belonged there in that kitchen. No matter how much he harassed him.

You feel so helpless in here, Angela said. So dumb and helpless. I talk to him. They said he could maybe hear me, so I talk and talk. You can't touch him, except for his feet. No one has touched the rest of him except nurses and doctors for the whole month he's been here and when they touch, they hurt him. She started to cry but stopped and rapidly composed herself. Yesterday they said his lungs were better and they could maybe bring him … a bit more up to the surface. You know, from the coma. Closer to consciousness.

That might not be a good thing. He's going to be in a lot of pain.

I just want his eyes to open. I want to know he sees me. She wiped her nose with the back of her hand. His feet aren't too bad, she told Jon. The nurse said it was good to rub this cream into them. She took down the tube of ointment, showed it to him and uncapped it. Jon watched her palm a little blob, then smooth it gently over one of Sean's feet. Slowly, gingerly, he sat down beside her on the end of the bed, waited a few seconds, then held out his hand for the ointment. He squeezed out some white cream, hesitated, shuddered slightly as the tips of his fingers met Sean's ridged brown flesh, pulled back. Angela was using long, gentle, practiced strokes and Jon took a deep breath and imitated her, running his palms again and again over Sean's soles and between his toes, willing the cream to fulfill its soothing ministry and soften the hardened flesh.

It's nice to be able to do something that feels good to him, Angela said.

Jon fought a stab of shame. This tending the sick endears them to us, he said after a moment. She looked at him inquiringly.

Under his breath, he added, Us too, it endears.

After Jon left, Angela sat by Sean and talked. She tried her usual tack. She told him that no one had worn purple much for years but it was one of her favorite colors and she wished it would come back. This season was sort of fluorescent—lime, which she hated, and bubble-gum pink—but at least what Piqué carried was different, more offbeat—it was always a tightrope walk between feeding the appetite for what was popular and being original. Even people who said they wanted to be original really wanted to wear stuff they'd seen somewhere else. She explained to the silent prone form on the bed that the houses in Paris had gone off the radar and New York was the real fashion center now. Everyone takes it so seriously, she said. Remember when I told you it's all just a joke? It is, Sean. At least, it should be.

His eyes opened, but it was on vacancy, and they flickered closed again almost instantly.

She stopped speaking and tried to simply be present in the room with Sean, to somehow transfer some of her own life force to him. Angela had never meditated or anything like it, but Kathryn posted a lot of aphorisms about mindfulness and staying in the present on Facebook, and at this moment, in this room, those aphorisms felt powerful. The things she couldn't do for her mother, hadn't even thought to do, Angela would do now for Sean. She was glad he didn't seem to be in pain. She willed him on in the struggle, the fight against the thing that wanted to claw away his flesh and turn him into cold clay. At least he was all right now. His eyes were closed, not squeezed shut against pain, but simply closed, and she could imagine his face relaxed and healed under the bandages, his dear, pudgy, unfinished face, and she was sitting beside him ready to receive his spirit— this was something else she remembered from Kathryn. In the presence of suffering, Kathryn had said when Angela told her about Kim's death, you need to empty yourself. Get rid of your own selfish, irrelevant grief and make your mind and body into a receptacle for the other person's soul. Angela would do that. She would create a place of peace for Sean to enter.

His eyes were slitted open. He was looking at her. She stifled a gasp. And you said what if they weren't joking, those fashion people, she said. Sean. Do you remember saying that?

He was still looking at her. He recognized her. He had heard her words. She wanted to hug him, but she wasn't sure where she could touch that wouldn't hurt. She was grinning and couldn't stop. Oh, Sean, she said, I knew you were in there. I see you in there now. You're smiling, right? Please tell me you're smiling.

His eyes stayed fixed on hers for several seconds, then drifted shut.

CHAPTER FORTY-NINE

The next morning, Angela got off the elevator. Bonnie was at the desk in the center of the ward, and she hurried to intercept Angela as she headed for Sean's room, placing her short squat body in front of Angela like a powerful little tank. Let's go in here, she said, gesturing toward the consultation room. Why? Angela asked. But she followed the nurse. Inside, Bonnie turned to face her. I'm so sorry to have to tell you this Angela, but Sean's gone. He went in the middle of the night.

Angela stared at her stupidly. He's someplace else? He left? You moved him?

Sit down, hon.

I don't want to sit down. If she kept standing what Bonnie had just said wouldn't be true.

He died, Angela, of a massive infection. Sometimes infection just does that.

But he was getting better. He opened his eyes yesterday.

Infections can come on quick. The body is so exhausted from how hard it has to fight to regulate itself after a burn. Sometimes it just all happens so fast it doesn't matter what we try and do.

Angela sat down and began to cry, cry as she'd never done during her lonely childhood or for her own mother. Bonnie sat quietly beside her saying I'm sorry, Angela. I'm sorry. I didn't realize how close you were to him.

I wasn't. Angela caught herself, took several long, deep breaths, blew her nose.

Bonnie waited. After a few minutes, Listen, do you know anyone we can contact?

No.

His family hasn't responded to us. Do you know who can make the arrangements?

Angela stared. Then she put her hands over her face and began crying again.

In the end, after she'd finally calmed down, it was Stocker Angela called. Within the hour, he had bustled in, taken one look at her, told her to go home, and sat down to talk to Bonnie. Angela learned later that he'd called the funeral home, explained that Sean had been out of touch with his family for years but no, Sean wasn't indigent and he, Stocker, would pay for a decent burial and all other expenses.

CHAPTER FIFTY

Sean's room was so small you could barely take three steps into it before your knees came up against the bed. There was nothing you could do in that room that you wouldn't be doing on the bed, Angela thought—the super having just let her in to go through Sean's belongings and salvage anything worth keeping—whether reading, writing, or watching the funky old television. You couldn't walk around that bed; to get to the room's far side, you'd have to crawl over it. There were no sheets, nothing but a thin, olive green blanket, left by a previous tenant or picked up who knows where, and a very large pillow: Perhaps Sean had wanted something he could burrow into at night.

In the drawer of a chest tight up against the wall, she found two pairs of underpants, gray from washing and wear. A wire hanger on an exposed overhead pipe held a pair of gray slacks and a shirt with white and pink stripes: Sean's dress-up clothes.

In the cubby that passed for a kitchen, Angela saw a sink, hotplate and tiny fridge, which she opened to the sour scent of old milk. By the sink were a towel and washcloth and on the edge a toothbrush with toothpaste caked onto the flattened bristles. There was something about this scene of Sean's lonely ablutions—the bathroom was down the hall and Angela guessed it was filthy and he used it only when absolutely necessary—that spoke so strongly of Sean's marginal life that she wanted to weep. She went back to lie down on the bed, pressed her face into the pillow and inhaled the familiar fusty scent. A spiral notebook lay on the chair that served as a bedside table, and she sat up cross-legged and opened it. On the first page it said, Spuds. Peel AWAY from you. Cut out eyes. Lettuce: tear off outer leeves or slimy or with brown on them. Halfway through, there were pages and pages of sketches: A brown leaf was pressed into the book, and Sean had tried to copy its tracery of veins. Further on, there were birds, drawn perhaps from memory, perhaps observation. Sean had worked hard on the three-toed feet, which repeated again and again, along with sketches of wing shapes and feathers, below which he'd written: SPARROW. ROBIN. PIGEON. The images had a moving and unexpected delicacy. A photograph fell onto the bedspread, clearly a family portrait: two people seated, three younger ones standing in the back; one of them was Sean. He must have been moving, because his face was blurred.

Angela stopped a few times on the way home. Once she was in the half-empty apartment she'd be leaving soon for California, she dropped her purse onto the table. She cleared some clutter—a paperback mystery, a wine glass, some loose change—from the shelf behind her bed, wiped the shelf off with a wetted paper towel, then a dry one, and covered the bare wood with a purple silk scarf. She went back to the table and pulled Sean's family photograph from her purse, set it down in front of her, and circled his face three times with a purple sharpie. Then she slid it into the wooden frame she'd just bought and put it in the center of her shelf. Sean's notebook went to one side, and a vegetable peeler with a half-melted handle someone had rescued from the floor of the soaked and blackened restaurant to the other. Next came a saucer holding a crust of bread and some grains of salt, so that Sean would never go hungry, and then Angela made him a gift of her feather earring, the one with a drop of dried blood where Stocker had torn it from her ear. She contemplated her work for a few minutes, then completed it with Sean's flattened toothbrush.

CHAPTER FIFTY-ONE

The cat was hungry. It crept into the corner of the dream. Sitting in the alley behind the restaurant, Stocker had dozed off. He was stirring stew and somehow the cat was in the stew now, paddling softly in the liquid, everything floating around her like the things Alice saw during her fall into Wonderland. Angela was there too, her hair swirling like seaweed. He started awake.

He hurt people. How badly had he hurt Angela while thinking it was himself being hurt, being defensive and afraid she'd leave him? Worse than that, far worse, he had killed Sean. Fuzzy Bunny had died because of Stocker's faults and his dirty kitchen with the hot spattering grease. Fuzzy Bunny's body was all burn. Almost. What did they say? Forty percent? How much burn could a person survive? And how deep, how far into the layers of skin, into the meat, did it go? Did the fire char Sean's bones? Stocker knew how it must have hurt, he knew Sean must have been in agony. But doped up. What was the fucking word? Sedated, and ultimately drifting into sleep, then into death. So quietly, like the little mouse he was, like the baby mouse Stocker had kept in a shoebox once as a boy because he'd had some idea of saving it—a dumb idea; he knew mice were vermin. But this one had been so little. It barely moved. He gave it water and crumbs but it didn't touch nourishment. He remembered something about monkey babies deprived of their mothers responding to a wired shape covered with cloth, and put a stuffed animal in the box with the mouse, a small gray and white dolphin. When he looked into the box in the morning, the mouse was dead, huddled against the dolphin. What struck him most was the creature's absolute silence and lack of complaint. You couldn't even call it resignation because it had no experience of the world, nothing to tell itself about its own plight. It just lay against the toy dolphin and waited and expired. Sean had stopped breathing alone in his hospital room. Stocker knew Angela had been sitting beside him for hours every day, but still Sean had died alone.

It wasn't just Stocker's habits that had killed Sean. It was who he was, his essence. Because he was dirty and chaotic to the core and his kitchen was a reflection of his unclean soul. So the place where he was king had turned into an inferno with Sean trapped inside. Stocker's Stockerness had killed Sean.

Angela was never coming back, and at the thought emptiness welled up inside him like Cherry's dark blood.

Stocker wasn't impermeable any more, and that meant the thing he'd always pushed to the back of his mind was obsessing him: the blood on his father's assaultively jet-black hair, the white that meant he'd hit through to bone, the knowledge that his father hadn't survived the blow.

It was a cool March day. He drew his jacket closer around his body, and reached in the pocket for a cigarette. He saw himself walking along the road after his father's death, so vulnerable, so membrane-transparent that the sun seemed to shine right through him. The sky was blue, the birds wheeled above him singing, shouting and chattering as if nothing had happened, as if the man whose hands had dealt out hurt and death all the years of Stocker's life weren't lying on the kitchen floor, his hair matted with blood, red against black like the colors in a bullfight painting, and at the wound's center, a deep pit, another kind of blackness. He could still hear his mother screaming. The grass shone, the world was innocent, but in this innocent blue world he, Stocker, would never be innocent again. He had drunk Cherry's blood. He had taken up the heavy skillet and staved in his father's skull, and been glad, glad and free and so happy he wanted to sing. Life was everywhere and he, Stocker, was the bringer of death. Where would he go now that Sean was dead? What would he do with his tainted self? How could he prepare food for others to eat with his hands so thick with blood?

Angela had sat in his staff room and eaten, had run her tongue around her lips to remove the last vestiges of grease from his cooking, had walked beside him with her hand threaded through his elbow. He had prepared morels for her, cleaning them carefully, sautéing with butter and wine. And suddenly there she was, turning onto the alley from the sidewalk in a bright flowered dress. She was an illusion surely, he thought, summoned by the sheer force of his longing. But, no, she was real, she was Angela, she was lowering herself onto the step beside him, slightly off balance, tottering on those familiar suicide-leap heels.

He put his hand around her bony ankle and she didn't move away. He said, Some shoes you got there, girl.

You like them? I'll wear them to your funeral someday.

It was meant to be jocular. He grunted.

Because you know I'll be there.

You and the worms.

She sat down beside him.

He wanted to say the sooner the better. He imagined her standing over his grave, the sharp heels that propelled her graceless graceful walk sinking into the earth while he disintegrated in the darkness below her. The thought was comforting.

You could piss on me, Angela. That'd be a kick.

Her laugh was brief, bitter and sad. I know it's been hard. She was searching for words. I know how you must be feeling about Sean. She paused. He knew you were trying to teach him things, how to survive even. He loved you. Stocker looked away from her. She went on, You'll rebuild. You'll serve food here again. The dining room's not too damaged, and you have insurance. Hey, everyone knows you're irrepressible.

She was trying to make him smile and he obliged. Sure. I'm like one of those rubber balls you throw in water and they keep bobbing back up—again and again, no matter how hard you throw.

They were both quiet. He took his time with this one: Are you coming back to me, Angela?

No.

But she took the cigarette from his lips and inhaled just as she always had, and they faced the alley together. Sooty trees, tangled weeds, the glint of discarded soda cans. He would hold the peace of this moment in his mind for the rest of his life: Angela beside him on the step, their shoulders close but not quite touching. It would be the last thing in his consciousness ten years later when his burdened and fractured heart finally gave out as he stood over the stove stirring stew.

My brother had his baby, Angela said. Did I tell you before? They're calling her Angela.

We're not going to be together again ever?

Did you hear me?

About the baby? Yes. That's good. I'm happy for you, Angela.

I'm going back to California.

She waited but Stocker was silent.

There's nothing here for me any more.

He wanted to say, I'm here. Instead he asked, What will you do?

I don't know. There's a lot of Vietnamese people in the Los Angeles area, and my brother lives not too far from there, sort of in the suburbs. I can maybe stay on his sofa for a while and help with the baby. Maybe I'll meet a nice Vietnamese guy. Hey, I'm kidding. She handed back his cigarette, touched his knee lightly and stood.

Okay, he said. Goodbye then. He didn't look up.

She hesitated. We'll always be together, Stocker.

He whispered I know, but she was already walking away from him, picking along the alley through dog droppings and broken glass. At the sidewalk, she turned, raised her hand and mouthed a goodbye.

CHAPTER FIFTY-TWO

Within a month, Jon had secured a job at a West Village restaurant that was everything he'd always wanted: the obsessively meticulous head chef, the radiant dining room, the spotless kitchen with a section dedicated to his desserts, the two ambitious youngsters there solely to do his bidding. For a week or two, he was in his element, but then the place began to irk him. He started making joke desserts. He created a model of the Leaning Tower of Pisa delicately worked in hand-made fondant as a centerpiece. He scattered golden capsules you had to crack open with your teeth across the customers' pristine dessert plates. Sugar butterflies hovered over brittle sugar flowers. Every inch of every dessert was fussed over, every curl of chocolate, white or dark, arranged, every dollop of cream given a cute little curling tail—and the cream wasn't always cream, but sometimes whipped sweetened turnip. From the kitchen, he watched as diners exclaimed over their ridiculously over-defined desserts. Oh, they said, before lifting their forks to shatter meringue or smear crème anglaise, that's just too pretty to eat. And what had he accomplished, he'd wonder as the sticky plates returned to the kitchen. Whom had he fed and what had he done that mattered? His customers' playfulness wasn't the playfulness of children, but of wealthy, satiated people who needed a constant stream of cleverness and novelty to stimulate their jaded senses, and who liked to view themselves as the cognoscenti, the lucky souls who had discovered the exact right place at the exact right moment. He thought of Crystal sometimes, her warmth and scent, the crescents of flesh under her arms as she lifted Stocker's heavy plates, and of Karen, Katie and Dot. Crystal was back in Alabama, that much he knew, and the Scots, father and son, had left the city. Jon lasted a month while the diners consumed his mockery and venerated his contempt, and then he quit.

He didn't need to work for a while. He had money. His days and evenings were his own. He took long walks. He visited art galleries. He had the idea of re-reading Ulysses but abandoned the book a quarter of the way through. Sometimes he thought about Keith, how Keith would have teased him during the stint at his brilliant Village restaurant and fully understood the aversion and distaste that had driven him out of it. Jon had always hated the idea of being permanently linked to anyone when what he wanted—needed—was to be light on his feet and unencumbered. But perhaps it wasn't dependency Keith had offered, but gentleness, respect and companionship. Keith, who had needed Jon and whom he had betrayed.

Jon was on one of his solitary walks on a bright May morning when it began to rain—drops falling from a clear sky, sun and clouds contending. He leaned his head back and tasted the rain, sooty-silvery on his tongue. There ought to be a rainbow, and he stopped to peer at the sky, but he couldn't see one. And then the clouds darkened, the drops multiplied, and it was pouring. He remembered Keith as he had first seen him at the bus stop, his face shiny and glazed with water and how he'd come in gratefully under the shelter of Jon's umbrella. Now he knew where he was going. He began running, water pouring mercilessly over his head, the bottom of his jeans dragging against his ankles, his red trainers squelching and saturated, running and laughing while the rain pelted him, racing through street after street until he found himself in front of Keith's dental practice. He leapt the concrete steps in front, pushed open the smooth black door with its heavy gold knocker—Keith's practice was an exclusive one—and raced up the stairs to the second floor. Outside Keith's office, he hesitated, bent double, catching his breath. Then he straightened, combed back his sopping hair with his fingers, tried to wipe his face with a handful of soaked tissues, and opened the glass door.

From the tightness of her smile, it was clear the receptionist remembered who he was and knew something about what had happened between him and Keith. Perhaps she had comforted Keith while he grieved: Keith's ability to evoke empathy and affection was effortless and without limit.

I just need to talk with Keith, Jon said. When he has a moment.

That's fine. Her face was expressionless. After this, his next appointment's not till noon. Go ahead and wait. She nodded toward the waiting room: in one corner, a circle of child-sized chairs, toys on a low shelf, an open coloring book and some crayons abandoned on the floor. He sat down across from a woman engrossed in checking her mobile, ran his fingers through his hair again and caught his breath. There was an odd sound coming from behind the door of Keith's operating room. A child was humming under the drone of the drill, Jon realized, and Keith was humming along with the child. And then Keith laughed. Keith's laughter. The sound sent a current of warmth along Jon's bones. He remembered all the teasing: Keith calling him a persnickety old fart and a prize racehorse requiring endless maintenance. And other things: Keith huddled under their blankets, hot and damp with flu, used tissues scattered all over the bedspread. Keith rubbing his feet—a favor he, Jon, had never returned. Keith mystified by the Czech movies Jon insisted they watch together and his good-natured attempts to enjoy them. The sound of football games, and how irritating he'd found them. Hearing that laugh—and the child's light laugh twinning with it—he realized that when Keith came out into the waiting room, he might not be pleased to see him. He might stiffen with the anger Jon knew he deserved, summon up the protective carapace he'd created for himself through their weeks of separation. Perhaps he had a new lover. If so, he, Jon, deserved it. He'd been a shit, a dried up, self-centered, desiccated turd. He had left the man who loved him to face a terrible illness alone, pushed him out of their apartment and consecrated it entirely to himself, protected and impeccably ordered. Under its last dust.

But it didn't matter. He refused to let it matter. However Keith reacted right there in the waiting room, he, Jon, would win him back. He would make a mission of it because he had to, because at this moment he wanted to put his lips to Keith's warm neck more than he had ever wanted anything in his entire life. He was shaking with the extent and depth of his wanting. He would do whatever he had to—beg forgiveness, grovel, tease, flirt, adopt a dog, adopt a baby, become a football fan and fry up chicken wings for every game through the entire season. He would wipe his lover's butt, if necessary, and decorate his sick room with flowers and photographs as Ted had done for Leon. Or, given a longer, happier narrative, he would sleep beside Keith every night, greet him with coffee every morning, and restore their placid life of meat loaf and doughnuts, sitcoms and squabbles—all the dull ordinariness and disheveled warmth that he finally recognized for what it was: love.

The drill stopped and Keith's voice sounded in the silence. Okay, he said to the child in his chair. Almost done. What shall we sing now?

Advance Priase for Stocker's Kitchen

"This isn't an easy book. But I don't want an easy book, I want what Juliet Wittman has written, an agonized and lyrical story filled with people who are often damaged, often inspired, always fascinating. I love how the author takes a troubled soul—Stocker is only one example—and develops a character we want to know, someone we root for and suffer with and learn from. Stocker is "short and fat and vulgar," a guy with "no peace or order to his life." But in his kitchen, and in his romance with Angela, he's brilliantly alive. So is Angela. So are Keith and Jon. So is everyone in this exuberant and gorgeously-written book."

~ John Thorndike, author of *A Hundred Fires in Cuba* and *The Last of His Mind*.

"Juliet Wittman's timely novel casts a clear eye on life in the professional kitchen. Her prose revels in the tactile pleasures of working with food and the romance of lives devoted to craft. But it never shies away from the toxicity of that culture, nor the mental health issues that its characters, like so many cooks, must deal with. In Stocker she has created a character with a distinctive voice. After reading the novel you want nothing so much as to try his food."

~ John Kessler, long-time dining critic for the *Atlanta Journal-Constitution*, award-winning writer, and chairman of the James Beard Foundation's journalism awards committee.

Acknowledgements

Many thanks to those whose feedback, advice and encouragement helped bring *Stocker's Kitchen* to life:

Ellen Gault, Caryn McVoy, John Thorndike, Dana Kaersvang, Rob Duray, Teri Rippeto, Eric Izant, Paula Wenger, Emma Messenger, Judy Anderson, Jeff Lukes, and my dear husband Bill Blackburn.

And special thanks to April Eberhardt, the most insightful, supportive and indefatigable agent a writer could possibly have.

Also by Juliet Wittman

Breast Cancer Journal: A Century of Petals

Winner of the Colorado Book Award, and named a finalist for the
National Book Award

•

"Informative and riveting."
~Washington Post

•

"Ruthless, insightful, funny, uplifting and informed."
~The Denver Post

•

"Juliet Wittman has written an extraordinary book."
~Laurence A, Marschall, The Sciences

•

"This book is terrific for a number of reasons, but mostly because
Wittman is smart and funny and wise."
~The WomanSource Catalog & Review

•

"A wonderfully written book you simply cannot put down."
~Minnesota Women's Press

37923650R00186

Made in the USA
San Bernardino, CA
05 June 2019